THE SPIDER IN THE LAUREL

MICHAEL POGACH

RAGNAROK
PUBLICATIONS

CRESTVIEW HILLS, KENTUCKY

THE SPIDER IN THE LAUREL

Ragnarok Publications | www.ragnarokpub.com

Editor In Chief: Tim Marquitz | Creative Director: J.M. Martin

The Spider in the Laurel is copyright © 2015 by Michael Pogach. All rights reserved.

Published by Ragnarok Publications
206 College Park Drive, Ste. 1
Crestview Hills, KY 41017

ISBN-10: 1-941987-58-3
ISBN-13: 978-1-941987-58-2
Worldwide Rights
Created in the United States of America

Editor: Tim Marquitz
Proofreader: Ryan Lawler
Publicity: Melanie R. Meadors
Social Media: Nick Sharps
Cover Illustration & Design: M.S. Corley
Interior Layout: Shawn T. King

For Coraline

ACKNOWLEDMENTS

I want to thank the following:

Stephen Mazzeo, Michelle Tooker, Daniel Schall, David Dill, and all past members of the AG writers group: muses, editors, conspirers, and more. Dr. Richard Wertime, for always pushing me. My brother, Adam, for never being afraid to ask if I knew what I was doing. My parents, Howard and Lisa, for always believing in me. My grandmother, Olga Tabak. Everything I write is just practice so that one day I may be able to tell her story. The good folks at Ragnarok Publications, for taking a chance on me. Most of all, I have to thank my wife, Colleen (and apologize for all the times I rushed off, saying, "I need to write this down").

PART ONE

RELIC ENFORCEMENT COMMAND

Then God said, "Let Us make humankind in Our image, in the likeness of Ourselves."

Book of Genesis, 1:26

Mephistopheles: When all the world dissolves...All places shall be hell that is not Heaven.
Faustus: Come, I think hell's a fable.

The Tragical History of the Life and Death of Doctor Faustus, by Christopher Marlowe, c. 1592

...to protect and defend the Citizens of the Republic against domestic threats both civil and fanatical, to uphold and enforce the criminal laws of the United Republic, and to guarantee the purity of our nation against all artifacts of zealotry.

Relic Enforcement Command Mission Statement, 2016

CHAPTER ONE

Rafael Ward was about to die.

It was a fact as sure as any in his textbooks. The fall of Rome in 476. Christopher Columbus in 1492. The formation of Relic Enforcement Command in 2016. Fact: The door at the end of the hall would be the last he ever walked through.

But it wasn't a completely unpleasant thought. There was something right about it. About this basement. The door. Like walking through it would be the final payoff on a debt owed.

Besides, he had to do it. There were things worse than death. Places worse than ash-filled urns. He thought of the Tower. One way or another he'd be there soon. Better to push on than to run away, to leave that debt unfulfilled.

His legs didn't move, didn't take him from that last stair down into the hall. He'd been taught to avoid basements.

"You can jump out a window or from one roof to another," Agent Compano, his recruiter and trainer, had said. "But in a basement you're stuck. It might as well be a coffin." Yet here he was, on his first solo operation, ordered into the cellar of an abandoned apartment building in South Philly. Ordered into darkness and dust and an almost ridiculous silence that pounded inside his head like waves.

He concentrated on his breathing like he'd been taught. "Control the aspects of the operation you can control," was another of Agent Compano's tips. "Trust us to take care of the rest."

Trust. It seemed a simple thing for Relic Enforcement Command, the REC, to ask. Trust them to control what Ward couldn't. What he couldn't control was that he worked for them. Quitting wasn't an option. Agents of the REC, even conscripts like Ward, were sworn for life. There was nothing to do now but take that next step off the stairs. Success or death. The REC's unofficial motto. All Ward wanted was to be just a professor again.

He squinted down the hallway that extended from the stairwell. By the remaining light from the top of the stairs he could make out two doors lining the left side of the corridor and one on the right. Even with his limited six weekends of REC training, he recognized the danger this setup presented: ambush.

Five minutes ago, as he'd approached the building, he'd replayed in his mind the last thing Agent Compano had told him in person. It was two weeks ago and he'd just been informed that his training reviews were approved. He was now an active Agent. She'd handed him an unremarkable black briefcase containing the items he would need to carry out his duties. In an uncharacteristic display, she'd placed a hand on his shoulder.

"It's simple, Professor," she'd said. "Collect the artifact, count the cash, and deliver the contraband to Command."

"What about the…" He'd wanted to say suspects or perpetrators but the words just didn't feel right, "…the bad guys?" That choice felt even worse.

"You let us take care of that," she'd said. "Just do what you're told. Operations like yours are simple. Good fun. You might even get to like it." The corner of her lip had curled like it was being pulled by a fishing line. It was as close to a smile as he'd ever seen from her. She actually meant what she said, he realized. To her operations like his were easy and fun.

Ward was not having fun. And he was certain there wasn't going to be anything simple or easy about what waited for him behind the door at the end of the hall.

His breathing finally even and under control, Ward reached beneath his black leather field jacket for his Command-issued RT40 pistol. The RT, or Republic Tactical, forty caliber weighed just over two pounds loaded, and at the target range it never felt an ounce more. But in the near dark of the stairwell its weight tripled.

Still, Ward found it a welcomed heft. A dozen clichéd lines raced through his mind, plucked from the pop-noir novels he'd been reading since grade school. Lines about, and by, characters like Terry Mack, Philip Marlowe, and Chili Palmer.

He waited in the dark, the narrative would go, reassured by the weight of the gun in his hand.

They were bad fiction from a forgotten era yet Ward loved them as much as the medieval history and literature he taught at Carroll University.

And here he was, clenching the knurled grip of the RT40, reassured of his safety by its weight in his hand.

He tried to ignore the fact that he'd never fired a weapon outside a range, not even during his military service—the two year mandatory Citizen's Duty everyone enlisted for after high school—which he'd completed just over a decade ago. But, as Agent Compano said more than once, he hadn't been recruited for his commando skills. In Professor Rafael Ward they had the perfect mole. He was one of the Atlantic District's leading experts in medieval European history, and thus in the illegal religions academically known as mythologies, of that era. He was exactly the type of person outlaw Believers would accept as one of their own.

At least they would so long as they didn't know about his childhood.

Ward put the thought out of his mind and chambered a round. He stepped from the stairway and began his progress through the hall. Dust rose around his foot making the floor shimmer. The room seemed to spin. All the comfort of the pistol in his hand drained away.

He became aware of his heartbeat at the same time as the desire to run returned. Both pounded. It didn't matter. There was no turning back. There hadn't been since he'd opened the door to his office near the end of the spring semester to find his officemate Ken Hickey fidgeting, wide-eyed on the couch. Ken, in his standard oversized khaki blazer and baggy trousers, had looked like a rumpled pile of terrified laundry. Standing in front of Ken had been two powerfully built men in identical black suits featuring black shirts and white ties. And Agent Compano.

She wore the same standard REC suit as her partners, but with a slightly more feminine cut and the addition of a red bar across her tie near the knot. Her brunette hair was pulled back in a tight ponytail. She was younger than Ward but her eyes asserted absolute authority. Once Ward was in the tiny office Agent Compano had asked Ken to excuse them. He did so, shrugging on his way out the door as if to say, "Sorry, dude. Hope you don't die."

Ward hadn't died. During a brief conversation in the office he'd been "volunteered" to join the REC. Just like he'd been "volunteered" to undertake this operation in this basement. And regardless of the "volunteering," REC Agents did not offer excuses. They did not fail.

Ward's thigh muscle pulsed in time with his heart. "Come on," he whispered. He locked his eyes on the door at the far end and forced his feet to shuffle through the dust.

As he approached the midpoint of the hallway a voice in his head announced: *The doors, Rafe. Check the doors.*

Ward's stomach tumbled over itself as he realized he'd been so focused on the door at the end he'd forgotten about the potential ambush. He shook his head and thanked the internal warning. He'd benefited from similar instinctive announcements before. He liked to think of it as his conscience, with a built-in alarm. A sentinel perhaps, for when the academic side of his brain lost track of the practical world around him. It was what kept him from dropping a coffee mug when he'd only placed half of it on the edge of his desk. Or from being run over when he stepped into the street while lost in thought about the day's upcoming lecture. It offered approvals and dissents for everything from choosing to study history, to backing off the purchase of a convertible yellow sports car which would have been near useless in the Philly winters, and likely would have been a money pit.

In this case the voice might well have saved his life. To find out, Ward pressed his ear to the closest door on the left. At first he couldn't hear anything over the pumping of his own pulse. He pulled back a little. This time he heard nothing. A good nothing. The kind of nothing that indicated there was no one inside waiting to kill him. In the limited light he examined the doorknob. A thin film of dust clung to it. He relaxed his hand and re-gripped his pistol. Agent Compano had never taught him to check for dust on doorknobs. That one was all him. He held back a grin but allowed a moment to congratulate himself. He then repeated the listening and doorknob check at the remaining two doors. Silence and dust. He continued down the hallway pressed against the wall, just in case.

At the end of the corridor Ward placed his ear to the final door. At first this one, too, produced only silence. Then, as he was about to pull away, he heard something. Not much. Maybe the shuffling of feet.

Maybe the ambush was in there.

Ward dismissed the thought before it could raise his heart rate again. Agent Compano, posing as Ward's contact and point person for what she called the relic black market, had set up this meet. Ward was an asset. She wouldn't have sent him into danger.

A conflicting thought came to him. An antithesis he would have titled it for his students. Agent Compano's first priority was to Relic Enforcement Command. To confiscating the relics that Believers used to inspire their insurgencies and terrorist attacks. The REC was the nation's key anti-Belief weapon. Bibles, manifestos, novels, videos, downloads, anything at all on the censor list, even tattoos and utterances invoking faith or gods—the REC tracked them all. But actual relics, these were the REC's priority.

Would she really care, Ward wondered, if I was killed during an otherwise successful operation?

He knew the answer but wouldn't allow his mind to form the word. Instead he focused on the door and on what he did know, the details of the operation as relayed via Agent Compano's encrypted text. He was to meet a man named Torres who would pay him ten thousand dollars in cash to transport an as yet unidentified artifact to an as yet unidentified location outside the Atlantic District.

The artifact and the location didn't matter. Ward wouldn't be keeping the cash and he wouldn't be taking the item anywhere but the REC's field office, known as the Tower, about four miles to the north. By the time Ward had arrived at the Tower, Torres would be in custody, likely in interrogation. By the end of the weekend he'd be feeding the Crematorium across the river in Camden.

Simple and easy as Agent Compano would say.

Maybe, Ward thought, disturbed at how naive he sounded even in his own head.

Either way there was nothing left to do but open the door and get this whole thing over with. Before he did so, however, Ward returned his pistol to the belt holster beneath his jacket. When drawn, Agent Compano had taught, the gun is all your adversary sees.

"Unless you intend to open the meeting with gunfire," Ward remembered her saying, "keep it holstered."

A gunfight was the last thing Ward wanted. He smoothed his jacket over the pistol and checked the hallway behind him once more. No movement. No open doors. There were only his own boot prints in the dust.

He inhaled, holding the breath as he'd been taught when lining up a target with a tactical rifle. He opened the door.

CHAPTER TWO

Four spotlights blazed on.

Disoriented, eyes burning, Ward put up his left hand to block the light, and reached for the doorframe with his right. Two thoughts came to him. First, this strategy was so simple he was amazed nothing like it had come up as a possibility during his training. Second, Torres had the advantage.

There was nothing he could do about the first thought. But the second, the advantage, had to be addressed. He had to regain leverage. He squinted at the floor as deep into the room as he could. He thought he could make out six or seven pairs of shoes split into two flanking groups at opposite ends of the room.

"This isn't going to be easy if I'm blind," Ward said, trying to keep his voice even but stern.

Another few seconds of radiance, then the lights dimmed and pivoted out and up. Ward pressed his knuckles into his eyes and tried to blink away the spots and stars from his vision. It took a moment for him to be able to see clear enough to realize it was actually only two spotlights, not four, that had blinded him. The rest of the room came into focus. It was about thirty-feet square with bare cinderblock walls on three sides. The back wall was submerged in darkness behind the lights. Chunks of broken cinderblock shards and other debris made up a number of small piles scattered throughout the room, mostly along the walls. It smelled of mold, something like wet dog.

With clearer vision came an understanding of just how effective the spotlight strategy was. He was flanked by four people, not six or seven. On his right stood a large, shaved-headed man in black military-style pants and sweater. The sweater looked like it was in distress from the man's physique, barely holding on. An assault rifle rested comfortably on his forearm. A smaller individual, possibly a woman, lingered behind the big man on the edge of the light.

On the other side, a man dressed and armed like the giant on the right, though not as robust, held an assault rifle against his shoulder, its stock balanced in his right palm. In front of him stood a bearded man with gloomy eyes, a heavy brow, and wearing a dark business suit. Arms folded. Scowling. This was the man in charge. Ward had no doubt.

Torres.

Ward raised his hands chin-high and took one step towards the pair on the left. "Maybe we can all step into the light a bit," he said, "and do this nice and friendly. What do you think?"

Torres took two unblinking steps forward. It was like the first tentative moves in chess, except here was Torres, at least a bishop, maybe a rook, facing off with a pawn.

Stillness and silence.

Ward became lost in Torres' beard. It felt like minutes. He swallowed, ready to give in when Torres finally spoke.

"Your weapon," he said, his voice full of bass and impatience.

During his two training operations, Ward had been the one in a position of authority. Two desperate Believers begging him to help them rescue their prized possessions from the REC's tireless hunt. He'd gathered a tooth, purported to have been Saint Anthony's, and a vial of cream-colored sand, pledged as some of the cremated remains of the Buddha. Ward knew neither was authentic. And from that, as much as the REC, he derived the confidence which gave him his authority.

Torres, however, was no beggar. Knowing that magic bones and shrouds didn't exist offered Ward no edge. And the REC was not close enough to afford protection, let alone authority, while outnumbered and outgunned. If things went bad he'd likely be dead before Agent Compano stepped foot inside the apartment building.

He removed his pistol with three fingers and placed it on the floor. The guard beside Torres slung his rifle over his shoulder and approached. He kicked Ward's pistol a few feet towards the corner. He then traced Ward's frame with his eyes before drawing from his belt a Citizen's Port, the roughly six inch by four inch standard issue portable computer and telecom device approved by the Republic. Everyone was awarded a CP on the completion of their Citizen's Duty if they were approved as a Citizen.

The large man motioned for Ward to raise his arms.

This was it. Agent Compano's plan, and Ward's life, hinged on this moment. She had warned him about it, but it hadn't come up in the training operations. Torres was no grandmother hiding a tooth in a coffee can. He had resources. And those resources were about to reveal whether or not the REC's technology was as advanced as advertised.

The guard wanded his Port over Ward's body, top to bottom then up again. It looked like a CP6, one of the newer models available. A bit faster and lighter than the standard issue CP. He was sweeping for any signal that might indicate an REC uplink, anything to prove Ward was not a legitimate Believer.

Ward held his breath. In the right hip pocket of his jacket was a new R1, a first generation Port model designed specifically for Republic officials. It was, according to Agent Compano, the most important item in the briefcase she'd handed him at the end of his training. Ward hadn't bothered asking about it. He'd assumed it was just a more powerful version of the CP. Now, however, he remembered Agent Compano saying something about its link to Command. What was it? A passive link? An unbreakable link? Undetectable?

Whatever it was, it was too late to do anything about it. Ward held his breath and waited for the guard to finish his scan.

The Port chimed. The shaved-headed man reviewed the results. He exchanged looks with Torres. The beard twitched. The guard returned to his post. The R1 had passed its test.

Ward exhaled and rolled his left shoulder, cracking some of the tension in his neck.

The sentry on the right side withdrew into the dark, returning with a small table. He placed it in the light, in the middle of the room, before resuming his position.

On the table sat a dark wooden box about two feet long and one wide. Certainly handmade, it looked to be a century old at least. A cross-engraved silver latch on its front refracted the spotlights, creating a small rainbow in the airborne dust.

Torres raised an eyebrow as if to say, "Get on with it."

Ward moved to the table, clenching his fist. Something was wrong. It was a panicked thought but he couldn't expel it. Torres was too cautious. The air was too acerbic. The thought of aborting the operation returned. He could wheel around and trace his own shadow back out the door, be gone in ten seconds.

Finish the operation. The voice in the back of his mind was steady and reassuring. The way a mother's cadence waltzed through a bedtime story.

Ward took a deep breath and knelt before the table. He lifted the latch. Its cool, thin metal calmed his nerves. This was not like the two training operations. This didn't have the feel of Jersey Shore sand masquerading as twenty-five hundred year old remains.

He opened the box.

Nestled in the plush interior was an iron rod, maybe ten

inches long, terminating in a petal-shaped spearhead.

"We're good?" Torres asked. His voice indicated an expectation of surprise.

Ward had to be careful. He was surprised. But not for the reason Torres thought.

He knew he was looking at what Torres believed to be the Spear of Destiny. The lance with which a Roman soldier supposedly stabbed Jesus at the crucifixion. A weapon that conquerors had sought and killed for over the many centuries before the Republic's Edict Seven legislated that there was no power residing in the sky nor in ancient artifacts buried in the Earth.

What Torres couldn't know was that this was the second Holy Lance Ward had beheld. The first had been presented to him at the university two years earlier with a mandate for authentication. It had arrived in an unmarked brown box. Inside was the famous Hofburg Spear which Adolf Hitler had possessed, and a scan code for Ward's CP. The scan uploaded instructions and a confidentiality agreement. It was signed by an REC research official.

It was a bit of an odd request. Ward had never heard of the REC bothering to validate contraband's authenticity. In hindsight it could have just been a test to gauge him prior to his recruitment. He'd apparently passed the test. The Hofburg Spear hadn't. A simple metallurgical scan had proven it fraudulent, a conglomerate of components from centuries too diverse and too young to have been present during the Biblical era.

This Spear of Destiny was not more promising. The typical

Roman spear of the first century BCE, the *pilum*, sported a conical socket and leaf-shaped blade that was close to a foot and half long. Ward surmised that what he beheld was actually a *spiculum*, a Roman infantry javelin that did not become common until the middle of the third century CE.

Ward reached into his jacket's hip pocket for his R1 to perform the standard scan of a suspected relic. "Almost. I just need to check—"

The guards raised their rifles.

Ward stopped, his hand immobilized halfway into the pocket. No one spoke. Seconds passed. He inched his hand out of the pocket, keeping his fingers splayed open to show he held no weapon. Sweat tickled his hairline.

"Maybe we should all take a breath."

It was a new voice, coming from that person in the shadow who was, as Ward had surmised, a woman. She stepped into the light.

She was a few inches shorter than he, wearing dark, pocketed pants, a black hooded sweater, and a shoulder-slung backpack. Her dark hair—it was difficult to discern color with the spotlights behind her—was short and rakish. It reminded him of...

"Let's allow Professor Ward to verify it's not tagged, shall we? After all, he was kind enough to let us scan him." She offered a perfunctory smile to Ward. "That'll be good, yes?"

Again, the only sign from Torres was a bobbing of the beard, but the guards obediently lowered their guns. The woman joined Ward in the center of the room, kneeling on the opposite side of the table. She leaned in close. To Ward she smelled like the park in spring.

She set her light eyes—blue or maybe green—in a glare that said: I don't want to hand this over to you, but I have to. "You better be as good as your reputation."

His reputation. A manufactured resume of lies concocted by Agent Compano on behalf of the REC and implemented into the nation's law enforcement network database to prove that Professor Rafael Ward had been smuggling illegal artifacts throughout the Citizen's Republic of America for years. He'd been forced to memorize dozens of his own supposed activities, moving saints' finger bones and vials of prophets' tears and so forth from District to District to keep them out of the REC's reach. According to the files his identity was unknown by the REC. He was listed as Codename: M.

Ward liked to think the M stood for Marlowe or Melville.

He mustered all the confidence he could, all the confidence of the criminal called Melville, and forced a half smile. "I am."

The woman raised an eyebrow. Ward couldn't tell if it was curiosity or skepticism. In either case he didn't want to test how far he could carry his bravado. He chose instead to deflect. "Who are you?"

"MacKenzie."

"Okay, MacKenzie," Ward said, knowing they'd be expecting him to ask more questions. "Where do you need me to take this?"

"Just scan the Spear. Then we'll discuss the details." Her tone was harsh yet seemed forced.

He removed the R1 from his jacket, tensing as he swiped a finger across the screen to start the program. The R1's second test was about to begin.

"Nice toy, Professor," MacKenzie said, bending in as if to get a better look. "You know, if Torres hadn't done his homework I might think you were REC. I've only seen Ports like that in the hands of Agents."

This close he could make out faint freckles on her nose. He found himself examining the rest of the lines and curves of her face.

The Spear, Rafe.

Yes, the Spear. He and Agent Compano had prepared a plan, a script, in response to an observation like hers. What was it? Where had it gone? She just reminded him so much of...of who?

"Professor?"

MacKenzie spoke the word softly, but with concern. Her hand crept towards whatever weapon was hidden behind her back.

Ward cleared his throat and pulled back. The words he needed returned.

"Look, if we're moving cash and artifacts," he pointed at the box, "in a basement, then I can buy a Republic-issue Port in an alley, can't I?"

She pursed her mouth as if biting the inside of her lip and nodded in agreement.

Second test passed. But he couldn't let himself be distracted like that again. He focused on the Spear, refusing to look MacKenzie in the eye. He lifted the artifact a few inches out of the box and passed the R1 over the length of it. The metal of the Spear was warm and smooth, in far better condition than should be expected from a two thousand year old memento.

The scan complete, he tapped a four digit code onto the screen and waited. Three seconds. Two. One.

The readout indicated that the Spear was GPS free. It also confirmed the Roman design. It was not, however, of Iberian ore, as would be expected—as would be required for it to be a legit relic—of a late BCE Roman weapon. Its iron was Britannic, specifically from the Southeast region called the Weald. Ward knew that Roman mining in this region did not get underway with any serious commitment until the middle of the first century CE.

Authentic? Of course not. Edict Seven always wins.

But it was Roman. It was ancient. And that was enough to make Ward's hand tremble just a bit. Regardless of his new position as an REC Agent he was still an academic. He wondered what stories the Spear might tell, as if it could feel the question through his fingers and maybe answer his thoughts.

MacKenzie leaned her head in beside his. "The Spear of Destiny," she said, her breath minty. "Can you feel it, Rafael? Your hand there on the Spear, the actual surface which pierced the Savior?"

Ward grinned. Definitely a Believer. "It's Rafe, please." He placed the Spear back into its chest.

"Are we good?" Torres interrupted. The glare above the beard indicated that he was growing impatient. Or maybe jealous.

MacKenzie hopped to her feet and slipped back into

the shadows, returning quickly with a large green duffle bag. Ward took the bag and opened it, his eyes still on Torres. This time the bearded man looked away first, giving Ward leave to examine the contents. Inside was a pile of cash and a black Citizen's Port, a CP2, with a yellow stripe down its back.

"The Port is locked to incoming," MacKenzie said. "You'll get a text tomorrow with the destination."

Ward acknowledged the instruction and proceeded to count the cash. "Always count the money," Agent Compano had said. "Smugglers, even compassionate ones, work for the money. If they don't believe the money's important, they won't believe you. And that, Professor, is how operations get blown and Agents get dead."

"You are an interesting man, Professor," Mackenzie said as he finished counting. "I wouldn't pick you for a smuggler. Or a Believer."

"How's that?" Ward asked when he'd finished counting the cash. He placed the box inside the bag, zipped it closed, and stood, taking note of just how far to the right his pistol laid.

"You just don't seem the type to risk your life for a thrill."

Ward extended the duffle bag's straps and slung it over his shoulder. "Well, it's for cash and the cause, not thrills, right?" Another scripted response.

One of the guards tilted his head and touched his ear. He approached Torres and whispered into his boss' ear.

This isn't good, Ward thought, but held his ground. If there was a problem, making a move for the door would only exacerbate the tension and danger.

"You shit," Torres said, pulling a pistol from behind his

back.

MacKenzie jumped away from the table as the guards lifted their rifles.

Ward raised his hands and took a step backwards. His breath caught in his throat like a gulp of water down the wrong pipe.

"There's cops outside," Torres said. He took a step forward. "What did you do?"

"What?" Ward said, confused. Standard REC procedure, he'd been told, was to clear the operation zone of all police. No other agencies were allowed to interfere with an Agent. He felt panic building like bile in his throat. He blinked, holding his eyes closed for a two-count while he exhaled. How fast could he drop and grab his RT40? How many steps from the door was he? Nine back and one to the side? Ten and two?

"You didn't think there were just four of us, did you?" Torres raised his pistol.

Ward's chest clenched. "Wait," he shouted. "I'm not a cop. I'm not a cop." His voice repeated the phrase like a skipping record. They were the only words he could find.

One of the guards took a step forward, leveling his rifle at Ward's head. MacKenzie melted into the darkness. Without taking his eyes from Ward, Torres asked the guard beside him how long they had.

The big man touched his ear again. "Ninety seconds."

"Either you're with the cops," Torres said, taking a step closer, "or you're careless and let them follow you. Which is it?" He cocked the hammer of his pistol. "One gets you killed, the other gets you beaten and left for them."

The black hole of the gun's barrel was immense. It swallowed Ward's thoughts, leaving him able only to stare.

"They're in the building," the guard said.

"Torres," MacKenzie shouted from somewhere.

Images of the building from Agent Compano's recon files shuffled through Ward's mind. The entrances, exits, breach points, and dead ends. There had to be a way out. An explanation he could offer to buy time, if not yet his life. The images zoomed into the building itself. He saw the empty rooms, the stairs, the doors, the dark hallway.

The footprints.

Yes. That was it. How did Torres' people get in without leaving footprints?

"Did you check the side rooms in the hall?"

Torres cocked his head like a dog.

"When I came down the stairs," Ward continued without waiting for an answer, "there were already footprints in the hall, in the dust, back and forth. Only one set. Not enough to be yours. Someone's in one of those rooms."

Torres glared at the guard.

"It was empty," the large man said. "No prints."

Torres stared. Ward could imagine what he was thinking: Was it a bluff? Could he leave Ward here to get caught? Could he trust to show him whatever escape route they had planned? What about the money? The Spear?

"Torres!" MacKenzie's voice seemed farther away than it should.

Torres lowered his pistol a few inches. Ward exhaled. The dark man's eyes were relentless.

Ward hedged a little to his right.

Torres lowered the gun to his hip. "If I find out you led them here—"

The room exploded.

CHAPTER
THREE

A phone rang. That long, mechanical tone like an extended beep. But continuous. It didn't come from a single point. Instead it filled the air. Filled the room. Filled Ward's head.

He opened his eyes. He was lying on his stomach in the dark, his chest squeezed as if by a giant fist. The ringing shrank to a droning in his ears. He tried to pick himself up but collapsed with a shooting pain through his left side. He sucked air and nearly choked. Two thoughts appeared between coughing spasms. First, he'd landed on the small table, smashing it to pieces. Second, his RT40 had somehow made it back into his hand.

He rose to a knee. The bag containing the cash and the Spear was still slung over his shoulder. He adjusted its weight and looked around. The room was dark. Murky. Only one spotlight was shining, glaring up at the ceiling through a film of smoke. The buzzing in his ears began to dissipate but he still couldn't see more than a couple feet into the white smoke.

White smoke.

Fires don't make white smoke. Standard issue police smoke grenades do.

Ward twisted around trying to find the door but couldn't get a bearing on his position in the room.

"Rafael!"

It was a woman's voice. It occurred to him that she'd been yelling his name for some time. The woman with the freckles. What was her name? He tucked the pistol into his belt holster and crawled towards the voice.

The floor was a labyrinth of debris. Shards and splinters and... Was that a hand? Ward looked away, fighting to keep his eyes open.

Gunfire detonated all around him.

At the first shot, a single, unbearably loud explosion, Ward pressed flat to the ground. As more blasts followed his understanding of the layout of the room danced away like a soda can on a firing range.

Another salvo thundered. *Forget it*, he thought. *I'm just going to lie here and wait for the cops. They're on my side.*

It was logical but when the next volley of shots ignited, Ward's body forgot logic and began crawling again in the opposite direction. Towards the voice. As he got farther from the gunfire the smoke dissipated enough to get his bearings. He'd crawled nearly the length of the room. And though he couldn't help but flinch at each gunshot he was able to discern a single shooter inside the room and three or four outside. Shouting barked unintelligibly between the shots.

Ward continued crawling over the bits and pieces of what was probably once the door, trying not to imagine the same type of damage being inflicted on his own body. He forced his mind to assess the situation as he crawled. With only one defender in the room, the cops would be inside in matter of moments. Whatever exit he was going to find, he needed to do it now.

"Rafael." It was the woman's voice. MacKenzie. That was her name. He couldn't see her but her voice was certainly ahead, no more than a few feet away.

Ward clambered faster, telling himself that what he'd just splashed through wasn't blood.

A hand reached through the smoke and darkness, grabbing his shoulder. He bleated like a child.

"Come on, we have to go. Now."

Ward squinted the scene into focus, finally understanding how MacKenzie had escaped the explosion. She squatted inside a roughly five-foot-by-five-foot hole cut out of the cinderblock back wall of the cellar. He let MacKenzie pull him into the tunnel, squeezing past as she fitted a faux cinderblock wall into the opening. It would buy them some time, but not much.

With the tunnel entrance sealed they were in complete darkness. Ward found his voice. "Now what?"

"Now we get the hell out of here. You still have the Spear, yes?"

"Yeah." He reached for the small tactical flashlight he

kept in his jacket's left breast pocket.

A hand grabbed his. It was warm and sweaty. "No lights. I have night-optics. Just don't let go."

"What about the others?"

"Torres is out." She pulled on his hand. "He tried to get to you but there was too much gunfire to go back. Maley's dead. Harrigan'll buy us time to get out of here."

She led Ward ahead, leaving her companion behind to die. Either in the gunfight or at the Crematorium. It was the kind of sacrifice only a Believer would be willing to make.

Ward put out his free hand to help guide him through the darkness. The walls of the tunnel were softly packed dirt, dry and with the smell of decay whenever it crumbled between his fingers. The floor felt similar beneath his booted feet. Occasional wooden support beams introduced themselves to Ward's head or shoulder every so often. He grunted each time, and was hushed each time by MacKenzie.

The tunnel felt old. It was certainly, Ward concluded, not the product of Torres' handiwork.

In the darkness, he saw textbook pages from his youth flitter by like a flip book. Chapter after chapter on the War of Reclamation, the revolution which birthed the Citizen's Republic of America—the new, secular nation encompassing the previous United States of America, Canada, Greenland, and much of old Mexico. All the corruption of fundamentalists and foreign meddling was eliminated. Yes, it took religious Believers setting off three nuclear bombs in Washington D.C. to start the war, but every school-aged child of the Republic knew that the Reclamation was the best thing to ever happen to America.

Ward's mind stopped the flip book on a particular image, a photo that had given him nightmares in his earliest school years. It depicted a tunnel or perhaps a mine shaft, dark as death in the background. The foreground featured human bones. Its focal point was a single, grinning, pearly white skull.

The caption beneath the photo read something like: *Vigilance helps the Republic turn Believers' tunnels into graves.*

Even scuttling frantically through the dark, Ward couldn't help a chill at the memory.

His toe caught a root sending him tumbling face first into the earthen wall of the tunnel. He reached out, managing only to brush his fingertips on MacKenzie's back before hitting the ground, the air vacating his lungs. He was promptly covered in a shower of debris from above.

"Up," MacKenzie said, her voice wooden.

Ward felt her hands on his shoulders and curled himself into a crouch. "Just a second," he huffed, air slowly re-inflating his chest.

"No time," she said, grabbing his hand and pulling him along.

As they scrambled through the tunnel, the dirt and pebbles crumbling occasionally onto his head made Ward wonder if the whole thing might collapse. Would it be just a rumble, unnoticed on the streets above, followed by eternity in a dirt grave? Or maybe the whole building would implode into the void of their tunnel, like the church demolitions after the Reclamation. So much stone and mortar reduced to nothing more than rubbish. The systematic Cleansing of the Republic.

A lesson in pure industrial efficiency.

He remembered watching the recorded demolition of Boston's Old South Church on television after school one day. It was part of the tenth anniversary celebration of the Cleanse.

"But it's such a cool building, Mom," he'd said, popping a chocolate chip cookie into his mouth. In his memories home always smelled of fresh cookies.

"Yes, Raffi, but churches like that... That's where the people who started the War of Reclamation built their bombs. That's where their priests convinced us they were gods." As she spoke a graphic showing the countdown ticked away on screen. Ten seconds. That was all they gave for the almost two-hundred year old edifice. Nine. Eight.

"But there aren't really any gods," Daniel, Ward's older brother, had chimed in. "Right, Mom? Not really?"

His mom had gotten up then without answering and gone to the kitchen for the next batch of cookies.

Three. Two. One. And the Church was nothing but rubble and a cloud of dirt rising up to what was, by law, an empty sky. It could have been made of nothing more than the loosely packed earth through which Ward and MacKenzie currently fled.

From somewhere in another room of Ward's memory, he could still hear his mom's voice floating on that chocolate chip aroma. "It sure was pretty, wasn't it?"

Another smack of his shoulder against a wooden beam shook the memory from Ward's mind. Where were they? He'd lost track of the turns. Eight? Twelve? MacKenzie's hand still held his, but her grip was less militant as they shuffled through the darkness. Even with the directional changes Ward estimated they had to be fifty or so yards outside the apartment building. Maybe even beyond the perimeter the cops would have set.

The cops—why had they broken protocol and interfered? Ward replayed the moments before his entry into the building. Had he tripped a security alarm? Been seen by a neighbor sneaking into the building? Trailed by a suspicious cop who hadn't gotten the memo?

A squeeze of his hand told him to stop. MacKenzie let go. The grating of metal on metal forced Ward to flinch and squeeze his eyes shut. When the sound ceased, he reopened his eyes to two perpendicular lines of light breaking through the darkness above. A second later the trap door popped open.

Squinting against the light Ward found MacKenzie's face—her eyes obscured by plastic-framed sunglasses—only inches from his. She removed the night-optics lenses and dropped them into a side pouch of her backpack, then heaved herself up and out.

"Come on, Professor," she said, reaching out a hand. "Unless you want to stay in that hole."

Ward took her hand again and climbed up. They appeared to be in another empty basement. A flickering fluorescent tube in the ceiling provided the only light. Two doors waited on opposite walls, one behind each of them.

When he brought his attention back to MacKenzie, she was glaring at his midsection. Looking down he saw he was still holding her hand. He let go, quickly finding his pockets. She closed the trapdoor and locked it with a bar that had been lying to the side.

She examined Ward up and down, perhaps trying to decide what to do with him next.

"All right, what the fuck happened back there?"

"I don't know." Ward stuttered the first word. "I told you, I was alone. You were all there first, and clearly you had people watching the outside. Did I bring the cops? You tell me."

She made a face.

Ward felt a moment of panic. She wasn't buying it. He clenched his fist, not sure if he should rush her or try to escape.

"Okay," she said, her tone giving nothing away. "We should be past any police activity. You can still move the Spear?"

Ward exhaled. "Of course."

"Then nothing's changed. Wait for Torres' text. I'll let him know we're still good. Take that door behind you. The third door on the right will lead you to the stairs. Go up one flight, then left. You'll find your way from there."

"And you?"

"And me what?"

"You know where you're going?" He cringed as the words came out of his mouth. He sounded like Professor Ward checking up on a helpless freshman.

"Yes," MacKenzie said. "I know where to go."

"Wait. What about—"

But she was through the door. Ward thought about going after her until a siren a couple blocks away, maybe less, prompted his feet to march towards the door MacKenzie had indicated. On the other side he wiped a layer of grime from his forehead and followed MacKenzie's directions. The hallways were wide, tall, and only occasionally lit, forcing the use of his flashlight. Piping and utility conduits ran along the walls, probably once covered up by drywall.

After his left at the top of the stairs, Ward faced a locked door. It gave way under a hard kick. Two steps inside he realized where he was—a locker room in the old football stadium.

Shining his light about revealed walls and lockers, row upon row of them, painted a faded green. On the back wall of the locker room a mural of an eagle's head in profile offered a silent reminder of a lost era. A time of huge social gatherings, sporting events, and good-natured competition. Ward, like a lot of other children who grew up in Philadelphia, had once taken a tour of the stadium after its conversion to a detention facility. Professional team sports had long been abolished by then. It was a school trip. Second, maybe third, grade. It was intended to scare the children, to make them remember that Faith was a false father and that evil Believers would inevitably end up in just such a prison.

It was only a few years later, though, that the Crematoriums were introduced. The prisons went vacant, once again sitting empty like they had after the death of professional football. Sitting empty to this day, waiting for a new Cleanse to wipe them away.

If his memory was true, it was Ward's fifth grade class trip that had taken them to the brand new Camden Crematorium.

His eye was drawn to the left. Scrawled across some lockers there, in dark spray-paint, were two words: God lives.

The battle cry of Believers. It had been a long time since

anyone had seen such graffiti in a public place. No one dared spray those words anymore, not with the REC lurking around every corner, watching every security feed, keeping its fingers in every social network.

Probably, Ward thought, *the last words ever articulated by some former prisoner.*

Another siren reminded Ward that he had to avoid being picked up by local cops. His REC identification was in the console lockbox of his car, as he'd been instructed to do on all undercover operations. Without it in hand he risked an overzealous officer executing him under the authority of the Chamberson Act, an initiative allowing local authorities great latitude to act in the interest of the Republic if they felt a terrorist attack was imminent.

The best plan, he decided, was to wait until the roads cleared. Maybe two or three hours. That would leave plenty of time to deliver the contraband by the twelve hour deadline, and still have time to go home, shower, and maybe even nap before class.

He made his way to the corner of two rows of lockers and settled in, using his jacket as a cushion. He intended to get comfortable, nothing more, but was asleep in less than five minutes.

CHAPTER
FOUR

Ward jolted awake, the feeling of falling and a dreamed
woman's face fleeing into the murky corners of the
locker room. His hands, dashing about on their
own, verified possession of the duffle bag. He blinked away
the rest of his exhaustion and climbed to his feet.

It was a little past seven. Later than he'd planned to sleep,
but still within the twelve hour deadline for delivering the
contents of the duffle bag. He stood, stretched, and found
the exit from the locker room. A barely legible sign, its paint
faded, led him to a long hallway. A second decrepit posting
at the end of the too silent corridor pointed him out to the
prison grounds. The former playing field. Now, decades after
the last prisoner had breathed this air, a generation after the
last professional athletes tore up this grass, the only remnants
of people were a handful of guardhouses and stockades, barely

more than propped up corpses. Ward marched through this decaying gauntlet of buildings and barricades, finally making his way out of the stadium by slipping beneath the remains of a brittle barbed wire fence.

Three blocks away he found his car, a Dodge Dash, in the same condition he'd left it: a six year old scraped and dinged hatchback with a faded almond pearl paintjob. It was an ugly thing with a profile like an elderly turtle. Not for the first time he lamented that unpurchased Republic Motors convertible. With only two other manufacturers still alive in North America—Dodge and Ford—the government owned RM had vaulted to the top of the food chain, making its cars the desire of every Citizen. Ward's Dodge Dash, on the other hand, was about as cheap a vehicle as could be had. It cost less than some e-drive motorcycles.

Ward repeated his feel-better mantra: *that yellow convertible would be no good in the Philly winters. No good.* He sighed and slumped into the Dodge's driver seat.

The Dash started by pushbutton, as all e-drives did. Without keys, automobile security was handled by the owner's Port which was synced to the car's computer. As long as the Port was on your person, the doors would open and the car would start. At least that was the theory. Ward's car, however, had been having a little trouble in that department, sometimes taking three or four stabs at the start button for it to get humming. He didn't use the car much, as he lived within walking distance of the university, so he'd never put any serious thought to trying to get the issue fixed. One day the car just wouldn't start, he figured. And that would be okay with him.

But with the REC now pulling his strings he'd probably have to get it looked at. *Maybe,* he thought, *he could get them to cover the repair bill. Or even buy him a new car.* That yellow convertible zipped through his mind again. He waited for it to go, then pushed the start button. First try, the car thrummed to life. He let its magnetic drive hum a moment while he rubbed his eyes. It was a calming sound, like an air conditioner or a refrigerator purring along at night. White noise. It was tempting to just close his eyes for a second.

No. He had to go. North. The field office. He put the car in drive and pulled away from the curb, thinking about that shower waiting for him at home.

———◆———

The REC's Philadelphia field office, the Tower, was a stainless steel fortress that caught the sun like a beacon anytime between dawn and dusk. Now, however, with a husky haze keeping the day's light from the jagged urban horizon, it sat like a stone in the heart of the city.

Ward drove into the Tower's underground parking structure, paying little heed to the rows of Republic District flags lining the four sidewalks of Center Square, the capital of the Atlantic District. He didn't even look at Republic Hall, an impressive limestone-clad edifice built in the Second Empire style to resemble the old City Hall that once called this Square home.

He parked in one of the designated parking spaces on the first level below ground as he'd been instructed by Agent Compano. He got out of his car and plugged it into the recharge station as he was required to do for each visit to the

Tower. And he walked across the parking level, silent but for the echoes of his own footsteps, to the door for the only available stairwell. Ward removed his ID card and passed it in front of a sensor to the left of the door. The ID card was linked to his R1 and also required a facial scan by the camera above the door. He looked up, holding the pose for a two-count. The door clicked open.

The stairs took Ward up one flight and delivered him into the Tower's main atrium beside the street-level front entrance. Walking into the atrium was like walking into a chrome box. It was a breathtaking three stories high, and it shined like the exterior of the Tower did in the sun.

Ward stood to the left of the main entrance, a sliding glass door that led into Center Square. Ahead of him was a row of subway-style turnstiles. Next were body scan booths like in an airport. And beyond these was an open courtyard. Glass cubicles lines the wall on the left. Computer terminals lined the wall on the right. In the middle stood two information kiosks. Past those the courtyard became a maze of decorative columns, benches, and three fountains. The far end of the atrium was lost beyond these obstructions.

The clutter beyond the courtyard, Agent Compano had explained, was a defensive tactic, much like the way medieval castles were built around spiral staircases, making it difficult for invaders to fight their way up. Any hostile group would be forced to make their way to the elevators and stairs at the far end by passing through the vulnerable courtyard. If they made it through they'd then be split up by the multitude of strategically designed funnels, all the while being herded towards security forces at the back and picked off by snipers in the hidden rafters above.

Looking up, Ward saw no snipers. Not surprising. What he did see—what everyone who looked up saw—were two banners, each at least twenty feet high and thirty wide, hanging from the ceiling. The first was in honor of the fallen during the War of Reclamation. The second listed the names of REC Agents killed in the line of duty.

He passed through a turnstile with the swipe of his ID, then marched through a body scan booth. Behind the booth waited one of only two security personnel Ward could see, a tall man in his mid-forties. He wore what looked like a modified police uniform. The other security guard, stationed at the far booth, was a woman of about the same age, with platinum blond hair and neck too thick for her frame. Neither looked overly vigilant.

Most people entering the Tower would have been pulled aside by one of these security guards for a physical body search. But not Agents.

"You don't want security guards getting their hands on whatever contraband we bring in," Ward had said to Agent Compano on his first visit to the Tower.

"Correct," she'd replied as if that was obvious and should have remained unspoken.

As Ward maneuvered through the courtyard, he heard the front door of the Tower slide open with a heavy *shush*. A man screamed.

Ward spun. An Agent in black tactical gear and two police officers were trying to drag a wailing hulk of a man inside. It took a cop on each of the man's tree-trunk-like ankles to break his grip on the side of the door. The prisoner's left shirtsleeve was torn off, presumably in the struggle, revealing a bulging arm covered in tattoos. From at least the elbow to the wrist, bright colors and deep blacks swirled about in a collage of ink. Ward could only make out two distinct images in the inked-cacophony: a bejeweled cross and a version of Michelangelo's *The Creation of Adam* drawn with skeleton hands.

The tattooed prisoner next grabbed on to a turnstile stanchion. One of the police officers brandished his nightstick. He offered a warning blow to the prisoner's shoulder. The nightstick seemed to disappear into the man's flesh like being swallowed by a pillow. The man lost his grip, but his thigh caught in the turnstile's bar. He howled. Without a word, the other police officer drew his nightstick, and the pair beat the prisoner into near unconsciousness. In total the drubbing, complete with the sickening sound of reinforced polymers slapping against meaty flesh and cracking the bones beneath, took only a few seconds.

As they dragged the tattooed man into the courtyard, the Agent with them motioned in Ward's direction. No, beyond Ward to where a half dozen more Agents in tactical gear emerged from behinds the columns. Above, Ward detected darkness moving within darkness in the rafters and crossbeams. The Snipers. It was an impressive response, confirming everything Agent Compano had said about the atrium's design.

The wave of reinforcements half-dragged and half-carried the prone prisoner through the rest of the courtyard. The two police officers, still without speaking, exited the building through the main entrance. As the prisoner was towed past him, Ward couldn't help but shake his head and wonder if this man would have been arrested if not for his obvious tattoos. *There could be no stupider declaration of one's Belief,* Ward thought, *than such enormous displays of illegal body ink.* Agents and police knew what to look for when they saw long sleeves and turtle necks in warm weather. And in the winter all it took was a sleeve to kink while reaching for a coffee to betray a Believer's mark.

Many Believers sported some ink, of course. Small crucifixes or a bit of Latin script. Ward at least understood these. They were generally placed covertly, personal declarations not public announcements. Those with brazen canvas painted on their bodies—like the prisoner ahead of him—might as well, he mused, have clocks tattooed on their foreheads. They were going to be caught sooner rather than later.

The procession continued to the back wall of the atrium which featured a line of four elevators flanked by a stairwell door in each corner. Ward followed most of the way then hung back while the Agents and their prisoner waited for their ride. None of them spoke other than the occasional moan from the bulky, limp prisoner. When their elevator arrived, two of them piled in with the prisoner. The rest resumed their posts.

Ward didn't want to think about where the tattooed man was going. Down. Interrogation. Just one step from Cremation.

Ward was going up. Elevators one through three, counting from the left, accessed the first five floors of the Tower, and the whole of its substructure. Only elevator four had access to the top five floors. It was also the only one without a call button. Instead, a round depression in a black inset sat where the call button should have been. Ward placed his thumb in the depression and winced. The inset lit up. There was a momentary hum, then the elevator doors opened. He removed his thumb from the pinprick DNA scanner and held it up. A drop of blood beaded in the center of his fingerprint. He licked it away and stepped inside the elevator where he pressed the top button.

The tenth floor of the Tower was laid out like a barbell with the elevator in the center of the bar. Twenty feet to the left and right waited unmarked doors. One was to Logistics and Control. L&C. The other was to Commandant Gaustad's office. The floors, walls, and ceiling, like downstairs, were gleaming steel except for the window facing him when the elevator doors opened.

From the outside it was the only inconsistency in the Tower's sheer stainless steel façade. A ten foot round window in the top floor of its western face. To those standing in the square it appeared the Tower was watching Republic Hall.

This was Ward's third visit to the Tower. His third trip to the tenth floor. And like the previous two he stood transfixed. Only when the elevator, whose doors he was holding open, dinged, did he step out and walk to the floor-to-ceiling window. His first two visits had been at night. It had been bright inside and dark outside, essentially making the window a mirror. But this morning it was transparent. He could look out on the whole city. His heart throbbed in his chest. It was like looking out a stained glass rose window in one of Europe's

Gothic cathedrals.

He'd always found it curious that such a feature should figure so prominently in the tallest building of Center Square. He'd even made the comparison in class last semester of the field office and City Hall to Saint Peter's Basilica and the Castel Sant'Angelo. It had started as a simply discussion of rose windows. Then, as he'd pushed an image of Center Square onto the classroom's projector, he was struck by how similar the layout of the Square was to Vatican City. The Dark City. It was a logical analogy, with the Castel connected by a fortified passage, the Passetto di Borgo, to the Basilica in order to serve as a bastion to protect the Pope and Vatican City if attacked. And Ward was sure there was a similar contingency plan involving Republic Hall and the Tower. The problem was, he'd said so out loud.

The boos and hisses his students had flung at the mention of the Dark City had turned into absolute silence. Shock. It was one thing to name the Dark City. It was quite another to compare it to the Atlantic District capitol.

He'd received a reprimand from Dean Markinson for the incident. And he'd told his office-mate, Ken Hickey, about it. Ken had thrown himself onto their couch and said, "Shit, Rafe. They don't have to just reprimand you for that. They can terminate you."

Ward had nodded. He'd felt numb.

"No, man," Ken had continued. "I mean terminate. They could call that treason. I heard there are still Labor Camps out west, like in the Southwest District or something. Or, you know, the Crematorium, dude."

Nothing more than a reprimand had come of it, of course. The REC already had their eye on him. It was only a week later that Agent Compano had been waiting in his office with her offer for him to "volunteer." Though now that he replayed the incident, Ward wondered if she'd chosen that morning because the official reprimand made good cover. Tangible evidence in his file would go a long way towards proving religious sympathies. Or maybe it was that particular morning to get their hands on him before he could say something in class that was even stupider.

What did it matter? He was here. Agent Rafael Ward. He put the whole thing out of mind and looked out the window on Philadelphia. The city below was barely rubbing the sleep from its eyes. A few men and women in business suits were walking through Center Square with that zombie-like gait that infected people in the early morning. None appeared to greet each other with a wave or a word as they passed. Business as usual on a Friday.

What would Citizens say, Ward wondered, when they saw the tendrils of smoke rising from the apartment building the police had nearly destroyed last night? Or when they smelled the charred wood, plaster, and paint lingering over the neighborhood for days?

Nothing, that's what they'd say. They'd take it all in and let it make them feel safe because when the cops and the REC take action they always succeed. And they always make the Republic a safer place.

Ward pulled himself away from the window and considered his options. His orders were to go left to Logistics

& Control. But after the chaos of last night he considered, for a split second, turning right, banging on Commandant Gaustad's door and demanding an explanation for last night's police interference. It was a ridiculous thought. Commandant William Gaustad was the head of the Atlantic District REC. He was the brains behind the Great Cleansing. He was the power behind the REC's termination of dozens of terrorist plots. It was likely he would be the next Republic-wide director of the REC. Speculative news feeds even claimed he stood a strong chance of winning the presidency at the next election in five years if he chose to declare. Banging on the Commandant's door would reward Ward, at best, with only the echoes of his yelling. At worst, he would be taken by security back down the elevator to one of the lower levels.

The fact was, if he was going to complain to anyone it should be Agent Compano, but she'd made it very clear that she would contact him, not the other way around. Under no circumstances would he message her. That left only one option. Ward turned left. Another ID scan opened the L&C doors to reveal what looked like a bank lobby. A series of teller-style windows lined three of the room's walls. Each window-station was made of mirrored glass reflecting more than a dozen Rafael Wards.

"If they stay mirrors," Agent Compano had said during Ward's first initial trip to L&C, "you're doing a good job. They're busy logging info and handling operations back there. They're the ones who clear op zones of police and other potential interferences. All communications are run through here. All network and tactical support comes via this room.

You don't want to ever see their faces."

Ward approached the first window on the left, revisiting his earlier thought about demanding an explanation for last night. L&C was responsible for the operation zone. Maybe he could find out here what happened by knocking on one of the windows.

As he neared a panel in the wall beside the window should have slid open revealing a small computer terminal. Beneath that should have been a drawer that would open when he was finished inputting his report.

The panel didn't open.

The window in front of him cleared revealing a middle-aged woman wearing a headset. She was clearly in her forties, yet her face was unnaturally smooth. No wrinkles. No lines. She waved Ward forward. He was frozen, unable to move. A line from a poem, something about being pinned to a wall, wriggling, came to him.

"Agent Ward, you are not scheduled this morning." The woman's voice sounded mechanical.

"What? No, last night's operation—I have contraband to deliver."

The woman touched two fingers to the headset at her ear. She nodded. Nodded again. She looked at Ward, unblinking, typed something on the console in front of her, and nodded once more. "Agent Ward, there is no record of an operation last night. You—"

"No record?" Ward's voice hit an uncomfortable high pitch. "Lady, I got shot at. The cops blew the Clean Zone, and I-I…"

You what, Rafe?

"Agent Ward," the tech said, her lifeless tone somehow calming him. "There was no operation last night. There was no police action last night other than residential security around a gas-leak explosion. There is no contraband. Agent Compano's update is thorough. You have been requested to conference directly with Commandant Gaustad."

Ward's mouth began to form the word "what," but no sound came out. Conference directly with Commandant Gaustad? It had to be a mistake.

Ward finally found a single word. "Now?"

"Now."

The woman held her stone-faced visage as the glass mirrored, leaving Ward staring at his own gape-mouthed face. He was sure his thoughts echoed the woman's behind the glass: I look like an idiot.

CHAPTER
FIVE

No handle adorned the immaculately polished stainless steel door to Commandant Gaustad's office. Ward stood a moment, wondering if he should knock. He raised his hand waist high and paused.

It had to be a mistake, right? *What reason,* Ward thought, *could Commandant Gaustad have to invite a rookie Agent into his office?*

A soft click was followed by the door sliding aside. At first Ward didn't look into the office. He couldn't. His eyes locked to the polished floor but this paralysis lasted only seconds. With a similar strength of compulsion he lifted his gaze. The Commandant's office spread before him almost like magic. It was twice as long as it was wide, with a ceiling much too high for the construction of the building.

Once more this morning his mind sidetracked to

architecture. He remembered his undergraduate studies of medieval cathedrals, the way he used to scroll through image after image of grandiose naves gaping impossibly high within those stone behemoths, wishing someday he'd be able to apply for an international travel ID. To actually cross the threshold of one of those cathedrals.

Ward stepped inside. He might well have stepped into his own daydreams from those undergraduate years. Everywhere he looked was art. Draped on the walls, sitting on pedestals, even hanging from the ceiling. There were no museums anymore—none containing works from before the birth of the Republic, anyway—as their buildings and collections were looted or destroyed during the Reclamation. What pieces had survived were so often of a religious nature that they were deemed contraband and taken to the Crematoriums, or smuggled into the shadows. Most Citizens' experiences with art came through Republic approved history lessons and data streams.

This room, however, was a gallery unlike Ward had ever seen. On his left was David's *Napoleon at the Saint-Bernard Pass*. On the right was Bosch's *Epiphany* and Rubens' *Prometheus Bound*. Sculptures ranged throughout. Ward didn't know this medium as well as he knew the paintings, but he was sure that was one of Michelangelo's *Slaves* in the center, and maybe Rodin's *Monument to Victor Hugo* closer to the head of the room. Smaller pieces filled the voids between the large ones. Ward couldn't go three steps in any direction without touching a pedestal showcasing a sword, a breastplate, a dish, or a codex.

Look at them all, he thought. Saved. Yes, hidden here in

the Tower. But survived. It almost didn't matter how or why, only that they'd been spared the fire. And what if they could be displayed? Forget Belief, religion, and law. Forget Edict Seven. What if the people could be allowed to see what men and women once could do?

A dais along the right wall beneath an array of bronze double-bladed axes, Minoan *labrys*, drew Ward's attention. It was topped with a glass case holding two golden bees, wings flexed back. Though only a few inches long, each featured glittering ruby inlayed wings.

Ward's mouth dropped open. He'd seen drawings of these French masterworks, but to his knowledge the bees themselves had been lost since they were stolen from Paris' royal library more than two hundred years ago.

"The only extant examples of Childeric's Bees. Beautiful, aren't they?"

Ward nearly jumped at the voice.

Commandant Gaustad stood before his desk at the head of the room. Had he been there the whole time?

The Commandant was a large man with a salty military buzz cut and the build of a fighter that denied his sixty or so years. His black and silver uniform fit as if it had been constructed around his frame, the way the bronze skin of a colossal statue might be placed on its steel skeleton. Braided silver epaulettes, absent on other REC apparel, left no question of the man's rank. The dark line of a scar on his neck, barely peering out above his collar, added an almost inhuman level of gravitas to the man's stature.

Ward solidified to attention. "Yes, sir," he said, unsure if he should salute.

"Relax, Agent Ward. You're not being censured. I wanted to speak with you, to congratulate you for last night. That wasn't an easy first assignment. Come, sit." Gaustad indicated a chair opposite his desk. He then sat in his own plush high-back chair and waited with his elbows propped on the desk, hands folded.

"Thank you, sir." The walk to the chair might have been a hundred yards.

The way the Commandant watched him remove the duffle bag from his shoulder and settle into the chair unnerved Ward. He imagined it was the same way he watched everything, from strategic reports to Agents' conduct assessments.

The Commandant took a breath as if about to speak, the pause allowing Ward to notice an object on the desk. He turned his head slightly, trying not to appear distracted. The Hofburg Spear? He couldn't help but stiffen.

Ward pulled his eyes from the artifact and returned them to Gaustad. The Commandant did not speak. He offered what might have been a smile and nodded his head towards the Spear, giving Ward permission to examine it. Ward hesitated.

"Please," the Commandant said, waving his hand.

Ward leaned forward to get a better look but didn't touch. Yes, it was the Hofburg Spear. There was no doubt. It'd been in his possession for over twenty hours before he'd returned it two years ago for cataloguing and Cremation.

"You seem surprised," Gaustad said, his voice betraying something like amusement.

"Yes, sir. I thought this artifact had been destroyed. My

report on it for the REC was thorough? Was there—?"

Gaustad's hand came up like a crossing guard. "No, Agent Ward. You did everything correctly. Exemplary, in fact. I've had my eye on you for a while. As for this," he passed his hand over the Spear, "it was prudent to keep it. Actually, as you are now aware, I have kept a number of artifacts over the years."

"But why?" Ward regretted his words even before he had finished saying them. You do not question an REC Commandant.

"Agent, what was your analysis of this artifact?" The Commandant tilted his head towards the Spear. There was no anger in his voice. There was, however, a tone which made Ward's stomach tighten.

"It was not authentic, sir. None of its component pieces were old enough to have been present at the purported time of its..." he paused, searching for the right word, "its mythological endowment. But still, sir, possession of any relic, authentic or otherwise is illegal. You...it..."

Gaustad waved his hand again. "Can the Republic commit a crime, Agent?"

"No, sir," Ward said, careful to measure his voice with the appropriate amount of pride the Commandant would expect from a Citizen and an Agent. "The government defines and enforces law. If it engages in activity that had previously been deemed illegal, then that activity can no longer be regarded illegal as a definitive statute. There must either be a reason for the rescinding of the law, or a nuance of the law that the average Citizen is unable to comprehend."

"Then, Agent, have I broken the law by storing illegal

artifacts, relics, in this secure office at the heart of an impenetrable REC fortification?"

"No, sir," Ward said, recognizing the rhetorical quagmire he'd stepped into. "You have chosen, if I may presume, to enforce Edict Seven by locking away illegal artifacts rather than cremating them. The artifacts in question are removed from endangering the lives of Citizens by inciting the irrationalities of Belief and Faith."

"And why would I choose internment over Cremation?"

Ward thought for a moment. There was an answer, a logical response, but it eluded him.

Gaustad pulled his elbows off the desk and leaned forward. Ward couldn't help but stare at the scar on his neck.

"Agent Compano's assessment of you is quite accurate. Smart and resourceful. You're a good asset, Agent Ward, but you do not yet see the big picture."

Ward's hands ball into fists. He didn't like being on this side of a lecture.

"The reason to keep certain artifacts," Gaustad continued, "is to prevent their martyrdom. To, let's say, keep an ace up the sleeve. What if, and I am sure it is unlikely, an insurgency of Believers was to rise up and to seek a relic to hold at the head of their new revolution? What if they were to go in search of this Spear of Destiny?" He opened his palm toward the Hofburg Spear. "Or the one in your bag? Would anything we say or do convince them that their cause is false? That their deity is the invention of primitive minds searching for answers to questions which the Republic, through science and logic, can now provide?"

"No, sir," Ward jumped in, embarrassed by his schoolboy-like eagerness to respond.

"Continue."

"Yes, sir. Our possession of that very relic which they seek can serve to refute their claim of righteousness, as surely they must believe that no 'aberrant' government could possess such a 'holy' object. And in the event that refutation of righteousness is not possible or prudent, the artifact in our possession could be shown to be the fraud that it is, with science proving its inaccuracy to the period of its supposed origin."

Gaustad rubbed his chin. "Good. You reflect well on Agent Compano. Now," his tone became more conversational, "to last night. You seem dissatisfied. Did you want to log a complaint?"

Ward stared. Could he complain to the Commandant?

"Come now. It's just us two men here. Two Agents. Let's not worry about rank, shall we?"

It was another trick, a trap, but Ward couldn't see the answer or the exit. He took a deep breath as if preparing to take a punch. "Yes, sir. Why were local police allowed in the Clean Zone? Agent Compano explained how important the Clean Zone is for our operations. At first I thought it was a mistake, but it didn't feel like a random discovery by some cop."

Gaustad stood. "Why not?"

"The force with which they breached the room, sir."

Ward felt awkward still sitting with the Commandant looming over him. He exhaled purposefully, crossed his legs, and pushed his fingers through his hair. Forget undercover Agents, he thought. If Commandant Gaustad stared at each suspected Believer like this, he was sure the criminals would confess all their actions and hand over all their contraband.

Finally, Gaustad raised his palm inviting Ward to stand and continue.

"And the timing of it, sir," Ward said, not sure if he was about to overthink himself into serious trouble. "The assault commenced just moments after my verification of the artifact. I've got to figure that the scan was monitored, right? That would mean that the assault was coordinated by Command."

Gaustad began a casual pacing of the room. Ward scurried into stride, a half step behind. Gaustad meandered around a handful of podiums, letting his silence charge the room, pausing before a wall-sized tapestry. Pagan women danced across the cloth beneath a garlanded chandelier, their bodies appearing drawn to an altar at the center. One of the characters, her hair bound up beneath a laurel wreath, looked so much like MacKenzie, even down to the powdering of freckles, that Ward couldn't help but stare.

As if there'd been no lapse in the conversation, Gaustad said, "Correct. You are also correct that you deserve an explanation and an apology. This is why I asked to meet you here. The truth is that the operation was potentially compromised. Your contact, Torres, had been working for us for eleven months, gathering intelligence on that congregation's holdings and locations."

Ward's shoulders straightened as if he'd been dosed with a small charge of electricity. He never would have guessed Torres was a traitor. MacKenzie and the others seemed to trust him completely. And it brought up another question. Why had Agent Compano not alerted him to the situation?

Sure that the answer was well above his pay grade, Ward chose not to ask it.

The Commandant turned from the tapestry and surveyed the room as if looking for something. He smoothed out his uniform and moved into the center of the room.

"We had reason to believe either his role had been exposed, or he had double-crossed us. In either case, once the presence of the contraband was verified by your scan, I instituted the exfiltration in order to secure both the artifact and you and to remove Torres as an obstacle before he could blow your cover and our greater mission. The use of local police was to create the illusion of a random sweep rather than a sting."

It sounded logical, but felt wrong. Again, the question begged to be asked. Why had Ward not been notified of the depth of the situation?

"Unfortunately," Gaustad said, the addition coming so quick it sounded like an excuse, "local law enforcement was, shall we say, over enthusiastic in their actions. Rest assured, however, we have Torres. In fact…"

Gaustad paused as if considering something. He smiled. Ward decided that he didn't like the Commandant's smile. It was somehow sinister, the way the music in a film could make your hair stand on end.

"For now, Agent Ward," Gaustad said as if waving the previous thought aside, "I offer my personal, and official, apology."

"Thank you, sir."

"Now let's take a look at what you've brought."

The Commandant returned to his desk, resuming his

place in his throne-like chair. Ward followed, also sitting. He removed the box from the duffle bag and placed it on the desk, unsure if he should open it. Gaustad tilted his head as he examined the box, before locking his focus on Ward. Not knowing what else to do Ward raised the bag, tilting it forward so the Commandant could see the money and the yellow-striped Port. Gaustad barely looked at them, his gaze passing back to the box.

Finally the Commandant leaned back and nodded. Ward took the cue and turned the box to face Gaustad. He flipped the latch and opened it.

"It's not as attractive as the Hofburg version, is it?"

Ward again studied the Spear displayed on the Commandant's desktop. Partially wrapped in gold leaf, he thought it actually bordered on gaudy. MacKenzie's Spear, on the other hand, was elegant, dignified, but he wasn't going to push it.

"No, sir."

"Mmm," Gaustad said, raising an eyebrow. "Now, your report on the night's events…you are prepared to report, yes?"

Ward acknowledged that he was. Gaustad removed his own R1 from a drawer and set it on the desk to record. Ward proceeded to relate the night's events. For a brief moment as he mentioned MacKenzie, his stomach did a somersault, like he was afraid. He coughed and choked the feeling away. The report continued, the feeling quickly forgotten.

While Ward spoke, Gaustad sat quietly, perfectly still. Only his eyes moved, sometimes closing for a moment, then re-opening and focusing on Ward. Sometimes looking at

Ward's face, sometimes his chest, and sometimes his hands. But always on him.

When Ward finished his report Gaustad leaned over the desk and closed the box.

"Fine job, Agent."

He rose. Ward once more followed suit, prepared to salute, but the Commandant continued.

"One more thing, Agent Ward. As I said, we have Torres, but the woman—this terrorist MacKenzie—has thus far eluded capture. According to our intel she has information on more artifacts. I'd like you to find her. Reinitiate contact. Gain her trust. Gain her congregation's trust. I want the location of all her holdings. We need to know everything they have and everything they know. Understood?"

Ward felt his eyes go into a spasm of rapid blinking. Find MacKenzie? Yes, of course yes.

Infiltrate a congregation of Believers? Terrorists? No, of course no. He was an academic not a spy. *They came to me*, he thought. *They gave me the contraband. How am I supposed to find her?*

"Agent."

It was a prompt, not a question. There was no reason for the Commandant to question. Agents followed orders.

"Yes, sir."

"You'll receive more detailed instructions tomorrow. A little time is good. If you stumble across each other too soon, she'll be suspicious. Agreed?"

Another non-question.

"Yes, sir."

The salute, Ward knew, should come next. Yet his body was locked. The desire to leave, abruptly tangible, pulsed in his temples. The Commandant, however, his attention already back to the box, didn't appear to notice this lack of decorum.

A second or two passed before Ward's legs, seemingly on their own, walked him towards the exit. The art and artifacts in the room rolled by as if he were passing them in a car. The fingers of his left hand brushed a marble pedestal, the fringe of a tapestry, the cold glass of a display case, the rim of a large vase which had been, from the fissures climbing its length, recently reassembled.

His feet stopped. "Have any of them, sir," Ward heard himself say, somehow not sure what the next word was until it passed his lips, "ever been real? These artifacts, have any of them even been period authentic?"

He turned to find the Commandant frozen halfway between sitting and standing.

"There's only ever been…" Gaustad's eyes widened as he spoke, appearing as surprised by his answer as Ward had been by the question.

"Sir?"

Gaustad shook his head. Was it a negation? The clearing of a thought?

"Death, Agent Ward. The only truth in a relic is death." Gaustad dropped into his chair. "You have your orders," he said, focused on something in the corner of the room.

The door slid open. Ward looked at his fingers, the tips still resting on vase's rim. He recognized it as Greek, about twenty-six hundred years old by the black figures painted around its circumference, yet something about it seemed incongruous with this analysis. The proportions. The glaze. It wasn't Greek, it was—

"Is there something else, Agent?" The Commandant's voice sounded stressed and tired.

Without turning Ward continued to the door. "No, sir."

CHAPTER
SIX

If there was such a thing as sleep-lecturing Professor Ward was doing a masterful job of it. For the last three and a half hours he'd muffled the conscious division of his brain—that arena screaming, "Look at the clock." The books, the history, the research, the legends had all taken over, had dragged him through the morning into the afternoon.

After his discussion with Commandant Gaustad there hadn't been time for a shower. Instead, he'd parked his car on the street in front of his apartment and walked the three blocks to campus. After a brief stop in the restroom to wash his hands and face of what seemed like a year's worth of grime, Ward made his way to his office.

Ken hadn't been there, which was good. Ward wasn't in the mood to talk to anyone else yet. He closed and locked the door and opened the middle right drawer of his desk.

He took out his emergency bottle of Louisiana Bourbon and poured two fingers into his emergency non-coffee mug taken from the same drawer. He plopped into his chair, leaned back, and held the mug under his chin like it was filled with a hot drink on a cold day.

After a few moments he'd downed the bourbon. It had a bite but not nearly as much fruitiness as he preferred, which was why this bottle was stowed away in the emergency drawer. He shivered, coughed, and put the emergency provisions away. Then he'd taken off his field jacket and shaken it out, as if that would cleanse it of last night. He draped it over his chair and retrieved one of the three sport jackets hanging on the back of the office door. The black one with the thin white pinstripes. This he put on and declared himself ready for class.

Now, he let himself drift on auto-pilot through a repeat of his lecture from the previous class period.

"Charlemagne then, in the deal he'd brokered with Pope Leo, was crowned Imperator Romanorum, or Holy Roman Emperor, on the ancient Christmas holiday in 800."

The words kept coming. He could have been reciting song lyrics and neither he nor, likely, his students would have noticed. He finally allowed himself to seek the clock over the door.

How could he be ten minutes behind where he was last class?

It was too much. He wanted the day to end. The meeting with Gaustad, the way their final exchange just hung in the air. The grimy clothes he was still wearing. He'd never been the most professional of dressers, but his standard classroom attire of a buttoned dress shirt and a sport coat were a far cry from boots, dirty jeans, and sweat-soaked t-shirt. Yes, he had on the nicest of his sport coats, but putting a bow on a shitty gift, he'd once heard his father say, wouldn't make it a better birthday.

If he could just get through another twenty-five minutes…

But Gaustad's orders were making that impossible. Infiltrate. How does a university professor infiltrate what might be a small army of insurrectionists? How does he get the girl to trust him?

On any other day, a lecture like this would find Ward acting out the parts of the players, seeing and feeling their emotions. He'd sometimes employ one of his students to take the role of Pope Leo and crown him at the altar of his desk.

This afternoon, however, he couldn't concentrate.

"So, that's it? They made him emperor, and then he died?"

Ward stopped. He scanned the room. Who said that? What had he said to prompt the outburst?

His gaze landed on Andre Richards, a plump junior who wrote down everything Ward said, even the sarcastic quips.

"What was that, Andre?"

"You went from the coronation to his death. Nothing else happened?"

Ward looked from Andre to the clock and back. Images of the treasures in Gaustad's office shuffled through his mind. The tapestries, pottery, paintings, and sculptures. Interspersed with these were flashes of the woman from last night. The Believer. The criminal and terrorist who'd saved his life. Her eyes. Blue or green? Or maybe some exotic coppery tint?

He willed himself to focus. To choose any one image and end the mental slideshow. The image his mind grasped on to was the golden bees. Childeric's bees. They'd come up an article recently. There'd been an occasion. What was it?

"Do you all know what this past May was?" he asked, finally remembering.

No one answered. Ward let the silence hover a moment before continuing.

"It was the four hundredth anniversary of the discovery of one of the greatest treasure hoards in history," he said. He followed this up by telling the story of the deaf, mute monk, who while working on restorations of the Church of Saint Brice in Belgium, had discovered the thousand year old tomb and treasure of the first Merovingian King, Childeric. He couldn't remember the monk's name but that didn't slow him. He pushed image after image from his Port onto the classroom's display. Swords and coins and jewels the size of apples. He made sure to show a drawing done during the reign of Louis XIV of the golden bees which were discovered in the hoard. Until this morning, that drawing had been the only example of the bees Ward had known to exist. He wished he'd taken a photo of the real ones with his R1.

An energy gripped Professor Ward. It wasn't so different from the adrenaline he'd felt last night. Only he knew this feeling. It was the classroom. The engagement. The moment. He felt like himself again.

He climbed on top of his chair and reenacted Childeric's speech at the end of his exile. He pulled students from their seats to play Childeric's son and daughters as the monarch declared his succession near the end of his life. He acted out the nameless deaf, mute monk's discovery of the treasure in the mid-seventeenth century. His students cheered. They passed imaginary jewels and pieces of gold to each other. They tapped their own university-issued Ports together, beaming images of the real treasure from Port to Port. They even pretended to fight over the treasure in a manner Ward imagined was far more realistic than they knew.

In time Ward looked to the clock. They'd gone six minutes past the end of class.

He settled everyone down by reminding them of their reading assignment for Monday, and then watched them pack up and filed out of the room. Many of them were still arguing over which jewels they would trade for how many gold coins. Inexplicably one pair were doing their haggling in mock-pirate speak.

"I'll give you twenty coins for your ruby, me bucko," Fern Clemmens said.

"Yar, that be not even close, matey," David Childress replied from beneath his mop of blond hair.

Ward shook his head and made his way out of the room, last to exit as always. This time when he entered his office Ken was waiting.

"There he is," Professor H, as the students called him, announced in his ever-exultant, somewhat shrill, tenor. "We on for tonight?"

Ward smirked. Of course they were on for tonight. Happy Hour at The Barrel, a bit of a dive bar a block from campus, just one block further from Ward's apartment. They went every

Friday, usually staying until students began rolling in around nine. Though there'd been plenty of nights they'd closed the place down, leaving precious few minutes to get home before the fall of curfew. There'd even been a few nights they'd come far too close to taking home, or going home with, a current or former student.

Ken stood and swept up a pile of papers and books from his desk. "I thought so. I'll have a margarita waiting for you."

"I'm not drinking a freakin' margarita," Ward said. "And I need to go home for a shower and a nap first."

"Ah, bullshit," Ken said, his used-car-salesman smile beaming triumphant. "I'm heading over now. I'll save you a seat."

Ward knew Ken wasn't actually going now. It was only half past three. The banter was part of the game. The Friday ritual. But Ken would likely be there in an hour with some ridiculously colored margarita sitting in front of the empty barstool beside him.

"Whiskey and soda," Ward said.

Ken headed for the door. "Margarita it is," he shouted then was gone.

———◆———

Ward got to The Barrel a few minutes after six. He felt better, having stopped home for a shower and to eat the last two slices of leftover pizza in his fridge. But he still promised himself he would only stay for two drinks tonight. He even believed the promise would hold up.

The Barrel was a typical restaurant/bar. Upon entering, the restaurant section, consisting of about two dozen tables, spread to the right. To the left was the bar area. The bar itself was L-shaped and made from a dark wood coated in a thick, glossy polyurethane. It featured a brass foot rail and about twenty chairs. A handful of high-top tables filled the rest of the space.

"There he is," Ken said, upbeat and shrill as ever. A quickly melting frozen margarita sat before an empty stool to his left. He raised his own class. Inside was a concoction that Ward could only guess was a Bloody Mary or some similar drink. "I was wondering if you'd make it."

"Just needed a shower."

Ken grinned. "You win this time. Next week, you come early and get the seats."

Ward offered a laugh. They both knew he'd never beat Ken here. And there was never any reason to worry about not having seats. Not this early. At present there were a couple families having an early dinner on the restaurant side. And at the bar the only other people were Carrie, the bartender, and an old man sitting a number of seats away by the corner.

Ward took a sip of the margarita and grimaced. On cue, Carrie came over, a rocks glass in her hand.

"You want a real drink now, Rafe?" As always she was wearing an impeccably tight, impeccably low cut black shirt. She grinned and went to work making Ward's beverage without waiting for a reply or an order.

Ken elbowed Ward in the ribs. "Come on," he said, tilting his head towards Carrie.

She wasn't yet in her mid-twenties. Her blonde hair was usually pulled back but tonight it was loose, hanging in her eyes and to her shoulders. She bounced when she walked, like a dancer always between moves.

On any other girl Ward would have thought her tight shirt would have bordered on tawdry. On her it was somehow elegant.

Ken teased Ward endlessly about her. On just her second or third week on the job, she'd made it plenty clear that Ken had no chance with her. So he'd taken to encouraging Ward, and digging for the vicarious thrill of hearing gossip that never actually came.

The truth—which neither Ward nor Carrie ever shared with Ken—was that they had spent a night together. It was over a year ago. And there hadn't been a repeat. Her age was part of it. She wasn't too young for Ward, but she also wasn't quite old enough for him to not think of her as in the same category as his students. The other part of it was simply that the pair had made it clear to each other that night was all physical and fun. Nothing more. No need. No desire to own a part of the other person. No pitter-patter as an ex-girlfriend of Ward's had once said.

And the best part was there'd been no awkwardness afterwards. No regret. No avoided eye contact. Just an occasional shared look between them, maybe a wink, when Ken started pushing Ward to find a girlfriend. Carrie even sometimes got in on the act, digging away at Ward for his bachelor lifestyle. She'd even offered to set him up once or twice with a friend. But the fact was Ward liked living alone. He liked not having to worry about someone worrying about him, especially now with his new night job working for the

REC.

Ward thought of MacKenzie. He hadn't meant to. Her face, freckled and streaked with dirt from the tunnel, just popped into his head. Before he could process it, however, Ken dug his elbow into Ward's side again and gave his car-salesman grin.

As if reading Ward's desire to end Ken's needling, the old man at the end of the bar suddenly slapped his glass down on his coaster. "A pint for the road," he said. No, not said. He almost sang it.

"Oh, right," Ken said. "Rafe, this is Gabe. He's been keeping me company till you got here."

Ward offered a polite hello and was about to turn away from both men when he found himself staring. The old man was beyond old. Eighty? A Hundred? It was impossible to tell. But his eyes were bright. There was no rheumy dullness there. The more Ward examined the old man, the more he found himself being drawn into the crags and gullies that lines his face until he was no longer sure that Gabe was an old man. Had Ken said Gabby? There was something about the man's cheekbones, the way his chin tapered that was just so...feminine.

"Here you go," Carrie said as she brought Gabe a new glass of beer.

She blocked Ward's view of the old man for a brief moment. When she stepped aside, Ward felt an almost vertigo-like dizziness. Gabe was undoubtedly a man. Grizzled and masculine. Ward shook his head to clear it.

"Nice night?" Gabe asked.

Ken said something, but the old man—yes, still definitely a man—was staring right at Ward, somehow indicating that it was Ward's duty to answer, not Ken's or anyone else's.

"Yeah," Ward said. "Pretty nice." It was, actually, a bit chilly for this early in the semester, but the sky was clear and bright. It really was a great night for a—

"A walk then," Gabe said.

"What?"

Ken chimed in, "He said it's a nice night for a walk."

Ward didn't think those weren't the words the old man had said.

"War's coming," Gabe said, his mouth near the rim of his glass, but his eyes locked on Ward.

The vertigo returned. Ward tried to blink it away. "What did you say?"

Gabe downed a gulp of his beer. "I said, young man, there's more coming."

Ward was certain this time that wasn't what Gabe had said. But before he could push for clarification, Carrie appeared before him. She placed his whiskey and soda on a coaster before him. "You look tense, Rafe," she said. "Want to talk about it?"

"I'm good," Ward said.

Before he could turn back to Gabe the front door swung open, crashing into the wall. A half dozen college students bound in, raucousing their way up to the bar. Ward tried to refocus his attention to the old man but the seat at the end of the bar was empty.

"Where'd he go?" Ward asked Ken.

"Who?"

Ward wanted to shake his office mate and scream, "The old man, you idiot. Where's the creepy old man?" But it suddenly occurred to him that there might not have been an old man. What had he looked like? Had he spoken? No. It was an old woman. Wasn't it?

Ward's thoughts rolled until, somehow, they landed on the shower he'd taken that afternoon. It should have relieved some of the shock of last night, and the stress of this morning. But it obviously hadn't. In fact, each time he blinked, bursting images—there and gone before he even realized it, like flashes from a camera—of severed hands and spattered blood assaulted him. Part of him wanted to get up and leave, to run home and hide in sleep. But he was afraid sleep wouldn't keep the images at bay. So he contrived a grin to go with his insistence that he was fine. He would put his trust in the power of alcohol to make his sleep later that night an empty one.

Ward downed his drink without tasting it. He felt the burn, though. It was good. Not enough yet to shut out the memory of last night's gunfight but it was a start. He pushed the glass forward.

For a brief instant, Ward found himself trying to remember something. Or was it someone? He looked off to the far end of the bar, now populated by a handful of jocks in hoodies and their girlfriends. Hadn't there been...

Carrie was standing in front of Ward wearing a mischievous grin. How long had she been there? She swiped his glass off the bar, mixed him another, and poured herself a shot of vanilla vodka.

"Happy Hour," she said, raising her glass.

Ward took his from her other hand and waited for Ken to raise his drink.

"Happy Hour," they repeated together, and drank.

CHAPTER SEVEN

Ward's apartment was the third floor of a converted century-and-a-half old Victorian home. It was the corner house on the last street in the area that still showcased the obsolete style. When walking home, either from class or the bar, he almost always paused to take in the sight of his favorite part of the building, its spired cupola rising on the southeast corner.

Tonight he didn't pause or look up.

It was late. He wasn't sure what time but curfew couldn't be more than a few minutes off. Still, he'd walked the four blocks slowly. Something gnawed at him. It wasn't the gunfight. He'd succeeded in burying the most disturbing images from last night under a pool of at least five whiskey and sodas. It was something else. An important detail he'd overlooked before the gunfire, or after. Or maybe this morning at the Tower. It was a feeling like a necessary word impishly dancing away from his tongue. The image of an old man bobbed through his mind in the wake of the lost word, then was gone. As Ward passed beneath the cupola, he gave up, deciding to forget it. To deal with it tomorrow.

He entered at the side of the building, his apartment the only one in the house with a private entrance and stairwell. He bounced up the first flight. The second flight, however, seemed steeper and longer than usual. His chest and legs begged to take the remaining steps deliberately. Obediently he slowed his pace.

Finally he reached the small landing before his door. He unlocked it and let himself in, nearly losing his balance when the door swung open. The apartment opened into a combined foyer and dining room. Ward flung his jacket onto the small folding table against the left wall below the bronze laurel wreath and plaque he'd been given by the university upon his appointment as Professor of History. Ward nodded at the plaque the way you might towards a passing acquaintance. He then had a moment's trouble with his holster and gun but was finally able to disentangle himself from them and drop them on top of the jacket.

Now free of the constraints of his job, Ward made the familiar walk from the dining room to the kitchen for a glass and back to the dining room. In the corner opposite the laurel wreath waited a second folding table laden with half a dozen bottles of inexpensive, though not cheap, whiskeys and bourbons. He grabbed a green-labeled bottle from the back and filled his glass halfway.

One more should take care of the night, he thought. As well as the nagging feeling that he'd forgotten something. He took a sip. Its aroma was smoky. The taste was sharp. He held it in his mouth a moment before gulping it down, letting it spread first a chill then warmth through his chest.

His legs took over from there, carrying him to the foremost room in the apartment, the one built into the cupola. It was his favorite part of the apartment. An octagon of bookshelves jutting out from the rest of the building. The only spot in the apartment from which he couldn't see a television.

And, of course, there was his chair in the middle. High-backed and firm, it embraced him like a giant pillow. It made him think of sleep. And of dreams.

The boy knew something was wrong. It wasn't the couple dozen people in his house; he understood life and death and funerals, at least enough for an eleven year old. It was something else. It was like watching a video-game split-screen—one eye saw the first person player view, the other saw a third person doll-house-with-the-roof-removed view. There was Aunt Ginger by the deli spread. There was Patti and Michael. That must be Uncle Roger with his face buried in the fridge. He could even see himself, little Raffi, pushing through people with his arm outstretched, not caring if he was touching leg, buttocks, or groin.

But it wasn't the view that was most disconcerting. It was the air. Somehow dense. Musty. Smoky.

Where was Mommy?

The boy ran upstairs, elbowing past Grandpa Walt. His first-player view saw Grandpa grab the banister to keep from tumbling over. The doll-house view saw the boy's head bobbing left and right and left again. Where was she? Which room? Which door?

Mommy's. Yes, of course. He tried the door. The knob was hot. He snatched his hand back, covered in embers and ash. The air grew sharp, like inhaling needles. He coughed.

He was at Daniel's door. He hadn't turned to it, hadn't walked down the hallway. He was just there, his hand on the knob. It was cold. He heard Mommy's voice from inside. The split-screen view blinked out. It was his eyes now.

The door opened.

His older brother's room hadn't changed, not in a week. The same toys lay on the floor. The same sheets crumpled unmade on the bed. It was as if the brothers had just finished playing and left it all to await their return.

A die-cast fire engine on the shelf burst into a tiny flame. Raffi recoiled.

He faced the bed. Again he hadn't moved.

The rest of the room melted. The greens and blues of the bed sheets, the yellows of the curtains, the oranges and browns and reds of the toys merging together like candle wax until there was just the naked bed. And a woman kneeling before it.

Her back was to him but it was as if he could see through her. She reached her hands to her chest and folded them together. She spoke soft, confusing words he did not understand. She was reading them. An old book lay open on the bed, a book he had never seen before. She turned a page and refolded her hands. After a few more words she raised her voice.

"It's okay, Raffi. I just miss him. I miss them both. This is how people used to say goodbye."

But it wasn't okay. It was wrong. It was called Prayer. They'd been taught in school what to look for. How to recognize Prayer, and Worship, and Faith. Those three Bad Things which would only lead to more lies, more wars, more crusades, more deaths.

"Don't you want to say goodbye to your father and your brother?"

Mommy turned. Her eyes were empty. Tears drained from black, bottomless sockets. Wrapped around her left hand was a silver chain, its pendant closed in her fist. Raffi knew what it was. He knew it was one of those Bad Things. That's why it was kept in the back of Mommy's closet, farther back even than where she hid birthday presents.

She opened her fist and laid out her palm. "Take my hand and say goodbye." Smoke leaked out with her words.

The boy backed up.

"Raffi." It sounded almost like a question. Almost like her real voice.

He backed up another step, his feet sticking to the waxy emptiness of the room.

"Raffi." Her voice was so smooth. He wanted to roll himself up in it like a blanket but it was wrong. The whole thing was wrong.

"Rafael," she screamed.

The boy spun and ran, through the once again solid hall, down the stairs, into the living room. The people were gone. Instead, the living room was populated with dozens of unfamiliar potted trees, their branches groping blindly about the room. He banged into one and they all toppled over, the pots shattering and the trees splashing as if they were made of water. He grabbed the phone. One. One. One. It rang twice. On the third, someone picked up.

Ward woke to a scream. His own?

He was sweating, but he was also, somehow, comfortable for what felt like the first time in weeks. He knew the dream. And familiarity was welcome after the stress of what he'd been through in the last twenty-four hours.

He'd been visited often by the dream over the years. As a teen it was one of the main causes of his insomnia. Or maybe it was just a symptom. Either way, once he entered the military after high school it came less frequently. By the time he'd completed his studies he would often go months, even a year, without experiencing it. Or, at least, without remembering having dreamed it. And now... How long had it been since the last one? Two years? Three?

But there was something different about tonight's dream. Something new. He tried to recall. There was the lucent image of his mother. The fire. The phone. These were standard to the dream. What was different?

Ward realized he was still holding his not-yet-empty glass. He took the last sip of the bourbon, sucking his teeth as it went down. The answer began to float along in his consciousness like a child's newspaper boat. Not coming towards him, though. Rather it seemed to be moving parallel to his mind, again like that word you want to say, that you can see and taste and hear but can't find the sounds to make.

The stream changed direction. He reached for it but the more he stretched the farther away it drifted. It was as if he was squinting into his own psyche, narrowing the focus until there was only a small tunnel of light chasing the solution down a drain.

He stood and looked at his watch. It was after one. He went into the kitchen for something to eat. There wasn't much in the fridge. He'd finished the pizza that afternoon. His options were half a block of cheese, ketchup, a jar of salsa, and two bottles of water. The freezer was bare, absent even of frost. And the cabinets contained only a box of pasta and a bag of croutons.

There was, at least, an apple on the counter. It wasn't quite what he was in the mood for but it would have to do. He traded his glass for the apple, weighed it in his hand, and took a bite.

"Remember!"

Ward nearly dropped the apple at the sound of his mother's voice. Imagined, of course, he told himself. Still, he stepped into the dining room and looked around. He peered into the reading room and down the hall towards the bedroom and bathroom. The apartment was empty. He was alone. He waited. Listened. There was nothing.

"Remember what?" he whispered to nothing. To the bottles of alcohol. To the laurel wreath.

None of it responded. It didn't matter. He knew. Remember the funeral.

He went back into the kitchen and sat down.

It had been only weeks after his eleventh birthday. A Wednesday. The house full of people. He could tick off their names like taking role even though he hadn't seen one of them since.

The fire.

No, that was the dream. Not the memory. He needed the

memory. He closed his eyes.

His father and Daniel had been killed in a car accident. Daniel was thirteen. Ward had discovered years later that the truck which hit them on Roosevelt Boulevard was fleeing two REC vehicles. According to the news archives, six people were killed in the pileup. The main cause of the deaths was that two of the vehicles had been old models. Gasoline models. The explosion of the first ignited the rest.

Ward directed his mind to the funeral, held at their house seven days after the cremations, as per Republic mandate. He pulled on the threads and strings and ropes of the memory of that day.

He saw his mother kneeling in front of Daniel's bed. He saw himself realizing that she was praying. He watched himself make a choice to enforce a law that, at eleven years old, he couldn't truly understand. He'd called the REC Emergency Hotline, then trudged back upstairs and placed his hand on his mother's heaving shoulder.

She'd hugged him, told him that she loved him. He could still feel the tickle of her hair, cut short in mourning as was the custom. He'd pulled back and told her that she was in trouble. He could still see her face, like illustrations in a book. On the first page her brow wrinkled and her mouth drooped open. On the second page her whole face smiled, except for her eyes. Then she'd squeezed him even tighter. On the third page she cried.

A voice then had come from downstairs, booming instructions for everyone to leave the house. His mother had kissed him on the forehead and, as two uniformed Agents entered, she'd pressed her hands into his.

"I love you, Raffi," she'd said. "Remember us."

Ward could still feel the bite of her fingernails. And something else. The cut of metal in his palm.

A gift. One he wanted to forget but which the dream always forced him to remember.

Ward opened his eyes. He knew he wouldn't sleep again until he held it. But he didn't want it to touch him. Time passed. He ate the apple. He threw away the core. He gave in.

Taking a heavy breath, Ward went into his bedroom, then to his closet. There, in the deepest corner, was a schoolboy's blue knapsack.

A strange doubt crept into his belly. *It's been years. Will it still be there?*

Of course it will, he argued with himself. Where could it go?

Yet the fear persisted, fueling his rapidly beating heart. He tore at the zipper, opening the backpack. From inside he pulled a crumpled blue shirt, Daniel's shirt, as cobalt and as fresh as when it was new.

Ward sat on the edge of the bed. *It's so small,* he thought.

He brought the shirt up to his face, careful not to let it unfurl and lose the treasure hidden in its folds. He inhaled. It smelled like cookies.

He flopped back on the bed, the knapsack on his chest rising and falling with his breaths. He fell asleep smiling.

CHAPTER EIGHT

Ward sat up, the blue shirt dropping into his lap. Had he fallen asleep again? Had a noise woken him? A voice?

The television mounted on the wall opposite the bed was the only light in the apartment. It flickered occasionally as the scene shifted or as images of war scrolled across the screen. The program was a retrospective on the famous 174th Infantry Brigade. After the destruction of Washington, D.C., it was the 174th, an Army Reserves training unit, which marched three hundred miles from near Lake Ontario to New York City to liberate the city from its occupying insurrectionists. The first great victory for the Republic. It was a well-made documentary. Ward, and the majority of Citizens he was sure, had watched it on its first run last week.

When the show paused for a news break—another report

on the chaos that was gripping Europe's streets, this one titled "Rioting in Paris"—Ward rolled onto his side and gripped the blue shirt like a pillow.

He should have slept through the night. In the past, when he'd been compelled to dig out the shirt and its buried treasure, holding it to his chest had always resulted in a refreshing, unbroken sleep. Why not tonight?

He waited, hoping an explanation would come from somewhere but there was only the flashing scenes from the television. Minutes passed. It could have been three or thirty. He was sleepy but unable to close his eyes.

Then, a sound—a creaking of the stairs? Ward jumped to the edge of the bed. A second sound, a tapping. Ward bolted to his feet and into the hallway. He waited.

Five seconds. Maybe ten. Everything was silent but he knew he hadn't imagined it. As quietly as he could Ward moved to the dining room and slid his pistol from its holster on the table. He pressed himself against the wall.

Someone knocked on the door. Ward nearly pulled the trigger.

He exhaled to steady his pulse and relaxed his grip on the pistol. He crept to the door and peered out the sight hole. A silhouette against the stairwell light waited, unmoving.

"Let me in, Rafael."

He knew the voice. The woman. "MacKenzie?"

"Now."

Ward opened the door wide enough for the woman to side-step into the apartment. She was wearing the same clothes as last night, holding her backpack in her left hand.

She'd apparently tried to clean herself up some in the last twenty-four hours but it looked like a rushed job undertaken with the help of a broken mirror. Soot still veined her face and caked her hairline.

He was surprised to see that her dark hair was actually a deep red.

"Is it safe?" Her voice was low, and she appeared ready to drop into a crouch at any moment.

"What are you doing here?" Ward shifted his body to prevent her from seeing the pistol.

"Can we talk without being monitored?"

Ward actually had no idea. It was not something he'd previously considered. He was gripped by the need to tell her to run. To dash the REC oath he'd been forced to take and tell her to get as from him as possible.

She needs help, the voice in his head countered. *Keep her close.*

Ward nodded, affirming it was safe. He pointed her to the reading room, closing the door behind her and following. She positioned herself in front of his reading chair but didn't sit.

"Are you going to shoot me?"

Ward looked at the gun in his hand. "What are you doing here?" he said again, placing the pistol on the bookshelf and turning on a small lamp in the corner.

"They got Torres," she said.

Ward almost asked who had gotten Torres. But he knew. The REC. For all intents and purposes Ward himself was the one who'd gotten the bearded man.

MacKenzie was describing what happened after she left the stadium. It took Ward a second to find his way into her narrative.

"They just bulled down the street like they knew he was in the van. At least two dozen of them. I couldn't do anything. I could hear him trying to start the van but," she peered out the window into the darkness, then back to Ward, "they pulled him right through the window. I ran."

She sounded like she was confessing her own crime.

"You walked here?" He was impressed she'd managed to evade the police after curfew, not to mention the Agents that were surely scouring the city.

MacKenzie dropped into the chair. "I did what I had to."

Ward was suddenly gripped by an emotion somewhere between elation and fear. Seeing her again wasn't a realistic expectation, no matter how much he now admitted he wanted to, even with Commandant Gaustad's orders. What he couldn't discern was whether he was happy to see her or happy that his job just got easier.

"So, what can I do?"

"I need a place to stay tonight. You're the best choice I've got."

"What about your friends?" Ward couldn't believe he was really her only option. At best, to her, he was a smuggler with a small conscience. Trusting him to move a relic was one thing. Showing up in the middle of the night and trusting him with her life was either foolish or desperate. And somehow, as if it had been arranged, she was playing right into Commandant Gaustad's plan.

"No. Can't be trusted."

"What do you mean? Why not?"

"The whole reason we came to you was Torres thought we'd been compromised. The Spear was no longer safe. We had to expedite our plans." She paused and ran her hands through her hair. "We couldn't trust anyone on the inside but us four. Now I'm the only one left."

"Torres thought you'd been compromised?" Ward couldn't believe it had been the bearded man's idea. *He* was the traitor. Commandant Gaustad had said so. But as this idea came to him, Ward saw the big picture. The Spear wasn't safe, MacKenzie said. That was Torres's chance to get Gaustad what he wanted. And what better way to convince a congregation they'd been infiltrated than by using the infiltrator.

"Last night is proof. That was no random sweep. They knew we were there." Her shoulders slumped. "Is the Spear safe?"

Lie.

"Yes."

"Thank God. Where is it?"

"Safe."

You are going to have to do better than that, Rafe.

"A safe house." The words were out before he could formulate any other idea.

Mackenzie scowled. "It's not here?"

"I couldn't just bring something like that to my house," Ward said, raising his hands like bad guys do in movies. "It's safe. I promise."

Her nose and upper lip wrinkled as if she'd tasted something tart. "When do you leave?"

What was a good answer? What would she believe?

"Tomorrow," he said. "Afternoon. Depending on when the text came." It felt wrong the moment the words past his lips.

She glared at him then scanned the apartment as if expecting someone to pounce out of the darkness. Ward wondered if it was actually going to happen.

"Okay. Put your hands down, Rafe. You look like an idiot." She grinned, more with her eyes than a full smile. "One more thing." She slumped into the chair.

"Yeah?"

"I'm going with you."

"What?"

"We pick up the Spear in the morning, and then I'm not letting it out of my sight. Whatever your plan was you're taking me along. Or sending me alone with the Spear. I don't care. Where it goes, I go."

Ward wasn't prepared for this. He still didn't know where they wanted him to send the Spear in the first place. At worst he thought she might ask for the details of how he moved his contraband. That he could have faked. But the Spear was gone. Whether Commandant Gaustad had delivered her Spear for Cremation or chose to confine it to his office or some warehouse, there was no way it would be allowed to leave the REC's custody.

"I don't know if I can do that."

"I'm not asking."

Grasping at anything to keep her from demanding to see the relic, Ward said, "I can't guarantee I can keep you safe."

"It's not about my safety. It's about the Spear. It might be the thing that can change," she hesitated, maybe looking for the right word, "all this." She swept her hand towards the window.

Ward didn't know what to say. He knew the foolishness of her zeal. No Spear of Destiny, especially not one forged too late to be anything other than some foot soldier's tool, was going to change the indoctrinated Citizens of the Republic, nor loosen the grip of men like Gaustad or President Barclay.

But how do you slow down a Believer on a mission?

You don't have to.

It was true. All he needed to do was keep her close. Keep himself necessary. He could promise the Spear, swear his support for her crusade, and perhaps learn everything the Commandant wanted to know before lunch tomorrow. At that point it was as simple as waiting for Gaustad's message, letting him know where MacKenzie was, and staying out of the REC's way.

Until then the game was to learn.

"Change it all how?"

"Come on, professor. You know the legends, the stories of what the Spear can do."

"An army of God, invincible with the Spear before it, huh?" He didn't mean to sound glib, but the look on MacKenzie's face said she was unhappy with his clear lack of belief in the artifact.

"All the people need to rise up and fight is a symbol. The Spear can be that symbol. But time is running out."

Ward wanted to ask why, what was going to happen so soon that time was running out. But before he could press for more information, she continued.

"It has to go now."

"Okay," Ward said. "Where? The Western Districts?" Rumors had been spreading about unrest, particularly in the Southwest. The news consistently denied, or ignored, the stories, but if there was any truth this could be a good time to find out. A new strategy occurred to him. If he succeeded in getting all the possible intel on MacKenzie and her allies—if he could add to that information on where and when a possible uprising was coming out west—maybe he could earn enough status within the REC to ask for a release from service as a reward.

It was a bit of a ridiculous idea but Ward grabbed at it, ignoring an altogether different emotion that tried to creep up as he accepted his role as MacKenzie's new betrayer.

"Europe," MacKenzie said, her voice low, but with a tone like she was announcing a destination a few blocks away.

"Europe?" Ward wasn't expecting this. Believers, as far as he knew, smuggled their cherished relics out of that growing mess, not into it.

"Torres said you could take the Spear anywhere," she said. Her eyes were pleading but her voice was strong and decisive. "He's gone. Maley and Harrigan are dead."

At the mention of MacKenzie's dead allies Ward thought of the severed hand he'd seen while crawling through the cellar. His stomach turned. His mouth became watery. It was all he could to swallow and hold back the need to vomit.

"There's no one else," MacKenzie was saying. "You're going to do this for me. You have to."

Ward knelt in front of her, confused by a sudden desire

to pledge his service to her. He choked back his nausea and said, "I'll try."

MacKenzie stared, a persistent, searching gaze. Another unexpected emotion announced itself—he was pleased to find her eyes were green. Grassy, bright, and flecked with blue and gold.

Finally she spoke. This time it was slow and even. "There is no trying, Rafe. You're going to get me to Paris."

"Paris?" Not just Europe but the center of the European shitstorm. Not a news update passed on the television without a segment on this most troubled of all of Europe's cities. Another riot in Paris. Believers take to the streets in Paris. Innocents killed in a terrorist bombing in Paris. Just last week, Agent Compano had shown him an REC intelligence update detailing the nationalization of the city's police force. Troops had been brought in. Paris had become a militarized zone.

MacKenzie shook her head as if aware of Ward's thoughts. "None of that other shit matters. You've got to make it happen."

"I—it's not. I don't know. That's not how it works. I don't smuggle people." Ward felt like he was babbling. "My contacts won't trust you. They trust me. Only trust me."

The dull ting of metal on wood caused Ward to look down. A pistol lay on the armrest of the chair, MacKenzie's hand resting on the grip. He hadn't even seen her move.

"Professor," she said, her voice slow and even, "I asked nicely. Now I'm telling you. Make it happen. Or start praying."

Her clenched jaw and creased brow were fixed and obstinate but her eyes told Ward it was a bluff. She was no murderer. He delayed his response, buying time to call her ruse.

Her lips pealed back to reveal gritted teeth and a relentless determination.

No, she wasn't a ruthless murderer. But she would surely kill for her convictions.

Ward folded.

"All right," he said, still not sure how to pull this off. "Relax. We're on the same side."

MacKenzie dropped the gun into her lap. "Yeah."

Her voice was softer but she still wasn't laying all her cards on the table. Ward was about to tell her it was okay, to try coaxing a little more information, when she continued, her eyes now almost apologetic.

"We'll take care of you when we get there. I promise."

"Who's 'we,'" Ward asked, surprised at his automatic response. Had Commandant Gaustad really augmented Agent Compano's training that thoroughly?

"My..." MacKenzie paused as if searching for a word. "Our counterpart congregation. I can't say any more yet. We'll pay whatever you need. Or set you up over there so you don't have to come back. Whatever it takes. We have to get him the Spear."

"So it's a 'him' now?" Ward was impressed with himself for catching the switch from singular to plural.

"He's..." she shook her head as if reluctant to say more.

Ward made a face. MacKenzie appeared to interpret it as reservation. She wiped her forearm across her brow and continued.

"You're a professor—you know about how priests used to work. They were leaders. They spoke for God. They helped people discover the Truth in themselves through His words. Not quite prophets but they had a better understanding than most people."

"And this man in Paris, he's a priest? Or a prophet?"

"I don't know. Not a prophet. Like a priest. Maybe." The last sounded almost like a question.

"Okay, so why does he need the Spear all of a sudden? Why risk it with me?" Now Ward felt he was getting somewhere. He envisioned this priest as the hoarder of all the remaining relics of the bible. A tall old man with flowing white hair and beard. Or was that a vision from an old movie?

MacKenzie dropped her head into her hands. "He said sending it here was a mistake. It was time to remedy it."

"Remedy it?"

MacKenzie's eyes flashed. It was defensive, the kind of look a mother would give if her child were threatened. Ward shifted his weight to relieve some of the pressure on his knee.

"Yes, 'remedy.' That's how he speaks. He's proper and," she paused. There was a compelling pride in her voice, though she seemed to be unable to find the right words to express whatever she was thinking, "people don't talk like that anymore," she said, softer, almost like a surrender.

Ward looked down at his hand, his fingertips about to bridge the few inches from his knee to hers. It was a simple, platonic, comforting move. He wanted to make it. He wanted it to be more than simple. He reached.

MacKenzie sat upright before his fingers made contact. He drew his hand back.

"Torres convinced me not to go. Wouldn't let me go. He

found you instead. And look what happened. I know it's not your fault but you have to help me." She looked at the pistol in her lap, but didn't reach for it. "You're going to help me." For the first time, it sounded like a question. A plea for help. Ward stood. He needed time. His orders were to follow her. But surely Commandant Gaustad hadn't meant for him to take her to Europe. Even if he could arrange travel clearance, the REC certainly had no jurisdiction overseas. There'd be no backup. No extrication.

He paced the room and looked out the window while replaying her words. For now it was all about time. Delay action as long as possible and learn as much as he could. Before he could ask another question, however, MacKenzie stood.

"Do you have anything to eat?"

Ward thought of the sad state of his refrigerator, ran his fingers through his hair and laughed. MacKenzie scrunched her face and tilted her head. Ward laughed harder.

They ate cheese and chipotle salsa in the kitchen and finished off Ward's last two bottles of water. They didn't speak, though MacKenzie occasionally brushed the hair from her eyes and offered an almost-smile. When they were finished he gave her a brief tour of the apartment, not much more than the two of them standing in the dining room with Ward pointing and naming the other rooms. He then suggested she sleep in his room. He would take the couch.

"I'm not going to sleep in your bed, Rafe." He started to argue but she silenced him. "I haven't slept in two days. The couch is fine. Make whatever calls you need to and let me know how we're getting out of here in the morning."

Ward agreed. "I'll get you some blankets and—hey, how did you know where I live?"

She lowered her gaze. "We had to make sure you weren't on the REC's radar. I mean reputation is great and all but it only goes so far."

"You spied on me?"

She feigned—at least, he was pretty sure it was feigned—being indignant. "It was my job. And I wasn't going to let the Spear out of my hands without knowing who I was giving it to." She spun and walked to the couch. "Are you going to bring me that blanket?"

The conversation over, he retrieved his RT40 from the bookshelf and scooped his jacket from the dining room table, tossing it all on his bed before getting a blanket and pillow for MacKenzie. She thanked him, then shooed him off when he didn't immediately withdraw.

As he got to the door of his bedroom he looked back. She'd already curled up on the couch and covered herself with the blanket. He could barely tell she was there. Without thinking he said, "I didn't get a chance to ask before. Is MacKenzie your first name?"

"Why do you go by Rafe?"

The question caught him off guard. "I um—it was a character's name in an old play my mom used to read to me. I liked it. I don't know. It was easier than Rafael."

"Your mom read to you a lot?"

"I guess. Mostly Shakespeare and stuff like that. She was a teacher."

"Interesting," MacKenzie said. "Goodnight, Rafe."

The conversation was clearly over. Ward shook his head. *Gaustad trusted me to get info from this woman,* he thought, *and I can't even get her whole name.* He let his eyes linger on the couch a few more seconds, then went into his bedroom and shut the door.

He sat on the bed between the jacket and the blue shirt. He could call it in. One-one-one. Let the police show up and take her into custody. The worst that could result was a broken front door when they stormed in and a reprimand from Gaustad for not following through.

Or maybe the worst was he'd be brought up on charges of duty violation. A vision of himself before an REC tribunal was pushed aside in favor of a far worse alternative: Three Agents perform a hard breach and have MacKenzie in custody in less than four seconds. Next they turn on Ward. He is pushed to his knees, a black bag drawn over his head. Within hours he is off to the same Crematorium which claimed his mother.

No, he was going to keep her close. Keep her talking. Earn that return to his real life. Go to school. Read. Teach.

He lay next to the shirt, pushing his jacket off the bed. The R1 in its pocket thudded to the floor, reminding Ward he needed at least to update Command on his houseguest. He exhaled, trying to gather the strength to sit back up.

What if, the thought encroached, *they did go to Paris, and never came back?* He could find a university that didn't monitor its classrooms. There were rumors that some of the Baltic States were at relative peace. Or the Middle East. Africa. Asia. Somewhere there had to be a place where he could teach students who weren't afraid to ask questions. Where he could read the *Aeneid* or even a bible in public without fear.

He closed his eyes thinking of all the books he could read while relaxing in a café or a museum or a park. The list grew and grew until all he knew were worn dust jackets and creaky spines.

He slept without dreams.

CHAPTER NINE

Rafe listened to MacKenzie walk around the apartment for some time while the venetian blinds over his bed brightened with the sunrise. He could hear her open and close the kitchen cabinets, pull books from his shelves, and in short order return them. He even heard her pad down the hallway towards the bedroom twice, though she never got close enough for him to see her shadow beneath the door.

He'd slept in his clothes, was sure he stank a bit of last night's whiskey, and was considering a shower when the bathroom door clapped shut and the sink's faucet turned on.

The immediate disappointment of this delay was quickly replaced with the urgent realization that he'd never sent his update to Command. More important, Gaustad hadn't yet provided and specific directions for this operation. What to do once contact was established with the terrorist who was now occupied Ward's bathroom. But who could he ask? He had no contact number for the Commandant. All he had was Agent Compano's number, a number she'd told him not to use.

Seeing no other options, Ward rolled over and dug the R1 out of his jacket. He selected Agent Compano as recipient and typed: "Have been contacted by target. Wants passage out of Republic. Paris. Please advise."

As he hit send it occurred to him that he had no idea if Agent Compano was even in the loop on this operation. If she even knew who the target was. At best he could expect to be plied with questions or maybe demands for more details. At worst he could expect the roof to be pulled off the house and Agents to swarm in killing them both.

It took only a few interminably long seconds for the Port to buzz. "11th & Pattison. 10a.m. Black RM sedan w/lights on," it read.

What did it mean? Bring MacKenzie to 11th and Pattison for arrest? Go alone? Was it a drop point for travel ID's giving them passage to Europe? The place he'd be black bagged for breaking protocol? The questions and options churned and roiled until Ward finally slapped his palms to his forehead and closed his eyes to force a moment of thoughtless quiet.

The water shut off. Ward placed the Port on the end table, and waited until the bathroom door opened to step out of the bedroom. MacKenzie, on her way to the living room, was still dressed in last night's clothes, though barefoot, and had her damp hair pulled back.

She looked over her shoulder. "You don't mind, right?"

Ward snapped his eyes to hers, not sure if he had been

staring at her hair, her feet, or her ass. With her head turned back like that she looked like an old fashioned pinup girl. He shook his head and told her that she was welcome to shower or browse his wardrobe for something clean. When she declined, he entered the bathroom.

He was halfway through the door when MacKenzie called from the living room, "I half expected you to turn me in last night."

The semi-accusation caught Ward off guard. He stuttered but couldn't find any words.

"I'm glad you didn't," she added, still from the other room. It was an obvious statement. Of course she was glad she hadn't been arrested last night. But Ward thought maybe there was more to it.

"Me too," he said, then rolled his eyes at how stupid he sounded. Without waiting for her to reply to closed the door behind himself.

The bathroom held the scent of something both woodsy and vanilla. Definitely feminine. Ward inhaled, enjoying the aroma for a brief second, then saw himself in the mirror. He snickered and twisted on the shower's faucet. He then got undressed and stared at the mirror while the water warmed. Not normally vain—at least no more so than he figured most men were—he found himself considering his attractiveness. He had a slight natural tan all year, as if he'd been at the Jersey Shore a week ago. It was a gift from his mother's South American ancestors. He was tall and dark. Women liked that, didn't they?

He flexed his shoulders and chest muscles. He was fairly

fit, especially after his training this summer, though there was a layer of flesh covering the middle of his frame that was a bit softer than he'd like. He sucked in his stomach and ran his fingers through his hair. His dark eyes couldn't help but seek out the one or two gray hairs in his sideburns. He sighed, and entered the nearly scalding water.

His muscles unclenched for what felt like the first time in a week, but he didn't linger in the stall. Once out of the shower it was a quick run with the toothbrush, during which he decided what to tell MacKenzie. They were going to meet his contact and find out the details then. She would, he hoped, recognize the authenticity of the statement, allowing for the trust Gaustad had ordered him to engender.

The quick respite over Ward exited the stall and ran a towel through his hair and over his body, then tightened it around his waist. He took one more look in the mirror, offered crooked smirk at his reflection then scoffed at having done so, and returned to his bedroom. He found MacKenzie sitting on the bed, his Port in her lap. Beside her thigh lay the blue t-shirt. Dangling from its folds, like a string of nectar from a flower, was a sterling silver necklace. The only thing left from his mother. His lungs deflated.

It wasn't fancy or otherwise adorned save for the small pendant which was still hidden within the shirt. A two-inch silver cross. It was inexpensive. It was illegal. For a Citizen it was interrogation then, at best, a prison sentence. For an Agent it was execution for treason. He hadn't considered this until now, mostly because he hadn't considered the necklace in over a year. Tucked up in the shirt in the back of his closet, it remained locked away in his mind. Accessible only when necessary. Only when the dreams came.

And even if he had thought about it, he wouldn't have done anything. He wouldn't have discarded it or destroyed it. He couldn't have. Emotionally, it *was* his mother. To him it was sacred.

"What the fuck is this?" MacKenzie said.

Ward couldn't speak. He stared at the necklace wondering if it required an explanation. She said something else, but he didn't hear. It was as if her voice was filtering in from another room.

He heard his mother's voice from last night: *Remember!*

He had remembered. There it was, right next to MacKenzie. But there was something else. One detail from that night…

MacKenzie stood. She held out his Port with her left hand. The Port! Ward looked from the device to her right arm curved behind her back. He had no doubt her pistol waited for a wrong answer.

"Explain."

"What?" he stalled. "What do you want explained?" If she'd deciphered his encrypted message logs, he was dead.

"Your scan. It says the Spear isn't old enough. It's a fake."

He exhaled. She hadn't found the messages. "How'd you log in?"

"Jesus, Rafe. It's a four-digit code, not some unbreakable cipher."

She was right. The messages were encrypted with the highest level of security the REC could device. But the device's login password was as simple as any other Port. It probably took her all of two minutes of randomly tapping keys before she hit on the right code. Why wasn't there a max-error lockout?

"Answer me."

"Relax," Ward said. He stretched the syllable to calm his voice. "It's nothing. Can you put the gun away, please?"

She adjusted her stance so that the pistol was now visible in her right hand but made no move to put it down.

"Okay. I changed the logs. The actual scan was good. Metallurgy from the first century BCE. Iberian. Totally authentic."

"Why?"

"Come on, really?" He tried to make her feel chided for asking. "Export. Anything pre-Industrial Era is automatically flagged. But there were some digs a couple years ago outside London that yielded a cache of Dark Age and older artifacts. Stuff the Republic had already cleared for transport. I was going to run the history of the Spear back to that excavation. Make it look like a piece that had been here for study."

It was a perfect explanation. He was impressed with his ability to not only come up with it but to explain so succinctly. MacKenzie, however, shook her head. She wasn't buying it. Ward held his breath, ready to launch to the side if she raised the gun.

Instead, her shoulders slumped. She dropped back onto the bed, placing the gun beside his pillow.

"I'm sorry. I just don't know who to trust anymore. I had to be sure, even with this." She lifted the necklace from the knapsack. The cross dangled beneath her palm. "It's pretty. You're more of a Believer than you let on."

"Yeah, I—can I have it?"

MacKenzie handed over the necklace. As the cold metal touched his fingers Ward became conscious that he was wearing only a towel wrapped around his waist. He wanted to cover his naked torso.

"It's a family piece?"

"It was my mother's. I…haven't spoken to her in a long time."

"I'm sorry," she said. "I haven't seen my father since I was still a little girl."

She stared at him. He looked at the necklace.

"So, where exactly is the Spear and what do we do next?"

Panic invaded his gut. He tried to hide it by cinching up the towel and looking away. He hadn't included a request for it in his message to Command. He could keep up appearances only so long as she was convinced that the Spear was safe and would soon be in her hands.

And then what?

Ward nudged the doubt aside. "My contacts have something set up. We need to get going to meet them. Down near the airport. Right by the stadium, actually," he said.

MacKenzie wrinkled her nose. "What about the Spear?"

"It's already there."

"Where?"

"With them."

"Who?" she asked, the smile gone from her voice.

Ward's mouth opened but he had no lies available.

"With who?" MacKenzie demanded.

"Our meeting's set. I can get you to Paris. You have to trust me."

"No, Rafe. Just because you have a cross, just because I didn't have anywhere else to stay last night, doesn't mean I have to trust you."

Ward put his hands out as if he was telling a passing car to slow down. He was out of options. "It'll be there. They'll have it." One more lie. It was all he had. "I promise."

She stared as if such scrutiny might verify his claim. After a couple seconds he began to fear she might actually have such an ability.

"Where'd you get the Spear, anyway?" he asked.

It worked. She looked away, maybe trying to decide how much to share.

"We had to make some sacrifices to get it."

Ward wanted to probe for more but the look on her face indicated that was all she was willing to share.

"I'll get you to Paris," he said, his own conviction in those words tasting utterly foreign. And sweet.

"Us, professor. You're coming with me."

Ward pulled the towel tighter around his waist. Had she said "we" last night? Had he? How far could he carry the charade until he ended up in the crossfire again?

"Are you kidnapping me?" he asked, trying to force a lightheartedness into their relationship.

"Yes," MacKenzie said, no levity in her response, and exited the bedroom, leaving the door open.

She waited in the hallway not watching, but not entirely

looking away either, as Ward dressed. He did so quickly, uncomfortably, nearly falling over while putting on a boot and twice dropping his jacket. Once set, he paused in the doorway, his mother's necklace calling his attention. Without knowing why he stepped back into the room and grabbed the silver chain, squeezing it in his fist.

"Ready?" MacKenzie asked.

Ward said that he was and stuffed the necklace into his pocket, wondering how anyone could be ready for all this.

CHAPTER
TEN

The drive into the city began quietly, with MacKenzie focused on the passenger side window. *They might have been heading down the shore for a family vacation,* Ward thought as they got on the Schuylkill Expressway. A few minutes later the weight of Gaustad's mandate for information pressed him to speak. To get MacKenzie talking he asked about her father. She, instead, talked about her mother bringing her to the Republic. She was a prominent Scottish psychologist, able to secure an exemption to the immigration lockdown due to her professional stature.

"But why come here?" Ward asked.

MacKenzie shrugged. "I asked her that, too. A lot. But she never really gave me an answer. Sometimes she would say things were unsure in Europe, even in Scotland. The new Republic seemed more stable. Other times she just changed the subject."

As they neared their exit from the expressway, MacKenzie finally steered the discourse to her father. Unlike her mother his request for immigration had been denied. He'd insisted they go without him, putting the safety of his family first. Her only contact with her father in the last twenty-some years, she explained, had been through letters.

"You mean, like handwritten letters?" Ward asked, navigating them onto the streets of the same South Philly neighborhood where they'd met two nights earlier.

"Yeah. Can you believe it," she said. "In a world like this, with all our technology, the only way I could tell my father I loved him was by writing it on a piece of paper and handing it off to someone to smuggle across the ocean. And you know what? He got every letter and wrote back every time. You tell me, Rafe, how can a girl grow up her entire life trusting the love of her father to complete strangers, and having that trust rewarded…how can that girl not believe in God?"

It was a rhetorical question. Still, Ward considered it before deciding he had no answer. "Do you still write to him?" he asked.

She was silent for a minute as if she hadn't heard him.

"We almost there?"

Ward turned another corner. They had a few blocks to go. He nodded. "What do we do when we get to Paris? Where do we go?"

"I don't know, exactly," she shook her head. "After New Mexico I haven't been given any new information."

"New Mexico? In the Southwest District?" Now Ward

was confused. What did New Mexico have to do with Paris?

"I don't understand either. He said New Mexico was the key."

"*He* again? The priest?"

MacKenzie looked at Ward as if she didn't understand his question. Then she nodded. "He said to bring the treasure from New Mexico to Paris. That's it."

"The treasure," Ward repeated. He thought a second. "You mean the Spear. That's where you got it—New Mexico?"

"Sort of," MacKenzie said. "The congregation who had it had actually moved to Amarillo a few years ago. About a hundred miles. Torres and I headed out there this summer. It wasn't easy getting through the Districts. You can't fly anywhere when you're on the watch lists. And no one in our congregation had any way to get us IDs that would hold up at the airports. So we drove. No freeways. We had to trade Jesus' ankle from the crucifixion to convince them to give us the Spear."

"You're joking," Ward said.

She glared at him but he continued.

"Crucifixion is at least five hundred years older than Jesus. Tens of thousands of people have been crucified throughout history. Maybe hundreds. You can't really believe you had a piece of Jesus' ankle."

"I believe," she said, flatly, "that the Spear is real and that it is needed in Paris."

Ward wasn't sure how to respond to this. Was she admitting that the ankle wasn't legitimate? Or was she just asserting that the Spear was? In either case, it wouldn't do to get into a theological or archeological debate. He needed info on her destination. She had to know where to go in Paris. Otherwise she'd just be running around a warzone with an illegal artifact in her hands. That couldn't be her plan.

"He never said anything else about where to take the Spear?" he asked.

"Clovis, New Mexico. That's it. It took a month to actually figure it out. Him and his damn puzzles. At first all I could find on the Web," her lip curled at the uselessness of the Republic-censored Internet, "was stuff about the stone age people who came to the New World being called Clovis people because that's where their spear tips and shit were found. We ended up having to hack police records to follow arrests in the area of Clovis before we finally struck on the congregation out there. We didn't even know what the 'treasure' was until we got there. But once they said they had the Spear of Destiny it was obvious."

Ward nodded through her description, then replayed her words in his mind. He grinned. *This priest,* he thought, *is a tricky bastard.*

"What?" MacKenzie said, her frustration causing her to fidget. "That's what he told me."

"You said your priest likes puzzles, right?"

"Yeah. So what?"

"He was giving you two pieces of info at once," Ward said, feeling for the first time since she'd knocked on his door that he was in control of a conversation. "I know where to go in Paris."

"Well, tell me," MacKenzie said, nearly shouting.

Ward smiled. Big. He couldn't help it. "Clovis isn't just a city in New Mexico. He was a man. A French king. The first real unifying French king, about fifteen hundred years ago."

MacKenzie seemed to brood on the revelation for a moment. "How's this any better? How's a dead king tell us where to take the Spear?"

"Where do you find a dead guy, any dead guy? Other than here, of course," Ward added, since burials had been outlawed in the Republic for over a generation.

"Cut the crap, Rafe. Where?"

"Come on, MacKenzie. A French king. Where do we go to find a dead French king?"

She leaned back in her seat, turning her face up to the car's roof. "A church."

"A church." He slowed the car as they approached 11th Street. "The Basilica of Saint Denis, if I remember properly. Northern Paris."

How amazing, Ward thought. *A church.* He'd never been in one; there weren't any in the Republic. To have the chance to actually see the architecture, hear his footfalls on the flagstones, smell the incense—forget Belief, forget God—to just stand there in the grandeur of what men could create.

He forced himself to stop fantasizing. He wasn't going to Paris. It was all a scam. Intel-gathering. Nothing more. He fixed his face to hide his disappointment.

"But there aren't any churches left," MacKenzie said.

"No, not here," Ward said. "But there was no Great Cleanse in Europe. From what I understand, even in the countries that have been Reclaimed, most churches still stand.

They're tourist destinations. Like the concentration camps after World War II."

MacKenzie didn't respond. Her face showed none of the exuberance Ward was feeling but there was something approaching hope coloring her eyes.

They parked half a block from the meeting place. Two other cars populated the street—the black RM—a luxury class, full size sedan, its lights on—at the corner ahead of them, and a white SUV, a Chrysler, the only other car manufacturer remaining after the gasoline purge, a few car lengths behind them on the opposite side. If a strike team was waiting, trying unsuccessfully to see through the SUV's smoked windows, that's where they'll come from, Ward figured.

Ward shut off the engine, and watched MacKenzie surveying the city through her window. After a moment she turned to him.

"Your necklace," she said.

Ward stared, unsure if it was a question or a command. She repeated herself. Confused, he fished it out of his pocket and held it in his open palm. She closed his fist around it, her hand encompassing his. It was thin and warm. But strong.

"Do you believe, Rafe?"

"Believe?"

"In this."

A chill tickled up his spine. He tried not to shudder but was unsure if he succeeded.

"The necklace?"

"What it symbolizes."

"What does it symbolize?" He hated the question before

he was done asking it. It was a trap as surely as Commandant Gaustad's rhetorical games were a trap. Only this one he'd sprung on himself. He could see her forthcoming answer. He could see his frustrated response. None of it would help. None of it would be by the script an REC Agent should know. None of it could be escaped.

She narrowed her eyes. "Religion."

Ward pulled his hand away. There was only one way he could respond to that. And that response had been part of him since he was eleven years old. "Religion is what turned the world into what it is, MacKenzie. It's what took my mother from me. It's what took you from your father, right? And you know what," he had to fight to keep his voice steady, the words pouring out as if they were being fed through him, "there's no such thing as religion. I've read the bible. I've got access. It's in there, in those university store rooms with the *Odyssey* and *Le Morte D'Arthur* and the *Mahabharata*. Do you know what the Old Testament, the Hebrew Torah, had to say about religion? Nothing. Not one fucking word because there's no word for religion in ancient Hebrew. And don't forget that your Savior, Jesus, was a Jew. He knew only *halakha*, the law, and *ya're Elohim*, the fear of God. That was it. Law and fear. Same as now. And where have they gotten us? Where have they gotten you?"

Ward couldn't tell if MacKenzie was trying not to cry or trying not to hit him. Her jaw was clenched and her throat seemed to be pulsating. But he couldn't stop.

"Religion," he said, "is one thing I think the Republic got right. It's nothing but a corrupted invention."

"You don't believe." It was part accusation, part question.

"No, I don't believe in religion," he said, lowering his voice. "I carry this because of whose it was, not the religion it symbolizes."

"Then what do you believe in? Just God?" The last word sounded like a plea, a hope that he would say something for her to cling to, something in him for her to believe.

"God," he paused and collected himself. His rant had nearly exposed him. "I don't think of it in terms like that. I just try to do what's right. Be good. Not holy." It was a comfortable explanation.

MacKenzie considered this for a moment. She shifted in the seat as if scratching her back on the upholstery. To Ward, the pause felt like his mother trying to determine which of the brothers had tracked mud into the house or eaten the last cookie.

"You're going to get us to Paris, Professor Ward," she finally said. "You're going to help me find that church. I don't care what you believe. I don't care if you think I'm bat shit crazy. You're going to help me." She reached for his hand with both of hers, placing one on top and the other beneath. "Say it," she said, her clenched jaw making it clear that in those two words was the threat of a gun.

"I'll help you find the church," Ward said. And despite knowing it was a lie it almost felt like he was telling the truth. "I promise."

"Swear it on the necklace. On whatever it means to you."

Ward opened his fist and looked at the silver necklace. It was heavier than it should have been.

"I swear," he whispered.

She nodded.

Ward blinked, holding the darkness a moment longer than natural. What was he doing? His ability to rationalize was lost. He was making promises to a woman whom he was delivering for Cremation. Whether it was here, to Agents inside a black Republic Motors sedan with its lights on, or later tomorrow, or next week in France, it didn't matter. There was only one end for her.

Ward found himself silently asking the car, the street lamp they were parked beside, even the buildings around them to at least let them go to Paris. Before this operation ended, to let them breathe the air within the walls of an ancient cathedral. He couldn't tell if it was the scholar in him or something else which made the plea.

"Let's go," MacKenzie said softly.

As they exited the car, Ward remembered the Spear. He had no idea if the Agents in the RM had it. No idea if there was a story in place to explain its absence. Not sure he'd be able to improvise a solution if she became agitated, Ward said the only thing that came to mind. "One thing. Whatever I say, whatever you hear, say nothing. Do not respond. Nothing. Got it?"

She didn't like it, that was clear, but she agreed. She waited for him to take the lead and fell into step behind.

CHAPTER
ELEVEN

The black-suit who got out of the driver's seat of the RM sedan was so clearly an Agent that Ward nearly faltered in his approach to the car. He was easily two-hundred-and-fifty pounds and made no pretense of hiding the submachine gun swelling his black suit jacket. He might as well be wearing a badge and name tag.

MacKenzie seemed to have the same idea, halting the moment he stepped from the car. Ward tensed, ready for her to flee or attack. Thankfully, she did neither.

"It's okay," he said.

She didn't move.

Then the back door opened and Agent Compano stepped out. She positioned herself behind the open door, a strange half-smirk on her lips. She wore a tan hoodie similar to MacKenzie's, and her hair was bulled back on a tight ponytail.

The sight of her made Ward's stomach turn. How was he supposed to keep up his charade with Agent Compano grinning at him like that? Why wouldn't she have given him a head's up?

Agent Compano didn't move. She didn't speak. It felt to Ward like everyone, MacKenzie and both Agents, were staring at him, waiting for him to do something. He collected himself as best he could but the first word out of his mouth caught and faded like the first word spoken before coffee. He tried again.

"Do you have what I asked for?" He tried to sound confident. In control. He knew they had something. He just didn't know what. Passage to Paris? Arrest? Execution?

Agent Compano said, "Good to see you, too, Rafael."

Ward's mind seized. How was he supposed to play this? Colleagues? Friends? He could feel MacKenzie glaring at him. There'd never been a training session on how to handle poorly disguised undercover Agents. Something in his brain pushed him to give the woman a name. What did she look like? An Elizabeth? Sarah? Gabriela?

"Hey, Em."

Em? What was that? Emily? Emma? Shit, did he just spurt a half-assed mirror nickname for MacKenzie?

"Short notice, but here you go," Agent Compano, now named Em, said with no more than a slight lift of her eyebrow at Ward's choice for her name. "Two ID's and passage set on an Innerspeed Corporation airline in an hour. Direct to Charles de Gaulle." She presented a beige envelope over top of the door.

Ward looked back. MacKenzie, motionless, was watching

the exchange intently, her hands behind her back. He took the envelope.

"And this," *Em* said.

She bent into the car, resurfacing with the Spear's wooden box. Ward could have collapsed for the amount of tension that gushed from his limbs.

MacKenzie maneuvered in front of Ward and grabbed the box.

"See you next time, buddy," Em said. Without any further words or acknowledgment, the Agents got into the car and drove off, barely slowing for the stop sign at the corner.

"Who were they, *Rafael?*" MacKenzie asked, the emphasis she placed on his full name—the name Em used rather than "Rafe"—was clear and dangerous.

"I told you," Ward said. "My contacts." He glanced over his shoulder at the white SUV. *This is it*, he thought. *If they're going to swarm and take us, it'll be now.*

The van remained motionless. He gave it a three count, then turned back to MacKenzie. The look on her face made it clear she wasn't buying that the departed Agents were on their side.

"She used to," Ward continued, grasping for the next words with each one that spewed from his lips. "I mean, she and I used to go out."

MacKenzie glowered. Ward couldn't tell if it was the ridiculousness of the lie or something else.

"Come on, we work through who we have to," he said, allowing the lie to run. "It's not like there's a smuggler's super store out there. Roll on in and pick out the model you want."

"You're ex-girlfriend looks like a cop."

"She's still kind of pissed at me, I guess. She always had that way of saying my name—you know, full name like when you're in trouble." It was the one truth Ward knew about all women in his life. His mother, his teachers, his girlfriends. When he was in trouble, he was *Rafael*.

She weighed the box in the palms of her hands. Was she considering his statement? Was she considering shooting him and leaving his body in the street?

"Come on," he said, not sure if he was hoping she would leave him. "We've got the Spear and the ID's. Let's get out of here."

Still, she didn't move. It felt like a full minute passed. A misty rain descended. She opened the box.

Ward's breath caught in his throat. His hand went to his hip, a half-second closer to the RT40 under his jacket, just in case the box was empty.

She nodded once and closed the box. Without looking at him, she tramped back to the car. Ward exhaled and squinted into the rain. The drops were dull, cool taps calming his nerves. He thought of a philosophy course he'd taken in grad school, a discussion of Schrodinger's cat. For a moment when MacKenzie had unlocked the box but had not yet opened it, the Spear had both been in the box, and not. Ward had been both alive and dead. It was an unsettling sensation. He took one more deep breath, rubbed the rain from his hair, put up his collar, and returned to the car.

She was settled, seatbelt on, when he got in. He handed her the envelope. She gave it the same look she'd given the

Agents but tore it open nonetheless.

"Not bad," she said, holding up one of the IDs.

Ward leaned over. It was his ID in her hand. The photo, he was pretty sure, had been taken by a security camera in the L&C offices yesterday.

"*Rafael* Jones," she said, again overemphasizing his full name again, but maybe this time playfully. "Nice."

"Yeah, what about you?"

She removed the other ID. "Oh come on."

He snatched it out of her hand.

"Hannah Jones. Looks like we're married." He was about to continue when the photo caught his attention. It appeared to have been taken outside his apartment just this morning. They'd been monitored. Would she notice?

"Brother and sister," she said. She grabbed it back.

"Okay, you got it, sis," he said, hoping she wouldn't examine the photo.

She didn't. Placing the ID into her pocket, she returned her attention to the envelope and withdrew a First Republic Bank debit card.

"Too easy to track us with this," she said. Before Ward could answer, she continued. "How much cash can you get your hands on?"

Ward tried to recall the last time he checked his savings online. He'd had just over twenty-one thousand dollars, if his memory was correct. Not a lot. Academics didn't pay any better now than it had in the old America. And despite his modest spending, that cache of funds still wasn't growing all that fast.

"Not much," he said. "I keep it all on the move so it can't

be tied to me."

He wasn't sure if it was the prospect of losing his life savings, or this trip suddenly so real, that made him reluctant to raid his bank account. In either case, he'd lied. Again. It was becoming too easy. And he was getting too good at it.

MacKenzie clenched her jaw. "Fine," she said. "We'll take as much as the card lets us when we get there, then we dump it. No trails."

Smart girl, Ward thought. He started the car down the street, keeping an eye in the rearview for the white SUV. It pulled out behind them and followed. Ward tried not to make his awareness of their tail too obvious.

"They gave us this, too," MacKenzie said, holding up a small yellow document. "Package clearance for one bag containing an Atlantic District University artifact on loan from The Louvre. Not bad, Professor."

"Thanks," Ward said, relaxing a bit as the white SUV fell farther back.

A block later MacKenzie asked, "What about coming back?"

"The ID's are encoded for re-entry," Ward said. It was probably a lie.

———◆———

The airliner was a recently introduced Boeing model 797R. It was clean. Its aisles were wide. And it smelled like a new car, that mixture of upholstery and adhesives making the air within thick and sweet.

Upon their entrance into the cabin Ward and MacKenzie, despite the flight being nearly full, discovered they were being treated to a row of four seats to themselves. MacKenzie took the window. She plopped her hand on the adjacent seat, forcing Ward to leave an empty chair between them.

She'd been silent through the security checkpoints at the airport. Only as they'd exited the car in the parking garage, and again when being forced to check her backpack with the Spear inside, had she appeared distressed.

The first incident had gone smoothly enough after her initial balk at Ward's instruction to leave their weapons in the car. He'd dropped his RT40 in the glove box first and watched as MacKenzie followed with her pistol and a telescopic baton. To this she'd added a six inch folding knife and a tiny bible from the thigh pocket of her black cargo pants.

He'd been surprised by this last item and had fought to keep his face impassive. It wasn't that bibles were unheard of, even with the punishment for possession beginning at two years of incarceration. It was that those who possessed them generally kept them hidden in vaults built into the frames of their homes, or buried beneath their basements. He couldn't remember the last time he'd heard of someone actually carrying one around.

Later she'd been visibly shaken after handing over her backpack, along with the package clearance certificate, to a security deputy at check-in. Ward had tried to alleviate her apprehension with a hand on her shoulder but she'd pulled away.

As Ward settled into his seat, he was content to let silence continue to be the theme until they arrived in Paris. Though he'd never been on a plane before he was realizing he didn't like them. The recycled air and the inescapable conversations from his neighbors were already giving him a headache. In addition, the stress of preparing to fly to a continent that was—according to public news outlets and REC intelligence reports—a bubbling crucible of fundamentalist angst, left Ward dreading the coming seven hours.

As they taxied onto the runway, the cabin became a tunnel-shaped concert hall brimming with discussions of quarterly reports, proposed mergers, and backroom takeovers. Ward rolled his fingertips against his temples. He was surprised at just how many people Innerspeed Corporation, the official info-tech company of the Republic, was willing to send overseas. How much profit could a Europe in chaos offer?

They were airborne in a few minutes. Ward squirmed, trying to get comfortable in his seat, trying to find an angle to lean that would alleviate his growing headache.

Something jabbed his thigh. He slid his thumb into his pocket. He touched metal.

The necklace. He'd forgotten it was in his pocket. How had the security scanner missed it? Maybe, he figured, the chain had been wrapped around the crucifix enough to mask its shape even under scan.

MacKenzie groaned as the plane leveled out. Ward stuffed the necklace deeper into his pocket and studied his companion. She was sitting stiff upright, her hands gripping the arm rests. Her jaw and the veins in her neck pulsed as her cheeks became almost ashen. Ward wondered if he looked as bad as she did.

"First time flying, too?"

She didn't answer and didn't unclench her jaw. It appeared

she was holding her breath.

"It'll be fine," Ward said, fighting to keep his voice even beneath the pulsing in his head. "We'll order some drinks when they come around."

She rolled her head to look at him.

"You don't look good," she said.

"I'm okay." It was like an instinct, his need to not show her any weakness.

"Anything I can do?"

Ward massaged the bridge of his nose. "Relax," he said.

She gave a quizzical look.

"No, really. You sitting there all tense like we're flying into the sun is stressing me out. If you can just breathe a bit and relax, I'll feel better."

MacKenzie made a face that said, "What are you talking about?" But she did as he asked, letting out a long whistle of a breath.

"See." Ward forced a smile. "Better already."

MacKenzie laughed. "No really, what can I do?"

"Just talk to me."

"About what?"

"I don't know. What do we do when we get there?"

"I have no idea." A moment later she continued. "You said it's the Basilica of Saint Somebody, right? You know where it is?"

"Roughly. We'll grab a map download when we get there. Unless you want to try to find it on your Port now." With his headache, he had no desire to go scrolling through his own R1. And he sure wasn't going to volunteer placing it in her hands again.

"I don't have one," MacKenzie said. Before Ward could question—*everybody* had a Port—she added, "I've been unplugged for about five years. We all have. No way to track us."

Smart girl, Ward thought again.

The steady thunder of the engines filled the next few minutes. Eventually, Ward said, "Tell me about your dad or something. Just give me something to focus on." He didn't know why he asked about her father but it felt like the right question.

"My dad?"

"Anything."

"I don't remember much," she said after a moment. "He told me stories at bedtime. That's really the only memory I have. His voice. I couldn't even tell you what he looks like. But his voice…'How about a story tonight? That will be good, yes?' That's what he used to say."

"What kind of stories?" Ward asked just to keep her talking. The sound of her voice lessened the throbbing that was consuming his skull.

"Bedtime stories. I don't know. Fairytales."

Ward perked up at this. Reading fairytales was the natural byproduct of studying history and literature. Along with the architecture, these folk tales were Ward's favorite part of the discipline. "Do you remember any?"

"Seriously? You want me to tell you a bedtime story?"

"Humor me. I did give you a place to stay last night."

"My hero," she said. "Okay, you've earned a story. Which

one do you want?"

"Whichever. Your favorite."

He said it nonchalantly but he wanted a fairytale. A good, old world yarn he could escape into for a few moments and forget the flight. He wanted, irrationally he knew, some undiscovered nugget, the kind that made up the backbone of the myths and legends he'd spent a third of his life studying. For every Little Red Riding Hood there was a truth which could divulge the secrets of its culture's past, if you had the will and the determination to do the research.

"Like Cinderella?"

Ward shook his head. "You don't strike me as a Cinderella girl."

She thought about it a moment. "There was one… I don't think it was a regular Mother Goose type. I've never heard it anywhere else. A princess and a spider…and a cauldron, or something." She paused. "I don't know, maybe it was supposed to be a king or a prince but he made it a princess for me."

Ward couldn't recall any fairytale about a princess and a spider and a cauldron. Maybe this was that undiscovered tale he wanted. More likely, he admitted to himself, she was probably confused. But even with a migraine he was up for a new story. He motioned for her to continue.

"Okay," MacKenzie said, dragging the word out. "So, there was a king—"

"Once upon a time," Ward interrupted.

"What?"

"You have to start with 'Once upon a time.'"

"Really? You look like you're dying and you're going to

be a pain in the ass?"

Ward let his silence be his answer.

"Fine. Once upon a time," she began, over-enunciating the words, "there was a king. No, wait. Not 'once upon a time.' My dad, he always used to say, 'Long ago, when it was still good to wish for a thing,' there was a kingdom with a castle right against the sea. And the king, a red-bearded king, had a daughter. The princess. So the king dies—and the queen was already dead; she died in childbirth—and there's only the princess left. And she's sitting on the throne, looking out the window at the sea, holding the king's crown in her hands and she hears a tiny voice say, 'I can –'"

"Do their voices."

MacKenzie's face scrunched as she tried to determine if he was serious. Ward wasn't sure himself but found he enjoyed watching her examine him.

"Fuck off," she said through a crooked smile. "So, the tiny voice says, 'I can bring your father back.' And the princess looks all around and finally sees a little spider peering out from the leaves of her father's laurel crown."

"Wait, a spider in a laurel crown?"

"Yeah, so what? You know this fairy tale?" MacKenzie asked, not hiding her doubt.

But he did. No, not the fairytale. "The spider in the laurel spins," the line went, Ward remembered from some dusty book. An actual book, he remembered that clearly. Not a download. "From there it was: something, something, something, then a bust of Apollo, the Greek god, is flung into a kiln to make, "lime for Mammon's tower."

"Mammon?" MacKenzie asked.

Ward started. How much of that had he actually said out loud? Mammon. Sometimes called a demon. Sometimes a devil. The spirit of wealth or greed. But not always. There was one medieval book where he was allied with Baelzebub, maybe even interchangeable with him, as a Lord of Death. He was rendered always as a great protector to his worshippers.

But what did it matter? Why was Mammon dancing in Ward's mind when all he wanted was to listen to a story and find some sleep?

"Nothing. Sorry," Ward said. He closed his eyes and imagined MacKenzie shrugging at him as if the listener was immaterial to the telling of the tale.

"Anyway," she went on, "the spider says again that it can bring back the king from the dead. All it needs is the princess to go get its magic cauldron. That will allow it to return to its true form as a person. A king of something or other, actually, I think."

"Sounds like a bad deal," Ward said, surprised at how strained, and how distant, his voice sounded.

"You sure you're okay?"

"Yeah. Keep going," Ward said, doing his best to let her voice soothe him.

"Okay," she said. He could hear her settling in her seat. "So, the spider tells the princess where to search for the cauldron and off she goes on the quest. She fights goblins, crosses swamps, and does all kinds of fairytale stuff. Then she finds the thing and defeats the bad guy, this big ogre. Oh, I almost forgot. Along the way, the princess's mother comes to her as a dove or some bird and warns her not to get the cauldron for the spider."

"Told you," Ward interjected.

MacKenzie went on as if he hadn't spoken. "But the princess, she doesn't listen, even though her mother—like a fairy godmother in those other fairy tales—keeps warning her. Keeps telling her the cauldron is evil. The spider is wicked and will take over the kingdom. She tells the princess the only way to destroy the cauldron and save the kingdom now that the spider is there is to make a believer out of a deceiver and let him sacrifice himself for the kingdom."

She broke off awkwardly and Ward opened his eyes. She was blinking as if putting the parts in order.

"I remember Dad's voice, like his actual voice for this part. But it's him doing the fairy godmother, or mother, or whatever…her voice. 'Find amongst your subjects the greatest of deceivers. Make him the greatest of believers. Then your kingdom will be free. That will be good, yes?'"

Ward snickered at the screeching voice she used for the fairy godmother. Had his head felt better he likely would have laughed until tears came. She smirked at him but didn't continue right away. He asked if she'd forgotten the rest.

"No, sorry. The princess brings the cauldron home but won't give it to the spider because now she's scared. She has her knights scour the whole kingdom giving everyone tests of loyalty. I don't remember what the tests were. But they tell her there's one man who didn't pass. So she tells them to bring him right at the end, just when she's about to give the spider the cauldron, so that if it doesn't come through with its promise, she'll smash the cauldron and figure out how to turn the believer into a deceiver.

"Meanwhile, the princess goes into the throne room and picks up the laurel crown and the spider asks if she has the cauldron. She says yes and has it brought in. But she won't let the spider go to it until the spider brings back her father. Then the spider says, 'Bring in the deceiver and spill his blood into the cauldron and you'll have your father back.'"

"Pretty dark for a fairytale." It occurred to Ward as he said this that it wasn't any darker than many. It wasn't so much worse than birds pecking out the eyes of Cinderella's step sisters, or carnivorous rape of Little Red's grandmother by the wolf. So did this story, this magic cauldron tale, feel so much…heavier was the word he was looking for. Heavy, as if with the weight of the forgotten truths of all fairytales.

"Yeah, it's not really a great happy ending kind."

Ward couldn't help but snicker at the apologetic look on MacKenzie's face. His headache, for a brief moment, lessened. "Spoiler alert," he said.

"Whatever," MacKenzie said, and continued. "So, the deceiver is brought in and the princess and him take one look at each other and fall in love, you know all fairytale-like. And the spider sees that there's no way she's going to spill his blood, so he leaps out of the crown and grows and grows until he's this giant half spider, half human monster and he comes towards the princess and the guy ready to kill them both and spill their blood into the cauldron. But then the dove, the dead queen, speaks into the princess's ear again and tells her there's only one way left to stop the spider. So, the princess and the deceiver, who now I guess is a believer because he's in love, they hold hands and jump out the window into the sea and drown to prevent the spider from gaining all its power and destroying the kingdom."

"What happens to the spider?" Ward asked, feeling like somehow he knew the answer but couldn't locate it. "Does it die?"

MacKenzie started as if she'd never considered the question. "I have no idea. But it doesn't destroy the kingdom. They all live on free and happy."

As MacKenzie spoke these final words the certainty that Ward knew more about the story began to evaporate from his mind. That fast he was left with nothing more than the aftertaste of an unusual fairytale. "Maybe the weirdest fairytale I've ever heard," he said, as before only half-aware he was speaking out loud.

"Rafe."

Ward turned his head. MacKenzie was watching him with an undecided expression. Ward could imagine. Was she about to chastise him, or slug him?

"You're an ass. Go to sleep."

PART TWO

THE
DECEIVER

Thou Shalt not Kill

Book of Exodus, 20:13

...small group of fundamentalists plunging the world into war. The Middle East Peace Accord is the most important step towards healing our September 11 wounds, the most important step towards fulfilling our vision of America as a beacon.

Jaime Nash, Acting Secretary of State, December 15, 2001

Sixteen hours after the surprise nuclear attack on Riyadh, there remain no lines of communication with Saudi Arabia or her allies. President Margulies reiterated at her press conference just a few moments ago that she expects a "complete and unconditional surrender of all of our enemies."

Tom Seldon, Fox Evening News Anchor, June 27, 2006

CHAPTER TWELVE

Their arrival in Paris was surprisingly uneventful. There was no security gauntlet to be traversed at the airport. No interrogations or examinations, just an ID scan and customs declaration. It was as if danger was inconceivable. There weren't even any posted police, armed or otherwise. Ward knew he should be concerned but he wasn't quite sure why. No one else exiting the plane with them appeared troubled.

He kept waiting for MacKenzie to say something about the lack of security but she didn't seem to notice. The pair moved through the airport in silence, helped along by bilingual signs, as if English and French were centuries old allies. They made only two stops: one to download a Paris city map to Ward's Port and the other to withdraw the maximum thousand Euro their debit card allowed. Then it was into a trash bin with the card and onto the Metro for Ward and MacKenzie. The simplicity of the trek ended when they exited the Metro car in the northern Parisian suburb of Saint-Denis. The Metro underpasses were labyrinthine at best, with minimal signs, not a single posted map, and no people to ask for directions, though this last bit was not surprising considering it was after one in the morning. Ward had expected them to surface from the subway within sight of the Basilica. Instead, even with the help of his R1's Paris map, they meandered about underground for almost ten minutes before finally finding an exit noting *Saint-Denis*.

It was twenty to two when they finally emerged to a cramped, cold neighborhood, dimly lit by yellow streetlamps. The façades of the buildings, most of them first floor shops built into Baroque or Rococo style row homes, appeared dirty and decrepit in the yellow light. The overabundance of peach colored window shutters felt like eyes staring down on them.

It was a disturbing introduction to the famed City of Light.

MacKenzie, who hadn't said much since the midpoint of the flight, fixed an uncomfortable stare on Ward. He, in turn, scanned the dark skyline in hopes of seeing one of the Basilica's towers or spires to help him get his bearings.

"Do you know where it is?"

"Would we be standing here like this if I did?" He regretted his tone but after the flight and the frustration of the Metro tunnels he had little patience. He was also exhausted. He'd slept on and off for most of the flight after MacKenzie's fairy tale. But it was not a restful sleep. And he now felt worse for it than he imagined he would if he'd stayed awake the whole time.

MacKenzie flashed a look, clearly holding back a dagger of a comment.

"Sorry," Ward muttered, examining the rooflines.

Finding no landmark he consulted his R1, which immediately located their position. A couple taps later and their walking route to the Basilica was revealed.

"It's a couple blocks this way." He pointed, embarrassed by the way he'd snapped at her and by the way his voice echoed down the street. He set off towards their goal.

"There's no one else out," MacKenzie said, stopping him.

Ward looked up and down the street. It was as deserted as the Metro tunnels. *Not a surprise,* Ward thought. At this hour, why would there be anyone else out? But now that she'd pointed it out he felt somehow exposed and vulnerable.

"There's a probably a curfew," he said. It was logical. Yet it came out like he was trying to convince himself.

MacKenzie glanced about nervously. "Let's get a hotel," she said.

Ward voiced his agreement but his feet didn't move. Maybe the fact that it was late and the church was closed was a good thing. They could just break in and find who, or what, they needed to find.

Or they could break in and get shot.

MacKenzie grabbed his wrist. "Come on," she said and led him up the street and around the corner, clearly choosing a direction simply for the sake of getting moving. It worked. A hotel presented itself a block later, in a more modern part of the city. Here, though the streets were paved with gray bricks giving it a classic feel, the buildings were all concrete and mirrored glass.

They could have checked his Port for something cheaper or closer to the Basilica but neither mentioned that option. MacKenzie strolled right into the lobby and up to the front desk.

A very round, very wrinkled woman wheezed a *bonjour* at them without looking up.

MacKenzie stopped mid-step and stuttered out a timid, "Ummm."

Ward moved in front of her. "*Bonsoir. Avez-vous une chambre pour la nuit.* Inexpensive…um, *peu coûteux, s'il vous plaît.*"

MacKenzie's mouth dropped open. Ward suppressed a laugh.

With a dismissive look at MacKenzie the concierge nodded and held out her hand for their ID's. They passed them across the desk. After proving their quality at the airport, their fake ID's should have posed no concern at a small hotel. But Ward could hear MacKenzie's trepidation in the way she shifted her weight and tapped her feet. His own anxiousness manifested in the clenching of his fists. He couldn't stop. The old woman, however, seemed oblivious, scanning the ID's and logging Mr. and Mrs. Jones in on her computer. Nearly a third of their cash went into the old woman's hand. With a raised eyebrow, she touched the bills only by the edges. Ward wondered how much they would stand out in Paris using cash.

"Room two zero one," the woman said with a harsh accent,

her rheumy eyes lingering on MacKenzie. She placed a room key—a metal square about two inches long, one wide, and a quarter of an inch thick, with a chip set in its center—on the desk before dropping her attention to her computer. MacKenzie grabbed it and followed Ward to the stairs.

"So, you speak French?" MacKenzie asked in the second floor hallway.

"Yeah, a little."

MacKenzie didn't respond, appearing to log this information away for future use. When they arrived at their room she maneuvered in front of Ward and unlocked the door by sliding the rectangular metal key into a slot beside the door handle. There was a click that reminded Ward of Commandant Gaustad's office. MacKenzie pressed the handle, pushed open the door, and peered inside before tapping the light controls to the right of the entrance. She made a quick glance into the bathroom to the left of the door, then marched directly towards the bed.

"I had the couch last night. Your turn." She flopped down, rolling the blanket over herself like a tortilla.

Ward didn't argue. He entered the room far enough for the door to close behind him and looked around. It reminded him of the dorm he'd stayed in over the summer while doing his weekend training sessions with Agent Compano. That room had been on a now defunct college campus up in the Lehigh Valley, about an hour's drive north of his apartment. He'd thought of it as "the closet." This one wasn't quite as small. There was, at least, the couch, and a half-sized sink with a coffee machine beside it. In a skinny wardrobe by the bathroom he found a couple robes and extra blankets and pillows.

He took these latter items and settled onto the couch. At first he found it strange trying to fall asleep without a television on. But the sound of MacKenzie's breathing, already steady and thick—like she might have been snoring underneath the blankets—made him feel at ease. He fell asleep without bothering to remove his boots.

———◆———

Ward woke startled. It was a feeling like waking up for school and realizing he'd forgotten to do his homework the night before. In fact, that's exactly what had happened. Like last night in his apartment he hadn't checked in with Command. He dug into the pocket of his jacket, which was now twisted around and beneath him on the couch, for his Port. Finally freeing it, he saw that it was a little after six in the morning. He held his hand over the screen knowing he should start a message. But to say what? They'd arrived. That was all he had.

He could, he figured, just report that they were in Saint-Denis. But a nagging thought told him they wouldn't be here long anyway. He tried to analyze that thought, to figure out why he felt so sure, but couldn't come up with anything. He pulled his hand back from the Port and stretched. He would report in later, justifying the decision by telling himself that if he gave their location now there was a risk for the operation being blown before any meaningful contact with MacKenzie's associates could be made.

He sat up to see if he'd woken MacKenzie. She was still engulfed in the bed's blankets. He took a shower, put on yesterday's clothes—they were all he had—and perused the room service menu and other guest services brochures. After a moment he decided to skip the hotel's overpriced breakfast. He then went to the bed to debate whether to wake his companion, the fugitive terrorist he would soon deliver for Cremation.

"Hovering over me like that," MacKenzie's said from beneath the blankets, "is going to kill all the goodwill you built up yesterday."

Her head emerged from the blankets like a turtle. Her hair was a mess, in spots sticking straight up. Ward laughed out loud before he could stop himself. She tried to give him a dirty look but with her hair like that it was a complete failure. He laughed full from his belly up through his chest.

When he finally caught his breath, and wiped away a few tears, he saw that MacKenzie had worked her way up to a sitting position. Her legs were crossed beneath her, the maroon, floral patterned comforter draped over her shoulders.

"Are you finished, Rafael?"

He nodded but couldn't stop grinning. She threw a pillow at him, then got up and went into the bathroom trailing the comforter like a cape.

"So, Professor French, I guess you should do the talking for now," she said through the door.

The shower turned on, forcing Ward to wait a moment before responding. "That's probably best, at least until we find your priest."

MacKenzie stuck her head out of the bathroom. "Do you think—no forget it." She pulled her head back into the bathroom.

"What?"

"Nothing."

"What?" he insisted.

"I'd really like," she said, pausing a second, "to buy some new clothes."

"You want to go shopping?"

Her head reappeared. "No, asshole. I've been wearing the same clothes for three days. I'm feeling a little grungy here."

"I tell you what. Take off your clothes…"

She gave him a look that threatened a beating.

Ward put his hands up. "There's supposed to be a laundry on this floor. Take a shower." He handed her a robe from the wardrobe. "Wrap yourself in this, and I'll go take care of the wash."

She withdrew without an answer. A moment later the bathroom door opened a few inches. MacKenzie's arm reached out holding her bundled clothes.

Ward found his attention drawn from the dirty clothes to her pale wrist. Up her wiry forearm. To her muscled bicep. Finally to her shoulder, lean and strong. There he saw something both expected and startling. The hint of a tattoo. What looked like the rolled end of a scroll of parchment.

She dropped the clothes to the floor.

He grabbed her fingertips before she could withdraw into the bathroom. The door opened a bit further, revealing MacKenzie naked, a towel wrapped around her waist and covering her chest, held in place with her right arm. She glowered at him, the look a combination of menace and amusement.

"You want something?" she said.

"What is it?" He wasn't sure why he was so intrigued. Maybe it was the simple fact that tattoos were illegal. That Believers generally kept them small to avoid being identified. And MacKenzie's, from what he could see, was significant, and seemed to be of high quality.

She tilted her head a moment as if unsure what he was asking about. Then she slipped her fingers from his grasp and swung the door all the way open. She turned her back and let the towel drape down. In the mirror he could see that she was holding the towel lightly to her breasts, covering almost nothing, to allow the slack necessary to expose the tattoo.

It was magnificent. It could have been a pen and ink drawing done by a monastic illustrator. The scroll unfurled from her shoulder blades down to the symmetrical dimples— the Dimples of Venus—just above the towel. The edges of the scroll, weathered and uneven, stretched to her sides. But what amazed Ward was the text. Two columns of flowing calligraphy that any artist would be proud of on a flat, inanimate medium, divided by the ridges and valleys of her spine.

Ward was transfixed. A moment passed before he was able to focus on the specific rather than the whole. The columns of text. Each numbered with Roman numerals. The Ten Commandments, he recognized, in King James English, with thou's and v's instead of u's. It was exquisite. True artwork. He wanted to ask where she got it, who was capable of creating such artistry. Then he noticed what was missing.

Number six, across her right shoulder from spine to

armpit, was blank. The Roman numeral VI, and nothing else.

MacKenzie turned, the towel still held to her chest, her right hand cupping her left breast. She looked Ward in the eyes. "You like?" she asked.

"It's beautiful."

She raised herself on her toes, closer to eye level. Had she been any other girl, had this been any other situation, Ward would have known the move to be an invitation. He would have grabbed her waist, slid his hand to the back of her neck and pulled her in for a kiss, knowing the towel would drop to the floor.

But this was not any other situation. She was not some other girl. "One's missing," he said.

Still on her toes, MacKenzie asked, "Which one?"

The towel, the eyes, the freckles, the tattoo. They were all a test. Weren't they?

"Thou shalt not kill," Ward recited. He couldn't help remembering that look she'd given him in his apartment when she'd demanded his help. Would she have actually shot him?

MacKenzie offered a wry, crooked a grin. "Be quick with the laundry," she said, and kicked the bathroom door closed.

CHAPTER
THIRTEEN

Two-and-a-half hours later they strolled down the street, clothes freshly washed and crepes cradled in their hands. *We could almost,* Ward thought, *pass for a couple on vacation. An Agent and a Believer who seemed to think her God's sixth commandment was the only one not worth keeping. What a couple.*

"What?" MacKenzie asked through a mouthful of pastry.

Ward looked at her confused, wondering if maybe he'd laughed out loud at the thought of them as a couple. It wasn't an unpleasant thought. She was nothing like the women he usually dated. Women he met in bars or online or with whom he was set up by a colleague. Women like Carrie. Caring and sweet but ultimately without any drive to their personality. The pattern rarely varied. Up to a month or two of pleasant dates and sex ranging from dull to rapacious to a furious quickie in his office—on top of Ken's desk, no less—between classes. Then one of them would simply stop texting the other. No hard feelings. In fact, there were rarely any feelings at all so far as he could tell.

But MacKenzie, she was all about feelings, of that much Ward was certain. With her they'd either go for the long haul or flame out in some kind of raging detonation. He liked the idea.

He said none of this to MacKenzie, of course, responding instead with, "Nothing." He popped the last bite of his crepe into his mouth as casual as he could.

She let the conversation drop.

It turned out to be a quick, quiet walk, with few pedestrians or even cars filling the morning. Those they did pass appeared to have no more concern for the two of them than they might for a plastic bag flitting about on the breeze. It was eerily similar to what Ward had witnessed from the top floor window of the Tower two mornings ago. Yet there was something different about it. When he couldn't place his finger on it, though, he let the idea drop.

Following the R1's directions, Ward led them from the cobblestoned main thoroughfare into an alley populated by trash bins and bicycles. Halfway through he caught a glimpse of something on the wall peering out from behind a wheeled dumpster.

"What is it?" MacKenzie asked, leaning closer.

Ward pushed the dumpster a couple feet along the wall, the motion disturbing its contents and flooding the air with the too-sweet stink of decomposing rubbish. Both Ward and

MacKenzie grimaced.

On the wall, in red spray-painted French, was the phrase: *Dieu est mort.*

"What's it say?" MacKenzie asked.

It said, *God is dead*, but Ward didn't translate for her. He was struck by this antithesis of the scrawled remnant he'd seen in the locker room in Philly. It was no nihilistic rant. And it was not old. It was, like in Philly, a message left by a revolutionary hand, meant for other like minds. But according to the Republic's news outlets it was the Believers who were the insurgents in Europe, the ones who would be leaving battle cries like this. The only other explanation—

"Hey, prof. What's so important?"

"Nothing," Ward said. "It's just graffiti. Come on. It should be up ahead."

MacKenzie looked from the wall to the final bite of her crepe. She wrinkled her nose and flipped the crepe into the dumpster then motioned for Ward to lead the way.

They exited the alley and halted. The view was beyond the insufficient words streaming through Ward's mind. Magnificent, spectacular, glorious. These were all soft, weak descriptions compared to the monument before him.

The almost thousand year old Basilica of Saint Denis was the first major edifice built in the Gothic style. Its spire on the southwest corner lunged into the sky almost a hundred feet. Its arched doors and windows beckoned all to step closer, to see what men had once built with nothing more than their hands and steel and stone. It was the same sandy color as the rest of the buildings surrounding the square yet the basilica lounged like a lion lording over its pride.

In the center of its West façade was the rose window. No simple porthole like in the Tower, this was stained glass, long one of Ward's favorite artistic mediums. He could remember hours at the university library in graduate school studying the rose windows of European cathedrals. In such masterpieces of colossal stone and soaring lines, the rose windows, and their smaller kin, were the touches that showed the true majesty of humanity's aptitude for beauty. Anyone could build a fortress. It took love to build these works of art.

This rose window was no exception. Powerful, commanding, watchful, yet somehow kind. It was a kaleidoscope of dozens of individual frames. Ward could identify the Zodiac, Adam and Eve, the Expulsion, and God at the center. No photograph could ever come close to the grandeur of the real thing.

He tried to imagine what Paris might look like through the rose window. How much warmer would it appear than Philadelphia? How much more colorful?

Slowly Ward's mind pulled back, allowing the entire square to fill his vision. It was replete with tourists the way a single cage at a pet store could be packed with dozens of mice. It looked like an unending assembly line of photographers, each one pushing into the center of the square as the previous completed his or her photos.

He was torn. Should he use his R1 to take some photos? He wanted to but knew they should do nothing to call attention to themselves. Or would not taking photos be what made them stand out?

"Rafe," MacKenzie said, nudging his elbow. "Do you

notice anything?"

Ward's muscles tensed. His legs flexed. He expected to see a bunch of men in black suits and dark glasses but it was the same everywhere he looked. Tourists. Caucasian, African, Asian, Middle-Eastern. Old folks on scooters. Families. Children romping about, their own crepes drooling down their wrists. Even what appeared to be a school trip.

Pushing past them went two little boys. The bigger of them was swinging a plastic sword above his head like a knight charging into battle. The younger one whined something, maybe in German, and tried to reach the pommel but it was held too high by his brother. Ward didn't catch the words but he knew the tone. The younger was complaining that it was his turn. The older was reveling in his superior size and strength. He could hear his own little Raffi voice in that same sing-song tone. "Da-an-nee-aal, it's myy tu-uurn."

The boys' mother soon plunged after them and the three were lost in the crowd.

"No. Just tourists and food carts," Ward said. "What…?"

Then he saw it. He saw Paris with the same clarity he'd seen Philadelphia yesterday morning. The contrast astounded him. There was no anxiety in the people's eyes. There were no cops on the corners. The phantom rogues and radicals of Republic news reports were absent. People weren't clinging to their wallets, guns in hand, in fear of desperate, revolutionary thugs. No one flinched when someone's bubblegum popped. The autumn air was chill but Paris didn't feel cold. It felt cheerful.

The back of Ward's neck tingled. With the sensation came

a memory. A pizza shop with Mom. One with those red vinyl seats. It was just before the accident. A Wednesday. Why would he remember that it was a Wednesday?

The accident! Yes, the accident was a Wednesday. Was the pizza shop the Wednesday right before? Was it the same day?

Forget the accident, his conscience insisted. *Find Clovis.*

But Ward was already tumbling down that memory-well.

It had been warm outside. No jackets. School, maybe, had recently ended for the summer. He and Mom had been out doing…doing what? It was evening free hours. Curfew was still some hours away. They'd stopped for dinner and Mom let him get two slices. One pepperoni.

Where were Dad and Daniel?

The girl who'd brought them their slices suddenly screamed into her hands. A cook, a huge man with pizza sauce splotched on his white shirt like bullet wounds, was leaned over the girl, nearly obliterating her from sight. He was whispering something.

A moment later the cook had said, "There's a situation. Everyone has to leave."

One by one the patrons stood and marched to the exit. Raffi had tried to remain planted in his chair long enough to finish the slice but Mom had grabbed him by the arm and yanked him along. On their way out he saw the cook throw a table aside and stare at a blue backpack that had been sitting beneath.

Outside, they'd crouched behind cars on the opposite side of the street. Ward remembered being angry that his pizza sat unfinished inside. There was shouting, and sirens somewhere far off getting closer. People began filtering out of the other stores on the strip.

A boy had ridden up then, perched on a black and yellow bicycle with high handlebars. He'd skidded to stop right in front of the beige car they were hiding behind. Through the car's window, Raffi watched the boy skip towards the pizza shop.

"Get back, sweetie," Mom had yelled.

The boy, a baseball cap sitting sideways on his head, wrinkled his nose as if to say, "Shut up, old woman. I'm a kid. Don't interrupt my life with your adult problems."

Mom screamed something about a bomb.

Ward couldn't remember the exact words but he could remember the tingle that had run up his spine.

The boy never broke stride. In a few seconds he'd emerged carrying a blue backpack.

"Forgot my bag," he'd said with a shrug. The boy had then taken off down the street, peddling so hard Raffi thought his legs might pump right off.

One forgotten backpack had evacuated a whole city block. It wasn't a frequent occurrence but it wasn't rare either. It was just the way things were. A fact of life in a country with terrorist Believers seeking to destroy the peace of the Republic. And vigilance was the duty, and pride, of every Citizen.

Where was that tension here in Paris? Where was the discord, the violence, the chaos the REC had told him about?

Lies. All of it. And how much more? The entirety of the Republic's propaganda machine stood clear in front of Ward as if he'd been standing there in the Party's news offices.

MacKenzie leaned in close. "Where are the cops and the riots and terrorists?"

"Exactly."

She stared at him, clearly unhappy with the cryptic answer.

Ward had a feeling that the longer they stayed overseas the more "truths" they might discover falsified. It was a difficult paradigm to accept, this new Europe that belied everything the Republic had ever taught. He swallowed it down like cough medicine, wondering what they'd learn next. Wondering what he'd be forced to swear to upon his reentry across Republic borders.

MacKenzie tapped his elbow. "Come on. Let's go inside."

"Will your friends be in there?"

"I don't know," she said as they approached a crowd hovering before the main doors. "I don't know anything about what comes next. We go find Clovis. That's what you said, right? Well, that's all I've got."

"What's that man's name," he lowered his voice despite suspecting that there was no Reclamation ban on religion here like there was back home, "your priest? You never told me."

"He's—his name is Simon." She stopped, her neck arched back, staring up at the archivolt above the north entrance. "Are they chopping his head off?"

The carved tympanum featured a kneeling man holding his head separated from his body. Above him stood another man, axe in hand as if ready to deliver another blow.

"You don't know the story of Saint Denis?"

She shook her head.

Ward wasn't surprised. Christianity's legends, and those of

other religions, had been the exclusive province of academics for nearly thirty years. Mythology. What once was a discipline for studying ancient pagans now encompassed all religious knowledge and relegated its presence within the Republic to libraries and storage cellars. As devout a Believer as MacKenzie might be she would have had little if any access to such stories as Saint Denis.

"He was executed," Ward explained, "for his conversions of the locals to Christianity in the third century. Legend says he picked up his severed head and walked six miles, preaching the whole way. When he got to this spot he finally lay down and died. That's why they built his basilica right here."

They passed through the doors of the cathedral as Ward finished his retelling. His words and his legs stopped. If the exterior was magnificent, the interior was transcendent. The vaults seemed ethereal. The nave was a tunnel into some level of consciousness he'd never been privy. The marble was as polished as cosmic ice. Ward felt like a cloud in the most perfect corner of the heavens.

"My God," MacKenzie whispered.

"Yeah," Ward breathed.

They'd only crossed the threshold by a few steps but already he felt himself shaking off an almost post-orgasmic chill. There was so much to gawk at, so many open spaces to inhale.

The nave in front of them thrust away to the East the way a camera shot in a film might pull away from the center of focus, its cross-ribbed vaulted arches rising more than fifty feet into the air. It terminated in the choir which was ringed by arched stained glass windows on both the floor level and the clerestory, the higher ones along the outer wall of the apse standing half the height of the cathedral. Six candles upon the altar, each some dozen feet tall, flanked a golden crucifix that reached almost as high. Statues, sculptures, busts, and glittering stained glass adorned every wall, punctuating the scene with too many details to focus on any one.

Ward knew he was grinning like an idiot boy on his birthday but didn't care.

Look at what men once could do.

He grasped MacKenzie's hand, pulling her forward out of the narthex towards the northern corner of the transept. "Look around for an entrance to the crypt," he said. "I've got to get some photos."

She acknowledged him and pushed into the crowds of tourists. Ward watched her for a moment, then removed his Port and began clicking. The triforium just above his head. The hearth-shaped marble tomb of Francois I. Centuries old cherry-wood colored misericords. A damaged marble column which legend said was disfigured by the flesh of a leper whose diseased skin was torn off and tossed aside by Jesus.

He bent and stretched to get his shots around the crowds. Effigies, tombs, *memento mori*. And windows. He shot every piece of stained glass he could. He might have taken a hundred.

The more he examined the cathedral the more he almost expected a priest—replete in silky black robes, pristine white collar gleaming—to part the crowd on his way to the altar. What could be more natural?

MacKenzie grabbed his shoulder, interrupting the

photography session. "Come on. I think it's this way."

He followed her deeper into the nave until they reached a sparsely populated spot before a closed door.

"That door," MacKenzie said, pointing. "It says to the necropolis, right?"

She was correct. But a glance into the choir showed Ward they didn't need to descend into the necropolis.

"Come here," he said.

"Did I get it wrong? *Crypte*, right? With an *e*."

"You got it right but look."

He took led her a few stops farther on, stopping in front of a marble sculpture of a Classical style temple surrounded by what he recognized as the apostles as well as the four cardinal virtues personified as women. He'd seen photos of the memorial before. The man and woman praying atop the temple were Louis XII and his wife Anne.

He pointed past the sepulcher. Ringing the rear of the choir into the ambulatory was a series of tombs topped with marble effigies.

"Cadaver tombs," Ward said. "The carvings are intended to show the kings at rest, yet still regal and holy."

"He's not in the crypt?"

"No. I'm betting he's lying right over there."

"You're a handy guy to have around, Professor," MacKenzie said before half-sprinting to the first of the tombs.

Ward grimaced at the scene she made darting through the church and followed at a less conspicuous pace. When he reached her she was studying a diamond-shaped sign on a brass post.

"Clovis." She jabbed her finger towards the sign.

Before he could read it, however, a family, lumbering like a single unit, blocked his view. Each one of the four—mother, father, son, daughter—was like a stuffed turkey with sausage limbs. He exhaled purposefully and examined the tomb. There was no doubt. This was certainly the tomb of Clovis.

The marble effigy showed a slight man without the wrinkles of old age. His hair and beard flowed even in the staid marble. He wore a tall crown and at his waist his right hand held a scepter. In his left he clutched between his thumb and forefinger what appeared to be a small cross. It was an exceedingly peaceful memorial for a man responsible for so much death. The king had conquered the whole of Gaul and was the first to unite all of the Frankish tribes. Such an accomplishment did not come without war, death, deceit, and treachery. And yet here he lay, an eternal pallid figure of serenity, immersed in the twinkling light of a stained glass window just behind them.

"It's stunning," MacKenzie said.

Ward agreed but was more concerned with who they were meeting and how he was going to pass himself as a Believer to a clergyman. "So, where's your priest?"

"I didn't say he was a priest. Not exactly."

"Whatever. Where is he?"

Ward didn't need her to speak to know the answer. Her face said it all. She had no idea. His jaw clenched.

"He's gone," MacKenzie finally said.

"I get that. But where is he?"

"Not him." MacKenzie pointed at the sign. "Clovis."

Ward turned. The obese family had finally tottered away. He scanned the first few lines. His heart sagged.

"See," she said. "Gone."

Ward was trying to put it all together when he noticed a man along the back wall of the ambulatory. The man was roughly Ward's age, wearing a dark blue suit and standing motionless, his eyes straight ahead. He held no camera and appeared ambivalent towards the art and architecture surrounding them.

"We've got to go," Ward said, grabbing MacKenzie's arm and pulling her around to the front of the choir. He positioned them on the edge of a large group of people exclaiming and gesturing in Italian.

"What the hell?"

The hell, as she put it, was that he hadn't done his homework. The sign told the story of Clovis' remains, brought to the Basilica from the Abbey of Saint Genevieve in the late seventeen hundreds, shortly before the French Revolution. During the war, revolutionaries had extricated the bodies from most of the Basilica's tombs, tossing them into a mass grave. They'd then covered them with lime. When the grave was dug up decades later, all that was left was a gray sludge punctuated by occasional bone fragments. Nothing was recognizable. The mess was placed into an ossuary and locked away in the crypt beneath the Basilica.

"I should've double-checked. I should've known better."

"Known what?" MacKenzie's voice was nearing frantic.

Ward quieted her with a scowl. Now that he'd identified one blue-suited man, he recognized three others with the same suit and blank stares at various spots throughout the Basilica. He couldn't know if they were security for the cathedral, French police, or even Agents keeping tabs on Gaustad's little project.

"We have to get out of here without drawing any more attention to ourselves."

MacKenzie didn't like this answer. "What about the crypts?"

"Don't worry about the crypts. Worry about the guys in the blue suits."

MacKenzie scanned the perimeter of the church, her eyes widening with each blue-suited man she saw. She flexed her hands. Her stance took on a hint of a crouch. She became a woman wanting to act. Run or fight. It didn't appear to matter; she was going to *do* something.

Ward had to counteract her adrenaline. If the blue suits were Agents, or some European equivalent, they didn't stand a chance.

"Your priest, Simon, he's careful, right?"

Bringing up the man's name refocused MacKenzie. She pressed her lips together as if considering. The conclusion found, she nodded.

"He told you to find Clovis but that's not much of a puzzle for anyone with Internet access, which I should've checked before we came here. I know the story of Clovis' tomb. I just didn't remember it. He would know it too, I bet. He must've had something else in mind."

MacKenzie thought on this a moment. "Yeah, okay. Where did the sign say he was originally buried?"

"The Abbey of Saint Genevieve."

"So, let's go."

"No, you don't understand," Ward said. "It's gone."

"Now a whole abbey's gone?"

"Demolished. It was closed in the late eighteenth century. That's why Clovis was brought here in the first place. The Abbey was torn down." Ward moved them to the side to better blend with the Italians.

"What's there now?"

"I don't know. I'm not even sure where it is. Somewhere on the Left Bank, I think."

"Okay. We get on the Metro and we look it up on the way." Ward shook his head. "It's probably just another church. Or at this point, maybe it's nothing more than a café. Clovis isn't really here, and he's not really there. We're missing something. There's got to be more to what your priest—Simon, right?—to what he told you. Think. What do you remember?"

"Nothing. That was it."

They were jostled as the Italians moved *en masse* to the transept, like six year old soccer players chasing the ball. Ward grabbed MacKenzie's hand and pulled her down the nave towards the entrance.

"His exact words, MacKenzie. Come on."

She yanked her hand from his, stopping them. She said, "He wrote, 'The road leads to Clovis.' That's it."

"You said something before about a treasure," Ward said, trying to see into every corner of the church at once without making it obvious he'd identified the blue-suited men.

"Yeah, in French. It was something like: Return the

treasure home, or return it to my house. What difference does it make if he never said where to return it to?"

Ward thought for a moment. "The part about returning it was in French? The rest was in English?"

"Yes."

Ward pushed words through his mind by the score, like sending photos from his Port to the screen in his classroom. It took twenty seconds before he found the right combination. He pulled MacKenzie in close so their foreheads were touching. "*Revenir a la maison, un cheri.* Is that it? Is that what he wrote?"

MacKenzie's eyes widened. "How the fuck do you know what he wrote?"

"It's the only translation that makes sense," he said. "Actually it's the best one to not make sense. You used a Port or some program to translate it?"

She nodded.

"Smart. He knew you didn't know French. He knew how you'd translate. It doesn't say go to New Mexico and bring the treasure home. It says: 'The road leads to Clovis. Come home, my cherished one.'"

"What about the treasure? The Spear?"

Ward had to make a quick decision. He was beginning the suspect that the Spear was never intended to be part of this, an idea supported by the fact that the thing couldn't be the real Spear of Destiny anyway. But telling MacKenzie that, especially after the way she reacted in his bedroom to the metallurgy scan, would not be a prudent move.

"Like I said, double meanings," Ward said.

He lifted his head from their huddle. It didn't appear any of the blue suits were watching them at the moment. His mind drifted to the priest's words, saying, 'My cherished one.'

"Hey," MacKenzie interrupted.

Ward forgot the priest. "I think you might be right about where they moved Clovis. Give me a second."

Ward accessed his map of Paris. It took only seconds to find what he was hoping for. He put the Port away and held out his hand.

Her head angled in confusion, MacKenzie ignored his hand.

"He's clever," Ward said, shrugging off her rejection.

"What are you talking about?"

"I'll explain on the way."

He led her out of the church, looking back once at the rose window as they reached the edge of the square. Even with the West façade cast in morning shadow, it was brilliant.

CHAPTER FOURTEEN

The moderately populated Metro zipped on its way with Ward and MacKenzie sitting in the back of the first car. Situated to the left of the vestibule door, facing forward, they were able to see everyone on board. Ward studied his map download while MacKenzie continuously repositioned her feet on the sticky floor, making a sound like a child smacking her lips over a piece of toffee. They were heading into the Latin Quarter. He knew the street they needed to find, but not exactly where on that street they were supposed to end up. He saw two strong possibilities named on the map. The church or the tower. But it could just as easily be some location he hadn't yet considered. He hoped it would become apparent once they arrived.

"I said," MacKenzie said into his ear, "where are we going?"

"Sorry. I was trying to figure something out."

"Okay, Professor. Did you figure it out?"

"Not yet. When we get there."

"Great. Where's there?"

"Rue Clovis."

"What?"

Ward was about to explain when the car slowed for the next stop. An irrational need to remain anonymous overtook him, quieting his words until the passengers around them settled into their places.

You are being watched, Ward's alarm-voice whispered in his mind.

The thought was so abrupt that Ward dismissed it as silly. Still, it hung there like—

"Rafe."

"Huh?"

"That guy at the front," MacKenzie directed his attention with a shrug of her shoulder.

It was the blue suit again. A woman this time. Mid-thirties. Medium build. Black hair. Her hands crossed in front of her crotch. Ward didn't remember her from the Basilica, but there was no doubt it was the same blue suit, albeit tailored for a feminine figure. The woman seemed to be scanning the crowd. When the doors closed she didn't take one of the nearby open seats.

"Cop or some kind of Agent?"

Ward didn't answer. What did it matter? He only needed to act concerned. Play the fugitive part. He wasn't the one in danger. So why did he feel so exposed? So vulnerable?

The woman now stood in the middle of the car. She wasn't

facing forward like most passengers. She wasn't looking at them but she wasn't *not* looking at them either.

Ward swatted his finger across the R1's screen to access the Metro lines.

The car slowed. Ward peered out the window to see where they were. Etienne Marcel. Five more stops before they were to switch lines.

"We should get off this subway," Ward said, convincing himself. "Get up and onto the streets."

He straightened in his seat, shifting his weight in preparation.

MacKenzie squeezed his hand. "No, not yet."

The car stopped. More people shuffled out. More people herded on. The woman in the blue suit remained in the middle of the car facing the rear. A dozen heartbeats. The car began to move. The woman touched her ear. A communications device? Or maybe she just had an itch. Ward couldn't tell but he knew MacKenzie wouldn't take the chance.

"At the next stop," MacKenzie said, leaning in to his ear. "Don't move until the doors are just about to close. Go to the right and stay close to me."

The assurance of her commands calmed Ward's breathing but they chafed at something below his ribcage. He was surprised to find he wanted to be the one in charge, the one keeping her safe.

"You stay close to me," he said.

The car stopped. Ward placed his hand on the back of her shoulder. She laid hers on his thigh. Fifteen or so people got off. The woman in the blue suit didn't move. Eight or nine people got on. As the last one hopped on board, just as the doors twitched in anticipation of closing, they bolted. MacKenzie got out clean, but the door slammed into Ward's leg, forcing him to stop and pull it free. He gritted his teeth and tried to match MacKenzie's speed. She was faster than he thought. Fifteen feet down the hallway she cut left around a group of backpackers.

Ward glanced back to see if they were being followed. There was a flash of blue but he couldn't be sure. He looked ahead. MacKenzie was gone. He passed an exit to the left. Two more exits waited ahead. Which had she taken? He chose the last one, barreling through a slow moving family, all notions of anonymity forgotten.

He was lost in seconds. Like last night, navigating the Metro tunnels seemed near impossible despite the number of Parisians marching along purposefully, unencumbered by the confusion plaguing him.

Alternating between a forced stroll and a near jog, he kept at it for a good five minutes, before frustration and leg pain forced him to slow pace. But there was no time to rest. He had to find MacKenzie. He had to get up to street level. He had to get out of these tunnels.

A turn brought him to a flight of stairs. It could have been the way out. It could have been the same flight he'd been up and down twice already. It didn't matter anymore. He went up. Checking behind as he climbed, he saw no blue suits. No one seemed to be paying any attention to him whatsoever. He cut around three more corners, then up another flight of stairs. A fourth turn, then a fifth. At last he saw what he wanted.

Sortie. An exit sign.

He emerged to a sun-blanched alley just off a main street. He leaned on the railing by the stairs and tried to get his bearings.

He was just off the Rue Rivoli, a major East-West thoroughfare no more than a couple hundred feet from the Seine, which he'd noted while mapping their Metro route. The Louvre, the former palace of France's kings, whose endless hallways displayed much of the world's greatest art, would be to his right. It took a determination Ward was almost surprised to find he had, to eschew the museum's treasures and march south instead.

This route took him into a shopping district. The streets were crowded in the same way Market Street might be in Philly, an anonymous push of people who cared little for other pedestrians. Only the next beckoning sign of neon mattered. And nothing short of outrageous attire or a car accident was going to pull the gawkers' attention from the gray marble edifices or the colossal-height windows hawking Paris' latest fashions.

It was an endless stream of shoppers and sightseers and pointing fingers. It was as disorienting as the underground.

Ward shoved through the crowds and across the street, steering south and trying to hide his growing limp. At last the mob grew more civilized in its pace and density as the river appeared.

He faced a limestone arched bridge packed with photographers snapping up memories of the Seine and the skyline. This would be the Pont Neuf, the oldest bridge in

Paris. On another day he thought, this would be the stroll of a lifetime. But today his focus was on recovering the wayward MacKenzie. Or was he the one who was wayward? It occurred to him that she was far more prepared for this type of operation that he. She was, in fact, exactly what the REC wanted of its Agents: smart, resourceful, and decisive. A far cry from himself, the academic who was quick only with historical factoids, not the assessment of a tactical situation nor the draw of a pistol.

Thinking of her in this way made him no longer wonder if she'd made it this far, or if she was still underground. He'd told her the street name. If she'd heard—*of course she'd heard!*—she would figure it out. Still, there was a strange nagging sensation coiling inside his belly. A familiar, though long absent sense of solitude.

He missed her.

It was a conflicting, aggravating, even embarrassing feeling. One that should not be fostered. His reason for finding her was to complete the operation, he told himself. He repeated the thought. Insisted it. Then pushed forward.

Once across to the Left Bank he walked along the river, thinking this route was the logical choice for finding MacKenzie, touristy enough to offer cover yet spacious enough to be seen. Minutes later the peaks and struts of Notre Dame peered above the buildings and trees. Against even his most adamant worries Ward found himself wanting only to stare at the grand cathedral.

Notre Dame was just as marvelous and ambitious as the Basilica of Saint Denis. Seen from this side of the river, however, it seemed more like a painting than an actual stone temple. Its buttresses and spires brush strokes to the sky.

To have the kind of carefree life that would allow a visit was a dream Ward didn't have time to indulge. He quickened his stride but managed only another few dozen steps before his pulsating leg demanded he stop.

Across a thin strip of grass was a small plaza. Ward limped forward, honing in on an unoccupied bench. As he reached the curb a marquee of carved wood letters beckoned. *Shakespeare and Company.* The famous bookstore and hangout of Hemingway, Joyce, and Pound in the 1920s. Ward's heart leapt at the literary treasure trove even more than it had at the sight of Notre Dame.

He approached the front window, a display of leather bound volumes the likes of which couldn't be found anywhere in the Republic. He had time to window shop, didn't he?

No. He had to keep moving. A glance back down the street revealed no familiar blue suits. Maybe he could spare just a minute to rest his leg—

A mustached man in a black pea coat, collar partially turned up, drew his attention. Leaning against a tree at the opposite end of the plaza, the man didn't fit. He lacked the aloofness of the blue-suits, as well as the interest of a tourist. He was purposefully casual.

Ward had no idea what other factions might be interested in MacKenzie or her priest. Some covert European version of the REC? Revolutionaries? Who were the revolutionaries here? Believers like back home? Secular Reclamationists like the ones he assumed painted the graffiti in the alley. Or some other cabal of which he was ignorant.

He thought of contacting Command. Doing so after having lost his primary target was certainly not ideal but he needed help. Maybe they'd abort and send him home. At first it was a satisfying thought. Then it became terrifying. What would happen to MacKenzie?

He forced himself to stop caring about MacKenzie's fate. He had one goal at the moment. Get away from the mustached man. The rest wouldn't matter if he got himself arrested or killed by whomever was pulling the mustached man's strings.

Okay, he thought. *Plan made. Lose Mr. Mustache. But how?* If he ran, with his throbbing leg, the man could easily overtake him. If he feigned ignorance he risked blowing the entire operation. Or being killed, knifed in the back by a man with a ridiculous mustache. He saw only one option. When the mustached man shifted his gaze to the river in an attempt to appear uninterested, Ward ducked inside the bookstore.

It could have been a storage closet at his university. There were no walls, only books. Shelves were barely visible behind and beneath the ramparts of spines piled almost thoughtlessly, and yet somehow lovingly, to the ceiling. An ancient woman— maybe a man—nodded as he entered. He thought of the way Hemingway described the store in *A Moveable Feast*: "… this was a warm, cheerful place with a big stove in winter, tables and shelves of books, new books in the window, and photographs on the wall of famous writers both dead and living. The photographs all looked like snapshots and even the dead writers looked as though they had really been alive."

As the words came back to him, a faded blue spine called

Ward's attention. In spite of the situation, in direct opposition to his operational training, he pulled it from the shelf and was amazed at the scent that came with it. It was like an old blanket from the back of the closet. The one your grandmother or great-grandmother had knitted. The one that wasn't used anymore, kept on the top shelf folded neatly, nothing else on top of it. It smelled of cinnamon and stale cake.

Ward held the book gently as if it were fragile china. *Murder in the Cathedral.* Eliot. One of his favorites from the Censored List.

Positioning himself so that he could see all who entered the store, Ward waited, the novel still in his hand. The mustached man didn't enter.

Maybe he could spare a minute to look around since he was already inside. It would give time for anyone trailing him to move on from the plaza.

He placed the book back on the shelf and rotated slowly, taking in the entirety of the store, and was caught by a precarious flight of stairs in the corner. As he approached the stairs, a couple came down single-file, forcing him to wait. With each step the couple took, the stairs groaned and coughed a plume of dust.

The way clear, Ward ascended and found himself in a study off to the side from more aisles of books. A small window, a small table, and a lounge chair not so different from his own populated the room. And, of course, books. But not so many as to occlude the warmth and cheer Hemingway had described. In fact, there he was—Hemingway, in a brass-framed photo above the table. Even in black-and-white, Papa's beard was as bright as summer clouds, as he stood frozen on the deck of some ship, probably in the midst of some great tale. And there, beside the window, was Joyce, his chin resting in the crook of his thumb and forefinger, his elbow on a polished desk. And there were more. Stein and Steinbeck and Eliot. The Lost Generation.

Ward hunched down, wincing a little at the pain in his leg, and peered out the window. The mustached man was gone. The plaza appeared clear. Ward relaxed. He breathed in the room and its history. It smelled something like cigars and genius.

"Agent Ward," a gravelly, very American voice said.

Ward flinched. His anger at allowing himself to be cornered drowned the need to know who knew his name. He spun. His first expectation was to see another blue suit. He faced instead the mustached man, and he was closer than Ward had thought.

The man reacted to Ward's move with a defensive thrust of his elbow. Before Ward could think, they were engaged. Quick jabs from the mustached man, mindless probes intended to buy time for evaluating an opponent, pushed Ward off balance. Ward countered not with wild swings but with controlled reactions. Muscle memories that Ward was surprised to find his body could recollect and apply. Remnants of self-defense drills from Citizen's Duty basic training all those years ago, combined with the recent refreshers under Agent Compano's guidance. But they were textbook parries he knew would only protect him so long.

Ward shot glances to every corner of the room. The stairs fell away directly behind the mustached man. Rooms of books lazed over the man's left shoulder. There was no way out of the study but around or through, him. The preliminaries were done. The mustached man backed up half a step. Ward tried to think. It was a mistake.

The mustached man blasted his left fist out forcing Ward to dodge awkwardly to the side. The man dropped to a crouch and brought his right knee up and into Ward's left. His injured ankle didn't hold. They both hit the floor. The mustached man rolled and flipped himself back to a standing position. Ward struggled to rise against the pain screaming in his leg.

His mind, far from being blank as per the cliché, was overloaded by movie scenes, literary descriptions, and murky recollections of unarmed defensive training sessions that were now fleeing ahead of the pain in his leg. He was nearly paralyzed by the deluge.

A fist crashed into his temple. He barely got his own forearm in the way of a blow aimed at his ribs. Decoys. The realization came too late. The mustached man's foot smashed into Ward's shin sending him to the ground again. Ward closed his hand on the nearest object, a book, and launched it. In flight, the dark red binding and yellowed lettering tumbled through the room in slow motion. Hemingway. *A Farewell to Arms.*

The mustached man deflected the hardback but his momentum slowed. Ward used the windowsill to lever himself back to his feet, groaning through the pain. He lashed out with three quick jabs. They bought him only a second. It was enough to recognize the move he should have made—a half-spin while still on the ground followed by a kick to the man's knee.

Too late. The mustached man was on him.

Fists were thrown in fast forward, most being deflected, but even these hurt. Soon they were grappled together, bouncing off a wall, a shelf, the desk. In the brief instant between jabs to his clavicle, Ward became aware that the man smelled like adhesive and bug spray.

They launched over the lounge chair, sending more books skittering across the floor. The arm of the chair caught the man's skull, and as they stood his eyes clouded over. Ward had two options: press the attack or escape. His training took over. He chose escape. He spun and made a leap to the stairs. It was the right move. It had enough speed. Still, the mustached man caught the cuff of his jacket. Off balance, they both plummeted down the stairs. The world spun, bounced, then flashed white.

Ward opened his eyes to a gathering crowd. He was sprawled on top of the contorted and still mustached man. Ward extricated his shoulder from the bottom step, which had split in two. Sound returned. He hadn't noticed it was gone until the shouting became discernible, like the din from a commotion blocks away.

He wanted to run. He placed his palms on the mustached man's chest and pushed himself to a kneeling position. He tensed, ready to sprint out of the bookstore.

His Port!

Ward froze. Someone put a hand on his shoulder. He shrugged it away. He reached into the mustached man's jacket. He found a Port. And a gun. The shouting grew closer. He shoved the pistol into his belt, the Port into his jacket pocket.

More hands pressed in on him. He had to go. He tried pushing through the crowd, but hands and voices seemed to be holding him back. Finally he grabbed a teenage boy, his blonde hair spiked and crusty, and shoved him into a stack of books, sending them soaring like shrapnel. The crowd gasped and parted.

Ward ran.

CHAPTER FIFTEEN

The sight of the neon green cross of a *pharmacie* a couple blocks from Shakespeare and Company offered as much relief as the medicine it sold promised. Ward stumbled inside, not concerned with decorum or anonymity. A box of pills fell from the shelf as he reached for a painkiller. Two more toppled over as he translated the strength of a different option. Finally finding the strongest painkiller he could, he straightened up and—

MacKenzie has the cash.

The thought struck him like another blow from the mustached man. With the cashier behind the counter peering over his glasses at him, Ward placed the box back on the shelf. He examined the boxes on the opposite side of the aisle hoping another customer would come in to provide the second's worth of distraction he needed.

As if he'd conjured her with his will and desperation, a tall woman in a beige raincoat traipsed into the store and marched to the checkout counter. Ward pocketed the painkillers and strolled outside, bounding into a hobbled jog as the door slid closed behind him.

A block down and one over, he ducked into a café and locked himself in the *toilette*. Four of the pain pills slid down his throat chased by a handful of water from the sink.

He stared into the mirror.

His forehead was bruised above his left eye, and blood was drying in his nostril and on his lip. He washed his face as best he could, then lifted his pant leg to diagnose the damage to his shin. Above the ankle it was a swollen mix of reds and purples. A doctor would tell him to stay off it for a few days, but that wasn't going to happen. He'd get some ice somewhere if he could. Otherwise the pills would have to be enough.

He rolled down his pant leg and checked the pistol he'd taken from the man in the bookstore. An RT40. Standard REC issue. Could the man have been an Agent? A tail? Backup? No. An Agent wouldn't attack him like that. They were the same.

Wait. Did the mustached man attack first? Who threw the first punch?

Ward shook the questions away. He needed information, not speculation. He pulled his Port from his pocket. The screen was cracked. It wouldn't turn on. The fall down the stairs, he assumed.

But he had a backup. His conscience had made sure he took the mustached man's Port. He pulled it from his jacket.

An R1. Had he really just beat the shit out of another Agent? Maybe killed him? Ward got that feeling in his gut, like when you see the car coming that's just run a red light and is about to hit you.

He swallowed hard and dragged a finger across the screen. An REC login appeared. He entered a dozen combinations of the four digit passcode but didn't have MacKenzie's luck. He balanced the Port on top of the toilette and splashed water on his face. It was cold. And it burned the bruise over his eye.

He ripped a handful of paper towels from a dispenser beside the sink, dried his face and hands, and blew his nose. More blood. He threw out the towels and picked up the Port. He tried again to hit on the passcode by luck. On his seventh attempt, the screen flashed. He was in.

The R1's standard functions were identical to his own. He tried the message logs. They were encrypted with a fingerprint access protocol.

I didn't know they could do that, Ward thought.

He tried the data logs to see if there was anything stored, any documents or downloads that might explain what was going on. He found only two files. The first was titled: RWard. It was a photo of himself taken by a security camera at the Tower sometime, he assumed, during his training.

The second file was titled: DWard.

It seemed ominous. What was the "D"? Detain? Death? He tapped the screen.

A video file opened. A blank screen with a time/date stamp of yesterday morning. Then it morphed into what appeared to be aerial surveillance of a mountain. The silent feed zoomed, revealing a quarry on the side of the mountain, some two hundred yards deep, of red stone and clay. It continued to zoom and pan until Ward could see the quarry was being worked by humans, not machines. Men and women in filthy rags swinging mute picks and hammers almost in rhythm. Digging for something too rare or delicate to be trusted to back-hoes or robotics. Maybe rhodium or tritium or maybe even just diamonds. Most looked as if they hadn't bathed in years. Yet, despite numerous bodies in various states of decay littering the quarry's strata and floor, each digger appeared strong and well-fed.

Ward knew he was looking at a Labor Camp. A still-active one if he was to believe the time/date stamp. A violation of one of the Republic's great promises: that such deplorable methods of treating enemies of the state would never again be sanctioned.

But what could that possibly...?

The screen zoomed again. Ward had to blink back a moment of vertigo. The picture settled on a single man some distance from the others. Two uniformed soldiers flanked him, rifles on their shoulders. The man's shaved head, his bare chest and back, his robust arms all were coated with grime and cratered with wounds and scars. Up and down this man heaved his pick with the metronomic power of one who has abandoned himself to his role.

One of the guards in the video cocked his head as if he'd been given an order from somewhere. He barked at the laborer. The man lowered his pick and straightened his bent shoulders. He turned his head like an actor awaiting his close-up. The screen zoomed closer.

Ward had never seen the man before. Yet there was something in his face that Ward recognized. Not the adult staring at whatever satellite was delivering this image but the boy the man had once been. A boy Ward had once known. His insides convulsed.

"Daniel," he said. His dead brother. Twenty years dead. Killed in the car accident that had also taken his father. The car accident that led to the funeral at which his mother was caught praying. The incident that little Raffi Ward called in to the hotline, making himself an orphan.

Ward grabbed the side of the sink with his left hand to keep himself from falling. It didn't make sense. It couldn't be real. But it was him. Daniel. Ward knew it with every drop of blood in his veins. And the time/date stamp. *Yesterday!*

Ward's head spun. He squeezed the edge of the sink and tried to force his mind to clear. It didn't help. He could feel the ceiling and the floor trying to swap positions around him. He dropped the Port—the Agent's Port—onto the tiled floor. He cupped his hands under the faucet until they were full then splashed the cold water on his face. It shocked his system. He did it again. Then drank and splashed more. The room slowed its motion. Rational thought began to return.

He needed to contact Command. To get an explanation. His picked up the R1 but only stared at it. Why would Command tail him? Why wouldn't they just send him this video? This great news that his brother was alive. It didn't make sense.

But it did. This mustached Agent wasn't here to share

good news. He was here with a warning. Ward started to put it all together. He hadn't checked in yet. He'd shared a hotel with MacKenzie. After offering his home to her. A home that had been surveilled close enough to get a photo of her for her fake ID on their way out yesterday morning.

The video was leverage. It was a warning. Do your job, it said, or this time we'll show you your *dead* brother.

Ward gagged, afraid he might vomit.

There was only one option. He would do it. He would follow MacKenzie to whoever or wherever Command wanted. Tell her whatever lies they needed him to. Then they could swoop in and take her and give Ward his brother back.

No.

If the REC, if Commandant Gaustad, was capable of keeping Daniel in a Labor Camp all these years, why would they suddenly just let him go once they had what he wanted from Rafe? He thought again of the carefree vibe of the courtyard outside the Basilica of Saint-Denis. Lie upon lie the Republic had told. Paris in chaos. Imminent terrorist attacks from Believers like MacKenzie. No more Labor Camps.

Then another thought. He imagined the mustached Agent tracking him across Pont Neuf, watching his own Port to see which way Ward turned next. Knowing that he'd stepped into Shakespeare and Company despite not seeing it. What was it MacKenzie had said about not having owned a Port in more than five years? Unplugged, she'd said. No one to track her. Ward recalled the way his R1 located their position last night to give them a map of Saint-Denis. Immediate.

Ward raised the Port, ready to smash it. But he had a

second thought. The Port was a useful tool. Don't destroy it. His hand danced from icon to icon. Swipe. Tap. Tap. Swipe. Tap. The Port's settings screen waited.

He'd be on his own.

He was already on his own. As far as the REC knew, his Port's uplink went silent in Shakespeare and Company. Let them think the same thing about the mustached Agent's R1 as well. There was only one path for Ward to take now. They wanted something MacKenzie's people had. Whatever it was Ward couldn't risk them getting it before him.

The plan was set. Find MacKenzie. Find whatever it was the REC wanted. Use it to negotiate Daniel's release.

He tapped the screen. The uplink to Command, and the Port's GPS function, were disabled. He slipped the Port into his pocket and splashed more water on his face. He shook himself dry and looked into the mirror. He barely recognized himself from even two days ago. He saw in his own eyes the same determination that had threatened him in MacKenzie's eyes. He found the vision satisfying in a way he'd never experienced before. He nodded to his reflection and left the café.

CHAPTER SIXTEEN

Ten minutes later, Rafael Ward turned right onto Rue Clovis at its eastern end, breathing harder than he would have expected for the soft incline of the Montagne Sainte-Geneviève, the central hill of Paris' Latin Quarter. He attributed the effort to his injured leg and paused a moment.

The quarter-mile-long street extending before him was a galley between walls of limestone, punctuated by a bell tower pointing up like a lighthouse in the middle of the south side. Tourists strolled through the galley in clumps of twos and fours.

Ward limped a block towards the tower, doing his best to act like a tourist. As he crossed onto the second block, eyes darting about for any sign that MacKenzie—or anyone else—was near, he felt someone fall into step behind him. He couldn't run. The pills had helped a little with the throbbing in his leg but he knew any attempt to sprint would only cripple him a dozen yards up the street.

He slipped his hand under his jacket, gripped the pistol, and spun.

It was MacKenzie, hood up, hugging the wall as she shadowed him.

"Are you okay?" He was surprised by the relief in his own voice. That emotion again—that absence he'd felt while they'd been separated. It disgusted him. It warmed him.

"Yes," she said. "I—oh my God. What happened?"

Ward's hand went to the bruise on his brow. It was still tender and now quite warm. He pushed aside his elation that she was okay. He had a mission.

"What is it, MacKenzie?"

"What is what?" She looked around, clearly trying to see if he was referring to something she'd not picked up on.

"Whatever you priest has?"

"Who said he has anything?" She hunched her shoulders and lowered her voice. "He needs the Spear." She shot looks at the tourists and locals strolling up and down the street. "He needs me."

"I'm not buying it," Ward said. "There's something else. Something worth going to New Mexico. Coming here. Risking all this. What is it?"

MacKenzie's eyes grew wide. It was that keep-your-voice-down glare Ward remembered his mother giving when he and Daniel got too loud in a store. He let her pull him closer to the wall, away from an elderly couple who had taken to passing closer to the curb when Ward didn't lower his voice.

"I don't know what you're talking about," she said.

"Bullshit."

"Fuck you, bullshit." Now her voice had risen to uncomfortable levels. A pack of teenagers, backpacks over their shoulders stopped to watch. A mother with a toddler on a harness and leash crossed to the other side of the street.

Ward could see MacKenzie calculating just how much of this she needed to take from him. Did she even still need him or could she just leave him behind?

If she walks away, he thought, *I'll lose any leverage I have to find whatever it is and rescue Daniel.*

"I'm sorry," he said.

She continued to glare.

"This," he said, pointing to the bruise on over his eye, "was an Agent."

"What?" Now it was her voice that was too loud. "An Agent? Where?"

Ward pulled her hand and led her past the teenagers, one of whom hooted something about abusive girlfriends. He didn't catch the whole thing. They stopped in a recessed storefront, a chocolatier with a sign in the window saying they'd reopen later that evening.

"Near Notre Dame," he said. "It wasn't the woman on the Metro, the blue suit. He cornered me in a book store." Ward watched her jaw unclench a bit. She believed him, believed the way he'd just acted was the stress of the incident. He wanted to try prying her once more.

"He asked where it was," Ward said, the lies coming as

natural as breathing now. "I thought he meant the Spear at first. But then he said something like, 'You haven't found it yet, have you?' I tried to run. I got away but," he pointed again to his bruised face.

"Jesus," MacKenzie said.

She touched her fingertips to Ward's brow then placed her palm against his temple. Her touch felt better than the water he'd splashed on his face. Better than the pills he'd taken. But it also felt like a knife in his ribs, knowing that he was going to betray her. He pulled away from her touch.

"What about you?" he asked. "You all right."

"Yeah," she said. "I thought I was being followed. I haven't run like that since high school." She combed her fingers through her hair. "How did they find us, Rafe? How did they track us all the way here?"

"I don't know," Ward said, trying to come up with another explanation. "Maybe your ID wasn't as clean as I thought. Or maybe the debit card. I told you, I don't smuggle people. It was a rush job. But there was only one of them. I think we're clear, at least for now."

It was a weak explanation but she seemed to buy it. To keep her from analyzing it too long, he said, "I was worried you wouldn't find your way here. That maybe you didn't hear me on the Metro."

"It took me a few minutes to realize that 'Rue' meant street, but I got it. I had to buy a map." She pulled a thick, folded wad of paper from her pocket.

"A paper map?"

"Yeah, it wasn't easy to find. Paper maps. Cash. It's like

home—they don't cater much to either here." She looked up and down the street, before stepping out from the store front to look at the tower rising over the street from the building next to the chocolatier. "This it?"

Ward didn't look up. "The Tour Clovis," he said. "It's all that's left from the Abbey of Saint Genevieve."

"Tour?"

"It means tower in French. The Clovis Tower."

"So, this is it, then." Again she looked up and down the street as if someone might materialize any second.

Ward had already considered the Tour Clovis as their destination but there was only entrance on the Tower's side of the street: the faded green doors of the Lycee Henri-IV, according to the yellow-lettered sign Ward had seen above the door before they'd stopped in the chocolatier's storefront. A secondary school. It didn't feel right.

"No, I don't think so," he said, also standing. He hadn't thought it all the way out yet, but now that he was looking up the street he was pretty sure he knew where they had to go. "I think we're heading a little farther up the road."

He stretched as if he'd been asleep for hours, making sure to flex and twist his leg. It still hurt but the pills were doing their job. MacKenzie, too, rolled her shoulders and arched her back. When they both had finished, Ward led them past the school and the tower.

"What happened to the Abbey that was here?" MacKenzie asked.

"It was torn down about two hundred and fifty years ago to pave this roadway." Ward stepped from the sidewalk into the street and tapped his foot. "It'd already been empty for a decade or two after being Suppressed during the French Revolution. It's a shame really. It was founded by Clovis himself after he converted to Christianity."

MacKenzie stopped walking. "Converted? I thought he lived in like the fifth century. Wasn't Europe already Christian."

"Christianity didn't always have the hold on Europe that it might have a hundred years ago. You have to remember, we're standing in the middle of ancient Gaul, conquered by Caesar in 52 BCE. Rome wouldn't become Christian for almost four hundred years after that. And neither the city nor its imperial provinces accepted the change overnight."

"So," she paused, visibly searching for the words to the questions that always accompany someone's realization that their version of history doesn't match the facts, "what was a pagan king doing buried in an abbey and then a cathedral? And," she added, "what does he have to do with the Spear of Destiny?"

"Nothing. Like I said, he converted. His wife, Queen Clotilde, convinced him to. He was Baptized at Reims on Christmas in 496. As for the Spear, I've got nothing. There's no connection I'm aware of. I've got to figure he put Clovis out there just as a landmark so you could find him."

An idea, a truth that would shed light on everything, felt like it was flitting just out of reach.

MacKenzie prodded Ward to continue walking. "So, what's here now?" she asked, pointing to the green doors.

"A high school but there was a new church built for Saint Genevieve just up ahead." As he said this the beige walls they had been walking beside gave way to the pallid hues of marble.

A moment later they rounded the corner to stand before a more modern, neoclassical structure.

"The Pantheon," Ward breathed, surprised that he could feel this stunned less than an hour after exploring the Basilica of Saint Denis and Shakespeare and Company, not to mention nearly being killed.

It took MacKenzie a moment to respond. "I thought the Pantheon was in Rome."

Ward heard but didn't immediately acknowledge her. He was taking in the scene.

Like the Basilica, a large square sprawled before the Pantheon. Here, however, due to the oversized nature of the building and the square, the tourists were spread out, making it seem less crowded. Teenagers covered the steps leading up to its massive marble columns, lounging, eating, chatting, kissing, and ignoring the tourists and photographers as if they were relaxing on their university quad. Another example of the Republic's lies about Europe's descent into anarchy.

More important than all of this was they appeared free of any surveillance.

"It is in Rome," he said, refocusing on MacKenzie. "This façade was modeled after Rome's Pantheon. It was built to be the kind of national mausoleum of France. See up there." He pointed to the inscription on the pediment above the columns. "*Aux Grands Hommes La Patrie Reconnaissante.* 'For great men, the grateful Fatherland.' Victor Hugo and Alexandre Dumas, Voltaire and Marie Curie. They're all in there."

MacKenzie nodded, her focus tilted up to the dozens of Classical-style sculptures in the tympanum, as well as the huge dome rising above the façade. This aspect of the Pantheon was higher and more ornate than its Roman inspiration, more like the dome atop the Republic's Capitol Building. Ward knew that its genius was actually in its triple-shelled construction and its oculus. He thought about explaining this feature to MacKenzie but stopped himself with the reminder that such things were generally only interesting to academics.

"Since when are you an architecture professor?"

Ward laughed. "I have to know a lot about a lot. History, literature, even architecture. I can't really lecture about the Dark Ages if I don't understand how and why they built their churches and castles. Plus," he said with a shrug, "I like this stuff. No one knows the histories anymore, especially of places outside the Republic. Citizens are so keyed in on their duty. Keeping clean. Staying anonymous. I think if we all knew more about how things once were maybe it might be different now."

"Maybe," MacKenzie said.

She started towards the stairs. Ward reached to stop her. He got her hip rather than her wrist. She frowned but with less annoyance in her glare than he expected.

"Hey," he said, trying to cover his embarrassment. "Will you even know this guy when you see him? You said you've never met him."

MacKenzie raised her eyebrow and proceeded towards the entrance without answering.

Unlike the Basilica of Saint-Denis, whose wide doors were held open for people to shove their way in, there was only one comparatively narrow entrance to the Pantheon. An usher, a gaunt old man in a blue suit, stood at the door guiding tourists inside in a more regimented manner than at Saint-Denis.

MacKenzie's steps slowed.

"It's okay," Ward whispered. "I don't think this fossil's going to give us any trouble."

"What if he's watching us? Setting us up for another Agent?"

Ward thought on it a moment but decided MacKenzie's theory just didn't feel right. "I don't think they would have stationed senior citizens at every church in Paris just in case we came by."

"Not all of them, Rafe. Just the ones we might hit."

It was a fair point. Still, it didn't track for Ward. He waited for his conscience to weigh in but it remained silent. He shrugged and continued to the door.

Inside, the Pantheon was laid out like the Basilica, though the nave was easily half again as wide and the transept didn't run as deep. And because this cathedral hadn't actively served as a church for any significant period since the nineteenth century, it was not encumbered by an ornate altar or pews, giving it a more open feel than might be expected.

The grooved columns present at the entrance were abundant inside as well. They stood like ushers, guiding the curious to the choir. But don't forget, they seemed to say, to explore the frescoes on the walls and the sculpted curves of the ceiling. Despite it all Ward found himself disappointed there were no windows.

There was, however, the pendulum. Designed by Leon Foucault in the middle of the nineteenth century, it looked like a giant tape measure ringing an octagonal table directly beneath the central dome. The pendulum's motion, seeming to change the plane of its arc across the table, was actually the first scientific proof of what had long been known: the Earth was a rotating orb not a ball held static in the heavens.

Ward led them to the pendulum, listening to their footsteps on the marble floor as if he were enjoying a concert. It was like every tourist was wearing tap shoes and dancing together to make the walls sing with their echoes.

MacKenzie appeared to notice none of it, not the poetry of the floor nor the distinguished pendulum.

"Which way?" she asked, the brass bob commanding not even a second glance from her.

Ward pulled his attention from the pendulum and searched for anything to indicate their next step. But there was nothing. No allusions to Clovis. No bread crumb trails to pick up.

Down, the voice in his head whispered.

"I think," Ward said automatically, "this time we're going into the crypts."

"Are you sure? You said Clovis was never here."

"Yeah," Ward said, unsure why.

"Okay," MacKenzie breathed. "I'll see if it's this way."

As she walked toward the transept Ward took a round of photos with his stolen R1, trying to get as many of the murals as he could. A dozen or so shots in, MacKenzie reappeared.

"Over here."

She pulled him towards a stairwell on the opposite side of the nave. A man in a dark blue suit stood motionless nearby.

MacKenzie nodded towards the man. "Another one," she whispered.

Ward tried to recall each of the people in blue suits they'd seen. Other than the one on the Metro, had any of them acted in any way a threat? Had the one on the Metro done anything other than stand awkwardly in the middle of the car?

"I'm pretty sure we're overthinking this. The Agent in the bookstore, he wasn't wearing a blue suit, MacKenzie. I've got to figure they're just building security. It's probably a standard uniform at all the tourist sites."

MacKenzie agreed but kept the blue-suited man in her vision as they proceeded to the spiral staircase into the *necropolis*.

The crypt began with a central chamber of limestone columns and an arched ceiling, all designed to show off the bricks of the master masons who built it. From this principal atrium, several arched tunnels reached out beneath the cathedral above. There were some tombs, like Voltaire's, present in this main atrium, his consisting of a white statue before the actual red marble sarcophagus. Of this one Ward took a photo.

The individual tombs in the catacombs were visible through brass grates, making each vault seem like a prison. They didn't know exactly what they were looking for but Ward figured there had to be some reference, no matter how veiled, to Clovis on one of the placards or tombs.

MacKenzie focused on the tourists. She seemed to be searching for a familiar face, though Ward doubted, from what she'd told him, this was a prudent strategy.

As they proceeded Ward counted off the names, famous yet

useless to their quest. Riqueti, Caprara, Braille, Rousseau. The Pantheon's architect: Soufflot. Before the tomb of Alexandre Dumas, Ward had to pause. Here was a man whose works, like the expatriates invoked by Shakespeare and Company, had once inspired generations. In the Republic, however, they were accessible only to those with authorization. Religious and un-American. The two worst offenses an author could enact.

"Who's this?" MacKenzie asked.

Ward knew not to be surprised but he couldn't hide his disappointment. "Alexandre Dumas. He wrote the best adventure novels of the nineteenth century. Maybe ever. You ever hear of *The Three Musketeers*?"

MacKenzie was silent a moment, once opening her mouth as if to speak, but then closing it again. Eventually, she said, "The Musketeers? Like with the 'everyone for each other' thing?"

Ward grinned at her misidentification of the motto as she continued.

"I think I remember my mother reading it to me when I was little. Before we left Edinburgh." She hesitated. "Is that it, 'everyone for each other'?"

Ward pointed through the brass portal at the flowing script epitaph carved into Dumas' sarcophagus. "*Un pour tous, tous pour un,*" he said. "It means—"

A voice from behind cut him off. "One for all, all for one."

CHAPTER SEVENTEEN

The man had gotten to within a few feet of them before speaking, his words causing them to spin in mirrored-arcs towards each other. Ward's hand went to the pistol beneath his jacket.

The man wore the same dark blue suit as the ushers upstairs. The same blue suit as the woman on the train and the ushers in the Basilica of Saint Denis. He was tall and slight, probably in his late fifties or early sixties but with a horseshoe of sparse white hair that made him seem older. His accented English identified him as a Frenchman.

Ward searched the man's face for a sign of his intentions but found the old man focused solely on MacKenzie. It wasn't a stare or a reckoning. It was something like disbelief. It was a man amazed by who stood before him.

Ward loosened his grip on the gun and moved in front

of MacKenzie, his right shoulder overlapping her left. "Who are you?" he asked.

The man looked from MacKenzie to Ward and back again. He said nothing. Seconds passed.

Ward tried again. "Simon?"

The man gathered a breath as if he might respond but MacKenzie spoke first.

"Dad?"

Ward felt his jaw flop open. "Dad?" he said.

The man smiled. MacKenzie exhaled hard. She moved toward the old man as if to embrace him but he held up a hand.

"Not here, Hannah," he said.

MacKenzie stopped. Her face fell like a child's atop a slide who's been told to wait and let others go first. The man moved sideways, motioning with his hand that they should follow. He led them back to the atrium, to Voltaire's burial, keeping them against the wall until a group of photo-happy tourists had cleared the area. He escorted them around the fence and behind a support column to the side of the philosopher's statue.

"Hannah," Simon began, but she'd wrapped herself around his torso before he could finish the word. His arms encircled her slowly, as if uncomfortable in the first seconds of the embrace. His shoulder's quickly softened, however, and he enveloped her in his wiry arms.

Ward had gotten over the initial shock of who Simon really was but he found the father-daughter display disquieting. He could understand MacKenzie's impulses but could they be sure who this man was after all these years? And why hadn't she told him that Simon, her "priest," was actually her father?

The two separated and Simon began again.

"Hannah, I am so pleased you are well but we are not safe here for discussion. I have not had a chance to complete the proper arrangements."

"It's okay, Dad. We have money. Whatever you need—"

He stopped her with a smile far wearier than his previous. "It is not money with which I am concerned. Oh, *ma cherie*," he said, his tone changing, "I am so sorry I have not been there for you. That I missed your mother's funeral. I wish…" He straightened his posture and coughed, "I wish there was more time for us but what is gathering simply will not allow it."

"Simon, right?" Ward interrupted.

The man nodded but didn't take his eyes from MacKenzie.

Ward continued. "Look, the fact that you haven't seen your daughter in—what, twenty-plus years—aside, what *is* gathering, what *is* there time for, and why do you have us running all over Paris?"

For the first time Simon shifted his attention to Ward. The Frenchman's gaze stalked him with an uncomfortable diligence. Ward's hands found his pockets.

"Young man," Simon said, too politely. "*I* do not have *you* doing anything. I must assume you are here by your own free will. Is that not correct?"

"Yeah, close enough," Ward said.

"Please do not mistake my caution," Simon said. "I am pleased that you are helping my daughter on her quest but now is not the time. I had expected you no earlier than this evening. Plans must be accelerated."

"You expected us tonight?" Ward couldn't help his raised voice or obvious incredulity. How could Simon have expected them tonight? Ward hadn't even known himself they were coming to Paris until yesterday. And MacKenzie hadn't contacted anyone since they'd been together. Had she? What about after they got separated in the Metro tunnels? No, any contact then would have led to a designed meeting, not a surprise introduction before the tomb of Dumas.

Ward became aware that MacKenzie and Simon were staring. He clenched his jaw and waved a hand in a half-hearted apology for the outburst.

Simon tapped a finger against his upper lip. He examined his daughter as if he could read her soul by the way she stood. "It is past lunch," he said. "You must be hungry. Find a café, maybe across the square. Eat. That will be good, yes? Come to my flat at half past one. It is on Rue Descartes, adjacent to the school. There is a brown door beside the La Celeste, a little bistro with a red awning. Flat C. Second floor."

He swung around the column, nearly disappearing from sight.

"I have the Spear," MacKenzie said.

The blue suited shoulder, all that was still visible of Simon, halted. The rest of him inched back into view, his demeanor an odd mix of emotions Ward couldn't identify.

"The Spear," he said, a peculiar nonchalance to his tone.

MacKenzie unslung her backpack. "Of course. Here." She held it out.

Simon kept his distance. He stared at Ward, his eyes

saying he knew something. But what he knew, Ward couldn't determine.

"Soon," he said. He rounded the column once more and was gone.

Tourists trickling in around them as if from a leaky faucet, Ward and MacKenzie exchanged looks. Neither spoke. They exited the building, pausing at the top of the stairs to look out across the square. The plaza was triangular, laid with various shades of brick forming patterns of diamonds and triangles pointing back towards the Pantheon. The plaza itself pointed away from the Pantheon, terminating in the converging one-way lanes of the streets that ran along its length. Standing at the top of the stairs the plaza seemed to be directing them ahead.

Ward tried to imagine the emotions MacKenzie was battling. It was a difficult enough scene to witness, knowing such a reunion could never occur for himself. But what exactly was she feeling as she held the father she hadn't seen in so long?

Other questions soon expelled the sentimental ones. How much did Simon know? What did he have to arrange? How quickly did the man's thoughts turn to his deceased wife—did such a regret ever leave a man? Could he be trusted? Was he even who he claimed to be?

More important, had he said anything to back up Ward's theory that there was some relic in play here? Something important enough to place a supposed Spear of Destiny back in the hands of Believer?

Ward couldn't think of anything specific other than the

look Simon gave when MacKenzie mentioned the Spear. It was a knowing look, not one concerned with the wellbeing of a precious artifact. It was almost amusement but it wasn't an answer. Yet.

At the bottom of the stairs MacKenzie pointed out a café beside a bank across the plaza. Ward held out his hand, indicating she should take the lead. He convinced himself that he did this out of chivalry and not a sudden desire to admire her shape before catching up. But he did admire.

"I'm not crazy, right?" she said.

More specificity wasn't necessary.

"He's your father, right? How could you not react that way? But are you sure he is…who he is?"

It was the wrong thing to say. He knew it as the words came out but he couldn't stop them. He expected to see her rage again, the same fury she'd exhibited when she'd hacked into his R1. Instead, she lowered her head, her pace slowing.

"How can I be sure?" she began. "I don't know his face. I never had photos. But he's familiar nonetheless. His words. The way he speaks. They're his words. The words from his letters." She stared at Ward, daring him to doubt her. "And his voice. When he said it—'One for all, all for one'—I remember that voice. The same as from the fairytale. That thing he said all the time, I think. 'That will be good, yes?' I can close my eyes and hear that voice tell me about Cinderella and the tortoise and the hare and…" She paused, as if recalculating to be sure. "It's him. My father."

Near the summit of the pyramidal plaza she stopped. They were still ten feet short of the white barricade posts that protected the pedestrians within from passing cars.

"Rafe," she said.

He stopped beside her. "So, it's Hannah, then? Your name?"

She looked at him like he'd just said night was day. "It's MacKenzie. Now look," she said, pointing.

He looked at the ground in front of her but saw only dirty bricks and a piece of chewing gum pressed with a shoe print. He opened his arms as if to say, "What are you looking at?"

"Clovis," she whispered.

Ward stepped around her and squinted at the ground. It took a moment, the Pantheon's shadow making the bricks blend together, but he saw it. Four bricks rimmed with a thin copper frame. Across the first two bricks was a single line of French,

"Clovis I, King of the Franks, here spoke:"

Beneath this was a flowing script almost obliterated beneath Ward couldn't guess how many decades of foot traffic.

"It's about our Clovis, right?"

It was certainly about their Clovis. Ward felt the breath leave his body, not as an exhalation, but as if he simply deflated. In the resulting vacuum, hundreds of pages and downloads of legend and folklore flooded in. So much began to make sense. Which, of course, led to a myriad of new, as yet unanswerable, questions.

"*Ainsi as-tu au vase à Soissons.*"

"Translate it."

Ward considered the phrase a moment. He felt he'd been in a dark library and someone had finally drawn the curtains letting in light to see the books around him. Finally, he said, "It says we need to talk a little more about your fairytale. Come on."

He grabbed her wrist and led them to the café, pausing at the barricades to allow a spurt of traffic—a boxy red sports car, a taxi, and a police car—to whip by quicker than Ward thought was safe for the narrow street.

He claimed a table on the sidewalk beneath the café's awning, settling into an uncomfortable metal chair with his back to the wall. MacKenzie sat facing the Pantheon, her mouth open, about to ask again, he was sure, for the translation. The arrival of their waitress—a middle-aged woman with a defeated crease across her brow—halted the inquiry.

In English, Ward ordered two *croque monsiuers*, two coffees, and a double-Scotch, a Glenlivet eighteen year. The waitress made a face at his language choice. MacKenzie made a face at his beverage choice.

"You don't like coffee?" he asked, knowing this was not her objection.

"The coffee's fine," MacKenzie said. "What's with the Scotch?"

"You want one?"

"Jesus, Rafe. This isn't really the time."

"You can't get real Scotch back home. I've never had it," he said. What he didn't say was that when he saw the Scotches listed on the menu, his molars began to tingle and his throat became parched.

MacKenzie shook her head and pointed back to the plaza. "Tell me about the bricks."

Ward looked up at the Pantheon. Its façade, massive and proud, seemed to revel in the slowness of eternity. Ward wondered what its longevity might allow it to tell of days like this in a century. Would all their efforts—the Reclamationists, the Believers, Simon, MacKenzie—be nothing more than a passing phase of humanity's short-sightedness?

MacKenzie cleared her throat.

His eyes still on the Pantheon he said, "The fairytale."

"What fairytale?" She was clearly confused.

"The one you told on the plane. I think it might be the key to what your father wants us to do."

"Come on. It's a kid's story."

Ward retrieved the R1 from his jacket and began swiping across the screens. No fairytale was simply a kid's story. The folk tales that evolved into famous children's stories began as accounts of everyday hopes, fears, and faiths, exaggerated for those who loved to dream. But there was always some truth at their core.

To explain, he wanted to show MacKenzie something. He just hoped the Internet here was uncensored unlike back home. He swiped and typed.

"Rafe?"

He let his outstretched finger tell her to wait while he continued searching. As he moved screen to screen an idea, a simple scenario, came to him. He could switch on the Port's GPS. Or better yet, send a message to Command. She'd never know what he was doing. He could give them the location of Simon's flat. Agents would swarm. Take him. Take what he was hiding. It would be over quickly, quietly. There'd be no more running. No more brawls in cultural landmarks. MacKenzie would never be in danger, never have to face an interrogation or a Crematorium. It would all be over.

Back home he could negotiate Daniel's release. Maybe even his own release from service. Be just a professor again.

He had two reactions to this idea. First, you can't negotiate if the other person already has what they want. Without Simon's secret relic, there was no way to guarantee Daniel a chance. Second, he'd never see MacKenzie again. This latter thought he found quite dreadful.

The competing ideas dissipated, replaced by a stern directive at odds with, yet somehow in compliance with, the operation:

Protect her.

"Damn it, Rafe."

Ward looked up. MacKenzie's impatience was bordering on anger. He refocused his attention on the R1. The image he'd been hunting for waited patiently on the screen.

She grabbed his forearm, her short nails digging in not accidentally, causing him to drag a finger across the screen and cue a different file.

"Don't ignore me."

There was a fire in her tone, a power of will that excited Ward.

"I'm not ignoring you," he said, reacquiring the photo he wanted. "I promise."

"Tell me what it says."

The waitress returned with their sandwiches and drinks. Ward took a long sip of the scotch. It was smooth with a tingling burn, a little fruity even. He shivered and smacked his lips. His veins coursed with pure energy. He knew he was grinning but couldn't stop.

MacKenzie tapped her palm on the table, not hard enough to draw attention from the other patrons, but enough to make it clear she was done waiting.

He rotated the R1 so she could see what he'd found. As she leaned forward he noticed the police car parked down the street.

CHAPTER EIGHTEEN

To a non-academic, the downloaded image on the R1 would have appeared to be a pen and ink drawing of some medieval post-battle scene. To someone with a rudimentary familiarity with religious texts it might have appeared similar in style to a monastic bible illustration.

It depicted a military scene of a dozen or so soldiers forming an arc around two men. Each of the soldiers was dressed in a, somehow, coherent mixture of Roman and Norse battle garb. The central figure stood taller than the rest, with a flowing mustache and thick beard beneath his *galea*, a Roman-style crested helm. In his powerful right arm he held an axe at waist-height. His other hand pointed to the second man who lay crumpled on the grass over his sword, an open wound gaping in his skull.

MacKenzie looked as if she wanted to ask a question

but couldn't quite find the words. She continued to study the screen, finally looking to the Pantheon before turning back to Ward and speaking.

"The one with the axe—that's Clovis?"

Ward scrolled the image so its caption at the bottom could be seen. It was Latin, but Ward was sure MacKenzie would make the connection.

She didn't disappoint.

"They're not the same language but…Soissons. That's on the brick, too. What is it?"

Ward took a bite of his sandwich. "It's a city north of here. That's French," he said, titling his head towards the Pantheon. "The illustration, that's Latin. They both say, 'Thus didst thou to the vase at Soissons.'"

"Okay. You lost me now, Professor. Who's doing what to which vase in some other city?"

"You may not recognize it as the same," Ward said, glancing over her shoulder. The police car was at the west end of the block. With the reflection from the sun he couldn't see how many officers were inside but there didn't appear to be any movement. *Maybe,* he thought, *I'm just being paranoid.* "But I'm pretty sure what's written on those bricks is the actual beginning of your fairytale."

She wasn't buying it. For a Believer, a woman on a quest that began with the Spear of Destiny, she was oddly skeptical. *Maybe that was the nature of ardent Belief,* Ward thought. It allowed for its own prescribed leaps of faith, required them in fact, yet drew definitive mortal lines there. A singular phenomenon, such conviction was thrown into chaos when the universe beyond those lines was introduced.

Ward wanted to write this epiphany down. It would make for a great classroom discussion. Though certainly not back home. The Republic—with its own unilateral Belief system—wouldn't allow it. A perfect example proving the theory. But now wasn't the time.

"Once upon a time," he began, holding back a chuckle at MacKenzie's what-the-fuck face. "Sorry. Okay, so I told you Clovis was the first king of France. A Merovingian, the name coming from his grandfather, Merovich."

"I've heard of them," MacKenzie said, her brow wrinkled. "Maybe in a textbook or a documentary or something."

More likely she'd heard it from her father. He guessed Simon had spent a good amount of time feeding his toddler daughter fragments of the legends they were now chasing.

"Well, Clovis becomes king when his father dies, five years after the last Western Roman Emperor is deposed. That's roughly the beginning of the Dark Ages."

"And he conquers France. I get it. Please tell me how this all makes sense out of us sitting here eating crock-whatevers in Paris."

"*Croque-monsieurs*," he corrected, receiving another glare. "Before he can complete his conquest of France—Gaul, actually, is what it was called—he has to go to war with Syagrius, the last Roman magistrate in the region. Do you want to guess which kingdom was his?" Ward couldn't help slipping into professor mode. MacKenzie, for all her stubbornness and skepticism was a great pupil.

"Soissons," she said, spreading her arms wide.

"Absolutely. One battle and the winner would be the undisputed king of Gaul. The problem was, Clovis' army was significantly outnumbered. So he goes to Remigius, the Bishop of Reims, the holiest man in Gaul. He asks for the Bishop's blessing and the power of the Christ-God to aid his army."

"The Christ-God?" MacKenzie cut in, clearly disturbed by this epithet.

"What do you call your Savior?"

"Jesus, the son of God." Her answer was definitive.

"To you," Ward said, lowering his voice. He was uncomfortable discussing the subject in the open. "But to many in the Roman world, or in the rubble left in its wake, Christ was simply another god in the pantheon. Especially in Gaul where Celtic gods still reigned and many tribes worshipped the powers innate in magical cauldrons."

"The magical pot from the fairytale," MacKenzie said, her skepticism obvious.

"Quite possible. And I'm sure you also know the most famous magic cauldron descended from Celtic lore. Its discovery was the goal of every Knight of the Round Table."

"The Holy Grail," she said. She didn't seem to be buying this either.

"The Holy Grail in France."

"The Holy Grail doesn't—wait, Joseph of…of…"

"Arimathea," Ward offered.

"Yes. After the crucifixion. I know this story. Joseph of Arimathea, Mary Magdalene, and Lazarus escape persecution in Jerusalem by sailing off in a little boat. They have a miraculous journey across the Mediterranean and they land in…well, France somewhere."

"Marseille."

"Sure. Marseille. And they had something with them. A holy treasure. I thought it was a memento, a relic of Jesus. I don't know, a lock of his hair or a fingernail or something. But the Grail. Come on." She shook her head.

"Hold on a second. I'm not saying that we're looking for the Holy Grail, or even that it exists. What's important here is the idea of the magic cauldron because it doesn't begin and end with the Grail. And it certainly isn't just an anonymous pot in a fairytale. You see, the Bishop offers Clovis his blessing on one condition. A relic once belonging to the Church was being held in Soissons. He asks Clovis to liberate it and return it to Reims. On the promise of this he blesses Clovis and his army."

"So, this is the magic pot? Vase. Whatever."

Ward bobbed his head in agreement as a second police car pulled in behind the first. Ward wasn't one to believe in coincidences. He certainly wasn't going to tally this up to one. Sure, it was possible the local police were just gathering for lunch or checking on the teenagers at the Pantheon. Maybe even following a lead on the incident at Shakespeare and Company but it could also be a distraction for the Agents who were already closing in. Agents who, perhaps, were able to track the R1 once it connected to the Internet. Ward gritted his teeth. It was too late to do anything about it at this point. Getting up now would only draw attention. Best to wait. And watch.

He took a large bite of his sandwich, indicating to MacKenzie that she should eat as well. He washed it down with the rest of the scotch, enjoying the burn in his chest and belly.

"After the battle," he said, speaking a little faster, "with Clovis having smashed his opposition, the king goes to his army's camp. He's already sent ahead a message that his commanders and his captains can take their spoils so long as the vase is left unclaimed. But he finds the church empty so he goes out among his men in search of it. They're all reveling in gold and silver and jewels, cheering him as he passes. Finally he finds one man, a captain of a small regiment in the army, sitting on the ground with the vase before him, riches spilling out over its sides."

"He kills him." She wasn't asking.

Ward found that each connection she discovered made her more attractive. He couldn't help a smile. It quickly faded, however, when a third police car, this one coming from the Pantheon to the east, parked at the corner, no more than thirty feet away.

For a moment, he panicked. They were outnumbered. Could they run? Fight? Why hadn't MacKenzie seen them? She'd know what to do.

He took a deep breath and held it. Something inside him, deeper even than his thoughts, tapped metronomic. An almost palpable rhythmic calm. His heart slowed to match the beat. No, he'd done the right thing by waiting. In their cars the police couldn't effectively be attacked. And if he and MacKenzie fled they'd be run down in seconds. The prudent move was to continue waiting. There was an exit strategy coming. He felt it. Not like a memory but rather an innate surety. He thought back to the fight in the bookstore. Though it had been years since basic training, and even then he hadn't excelled at hand-to-hand combat strategies, there'd been a definite proficiency to his actions and reactions. Trained movements as natural as catching a falling cup. He would trust them.

He exhaled and continued the story.

"Clovis asks for the vase but the captain refuses, claiming it as his rightful bounty. Clovis demands the vase but the man becomes irrational, spouting declarations that God has told him the vase must not leave his hands in one piece. So Clovis tries to take it. The soldier stands, hefts his battle-axe and brings it down on the vase with all his might."

"He breaks it?"

"He shatters it," Ward said, fanning his fingers out like an explosion. "The legend says it splits into four pieces. Clovis picks up the pieces, kicking aside the jewels and other treasures that were now spread all over the ground. He doesn't say a word. He just picks up the pieces and leaves."

"That means the vase is just some broken pottery now."

"Would it matter," Ward asked, "if the Spear of Destiny were snapped in half? Or if the Shroud of Turin were torn up? Would the pieces be any less sacred?"

"I guess not."

"They wouldn't."

The driver's side doors on the two police cars behind MacKenzie opened simultaneously. One officer emerged from each, squared hats pulled down low over their eyes. They convened at the front bumper of the closest car. The tallest one, bearded and broad, leaned in to the other, then straightened. He faced the café and addressed the radio receiver situated on his shoulder.

They were almost out of time. Still, Ward felt he needed to finish the story.

"But it's not over yet. You see, a year later, in preparation for another battle, Clovis musters his army on the Champ de Mars. While walking the lines of his soldiers he comes face to face with that same captain. He looks the man up and down, then pulls the man's sword from his hand and tosses it to the ground. 'You are not prepared for battle,' he says, 'you who holds your weapon so softly.' And when the captain bends to pick up his sword, Clovis brings his own axe down on the man's head, saying, *Ainsi as-tu au vase à Soissons.* 'Thus didst thou to the vase at Soissons.' The bricks over there say he spoke those words on that spot."

"Wait. Isn't the Champ de Mars where the Eiffel Tower is?"

Ward was impressed that she knew the name of the field on which the iconic tower had been built.

"It is. Champ de Mars means Field of Mars. It's the parade grounds where the army gathers, named after a similar place in Rome. Five hundred years ago French armies gathered in front of where the Eiffel Tower sits. But a thousand years before that Paris didn't extend much beyond the Seine. This hill was as good a place as any to muster an army. Of course I'm not going to claim that the man's blood pooled on that very spot."

MacKenzie seemed to be rolling the whole story over in

her head, finally uttering, "Jesus."

As the word past her lips, both front doors of the police car to the east opened, divulging a thick cop and short thin one. It was now four to two. The two officers from down the street began a slow march towards the café, hands on their holsters.

They had maybe twenty seconds. There was really only one option on how to play this. He just needed the officers to the east to come closer.

Ward leaned over to give MacKenzie directions. Before he could speak, however, she grabbed his knee under the table.

"Rafe, there are two cops staring at us," she said through gritted teeth. There was no fear in her voice.

Ward couldn't help his next thought: *this is going to be fun.*

CHAPTER NINETEEN

I f they timed it right, they could catch all four police officers by surprise. Ward could almost hear Agent Compano's voice instructing him as if in some tactical training session.

You sprint past the two coming from the Pantheon and, just maybe, find the police car still running. Then you've got a shot.

"There are two more behind you," Ward said, placing his hand on top of MacKenzie's under the table. "Move with me. Wait until the two coming to you reach the sewer grate. You see it?"

Her face scrunched up as if asking, "When did the professor become an action hero?"

When did I turn into something like a real Agent? Ward thought.

What have you ever done, he heard Agent Compano's voice

shout in his head, *to make you think this is going to work, Trainee Ward?*

It didn't matter. They didn't have time to doubt. He stared at MacKenzie. They didn't have time for him to explain. He was going to hold her eye until either she trusted him or the cops arrived. It took only a second. She nodded.

"As soon as their toes touch it, go. I'll be right behind you."

"Go where?"

Fifteen more feet. The officers from the east slowed their pace, letting their comrades from the west reach an equal distance.

"Their car," Ward said. He slid the Port into his jacket pocket with one hand and placed the other on his RT40.

"You're joking, right?"

He let his clenched jaw speak for him. He wasn't kidding. Ten feet.

"How'd they even find us?" she asked, as she placed her palms on the table.

Ward shrugged. How didn't matter. Not now. And he wasn't about to admit that it might have been because of the picture he'd just downloaded.

Five feet to the sewer. The thicker cop could have been the other's father. Ward guessed the young one, almost too young to grow a decent beard, was a rookie doing a ride along. None of the four had yet unhooked their holsters.

They reached the sewer grate.

Now, Trainee Ward, he heard Agent Compano bellow in his head.

"Now," Ward shouted.

MacKenzie pounced. She was up and running before any of the four officers had halted their pace.

Ward grabbed his plate, the sandwich plopping to the sidewalk, and flung it like a discus at the older officer. The plate missed its target but did its job of distraction. Ward charged, holding his pistol out in front like a lance.

MacKenzie had a three step head start and managed to lengthen it as Ward fought to clear the other tables on the sidewalk. He didn't bother looking back. They had enough distance from the western cops that the only worry would be if they tried shooting them in the back. Ward gambled they wouldn't.

He'd planned to go after the veteran officer, leaving the young one for MacKenzie to evade. She didn't need that concession. She threw a magnificent fake right, a cut left, then lowered her shoulder and slammed into the larger cop's chest. He never even tried to protect himself.

The younger officer, cheeks flushed beneath his boxy cap, was frozen mid-stride, his eyes wide. Ward could imagine the only thing he saw was the barrel of the RT40 bounding towards him. Ward sidestepped the immobile cop, delivering an elbow to just behind his ear.

The open doors of the police car beckoned. MacKenzie plunged into the driver's side of the still running car, forcing Ward to adjust his approach and enter the passenger side. They'd executed their moves perfectly. He could imagine the shock of the incident paralyzing Professor Ward. Even now, as Agent Ward, the whole episode might have threatened to overtake him had he not had the scotch to calm his nerves.

But Rafael Ward, on his own, caught between the REC and this beautiful fugitive, without a clear objective or extrication strategy, without a clue as to what was coming next, craved more of the adrenaline that now surged through him like a narcotic.

He liked this new him but even that thought was blown aside as MacKenzie sped them towards the scrambling officers to the west, Ward's door still flapping open.

"Which way?" MacKenzie shouted.

Ward's Port found its way into his hand as if the move had been practiced a thousand times. "Go past them," he said, his fingers dancing along the screen to call up his Paris map. "Swipe the door."

She did as instructed, hitting the lead police car more straight on than a swipe, careening them almost into the opposite curb. She had to struggle to right the car, finally doing so as they sped through an intersection nearly clipping a bus.

Ward finally got the map centered on their location. They were in a bad spot. Ahead, all roads led to the Luxembourg Gardens. To the right was the Seine. They had only one choice.

"Go left."

The car whipped around the corner. Ward nearly lost his hold on the R1 as they caught more of the curb than the street. A man out for a walk with a cat-sized dog fled into a tobacco shop, the dog fluttering through the air on its leash behind him.

Ward was about to call out the next turn when he realized his mistake. They were going the wrong way down a one-way street. Worse, the street curved right into the Gardens.

"Left again. Left, left," he yelled, surprised at his own hysteria.

MacKenzie, however, had it all under control. She cut the wheel hard one way. Spun it the other. Worked the handbrake. Smashed on the horn. In less than ten seconds she had them squealing tires through another corner followed by two more before slowing down to match the traffic around them.

"Not bad," Ward breathed.

She gave him a look which said, "Not bad, my ass. I'd like to see you do better."

"Where'd you learn to drive like that?"

She failed to hold back a grin. "Paris. Near the Pantheon."

He wanted to laugh. He wanted to bask a moment in the strange intoxication of the woman beside him.

He wasn't afforded the chance to do either.

At the next intersection, two more police cars—lights on, sirens off—sped into pursuit, the lead car nearly broadsiding them.

"Fuck," MacKenzie said, slamming on the accelerator.

Ward scanned ahead but saw no escape, no side streets or obstacles they could use to their advantage. He pulled his eyes from the traffic they were slaloming and whipped his fingers across the map.

He found what he was searching for.

"Stay straight. Faster."

"I can't outrun them."

A police car appeared on the other side of a small truck as they passed it. The driver tried to sideswipe them. MacKenzie smashed the brakes. The attacking police car skidded in front of them, continuing into a street lamp and a parked car. They sped up, cutting and drifting from lane to lane.

Ward saw their opening coming but they needed more speed.

"Faster. All of it. We're going left on my mark."

"It won't go any faster."

"Faster," he shouted.

He didn't know how she did it, but the car felt like it found one more gear. They gained another fifteen kilometers per hour.

"Get ready," he said. "No brakes. And watch the trees."

"What?"

"Now!"

The word wasn't fully formed on his lips when the whites and tans of the endless wall of buildings on their left broke into green. A small park ringed with trees was going to be their escape. Or their death.

MacKenzie churned the wheel to the left, her hands moving faster than Ward thought possible. Somehow they missed the first tree. The next two, however, stood like gateposts. He wasn't sure they would fit. His body clenched, his eyes squeezing shut.

The sound of the mirror exploding into a thousand pieces was louder than a gunshot. Ward breathed, not sure how long it'd been since he had. He pushed his eyes open. They were still speeding towards a wall of trees set in front of a building.

"Brake!"

The car tore up half the length of the park's grass as they skidded to a stop just feet short of a tightly spaced row of trees.

Ward exhaled and spun in the seat. None of the pursuing cars had made the turn. They were, he hoped, circling to a connecting alley. He turned to MacKenzie. She was holding her breath, staring at the steering wheel but clearly seeing nothing.

"You're amazing," he said.

"Am I alive?"

"Yeah, come one. We've got to go." He pulled her out of the car through his passenger side door.

They had maybe fifteen seconds to get out of sight. The police, he figured, should be coming from the alley access to the right. He led MacKenzie around the left perimeter of the park back to the street they'd just escaped.

"Wrong way," MacKenzie said, grabbing at his shoulder.

"It'll be clear," he said. He hoped he sounded confident.

They broke through the trees onto an empty sidewalk, gawkers circling from a safer distance. He was right. The police had continued *en masse* to try to flank them.

He slowed their pace and grabbed her hand. "Be a couple. Married. Whatever."

"Yes, dear," she whispered, adjusting her hand in his.

A barrage of shouting erupted behind them. They crossed the street as if ignorant of the chaos, orchestrated their way through a crowd outside a café, and darted around the corner. The sounds of the police remained tangled in the park.

After half a block a taxi rolled to a stop beside them. A young woman got out, ushering a sobbing toddler wearing a beret.

They got in the cab still holding hands, neither letting go for the duration of the ride.

CHAPTER
TWENTY

They exited the taxi a block south of Rue Clovis. At MacKenzie's suggestion they walked separately along opposite sides of the street to minimize the chances they might be recognized. With no sign of police or other surveillance they matched each other's quickening pace until the red awning of the La Celeste appeared. Ward, from the far side of the street, motioned for MacKenzie to enter. Once she was in he jogged to the café's red awning, taking a look up and down the street for any hint they'd been tailed. Seeing no one suspicious he joined her in the apartment building's narrow lobby.

The anticipation of seeing her father again—and of completing her quest, he was sure—left MacKenzie's eyes brighter than he'd seen them. But he knew caution was still needed. Especially after the conversation they'd had at the café.

"Just be aware," he said, as if there'd been no interruption to their conversation before the police chase. "I've also read accounts that say the Vase of Soissons is a Persian relic, or Hebrew, a Canaanite weapon, the Devil's baptismal, and even the Ark of the Covenant."

"Whatever," MacKenzie said. "I'm sure Dad will fill in the rest."

"Maybe. Look, I've studied this stuff for half my life. The stories of the Vase are vague, conflicting, and sometimes just impossible. There are plenty of accounts, even archeological reports, which claim it's simply a piece of Gallic artwork. Or Egyptian, or Greek. There's no way..."

Ward heard his own voice trail off, echoing up the stairs, as if it was someone else's.

"Rafe?"

No, he thought, *don't interrupt. I've got something here. It's—*

"Hey, Professor."

The thought was gone. Ward realized he was chewing his lip. "Sorry. I was reminded of something."

"Yeah, well," she said. "Let's stop guessing and maybe get some answers."

Ward agreed, unable to shake the feeling that he'd missed something important.

MacKenzie took the stairs two at a time. Ward found himself staring. He knew he shouldn't. But then, why shouldn't he? She was cute, with a great body—a dancer's body, Ken would've said—and that adorable, freckled smile. Okay, maybe "cute" didn't quite fit her aggressive personality but she was undeniably attractive.

"You coming?" MacKenzie was stopped halfway up the stairs.

Ward scratched the stubble on his chin and nodded. He took her lead, bounding up two at a time, hitting the top just a step behind. The smell of popcorn, burnt and stale, greeted him on the tiny landing.

There was barely enough room for the two of them to stand shoulder-to-shoulder. Two doors broke the monotone striped wallpaper of the hall. Simon's was at the far end. As they approached the popcorn smell was pushed aside by something else. Something sweeter, almost grassy. He inhaled. It was—perfume?

When had MacKenzie gotten perfume? Or had she been wearing it all day? The whole trip? It was delicious.

MacKenzie thrust her thumb at the door before them. "Do we knock?"

The door clicked open revealing a pale, wiry young man in the now familiar blue suit. The young man motioned them in with an outstretched hand, like a monk guiding them into a monastery. He closed the door behind them, placing his own back against the exit, the monk now becoming the bouncer.

The flat was small, opening into a rectangular living room with a kitchen to the right and a closed door in the middle of the left wall. The bed and bathroom, Ward figured. A flower-patterned couch sat along the right wall, past the kitchen. Two plush, high-back chairs—similar to Ward's reading chair—sat beside each other in the middle of the room, perpendicular to the couch, their backs to the door. Against the back wall was a shin-height coffee table.

There was no television but there were numerous framed photographs and paintings. Over the coffee table hung a bronzed plaque adorned by a laurel wreath. It was so much like the one in Ward's apartment he almost strode into the room to pull it from the wall and read its declaration. The surprise of the moment passed, however, leaving Ward with the recognition of the plaque as a generic token of academia, a simple statement of simple accomplishments for professors and museum curators alike.

He refocused his attention on the two men in blue suits huddled together before the reading chairs: Simon, his back to them, and a larger man, his face hunkered down nearly into Simon's shoulder.

Simon, without breaking from his colleague, held out his left hand, palm open and facing the room, indicating they should wait by the door. MacKenzie either missed the signal or chose to ignore it. She strode forward into the room, taking time before each of the many framed works while her father and the other man whispered.

Ward knew most of the pieces hanging on the walls, prints of various French artists: Delacroix's *La Liberte Guidant le People*, David's *Les Licteurs Rapportent à Brutus les Corps de Ses Fils*, and Poussin's *Et in Arcadia Ego*. There were others, too, which he didn't recognize, but they didn't hold his attention. MacKenzie did. She stood in front of a small wood frame to the left of the bedroom door. It contained a photograph positioned above a crayon-scrawled letter. The photo, partially obscured by MacKenzie, showcased a young girl with a charge of bright red hair. Ward didn't have to see anymore, or be able to read the letter, to know they were mementos for Simon of his daughter.

MacKenzie backed away from the frame, a narrow stream of tears on her cheek refracting the light from a lamp in the corner.

"*Ca suffit*," Simon barked, drawing Ward's attention.

Simon and the other man stood apart. The larger man, his lower jaw protruding, was not happy with whatever decision Simon had made but it was clear who was in charge.

Simon turned to his daughter. "Please forgive the wait, *ma cherie*, but the Pantheon was simply no place for a reunion."

The final words were barely out of his mouth before MacKenzie leapt across the room and embraced her father. The old Frenchman engulfed her. The other blue suit man, recognizable now as the security guard from the Basilica, stared at Ward.

After a moment, Simon pulled himself from his daughter's embrace. He held her at arm's length. MacKenzie wiped the back of her hand across her eyes while her father examined her from top to bottom the way you might check a painting for imperfections before spending a fortune to acquire it.

"Dad," she said, choking on her next words. She looked away.

"It is okay, *ma cherie*. Never fear your emotions. Your mother never did. It was the root of her beauty."

"Sir," Ward said moving around the chairs to face Simon, forcing the other blue suit man to back up against the wall. He needed information. That need was becoming physical. As he stood there, within arm's reach of the man who had the answers, he began to tremble. He felt like he had when the waitress was bringing his scotch. "I think I know what most of this is about but what I don't know –"

"What you do not know," Simon cut him off, "is inconsequential to what you do not believe." He settled into one of the chairs, motioning for his daughter to sit beside him.

"Look," Ward said, recognizing his mistake. He was in a den of Believers. There was no authority here but God's will and the voice of whom they believed spoke it. Clearly that was Simon. Ward softened his tone and played the only card he could. "The only thing that should matter is that your daughter is here. She's safe. Now, please, tell us *why* she's here."

"*Oui*," Simon said, "but introductions first. We cannot allow ourselves to abandon civility."

He stood, pointing to the big man and the boy at the door, successively. "My close friend Claude, and his nephew Henri."

"Enough," MacKenzie said. "We can be polite later."

Everyone turned to her. She focused only at her father. In one motion she rolled the backpack off her shoulder and held it out to him.

"The Spear."

Simon took the bag, shifting his attention to Ward. It was the same look he'd given in the Pantheon. It was both knowing and curious. Like the old man knew a joke was being played but was unsure how the subjects would react.

But Simon said only, "Thank you, *ma cherie*." He plunked the backpack on the coffee table, drawing a glare from MacKenzie at the lack of care shown for the relic.

Ward exhaled. He hadn't realized he'd been holding his

breath. *Simon doesn't know,* he thought. Clovis, New Mexico had been a misjudgment on MacKenzie's part. Then again, did Ward really believe Simon had no idea there was a purported Spear of Destiny only a hundred miles away?

"But there is one introduction we must attend." Simon paused.

Get out!

Ward tried to back away, realizing too late his error. By stepping into the square formed by the chairs, the couch, and the coffee table, he'd trapped himself. The large blue suit man, Claude, now loomed over his shoulder.

"Am I not correct, *Agent* Ward?"

Ward snapped his head towards MacKenzie. Would she yell? Turn her back? Attack? Would she even believe Simon? She did nothing. She sat motionless. Her face blank.

Ward's chest tightened. He should deny it but he had no words. It could have been minutes.

It was barely a second.

Her eyes blazed wide. Ward backed up into Claude. Then it was chaos.

MacKenzie screeched a sound Ward had never before heard. She launched at him, clawing at his eyes and throat like an animal. He managed to deflect the first couple blows until Claude wrapped him in a bear hug. The breath whooshed from his lungs. His chest threatened to cave.

MacKenzie's initial rampage became a series of focused strikes. Ward shifted his weight, trying to throw the Frenchman over his shoulder but MacKenzie prevented his forward step. Her face snarled so close that her features became distorted and dark. A screaming, spittle-laced tirade drove thought from his head.

Fists pounded his gut. A knee slammed into his thigh. More hands pulled at his jacket, going for his gun.

Ward put all his strength into a reverse elbow, catching Claude in the pelvis. The big man's grip loosened, giving Ward enough slack to pull one arm free. He countered blow after blow, deflected at best one out of three. He couldn't reach his weapon. He tried to turn, to let his body act as its own shield. Claude's massive fist pummeled his kidney.

His mind held only one thought: *fight back.* But something else inside wouldn't allow him to strike MacKenzie.

A foot crashed into his ankle. He crumpled to the floor. Another blow or two to his head and he knew he'd lose consciousness.

A voice, authoritative and commanding, bellowed through the room. The words echoed unintelligibly, but Claude's arms loosened and MacKenzie's weight against his chest vanished. He tried to stand. His leg failed. He collapsed again.

Hands pressed all around him, snaking their way through his jacket. Someone was taking the gun. It didn't matter. He just wanted to lie on the floor and breathe for as long as they'd let him.

CHAPTER TWENTY-ONE

The hands that tossed Ward onto the couch could have belonged to some Odyssean Cyclops. He didn't fight it, letting the hands dump him like a sack of a trash. His body crumpled over, mashing his cheek into a surprisingly uncomfortable cushion. Eyes closed he decided to play dead and listen.

The big man mumbled something in French that Ward couldn't make out.

Simon replied with a surprisingly calm tone, "In English, please."

Claude grunted, then said, deliberately, as if not entirely comfortable with speaking in English, "What do we do with him?"

"We put a bullet in his lying head and get out of here before his friends arrive." There was no compromise in

MacKenzie's voice.

Ward did his best to control his breathing. If they thought him unconscious he might learn something. Then again, if MacKenzie shot him while he was lying there…

He tried to adjust his position so that his shoulder was better set to lift him off the couch if it became necessary. He made the movement via a series of twitches that he hoped appeared involuntary.

The conversation went on around him as if no one noticed.

"Now, now, *ma cherie*," Simon said. "I do not believe the situation is as grave as all that."

"He's a fucking Agent, Dad," MacKenzie said. She was closer now. "What difference –"

"Your friend," Simon interrupted, "did help you make the journey here. He did keep other Agents from detaining you. And I dare say, from what I have heard, he nearly killed one of his own."

"He's not my friend," MacKenzie's voice seemed to rise. Had she been sitting and was now standing? "Wait—killed an Agent?"

Ward listened to Simon recount the altercation in Shakespeare and Company, wondering how the Frenchmen knew so much.

"Do I have that more or less correct, Rafael?" Simon asked.

Ward's shoulders went slack and he slumped into the stiff couch cushion. With no reason to continue playing dead he sat up and opened his eyes. His left cheek throbbed. There was a dull humming in his skull near his ears he hadn't noticed previously. He could taste the salty tang of blood in his mouth.

Gathering his bearings he saw Simon was sitting in the plush chair beside the couch. MacKenzie stood between the other chair and the couch, her arms crossed, her face scrunched in a confused mix of anger and disbelief. Claude stood beside the couch, an arm's length from his prisoner.

Ward wondered why they hadn't tied him up.

MacKenzie's voice hit a higher pitch. "What difference does it make? He's an Agent."

"*Oui*," Claude pitched in. "The end comes. He is not trustworthy."

"I believe, *ma cherie*," Simon continued as if Claude hadn't spoken, "that your professor ceased doing the work of his employer in that bookstore. Maybe, even the moment he took you in. He has, in fact, been declared a rogue, a traitor. A kill order has been issued." He motioned to Ward, making a face that seemed to indicate he knew even more than he'd already said. Then he added, "Rafael has as much incentive for our success as do you or I."

Ward winced. It was more than just the pain. Had Simon just admitted he knew about Daniel? It was all too much. His head pounded. He wanted a drink. With none available he reached into his jacket for the pain pills he'd stolen earlier. Claude stopped him with a hand on his shoulder.

"It's just medicine. She wasn't exactly gentle."

With his eyes Claude asked Simon for approval. The old man gave it with a twitch of his hand.

Ward readjusted himself on the couch and rolled his neck, letting out a sigh when it cracked. Relief crept up his temples. He shook three pills from the bottle, taking his time gulping them down individually. He needed to assess the overall situation. How much did Simon know? Would that prevent Ward from using the old man for leverage to rescue Daniel? What was the best exit strategy if the three of them did indeed decide to execute their prisoner?

After the second pill he concluded he didn't have many options. How much Simon knew didn't matter. It only mattered how much Simon could tell him. The overall goal to get his hands on the relic Gaustad wanted hadn't changed. And as for an exit strategy—his only real chance was the pistol they'd taken from him, which now sat next to MacKenzie's backpack on the coffee table behind Claude. It was a push, lunge, and grab away. That is, provided the big man both stepped aside and chose not to crush his skull if he went for it.

"How," Ward began, the word grating in his dry throat, "do you even know about the bookstore? About what the REC has declared?"

"Professor, do you believe that I have not had people watching my daughter from the moment she left my sight as a child? I knew what you were before she ever met you."

"Who *are* you?" Ward asked.

"Who the fuck are you?" MacKenzie snapped at him. She stepped to the couch, her arms dropping to her sides revealing clenched, pallid knuckles.

Ward's stomach flinched. Claude interposed himself, his hands up to prevent another attack.

"It is okay, Claude," Simon said. "Hannah, please." He motioned for her to sit.

The big man stepped back, resuming his post in front

of the table and blocking Ward's sightline to the gun. Ward ground his teeth, angry that he'd missed his window.

MacKenzie faced her father. She didn't sit. "Dad," she started.

Simon ended the plea with a tilt of his head. Her shoulders slumped. This time she sat, averting her gaze from the traitor.

"You ask a fair question, Professor," Simon said, leaning back in his chair like a father preparing to tell a bedtime story. "An important one. You see, I am simply a *conservateur du patrimoine*, a curator for the museums of Paris. All of us, Claude and Henri and more, just curators and security guards and art restorers. We are the invisible who keep Paris' museums and cathedrals pretty for the tourists."

"A curator?" Ward couldn't hide his surprise.

"*Oui*. And we have much to watch over since your Republic declared its reign. Look at how quickly Britain fell. Your history books tell that story, yes? Your Reclamation movement is on our doorstep—it has been for a generation. We are the ones who must ensure Paris' artwork, religious and otherwise, survives this age of radicals."

"*My* Republic, *my* Reclamation," Ward said. "I didn't make these things. Why are they mine?"

Simon folded his hands and watched his daughter as if not answering was all the answer that was needed. He was right, of course. That was what angered Ward the most. Shaking his head he focused his attention on MacKenzie.

Either oblivious or stubbornly ignoring the men, her eyes held purposefully to the floor letting the seconds pass.

Simon continued as if Ward hadn't asked his question.

"Your mother supported this cause as well, *ma cherie*. She was an artist by hobby. A brilliant painter. Did you know this? Her letters said he did not paint much after you and she left but I know it was always in her heart."

"She was a psychologist," MacKenzie said without looking up.

Ward wasn't sure if her tone indicated an affirmation or negation of Simon's claim.

"*Oui.*" Simon appeared almost ready to laugh. "She came to Paris to study her psychology. Yet she spent her hours between classes and exams sketching the wonders of Paris. I first saw her drafting Lenepveu's *Jeanne d'Arc* as she burned. She never painted it, though. A shame."

He paused, appearing to savor the memory the way one might savor a sip of brandy.

Ward squirmed, drawing a grunt from Claude warning him to sit still. He slowed his breathing against the uncomfortable feeling in his gut, an almost queasy sensation that was getting worse the longer Simon spoke of his wife.

"When her term was up, she stayed and we married. Soon," he said, his voice softer, "you were born." He breathed deep. A glance at Claude, who looked at his watch and nodded, confirmed they had time for whatever Simon needed to say next.

Ward, however, with his own life as well as Daniel's at stake, did not have time. Before Simon could start, he said, "How does the Vase of Soissons fit?"

Simon offered something between a smirk and grimace. "You are a smart man, Professor. All our stories are entwined.

Wait and you will be rewarded."

"What the hell reward does he get?" MacKenzie said.

"Hey," Ward started.

Claude slammed a gargantuan hand down on Ward's shoulder. He squeezed sending bolts of pain into Ward's neck. The message was clear: no more outbursts.

Simon went on, ignoring the interruption. "The story beings one year before I met your mother, *ma cherie*. It was a moment never recognized as it occurs, but known always in retrospect. Providence. Like that which brought you here today."

"But why did we have to leave? Why didn't you come to America with us?" MacKenzie asked, her voice cracking.

"Patience, *ma cherie*. I must tell you about the priest. You see, he was old even then when he entered my Pantheon near closing time, sought me out, and whispered three things. His name was Adrien, he had said. He had traveled from Italy under God's direction to find me. And he knew the location of a wonderful treasure. Naturally I asked him what this treasure was. He told me instead where to find it. Beneath my very feet, he revealed, in a hidden crawl space in the Pantheon's cellar the treasure had reposed for centuries. Abruptly, then, he exited."

"Sounds like a nut job," MacKenzie said.

"Claude thought the same," Simon said with a chuckle. "Yet he and I went below to search. And we found it, *ma cherie*. A sheaf of documents brittle with age. We spent a week studying those papers."

"And Guillaume," Claude added. He released his grasp

on Ward's shoulder.

Ward slumped, unable to prevent a quick gasp from escaping. He tried unsuccessfully to crack his neck, but was grateful at least that the nauseous feeling had subsided.

"*Oui*. And Guillaume." At the looks of inquiry from MacKenzie and Ward, Simon elaborated. "Another *conservateur* with whom we'd attended university. A good friend. The three of us examined and researched and translated those papers, taking no sleep for weeks, until finally we understood the revelation we held."

MacKenzie didn't seem to be listening. Her gaze shifted to Ward. The lines on her face spoke of open hatred but her eyes hinted of something else. She appeared about to speak. Simon leaned forward but she broke away, standing, stretching her calves and lower back, and pacing the room.

When she came to the picture frame she'd studied earlier, the one holding the photograph of herself as a child, she stopped. She touched her finger to wood frame before levying a glare at each of the four men in the room.

"How do you know we can trust him?" she asked, seemingly unconcerned with her father's story.

"I do not know it," Simon said. "But I believe he has come with you for a purpose. Providence. You must listen. The documents we found spoke of a wonderful and dangerous object. An artifact for which men have been dying for thousands of years."

"The Vase of Soissons," Ward said. But having reached this point in the story, he was dejected rather than heartened. The key to Daniel's freedom had been destroyed fifteen hundred years ago. Finding one shard would be difficult enough but legend said the Vase had split into four. Daniel simply didn't have time for this type of extended quest.

"*Oui*. The Vase," Simon said, betraying no surprise that Ward had figured it out. "But there was more. The documents were in Aramaic, Greek, Latin, and other languages which we'd never before seen. Each was of a different place. A city. A kingdom. Each a different era. Knossos, Ur, Jericho, Macedonia. The Vase made its way to Gaul with the caravans of Caesar. And everywhere it appeared in the records stood a guardian. Men who kept it safe and hidden from the eyes of those who would corrupt humanity. Remigius himself was such a man. You know his story, yes?"

The question was posed to Ward but it was MacKenzie who answered.

"The Bishop. He said," she waved her hand at Ward, "the Bishop thought the Vase was the Holy Grail."

Simon stood. He crossed the room, nearly brushing shoulders with his daughter, before taking up a position near the far wall. "Mmm," was his only response.

"That's not exactly what I said," Ward countered.

Another "mmm," rumbled from Simon's throat.

"What about us," MacKenzie asked. "Mom and I?"

Simon exhaled and nodded. "Soon, *ma cherie*. The story continues. We must, all of us, before long leave Paris. The final piece awaits our arrival."

At first Ward thought he meant the final piece of the story. It took only seconds, however, for him to understand what the Frenchman really meant.

"The final piece?" he blurted. "You have the others? All four? You found the tombs of Clovis' sons?" He shifted his weight to stand but scowls from both MacKenzie and Claude made him sink back into the cushions of the couch.

"*Oui*," Simon said. "And no."

"What does that mean?"

"Please, Professor," Simon said. "When we realized that the documents pointed to the pieces of the Vase of Soissons you can imagine we were excited. In discovering next that the Vase was a holy vessel far older than any Merovingian myth we became driven. Like you we went first to Clovis' tomb at Saint-Denis. And like you, we saw right away that we had erred. Providence guides, though. Bowed before Clovis' effigy was Adrien himself."

Simon rubbed his palms against his brow. When the seconds of silence threatened to become almost comical, he picked up the narrative.

"The priest asked us to kneel with him. We did."

"Some of us reluctantly," Claude muttered.

Simon expelled a heavy breath but did not look at his friend. "Adrien then told us the appointed time was near. He swore us to the completion of the quest we'd begun, touching his fingers to each of our foreheads. 'No matter how many years it may take,' he said. Thus he bound us, and then illuminated the true location of the first piece, the undiscovered tomb of Clovis' youngest son."

"Clotaire," Ward breathed. "But it wasn't in Soissons, was it?" He'd read much over the years about Clovis and his sons. How they'd torn apart their father's kingdom for petty jealousy. About their lost tombs and the treasures they purportedly held. The general consensus among historians was that Clotaire was buried in or near Soissons. Ward, however, had championed a theory in graduate school that his tomb was to the north, perhaps in Noyon.

"Correct," Simon said, his voice now indicating, Ward thought, pride. "The tomb was beneath the foundation of *le Château de Compiègne* in Oise. We excavated with hand tools. It took weeks of skulking around in the night but holding that one shard of pottery emboldened our resolve."

Ward kept his features impassive, though he was grinning on the inside. He'd been correct about the location of the Clotaire's tomb. It was to the north, just not quite as far as he'd presumed. Had he grown up in a country which encourage international travel, he could have made that discovery himself years ago.

Then again, had he grown up in such a country his father would still be alive. His brother would be free. And his mother wouldn't have gone to her death because of a boy's phone call. He put hand to his face and massaged the bridge of his nose.

"Providence," Claude said, the bass of his voice making it sound like a demand.

MacKenzie bounced her gaze from her father to Ward and back. She appeared about to speak but thought better of it.

"The next morning," Simon said, "when I arrived for work at the Pantheon there was a beautiful girl sitting near the back, sketching as if the world had never known strife."

"Mom," MacKenzie whispered.

Simon beamed. "We wed in six months. She too saw the importance of our quest, both for the conservation of art and for the Vase. Over the next year we translated, tracked, and researched the second piece of the Vase. And we were blessed with the birth of a daughter."

"Mom knew about all this?"

"Of course. We kept no secrets from each other. She was my closest advisor. But even so, with her wisdom, we grew careless. We rambled across Europe like foolish children chasing breadcrumbs. I even took you, *ma cherie*, on some of my forays. So foolish."

He inhaled, holding the breath a moment before expelling it from puffed cheeks. "It wasn't long before our exuberance and carelessness illuminated our faults. We had no mechanisms for security. We knew no methods for gathering intelligence. In unearthing Childebert's heirloom, the second of the shards, Claude was shot. We were all nearly killed."

MacKenzie asked, "How?"

"*La Police*," Claude said.

"Though their orders, I suspect, came not from the Prefecture." Simon paused, as if searching for words, or maybe for strength.

The mention of the second piece excited Ward's pulse once more. It meant that half the job for rescuing Daniel was done. It also made the possibility of seeing the actual broken shards of the Vase of Soissons—maybe even excavating the final of Clovis' sons' tombs—more real. Holy or not this vase was an artifact of history, a true witness to the life of Clovis. As a history professor it was a chance not to be missed.

A door clunked closed in the hallway outside Simon's flat. Everyone froze. Simon looked to Claude who made a motion to Henri at the door. Henri, looking something like a stick-figure come to life, peered through the peephole in the front door. He drew back, waited a moment, then leaned in to look once again. When he pulled back a second time, he glanced at his watch then nodded. Claude bobbed his head in return.

Simon watched the exchange between uncle and nephew with an odd look of entertainment, his lip half-curled in the beginning of a grin. He waited for Claude to indicate all was good before picking up the narrative.

"We held that second piece of the Vase in our hands the day after your third birthday, *ma cherie*. But with Claude in the hospital we saw the dangers awaiting us. Reclamation movements mirroring what had already occurred in America were growing. Paris was no longer safe." He dipped his head.

MacKenzie went to her father. She put a hand on his shoulder. Side by side they were nearly the same height. Their stances defiant, yet open, were identical.

"But the Reclamationists never did win here, did they?" Ward asked, thinking of the graffiti they'd seen in Saint-Denis.

"No," Simon said. "We remain a free nation. A moral nation. Though not by much. All those years ago, however, we thought it would turn a different way. Your mother and I," Simon said to MacKenzie, "decided she should take you somewhere more stable. America. It was not free, as you both know, but the war was over. We planned for me to come when my responsibilities to the Vase were complete."

"She never told me," MacKenzie whispered.

Simon kissed her hand followed by her forehead. "After you had gone we worked diligently and prudently, myself, Claude, and

Guillaume. Only a small cadre of others were involved, mostly without knowing the full depth of our goal. We hid knowledge of the Vase from all others. In this way it took ten years to find the third segment. It cost us dearly, though. Guillaume was arrested by your Republic's Agents here in France."

"No," Ward said, doing the math. "You're talking like fifteen years ago. There weren't any REC actions in Europe then."

"Like there are none now?" Claude said.

"What happened to Guillaume?" MacKenzie asked.

Simon shrugged, though it was far from a casual dismissal. "What happens to most men dragged off by Agents, their heads covered in black bags? Nevertheless, we now had three pieces of the Vase in our possession. We were close to completing our quest. But the fourth was most difficult. The papers we'd uncovered in the Pantheon all that time ago were damaged and incomplete, yet still enlightening." Simon and Claude exchanged looks again. "It took years. Finally, though, this past winter we succeeded. The final shard, Theuderic's, was found at Cologne."

"Wait, I thought you said we were going to the final piece," Ward said.

Claude raised his hand as if he might again slam it down on Ward's shoulder. Ward couldn't help but flinch.

"No one said you were coming," Claude said.

"Did you rebuild the Vase?" MacKenzie asked.

Ward shifted on the couch, trying to brush off the twinge of embarrassment he felt at balking.

Simon touched his daughter's cheek.

"No," Claude answered. "We hid the pieces."

"But they were stolen," Simon said.

Ward stood. "Stolen?" If they didn't have the Vase, he didn't have any leverage to use for Daniel's release.

A glare from Claude warned he had only seconds to resume his previous seated position. Simon, however, intervened, his raised eyebrow backing Claude off enough to allow Ward to remain on his feet.

"This past spring. From a locked vault hidden in the crypts below the Tour Clovis."

"I thought no one knew," MacKenzie said.

"It matters not," Simon said. "They are gone but we continued to study. To seek the truth of the Vase. To know what the thieves intended. We translated documents that referred to a revival ritual. Others which discussed the destruction of the Vase. Still more of which spoke of Heaven's wrath for one or the other of these actions."

Claude, still menacingly close to Ward, said, "We know where the last piece is. The fifth."

"Fifth?" Ward said. "There's never been any mention of a fifth piece. Four sons. Four pieces."

"*Oui,*" Simon said, moving to stand by the wall. "But we learned otherwise from many scrolls, some in Remigius' own hand. Others were by an anonymous scribe a millennium later. Both sets spoke of a fifth component of the Vase of Soissons."

Simon plucked from the wall a small picture frame hanging on the opposite side of the bedroom door as the photo of little Hannah. He walked it to the center of the room, shooing both MacKenzie and Claude aside. It appeared to be a print of a wood engraving. The original must have been quite eroded, for even in the reproduction many of the lines had diminished into the background. What remained, however, Ward recognized as the baptism of Clovis, with the Vase of Soissons beside him depicted as a clawfoot tub.

It was a familiar image to Ward, a key element of the Clovis legend—at least the Christian version which purported the king as a major force in the conversion of Europe. This particular woodcut was reminiscent of the Master of Saint Gilles' Renaissance painting of the event. The striking difference was that Clovis, unlike most other depictions, was not in the baptismal bath. He was standing beside it. The woodcut was also older than the Master of Saint Gilles' version by perhaps a thousand years, Ward guessed, based on the style and skewed proportions of the characters.

"That's Clovis," MacKenzie said.

"*Oui, ma cherie.* About to be baptized with the Vase but he is not able to enter the vessel."

"Because of the lid," she said.

"The lid," Ward whispered.

Yes, there it was. The baptismal bath, taller than it was wide, was capped with a handle-less lid. He'd never considered this. No stories of the Vase of Soissons mentioned a lid. Even the tales of the Vase's mystical nature and Clovis' attempts to restore it discussed only the four fragments he bequeathed to his sons.

But what was it, this fifth piece? A plug to keep the genie in the bottle? A lid for the Holy Chalice? Or was he being just as irrational as any Believer? Was he losing track of the only goal that really mattered? He had to save his brother.

This fifth piece was simply the means to do so.

"You begin to understand," Simon said.

Ward glanced up to find the old man staring at him. The look on his face made Ward wonder if Simon really did know about Daniel, if he did know that this fifth piece represented the only chance Ward had to regain his lost family.

"Well, I don't," MacKenzie said. "What good is the lid if we don't have the Vase? And even if we did have it, what the hell is it?" The rising frustration in her voice was mirrored in the deepening lines of her forehead.

"It is the one relic," Simon said. "The one vessel of God."

"What does that mean, Dad?"

"Those who stole the four pieces," Claude said, as if she hadn't asked the question, "they too know of the fifth."

Simon began pacing the apartment. "But not its location. Adrien told only Claude and I. It waits in his care for God's elect to arrive. Our quest takes us to it."

He looked at Henri, the stoic young man's arms folded in almost comical determination. It seemed like Simon might say something to him but instead he turned his back on Claude's nephew and meandered back to the center of the room.

"Is the old priest even still alive?" MacKenzie asked.

Simon and Claude, again, shared a look.

Ward was beginning to distrust their glances. "Hey look, the Vase is a wonderful piece of history," he said, trying to sound skeptical—confused by why he was finding it difficult to do so. "An important French artifact. But touched by God? And why doesn't this keeper just bring it here?"

"What the fuck do you know of it, Agent? How many

relics have you stolen and destroyed?" MacKenzie said.

"I've only been an Agent since the summer," Ward said. "It's not like they gave me a choice. It's do the job or they call it treason."

"Bullshit," MacKenzie said.

Ward didn't respond. He knew it wasn't a fight he could win. At least not yet.

"Does it matter, Rafael," Simon said, replacing the framed woodcut on the wall, "if you believe it to be real? Or does it only matter if those who will kill you believe it to be so?"

Ward opened his mouth but closed it just as fast. On this point the old man was right.

"So what is it then, Dad?"

"It is. That is all that matters. But I am no more than a messenger."

"Oh come on," Ward said. His academic brain simply couldn't let an answer like that stand. "It is? It is what? Holy? Biblical? Magical? What?" Ward could feel the others' eyes bounce between Simon and him as they waited for the old man's response.

"It is much older than the Bible," Simon began.

MacKenzie didn't allow him to continue. "It's older than God?"

"No," Simon said, shaking his head as if she'd asked a silly little girl question. "Genesis, though it speaks of the beginning, was written not so long ago."

"You're saying the Bible lied."

"The Bible, *ma cherie*, is a guide at best. God is Truth. He has always been. He has always shown Himself to His people in the form that they might best understand, be it a burning bush, carved tablets, or a pillar of clouds. Or perhaps a Vase. But I say again, I know only Faith. Adrien has the lid. He has the answers."

"How do you know Adrien has anything?" Ward pressed.

"Dad," MacKenzie said. "Why did you bring me here?"

Simon glowered at Ward, lingering upon him a moment before turning to his daughter. "As I said, I have kept an eye on you. Those sympathetic to our cause can be found even in America. *Conservateurs* by faith but academics by profession. Sometimes even auto mechanics and stock brokers. You were in danger. Friends had betrayed you."

MacKenzie glowered at Ward, her mouth open as if to speak.

"Not him, *ma cherie*. The one in charge."

"Torres? No. There's no way."

Ward spoke before considering whether it was a prudent idea. "It's true. Commandant Gaustad himself told me Torres was working for the REC."

MacKenzie spun and threw a punch at Ward before Claude could stop her. Ward pulled back but wasn't able to avoid the blow entirely. It glanced off his shoulder and impacted his jaw. The room went white. When his vision cleared, MacKenzie was still standing within arm's reach, her eyes still ablaze, but there was something else mixed in. She looked almost ashamed for her assault.

Simon placed his hand on his daughter's shoulder. "There is more," he said. "Adrien told me it was you who'd been chosen to unearth the final piece."

MacKenzie stared, digesting her father's words. At length she said, "But I didn't understand the letter. I damn near sent the Spear with him." She flung a pointing finger at Ward.

"Yet you are here," Simon said. "Both of you. Man and woman. Providence." He took MacKenzie by the wrist, drawing her in so he could whisper in her ear. Ward tried to close the gap between them to hear something of what was being said, but Claude made an impenetrable roadblock.

The old man opened his arms to the room and said, "We have been tasked with remedying that which the Vase has engendered."

The riddles and vagary had Ward's frustration about to breach. He turned his attention to MacKenzie. For the first time since his identity had been revealed her face held no hatred. It was confusion and…yes, it was that look she'd given him at his apartment, the one that had asked for his help.

His irritation subsided. "How?" he asked.

Simon rubbed his hand over his bald head. "We find the lid," he said, his words measured. "We use that which our adversary desires to draw him out, prompt him to bring the Vase to us."

"Then what?"

"We unite the five pieces," Simon said. "We make the Vase whole like when Clovis himself was young." He stared at Ward. "Then we destroy it."

CHAPTER
TWENTY-TWO

It had been twenty years since Rafael Ward made that phone call. Since he'd invited the police and the REC into his home to take away his mother. To complete what the car accident began and take away his entire family. In the two decades since he'd lived in three foster homes, one that was more a prison than a home. He'd done his Citizen's Duty, including firearms training, self-defense training, and most important, training in how to follow orders. He'd earned three degrees from the University of Pennsylvania, culminating in his PhD in Medieval Mythology. And he'd achieved his bronzed laurel wreath upon appointment to his position as a Carroll University tenured professor.

All of it had come and gone without forcing him to a crisis of self-reflection. He'd mourned his family, especially his mother. He'd battled his foster parents, particularly Mr.

and Mrs. Hadley with their "time out" cage in the cellar. And he'd accepted the censor committees and the need for him to pledge his adherence to the Republic Guidelines for the Study and Teaching of Fictitious Mythologies. And he'd managed all this—coped, a Republic shrink would have said had he ever gone to one—with only the occasional nightmare, a fondness for whiskey, and shoulder-shoving jokes with Ken Hickey about the ridiculousness of acronyms—"Careful Ken, or the RGSTFM might f-u-c-k you up," he was apt to slur at The Barrel.

In the last five months, however, that had changed. In the last five months, under the tutelage of Agent "Em" Compano he'd begun to muse about the rebelliousness of poetry. To discover his own dissatisfactions in the lines of Angelou and Hawthorne and Forche among others. He'd begun reciting to himself while brushing his teeth or grading an essay the lines from a Tennyson poem: "Theirs not to make reply, Theirs not to reason why, Theirs but to do and die."

He didn't dwell on why he recited it. Maybe it was this very quality which had kept him trucking along without imploding these last twenty years. The lines felt right so he whispered them to the mirror, or to the essay scrolling across his Port, or just to the pigeons as he walked to campus.

But as Simon spoke those four words—"Then we destroy it"—the dichotomy of the last five months hit Ward like the wind from a passing subway train.

Educator. Five years a professor. A devotee of history and the stories of humanity's epic success and failures. A man most at home with himself when reenacting the passions of generations long dead.

Destroyer. A gatherer of artifacts for the sole purpose of burning them to ash. A man agreeing to eradicate the only links to histories that are busy, as the quote goes, repeating themselves.

Now, standing in Simon's apartment, an emotion somewhere between panic and hilarity overtook Ward. The dichotomy of his two careers—both now likely forfeit—threatened to clatter into either a breakdown or a violent outburst. He looked for something to calm himself. He looked to MacKenzie but the frustration on her face was no less visceral.

"Destroy it?" They blurted at the same time.

"*Oui*," Simon said, making a face that was both smile and grimace. Was his tone apologetic? "The gift of a soul to return the beast—Ba'el, the bisected diarchy—to God."

Ward's conscience, that voice in his mind, gathered itself to speak, but then went silent. Ward begged it to tell him what to do. It felt like he was shaking a vending machine in his head, trying to get a stuck candy bar to drop.

Gift of a soul? Beast? God? All Ward cared about was Daniel. But as he thought this he realized it wasn't true. Something inside him—something deeper in his core than his internal sentinel—also cared about the Vase. About the Spear. About all the relics in Commandant Gaustad's office. No more should be cremated. It was a declaration rooted miles from his mind.

But why?

"Why?" MacKenzie asked.

Simon straightened his posture. Beside him, Claude crossed his arms like a statue, like an ironic mirror-image of his comical nephew at the front door.

The idea of destroying the Vase was becoming now, to Ward, inexplicably offensive. Worse, it was confusing. Yes, if MacKenzie destroyed it, he'd have no leverage for his brother's life but that wasn't it. He could feel a rage building in him at the idea of it being destroyed at all, even after rescuing Daniel. It was like he was being torn in two. One piece knew that the Vase was a bargaining chip but another piece could not be a part of the extermination of history.

"No," Ward nearly shouted. The room became uncomfortably warm. He wiped the back of his hand across his brow. He needed a drink. "No way this is why you brought us all the way here." He was barely conscious of the words he was using.

"Once again, Professor, I did not bring *you* here. I made arrangements to ensure that my daughter found her way back to me."

"Why? Because some priest fed you a line of crap about a magic Vase?"

"We have all been fed lines of crap. The only difference is who is doing the feeding and how hungry we are."

"Bullshit."

Ward approached the old man. He wasn't going to hit him but he knew he looked like he might. He was struggling to keep it together. Claude tensed, rearing like a bear ready to attack. MacKenzie took a step forward. Ward barely noticed. He relaxed his shoulders and wondered, nearly aloud, *What's happening to me?*

"It is okay, Claude," Simon said.

The big man backed up a step but didn't calm his demeanor.

"It's not okay," MacKenzie said. "He's an Agent. What if this was the REC's plan from the start?"

"I only concern myself with God's plan, *ma cherie*," Simon said.

MacKenzie made a face that reminded Ward of Daniel mocking Mom behind her back when she scolded them for playing in the house. The thought of Daniel, of Mom, felt like a post-whiskey chill in his core. His head cleared. His internal conflict began to subside. He recalled how he'd managed with the Hadley family. How he'd survived time out after time out. No food sometimes for days. And the "lessons" Mr. Hadley gave when he was angry—Ward learned fast to choose the belt not the fishing rod or the garden hose. He got through by focusing on the moment. By shutting out the pain or the hunger and just dealing with whatever was necessary to survive the moment. To succeed.

And right now he needed MacKenzie on his side. Without her he wouldn't be able to find the Vase. To save his brother.

"Hannah," Ward began.

"You don't get to call me that," she said, and strode to the opposite wall, ending his plea.

Ward put out his hands and turned to Simon. "Whatever part of this you think I'm supposed to play I'm not going to do you much good if she doesn't trust me."

"She will," Simon said quietly. "For now, concern yourself

with this, Professor. If the Vase is reunited with its lid, if it is thus wholly reconstructed, it can be then re-consecrated. Its powers renewed. Look at what Clovis accomplished with it in pieces. Imagine what it could offer someone were it complete."

"Come on, man. It's pottery. It belongs in a museum. It…"

"It what, Rafael?" Simon asked. His tone was gentle yet it dared Ward to finish the thought.

Ward shook his head. There was no point in arguing with a Believer, that much he knew.

"The Vase is much more than pottery," Simon said. "It is imbued with a power far beyond what technology can offer."

"Power from where?" Ward asked.

"From who?" MacKenzie added.

"Is not everything on this Earth of God?"

"Enough of the riddles," Ward said through his teeth. He needed real info, not superstition. Then again, as Simon said, did it matter what Ward believed or only what those who sought the Vase believed?

No, that didn't help. It was the REC after the Vase. They didn't believe anything. They wanted a symbol taken out of circulation. If Simon got his way Ward would just be doing their job—*his* job—anyway.

"You do not understand." Simon shook his head.

"Neither do I, Dad."

Simon exhaled. "Broken or complete the sacred vessel exudes power, like a battery or the way a radioactive debris gives off emissions. If mended, and if the proper ceremony is performed, it becomes much more."

"So these people who stole the pieces. They want what?

To carry the Vase before them like the Spear or the Grail or the Ark?" Ward asked. He wanted to play along, to find out more of Simon's plans and about who took the Vase pieces. But as he spoke his frustration—as happened with MacKenzie in the car when she asked what he believed—began to rise. "I mean, where do people even come up with ideas like this?"

"Professor, not every voice man hears is God's."

"What does that mean?"

"Time will reveal this truth."

"What the fuck are you talking about?"

"Enough."

"Dad," MacKenzie said, reaching out as if to touch her father's shoulder.

"No, Hannah," Simon held up his hand. "It is time Professor Ward listens. It is time you both listen. What you believe is immaterial. There is no time for doubt or for failure."

Simon motioned for them both to the couch. MacKenzie sat. Ward didn't want to but Simon made it clear he wouldn't begin until they were both on the couch. Ward gave in and sat. MacKenzie shuffled as far from him as she could. Claude remained a pillar beside the coffee table.

"You," Simon said, pointing with each hand at MacKenzie and Ward, "must destroy the Vase before it can be consecrated and the ritual completed. For God's sake, for all our sakes, you must not allow the completed Vase to be taken away or re-opened."

"Us?" Ward asked. "What happened to 'we'?"

Before he realized he'd done it he'd clenched his hands into fists. Anger caught his breath in his throat. Why was he angry? This was what he wanted. To be in the position to take the Vase himself.

Something soft and cool touched his hand, defusing his rage. He looked down. MacKenzie's hand rested over his. Her demeanor hadn't changed but this motion seemed to indicate that maybe she believed what her father had said about Ward's REC status. Or maybe she just wanted him to shut up.

"Where do we go, Dad? What's next?" MacKenzie asked.

Simon nodded the way the woman behind the glass in the Logistics & Control office nodded. It was less an agreement with an action than an acknowledgement that yes, you are doing exactly what I knew you would. It was another infuriating act. Had MacKenzie's hand not been on his Ward might have grabbed the old man and shaken him until more satisfactory answers rattled loose.

"A train, overnight, to Rome," Simon said, facing Claude then Henri.

"Tonight?" Ward asked.

"You will be told more once we have left Paris," Claude said, his tone indicating this point was non-negotiable.

Ward didn't like any of it. The secrets. The riddles. The Faith. He'd almost forgotten his headache and the throbbing in his leg. Both now returned. He rubbed his temples. It didn't help. He looked at the woman sitting next to him. An hour ago she wouldn't have questioned his motives. Yesterday she'd trusted him with her life. Now, even with her hand on his, she looked at him the same way he was looking at Simon. Suspicious and discontented.

"You said we have to draw out whoever has the Vase, get

them to bring it to us," he said, unhappy with the concession in his voice.

"*Le Traitre*," Claude said.

"Traitor?" Ward said, but then he understood. "The pieces were taken from a locked vault. It was one of your people. Who?"

"It does not matter," Simon said.

"The fuck it doesn't."

MacKenzie cut him off before he could say more. "How do we draw your traitor out?"

Claude pointed at Ward's chest. "Your Port."

"What?"

"You have disabled the link to the REC," Simon said. "Otherwise this conversation would have been interrupted long ago, yes?"

Before Ward could answer, Claude spoke again. "When we are ready, you re-enable the link. He comes to us."

"No, that doesn't make sense," Ward complained. "The only people who'll show up will be Agents."

"Exactly," Simon said, walking into the kitchen.

Dumbfounded, Ward could only sit and blink. He heard the refrigerator open and close.

As if the previous ten minutes hadn't happened Simon asked pleasantly, "Would anyone else care for a beverage?"

Ward shook his head. Had he misheard? MacKenzie shrugged, her bewilderment mirroring his.

"Are you okay with this?" he asked.

Her eyes fluttered from his chest to his mouth to his forehead. She slid her hand back to her own lap. Finally she brought her gaze to his.

When she spoke her words were measured and calm. "Can I trust you?"

There was a knock at the door. Everyone froze but Henri. The young Frenchman exhaled a heavy breath, placed his hand on the doorknob and said politely, "*Oui?*"

Something was wrong. Ward's instincts took over. He bolted to his feet. His mouth opened. He had to get Henri away from the door. A word touched his lips on its way out into the world.

It was too late.

CHAPTER
TWENTY-THREE

Henri opened the door, letting it swing wide of his body. His slender frame appeared little more than a stick figure in contrast with the towering man in the doorway. The man, in full black tactical gear including a visor-less helmet, held an R1 in his left hand. He looked from the device to Henri and back.

"Thank you, Henri," he said, his voice burly and detached.

In one motion he lowered the Port and raised his right hand, placing the barrel of a pistol against the pale skin of Henri's forehead.

In the few seconds since the knock on the door, no one in the room besides Henri had moved. A pause button could have been pressed on the entire apartment. Even the sound of the gunshot didn't restart the room.

The back of Henri's head exploding did.

Claude shouted his nephew's name.

MacKenzie flinched, then brought her hands to her mouth, a cry strangled in her throat.

Simon disappeared deeper into the kitchen.

Ward felt like he'd been separated from himself. Like he was watching his body act without need or interference from his mind. Instinct and reaction. He spun, shoving MacKenzie onto the couch and diving past Claude. As his knee hit the floor, he managed to hook his finger through the trigger guard of the RT40 pistol on the coffee table. He twisted around to the front of the room, bringing the gun up in time to see the grenade hit its first bounce in the center of the living room.

"Down," he yelled.

The sound of Claude flopping his big body to the floor was accompanied by the clanging of cookware in the kitchen.

On the second bounce, the grenade flared then began smoking. White smoke. A diversion. The man at the door, the Agent who'd just murdered Henri, would have his goggles and mask on by now. He'd be fanning out into the room with at least two other Agents.

Ward had no idea how he knew this. Had it all been a part of basic training? Had Agent Compano been that good an instructor? It didn't matter. His body was in charge now. His intuition told him their best chance was the thirteen rounds in his pistol. The placement of the front door centered on the wall made the position of ancillary Agents easy to pinpoint. A spray of three shots each to the left and right of the door should take them out. It was the first Agent, the tall one, he was unsure of. It was unlikely he would have entered the room in a straight line. But with the smoke, Ward couldn't see anything.

Two were better than none, he thought. He took aim to the right.

Wait.

Ward listened to the voice in his head, using the pause to reassess the situation. If the Agents were there to kill, then why knock on the door? Why toss the smoker? They could have destroyed the whole room with a single fragmentation grenade or breached with assault rifles blazing.

Why a soft entrance?

The answer came before he'd finished asking the question: to catch them shocked and immobile for abduction, not execution. For information. For the Vase.

Then why kill Henri?

Another quick answer: conspirators were expendable. Young Henri had signaled their location.

"MacKenzie," Ward said. The air in the room tasted like an empty pot left on the stove for hours.

"I can't see," she coughed.

"Stay down."

She didn't respond. Claude's hacking cough came from Ward's left.

"Stay down," Ward repeated to the Frenchman.

Claude also didn't answer. Ward had to hope he would follow directions and that Simon was smart enough to do the same.

The voice of the lead Agent slipped through the smoke. "That's good advice, Mr. Ward. You should all take it. Get on your knees. Hands behind your heads. You too, Miss MacKenzie. Off the couch." This last bit was to make sure they knew the Agents could see through the smoke with the help of their gear.

A motor clicked on, whirring eerily. In less than a minute the smoke was sucked back out the door into the hallway by a small fan, a simple gadget called a Breach Blast Ameliorator. Ward remembered a brief instructional video on its use. Maybe he had learned more than he'd thought from Agent Compano.

Ward secured his pistol behind his back. To his left, barely two foot away, knelt MacKenzie, her fear replaced by a trembling rage. Claude crouched to his right near the back corner of the room. Simon could not be seen. Ward fought the urge to peer towards the kitchen. The longer Simon's location could be concealed, the better.

The Agents, much as Ward had surmised, had fanned out in a predictable three-pronged pattern. The two ancillary Agents still wore their goggles and masks. They pointed submachine guns at MacKenzie and Claude. The lead Agent, standing a few feet in front of the chairs, had removed his headgear. He held only a pistol.

"Where is Simon?" the Agent asked, drawing out the words.

Ward slid his eyes to MacKenzie. She wouldn't give her father's position away, would she?

She didn't have the chance.

Claude stood, bringing an Agent trotting forward to within inches of him, a submachine gun pointed at his gut. Claude dwarfed the man. He glared right over top his head at the commanding Agent.

"I am Simon," he said.

The lead Agent exhaled, slumping his shoulders a fraction before straightening his posture. This was the only order his comrade needed. The smaller Agent jabbed the muzzle of his submachine gun into Claude's stomach. When the big Frenchman doubled over, the weapon came down on the side of his neck, sending him to his knees.

MacKenzie made a sound as if she too had been struck. She shifted her weight to stand. Ward reached out, placing his hand on her shoulder. He shook his head. She acceded. Ward left his hand on her shoulder. He needed to keep her calm. To begin a dialogue with these Agents. He needed to find out what the REC knew about the Vase. Did they know who had it? Did they know about the lid? Could he negotiate his brother's release without this fifth piece?

His hand on her shoulder served a second function as well. From here, if conversation didn't work, he could draw the pistol from his belt, aim, and fire in—he hoped—just over one second.

The lead Agent asked again where Simon was. Ward hesitated. Should he look to the kitchen to give Simon's location away? Would that be obvious enough to show his intention to work with the Agents? Would it be subtle enough to keep alive the chance MacKenzie would trust him?

It didn't matter. MacKenzie turned her head. All three Agents swiveled toward the kitchen. The move caught Ward off guard. He hadn't expected her to be that careless.

She wasn't.

It took MacKenzie just over one second to reach under Ward's arm, pull the pistol from behind his back, and bring it up to fire. It took her less than two seconds to push to her feet while squeezing off three rounds.

Her first shot missed the tall Agent by two feet, exploding the drywall behind him. Had she been stationary, especially from her knees, Ward was certain she would have hit the man in the soft spot of his throat between his clavicles.

Her second shot, aimed while leaping the chair, blew through empty air where the dodging Agent's head had been.

She unleashed her third shot without aiming, an attempt to disrupt the Agent by the kitchen from opening fire on the room.

Ward got over his astonishment and leapt to his feet. He had no choice now. The best case scenario was they could keep from killing one of the Agents and interrogate him. Worst case was they would all die. Either way, he let his instincts take over again.

Ward slammed shoulder first into the Agent by the kitchen, catching him in the hip. The two men thundered into the wall separating the living room and kitchen, the Agent's submachine gun caroming from his hands. The rest of the apartment erupted into an indiscernible racket which Ward barely registered. He was tangled with his adversary, exchanging blows while trying to regain his footing. After a half dozen jabs the two men separated and began maneuvering each other in a small circle like boxers. Neither attempted much defense. Working off a feint the Agent swept Ward's leg, sending him to the floor. Ward rolled over expecting to see a submachine gun pointed at his face. Instead, the Agent, weaponless, dropped a knee onto his chest, driving the air from his lungs.

The Agent stood. Ward, gasping, but having learned from his encounter in the bookstore, kicked out, catching the Agent's knee. The Agent hit the floor but managed to rotate himself on top of Ward. Two quick blows just below his shoulder blade nearly chased the air from Ward's lungs again. The Agent followed this by wrapping up Ward in a powerful neck and shoulder lock.

He's cocky, Ward thought, wheezing as much oxygen into his traumatized lungs as he could. *And strong.*

Ward thrashed his feet until he found the wall. He pushed, lurching the Agent up and back. When they came back to the ground it was Ward's weight crushing the Agent's chest. His grip loosened. Ward spun free, lurched to his knees, and threw a jab into the Agent's throat. The man collapsed.

Ward kicked the downed Agent's head, knocking off his helmet and revealing the face of a boy barely old enough to have completed his Citizen's Duty. He went limp. Ward scanned the floor for a gun. Before he could locate one, three bursts of gunfire caused Ward to drop. Someone rushed past him into the kitchen as another short surge of gunfire exploded the drywall above him. Chips and dust showered over him.

He peered through the falling debris at MacKenzie aiming the Agent's submachine gun towards the kitchen entrance. Claude stood beside her, blood dripping down his cheek. In front of them lay an Agent, his chest torn open by automatic fire.

"Dad," MacKenzie said, like someone afraid of the answer.

Something crashed in the kitchen.

"Here," a voice replied.

It wasn't Simon's.

MacKenzie tapped Ward's shoulder with her knee. He looked down. She was sliding his pistol to him with her foot. Ward pulled it into his belly and rose, finding himself standing face to face with Simon.

The tall Agent loomed behind the Frenchman, his arm around Simon's neck. The Agent's pistol was fixed to the Frenchman's temple. "I can take him or kill him," the Agent said. His face betrayed no fear or even disappointment in how things had turned out.

Ward couldn't help a moment, a fraction of a breath that stuck in his mind like the taste of burnt bread, in which he thought: *Could I have ever been as callous and efficient an Agent as this man?*

"And take one of you instead," the Agent added, his gaze falling on MacKenzie.

Ward retreated a step. Various instructional lectures, videos, and exercises collided in his head. These all clattered into the need for information. He needed a second to clear it all, to calculate his next move.

It took only half that. There would be no discussion. The situation had moved beyond that point. There was, however, a flaw in the Agent's tactics. Ward's fist clenched around the pistol still held against tight against his gut. There was no training for what he had to do. No instruction from Agent Compano or ancient lesson from basic training. He either could or he couldn't. A chill rolled from his neck down his shoulders and drained into his forearms. He was ready but he would need MacKenzie's help. Could she see it too?

As if she'd been reading his thoughts, she dropped the submachine gun. It clattered to the floor, drawing everyone's attention. Except Ward's.

The opening he'd seen was simple. In fact it was surprising that the Agent hadn't learned to compensate for his handicap. He was too tall. Simon didn't come close to offering the shield a hostage should. Ward raised and fired his pistol in a single motion.

The bullet pierced the Agent's left eye. His face lurched forward then flung back as the side of his head erupted in a mess of ruddy sludge. The rest of his body remained still. His pistol clunked to the floor. He made a face. It could have been a smile.

The Agent collapsed, his skull hitting the floor with a solid thud.

Ward lowered his weapon, unable to stop himself from looking at it. It was identical to the one he'd been issued by Command a month ago. That one had never been fired in the field. This one he'd held in his hand for less than a minute and it had killed a man whose blood now pooled inches from his own boots.

Ward's stomach convulsed.

MacKenzie gasped.

Claude's massive hand clamped down on Ward's shoulder as he made his way to Simon.

All of it, from the shot to Claude's approach was less

than two seconds. What happened next took half that time.

The Agent whom Ward had earlier incapacitated sat up and fired his submachine wildly in Simon's direction. The old man stumbled backwards in a clumsy attempt to dodge the attack. Ward brought his pistol up but found himself aiming at Claude. The big man leveled a knee into the side of the Agent's head and began pummeling his face. Within seconds the Agent's body was still except for its legs flailing with each of Claude's blows. Scarlet spittle rolled down the Frenchman's chin and sprayed into the air as he bashed the Agent's head over and over.

MacKenzie flew past Ward to her father who was lying half in the kitchen, his hand over his stomach.

"I am okay, *ma cherie*," he said, though his grimace said otherwise. He sat up.

Ward became aware of the dull thudding of Claude's fists against the Agent's skull. He cringed, unable to move. He watched as, with his daughter's help, Simon got to his feet and staggered to Claude. The sound of the big man's punches became a series of sickening wet slaps. Simon placed his hand on his friend's shoulder. The big man looked up.

"Simon?"

"Come," the old man said.

Claude stared at his hands. His knuckled dripped blood and lumps of flesh.

Simon made a move to the couch. Ward grabbed his arm. "There'll be more coming," he said.

MacKenzie shot him a glare that said, if my dad needs to sit, we'll let him sit. Simon, however, agreed with Ward's assessment.

"*Oui.* We can—"

He stumbled, dropping to one knee. MacKenzie knelt before him. He shook her off.

"Rafael is correct. We are not safe here."

As if on cue police sirens sounded in the distance.

Simon continued, "Claude will help me. You two go downstairs. Get a taxi."

"Dad, no."

"That can't be safe," Ward said.

His protest was dismissed with a wave. "We need only go a short distance. Speed is more important than concealment. Go."

Ward didn't like it but the decision was made. MacKenzie, with the mechanical motions of someone in shock, let go of her father's hand and crawled the few feet to where her backpack lay. She held it to her chest but didn't stand.

Not knowing what else to do Ward stepped forward, holding out his hand. MacKenzie stared as if she'd never before seen a human hand. After a moment she blinked, sniffed, and wiped the back of her hand across her mouth and nose. Then she rose, shouldered the backpack, and walked past Ward as if she hadn't seen his gesture.

CHAPTER
TWENTY-FOUR

The taxi took them two blocks. Ward sat in the front seat, asking the Baltic-accented driver questions about this building or that. He knew he was doing a woeful job of drawing the man's attention from Simon bleeding all over the back seat but short of threatening the already frightened driver, Ward didn't know what else to do.

Following Claude's directions they arrived on a street populated with small shops and cafes. Claude tossed a number of bills into the front seat and helped MacKenzie get her father out of the cab. Ward, after gathering Claude's cash and handing it to the driver with an apology, also exited the car. He'd barely gotten his legs clear when the taxi sped away, its tires squealing. He hurried to help with Simon but Claude was already half-carrying him into an unremarkable souvenir shop with a green awning. MacKenzie trailed, holding her father's hand.

Ward was left alone on the sidewalk in front of the gift store whose marquee said only: *Paris.* The rest of the block was just as generic. Next door, in the shade of the green awning, sat a number of sidewalk-set tables for a restaurant called *Le Restaurant Paris.* Ward couldn't help a glance at the nearest table where an older couple shared a bottle of red wine.

They could all use a bottle or two, he thought. *Especially MacKenzie.* He'd gotten a good look at Simon's wounds as they'd loaded him into the taxi, his shirt torn open and a bathroom towel wrapped around his abdomen. There was little doubt that she'd be mourning her father very soon. He wondered how she would respond. If it would be rage first, or that empty, mute, numbness. He could remember each so cold and clear from his childhood.

The sound of wailing police sirens converging drew the attention of the old couple. They looked at each other then turned their white-haired heads in the direction from which the taxi had come. *At least half a dozen police officers, Ward thought, are charging into Simon's flat right now, completely unprepared for the carnage they're walking into.* And any second from now the local precinct would get a call about the suspicious foursome a cabbie had just dropped off in front of a gift shop.

With a last look at the old couple and their half-empty bottle of wine Ward entered the store. Inside, a few customers were being hurried towards the door by a dark-skinned, pock-faced man. The man, apparently the store's proprietor, waited for the customers to leave, locked the front door, and hurried towards the back of the shop, gesturing for Ward to follow.

The shopkeeper led him into the stockroom behind the register. Claude placed Simon in a chair beside a stack of unmarked cardboard boxes. MacKenzie knelt beside her father, whose breathing had become shallow and stilted. His eyes were closed but not clenched. His pain was diminishing, being replaced by numbness. He didn't have long.

"He's going to be okay, right?" MacKenzie asked without taking her eyes from her father. Her voice carried a flintiness indicating she already knew the answer.

There was no reason for Ward to respond. He watched Claude, awkwardly aware of the sound of his own breathing and the mustiness of the boxes around them. The big man was talking fast and close into the shopkeeper's ear. After a moment the man handed him a set of keys. Claude wrapped his hands around the back of the man's neck, pulling his face close. He kissed him hard on the right cheek, then the left.

"Wait," he said to Ward, and raced off into the stacks of boxes. A few seconds later, a door opened and shut somewhere in the back.

"Rafael."

Ward turned, unsure if he'd actually heard his name. Simon's eyes were still closed but his lips moved just enough to repeat the word. MacKenzie lifted her head for the first time since they'd left the taxi, glaring at Ward as if saying, "Why the hell does he want you?"

Ward approached, kneeling opposite MacKenzie. The old man raised his head and made an attempt to shoo his daughter off. He lacked the strength to lift his arm but the message was received. MacKenzie, jaw clenched, stepped away to stand by the shopkeeper.

"You care for her," Simon said. He was weak, barely able to cough. His body convulsed and a trickle of blood drained over his lips. "I can see that but I need your promise, Rafael. The Vase must be destroyed. You will see to this above all else."

As Simon spoke Ward felt the old man's hand creep into his jacket pocket. When he reached for the pocket, Simon grabbed his wrist.

"Not yet," he said. "Promise."

Ward let his hand drop. "I promise," he said. Part of him wanted to mean it. Not because he believed but because MacKenzie would want him to mean it. A larger part of him, the part that made up his core—stomach, lungs, heart—couldn't care less if the Vase was eventually dropped into a pit, or a Crematorium, or just handed over to Commandant Gaustad with a bow wrapped around it. So long as he could trade it for his brother's life what difference could its final fate make?

Would they really let him and Daniel just walk away?

The answer was obvious. So obvious he refused to see it.

Simon licked his lips and pulled in a tattered breath as if preparing to say something else. A coughing seizure gripped him instead. MacKenzie darted back to her father, shoving Ward aside. She held his head back as the coughs faded.

"Dad," she said.

Her back was to Ward, her head dipped to the old man's ear. Claude reappeared, edging Ward farther from the older Frenchman. He stood over MacKenzie, his big hands dangling helplessly at his sides.

Simon's chest heaved twice. MacKenzie pulled back so she could see her father's face. He smiled. Ward imagined her returning the smile. Simon collapsed, wheezing something only MacKenzie could hear.

He became still.

MacKenzie's head bowed to her father's chest. Claude's shoulders heaved, then he turned and embraced the shopkeeper.

Ward, unsure what to do, crossed and uncrossed his arms. Before today he'd never seen a dead body. Not his mother. Not Daniel or his father. But now, in the space of a few minutes, he'd killed one man and watched three others die. He expected to feel nauseated again. Instead a cold knot formed in his chest, above his stomach. He had a job to do. He could mourn Simon but if it took the lives of a dozen more Agents, even a dozen Believers, he would pay that price to rescue his brother.

But what about MacKenzie?

"We have to go," she said, interrupting Ward's thoughts. Her voice was hardened glass. She surveyed the three men in the room, tears glazing her face. Her determination mirrored Simon's in the promise he'd elicited from Ward. The Vase above all else.

"*Oui*," Claude said. "Fernand will take care of things here." He motioned to the shopkeeper who bowed his head.

MacKenzie said goodbye to her father with a kiss. Claude led them out of the storeroom and into an alley that smelled of rubbish and urine. A white Renault hatchback, which had seen far too many fender-benders, waited for them, its engine running.

MacKenzie, the last one out of the store, was the first one

into the car, entering the back seat and closing the door before Ward could offer to sit with her. He got into the passenger side and stared out the window as Claude piloted them through the street of Paris.

Exhausted by the events of the last hour Ward had no energy to pull his Port from his jacket and try to figure out where they were going. He tried instead to keep track of their progress by memory of his map. It wasn't long, however, until he was lost. Claude was taking them on a circuitous route, a smart counter-surveillance strategy that Ward was embarrassed he hadn't thought of. Eventually, he gave up and stared out the window. He wanted to say something to MacKenzie. To tell her he understood what it felt like to lose a father. To be an orphan. Age didn't matter. Eleven or thirty, that emptiness was eternal.

All he could think of, however, were the awkward and often half-hearted phrases his family members had offered to him after the accident.

I'm sorry for your loss.

My condolences.

It'll get better, kiddo.

You know your dad loved you, right?

None of them helped. At best they'd only made a clumsy situation worse. What eleven-year-old knows how to respond to such platitudes? What could he say to her that wouldn't clunk just as gracelessly?

And, he was realizing now for the first time, that none of them spoke directly to the loss of his brother. Could they have known he was alive?

No. Coincidence. Nothing more. There are clichés for deceased parents. Not for dead brothers.

Claude took a right and the backdrop of anonymous buildings opened up into a gaping green woodland. The sudden change cracked Ward's reverie, taking only a moment for him to figure out where they were. The *Jardins des Plantes*, France's largest botanical gardens and home to a number of museums. The car slowed and turned down an access road behind a concrete behemoth of a building featuring row upon row of rectangular windows. It looked like a prison.

They entered a service bay, the car's tires and brakes howling on the polished floor. Before Claude could turn off the engine they were beset by two women and a man in the now familiar blue suits. Each rushed to a door to expedite their exit from the Renault. The name tag of the woman who opened Ward's door identified her as Lili, an employee of the *Grande Galerie de l'Evolution*, Paris' natural history museum.

The other woman pulled Claude aside while the man directed MacKenzie and Ward to wait by the car. Claude and the woman spoke until she put her hands over her mouth. Claude embraced her as she sobbed uninhibitedly. When she'd composed herself the woman reached up on her toes and kissed him on the cheek, then took the car keys from him. She waved Lili over and pointed the man towards a storage cabinet, then she drove the car back out of the service bay.

MacKenzie raised her eyebrows as if asking what the plan was. Ward shrugged and watched Lili hand Claude an envelope. The man, meanwhile, approached with a blue plastic first aid kit, his hand outstretched as if to touch Ward's forehead.

Ward pulled back. The man, his ID tag said his name was Marin, flinched and looked to Lili for instruction. Ward reconsidered the medical attention. It was likely this would be his only chance, for at least a while, to have his leg looked at. Another thought piggybacked on that one—who were these *conservateurs*? Coworkers don't have escape plans and emergency medical services prepped and waiting. Simon and Claude's circle was larger than they'd let on. He thought of the Underground Railroad two hundred years ago facilitating the escape of slaves from the Old American South to the free states of the North. Could the *conservatuers* be operating a similar network for Believers, some kind of a cross-continental Relic Railroad?

Claude brushed Lili and Marin aside while they were still deciding how to handle Ward's initial rejection of their medical attention. "We go," he said, positioning himself in front of Marin and the first aid kit. He nodded once each to Lili and Marin and offered a mumbled, "*Merci.*" He then exited the garage through a metallic door, not holding it for the Americans.

Ward and MacKenzie hurried to keep up, finding Claude halfway down a flight of stairs. He didn't stop, leading them from the stairs into a utility passage. From there it was a series of turns and short stairs down until the walls around them narrowed and went from plaster to bare cinderblock. Occasional fluorescent fixtures in the ceiling offered the only, somewhat inconsistent, light.

They had to be at least twenty feet beneath the basement

level of the *Galerie*, probably in an updated part of the ancient catacombs that ran beneath Paris, now being used as an access system for the museum and the surrounding gardens. The catacombs were extensive, some branches used as part of the city's sewer system, others still filled with the millions of bodies which had been buried beneath the city since ancient times.

Photos of this gruesome underworld were always one of Ward's students' favorite distractions during the semester. The workers who turned the tunnels from crypt to sewer stacked the bones of the deceased along the walls creating galleys of the dead. Entire walls, six to seven feet high, of femurs with a cross made of skulls inlaid at the center. Or perhaps random upper and lower arm bones. With a single child's skeleton pinned to the low-slung ceiling, an adult's scapulae positioned to look like wings, like the child was an angel.

Gruesome, the students would call it. *Memento Mori*, Ward would explain. He might even show them how to find a link to a story on the censored list—like Poe's "The Cask of Amontillado"—if they promised not to tell. As far as he knew, none of them ever did.

When the tunnel grew even narrower, allowing only for single-file marching, Ward tapped Claude on the shoulder.

"Where are we going?"

"Not yet," the big man said, his pace continuing unaltered.

The trek continued another few minutes until they reached a ladder embedded in the cement wall of a dead end.

Claude climbed first, unlocking the submarine-style portal at the top of the nearly forty foot climb. Ward offered

MacKenzie to go next but she declined. He ascended, offering his hand to MacKenzie when she reached the top behind him. Again she refused.

They had entered a small room lit by a flickering fluorescent bulb in the far corner. Ward thought of suggesting a moment to rest but Claude had them immediately marching again. They exited through a hollow sounding wooden door. Then down a long corridor of brick and fluorescent lights. The floor was unfinished concrete. They hiked up one more flight of stairs before Claude herded them into a dark room and pulled the door closed behind them.

The darkness reminded Ward of the escape tunnel back in Philly. No one spoke. Their combined breathing sounded like the wind buffeting through a partially open car window. Ward's hands fumbled through his jacket's pockets until he came up with his flashlight. The beam illuminated MacKenzie's knees, then made its way to Claude's chest.

"There," the Frenchman said, his disembodied arm pointing to the side.

Ward aimed the light, catching reflections of metal in reds and greens as he did. Claude followed the beam to a light switch. The single bulb that glowed on wasn't bright but it was enough to force Ward to close and rub his eyes. When he reopened them, he saw they were in a cramped concrete bunker filled with lawn mowers, drums of fertilizer, and other lawn care products.

"We are near *La Seine*," Claude said.

"At the far end of the *Jardin*?" Ward inquired as he put away his flashlight.

"*Oui.*"

"Now what?" MacKenzie asked.

Her tone struck Ward as angrily disinterested. It reminded him of Daniel, the way he would say those same words after Mom turned off the television or a video game because they'd used up their allotted play time. Such instances were always the younger brother's fault, at least in the mind of the older.

"We wait," Claude said. "One hour. Then we go one at a time. Twenty minute intervals. Alone they won't detect us."

Ward opened the envelop he'd been given in the service bay, and handed each of them a train ticket indicating they would be traveling in a "Comfort" cabin on the D car of the overnight train to Rome.

"Paper tickets?" Ward asked.

"Cash," Claude said. "No trace."

He sat on a metal drum and explained the route they were to take to *Gare de Lyon*, the train station across the river. While he spoke MacKenzie hunkered down on the floor, leaning against a wooden crate. When Claude had finished she turned her body just enough to make it clear she didn't want to talk. Ward climbed onto a riding mower and tried to get comfortable. The three of them passed the next hour in silence.

CHAPTER TWENTY-FIVE

Ward watched MacKenzie ignore him.

She sat huddled by her wood crate, her back to him. Other than an occasional heavy breath, followed by a shudder, she was perfectly still.

Eventually Claude exited the storage shed without any further instructions other than a thickly accented, "Twenty minutes." Though none of them had spoken in the previous hour it seemed somehow quieter without the big Frenchman.

Once the door clacked shut Ward returned his attention to MacKenzie. He needed her to trust him. At the least, he needed her to need him to finish the hunt for the lid. Without any survivors in Simon's flat to question the only way to find the Vase now was to do exactly what Claude had said. Offer the final piece to whoever had the lidless Vase.

Why, he thought, *didn't I take that bottle of wine from the couple at the café?*

After a few minutes he climbed down off the tractor and sat on the floor, legs extended, back against one of the mower's tries. He wondered what would happen when they got to Rome. Would there be a whole new contingent of blue suits waiting for them? Another old man—Simon's priest, perhaps—waiting to tell them riddles and scowl at them if they didn't immediately lap up the doctrine of the Vase?

The throbbing of his headache returned. He thought about the pain pills in his pocket. Two might help the headache. Four might combat the nagging soreness in his ankle. What would six do? Or eight? Would it offer anything like a dram of that scotch he'd had outside the Pantheon? Would—

MacKenzie was standing over him. He hadn't noticed her get up.

"Give me your Port."

It was the same tone she'd used in his apartment when she'd found the metallurgical report on the Spear. He watched himself hand her the R1. She held the device in both hands like someone trying to decide what to do with an awkward gift. Figuring he had nothing left to lose Ward was about tell her about the video file of Daniel. He didn't need to blurt out that he planned on leaving her empty-handed once the lid was within his reach. All he really needed to do was create sympathy. That could lead, if not to trust, at least to a working relationship that would be easier to exploit when the time came. He could tell her the only reason he'd joined the REC in the first place was because they'd extorted him with his brother's life.

It was a good first step. Logical, if deceitful. What he couldn't figure out was why he held back. Instead of enacting the sympathy plan he just watched MacKenzie look at the R1.

Then she smashed it on the concrete floor.

It sounded like a car had run over a child's plastic toy truck, followed by an echo that reminded Ward of Claude's fists pummeling that Agent's skull back in Simon's flat. The R1 bounced awkwardly to the side, rattling to a stop near the center of the shed. A piece of polycarbonate landed in Ward's lap. He whimpered. It was the only sound he could produce.

Silently, mechanically, MacKenzie hammered the heel of her boot onto the R1's screen. Again. A third time. The screen, touted as bulletproof, shattered. A fourth time and the Port shattered. Only two large pieces remained. The rest was debris and crumbs.

Ward looked from the destroyed device to MacKenzie. Her hair was tousled wildly, her face clenched in a manner that cautioned Ward not to chastise her decision to destroy the only link they had to maps, historical records, and the agency hunting them.

He didn't take the warning. He couldn't. It wasn't just her sacrifice in the destruction of the Port.

"What the fuck are you doing?" Ward pushed to his feet, barely able to contain his rage. His fear.

"I should kill you," she said. Her voice was low. She might have been whispering something complimentary, something sweet. But there was no mistaking her sincerity.

Ward tensed for an attack. He considered throwing the first punch. In fact he found he hungered to slam his fist into her throat. But MacKenzie turned her back and paced the shed, coming to a stop by the door.

"He said, 'Trust him. God's light shines on him even if his own eyes do not see it.' That's what he whispered," MacKenzie said, her voice unsteady. "That's what he wants me to do. But I don't trust you."

Ward took a heavy breath and exhaled. He was confused. Simon trusted him despite knowing what he was. MacKenzie didn't trust him despite her father insisting that she do so. And the one tool they had to advance them towards both their goals was now shattered and useless. The urge to vent his frustration returned, replaced just as quickly by the feeling that there remained a path to success, even if he couldn't see it.

Simon knew much more than he said. He'd ignored the Spear, despite, assumedly, not knowing what spear it was. He'd insisted the obvious traitor in the room—Ward—be brought into their confidence, yet he was oblivious to Henri's duplicity. Or was he? The only proof Ward had to offer of his trustworthiness was his actions in Simon's flat.

"They tried to kill me, too," he said.

MacKenzie didn't seem to hear. She put a hand on the door and leaned against it. "God's light," she whispered.

Ward knew he was in danger of losing her. To her grief. To her mistrust. If she didn't get on that train he was certain Claude wouldn't help him.

"Look, MacKenzie, I don't know what he meant either but you need my help," he said. When she didn't respond he made the decision to tell her about Daniel. "Fact is, I need your help too."

"Shut up," she said.

He scoured his mind for something to say. Anything to counter the finality of her words. To make her reengage the conversation. From seemingly nowhere a vision of her in the hotel bathroom came to his mind. In her towel. Just the towel and the careful, scrolling script on her back.

He didn't mean to say what he next said, only to say something. Anything.

"Tell me about your tattoo."

MacKenzie turned and stared. For a second Ward thought she was going to raise her shirt so he could see it again, her exquisite artwork minus one commandment.

"Are you fucking kidding?" She stared murder at him. "Twenty minutes," she said, then marched out of the shed, leaving Ward alone.

———◆———

In his solo time in the concrete bunker Ward did nothing other than count the pieces of the broken R1, and take six pain pills. They didn't help.

Without the Port he had no clock. No way to measure his third of an hour. He waited until he couldn't stand to wait longer, then exited the shed and made his way to the river. Soon he stood at the southern end of the *Pont d'Austerlitz*. This bridge across the Seine had been named for the site of Napoleon's greatest victory—his defeat of the Third Coalition—which resulted in the dissolution of the nearly nine hundred year old Holy Roman Empire. A short-lived emperor overthrowing a millennium of Europe's foundation.

Ward suddenly hated knowing all the history. He wished

for the ability to walk in silence through this city without the lecturer in his head reminding him of the academic life he'd forfeited.

He stepped to the edge of the bridge, the train ticket in his hand. He weighed it like a bar of gold.

Over his left shoulder he could feel the setting sun. He turned and found himself held for a moment by the sky, a thick cherry along the roof-topped horizon. It should have struck him as beautiful. Instead it looked to Ward like Simon's blood draping the city.

He refocused his attention on the Right Bank. The tip of the cupola atop the train station's clock tower peeked above the surrounding buildings declaring his destination. Ahead the stately arched bridge beckoned.

The city, he realized for the first time since they'd arrived, smelled like wood-burning stoves and pastries.

Ward looked at the ticket again. *They don't need me,* he thought. It was obvious that, even to himself, he was only trying to alleviate the guilt of his impending decision to abandon MacKenzie and Claude. The easiest way to save his brother was to find a public phone and make a call. Tell Command everything. Let Agent Compano take over and, when she had the Vase and all its pieces in her hands, he could ask for Daniel's release. He'd done his job. He would be rewarded.

This, too, was a lie. And he knew it. The truth was he was expendable to Agent Compano, to Commandant Gaustad, and to Claude.

The truth was that whether he handed the lid to Gaustad,

or pointed Command in the right direction, Daniel's life was over. No one who kept a man locked up for twenty years was going to let him go just because they got their hands on some pottery. Daniel was going to die in that Labor Camp. If he wasn't dead already.

That left only MacKenzie. Was he expendable to her? Probably. Ward didn't feel any surprise at that answer but he did feel pain. It was the shredding of that earlier emotion, that epiphany that he'd missed her when they were separated.

He peered over the edge of the bridge and battled the hurt that came with the thought of abandoning her. He squeezed it into a ball and tried to shove it down beside the guilt he'd been repressing for two decades. He thought of stretching out his hand and letting the train ticket float into the roiling Seine. He could sell the gun and purchase a new train ticket to anywhere in Europe. Maybe to Asia. Or South America. Anywhere where a book or a silver cross in your pocket wouldn't get you black-bagged. He could disappear from the grid the same way MacKenzie had done.

She will die if you abandon her.

"No," Ward whispered as the black water rolled carelessly along. "She has Claude. They'll be fine." It was a lie and he knew it.

They will both die.

Ward bowed his head. The whole thing was like a comic book. With that thought came the idea that maybe he should approach the situation like a comic book hero. Come up with a plan. Spring into action. Save his brother. Get the girl. Happy ending. He snorted a laugh and imagined his reflection, if the dancing Seine were kind enough to offer reflections, wearing a mask and a cape.

Ward shook his head. He was no hero.

Beyond that he'd never actually read a comic book. Daniel had been the one with the comic collection. And he'd guarded his comics jealously, as if their dialogues and animation cells were the plunder of millenniums past.

Ward remembered mounting an incursion into Daniel's room one night. He knew where the riches were, beneath a carefully lain blanket under the bed. It had felt like the darkest hour of the longest night, though it was probably not past eleven o'clock.

After an inch-by-inch opening of the door, and a forever-long belly crawl through the mines and obstacles his imagination made of discarded socks and un-put-away toys, he'd managed to get his fingertips on the blanket. It was so soft. Even today, so many years later, he could touch his fingers together in the night and feel the silkiness of that blanket and of its twin which had adorned his own bed.

The memory seemed to cry out, "Don't leave me under this bed. Wrap yourself in me and smile."

But no child is a stealthy as he believes. A warhammer-pillow had crashed down on his head. And blow after blow had chased him back to his own room, empty-handed and defeated.

Ward closed his eyes and let the memory of his brother float off. He inhaled the salty sweetness of crepes and éclairs and the river.

He made a decision. The Vase was the key. Gaustad wanted

it. Okay. Simon wanted it destroyed. Fine. He'd give Gaustad one chance to produce his brother. Then, with or without Daniel, he was going to extirpate the Vase from history. And Gaustad with it. But whatever was to happen he wasn't going to sacrifice MacKenzie. He wasn't going to do to her what he'd done to his mother.

When he opened his eyes the dipping sun shone a column of ruby light across the bridge. He put the train ticket into his pocket and was surprised to feel something else there. He'd almost forgotten Simon's hand in his pocket. He removed the object slowly as if it were a delicate treasure. The notion, it turned out, wasn't so far off.

In his hand was the photograph from the wall in Simon's flat. Claude must have grabbed it for his friend while Ward and MacKenzie were hailing the taxi. As he'd suspected, it was of MacKenzie as a little girl, barely a toddler, with a younger Simon, a full crop of rosy hair adorning his head. Behind them was a squared, whitewashed, maybe marble, church which Ward didn't recognize.

Simon was holding up little Hannah so that her face was even with his against the church's gleaming white arches. He was smiling at her the way a father does when he knows one day his daughter will have to learn she's not really a princess.

Ward couldn't help but grin. He'd made the right decision. He placed the photo into his jacket's inside pocket, careful not to crease it, and followed his own shadow across the bridge.

CHAPTER
TWENTY-SIX

Ffrom the street the blockade of concrete and windows
that was Gare de Lyon could have been a palace, a
museum, or even a warehouse. Inside it was every
train station Ward had ever experienced. A generic push of
people rushing to board a train, buy a croissant, or just find a
spot to mill about. A handful of potted palm trees and endless
panes of light-bearing glass above a trellised ceiling kept the
station from feeling too gothic.

Ward made his way through the station with his head
down and collar up. After the fight in Shakespeare and
Company and the car chase outside the Pantheon he figured
he had to be a wanted fugitive by now. If the train stations of
Paris were anything like the one's back home there would be
cops and transport security stalking every hallway and corner.
There would be enough security sensors to get a fifty percent

angle on his face no matter how invisible he made himself. He had no option but to hunch into his jacket and hope that Paris continued its pattern of being the opposite of what was expected in the Republic.

Somehow he made it to the train even without a pair of dark sunglasses and a fedora to complete his dime-store novel disguise. His hope about the freedoms of Paris had proven accurate. There were no cops. No Agents. No conductors checking IDs. All he had to do was scan his ticket and step on board. As far as he could tell not a single person even looked twice at him.

Ward made it to their cabin just as simply as he'd traversed the train station. A cliché about being too simple crossed his mind dissipated. As he placed his hand on the handle of the cabin's sliding door, however, his gut did a quick somersault in fear that one or both of his companions wouldn't be there. Then what? If they'd been captured, surely the cabin was compromised. He should run.

His conscience didn't intervene this time. It didn't have to. There was no running. He was here. Whoever he'd once been was gone. And whoever he was now was going to keep MacKenzie safe. With Daniel thousands of miles away in a Labor Camp that would likely never let him go, keeping MacKenzie safe was all he had left.

He slung open the door. Claude and MacKenzie sat opposite each other on blue-cushioned benches running the short length of the compartment to the exterior wall of the train. Neither spoke.

The cream-colored cabin was small, its focal feature a

tiny window peering at the train on the next line. There was a sterility to the room, the way hospitals gave the impression of untidy cleanliness.

Ward locked the door behind him and breathed the uncomfortably thick air. There was no hiding the tension between Claude and MacKenzie on opposite sides of the room, in opposing corners: MacKenzie by the door, Claude squeezed into the corner by the window.

MacKenzie pulled her knees to her chest allowing Ward room to maneuver. Claude acknowledged him with a nod. Both stared at him as if relishing the distraction from avoiding each other's gaze.

This is going to be an uncomfortable night, Ward thought. He sized up the cabin, trying to figure out where he would sit. Better, where he would sleep, as each bench was only wide enough for one. A moment of comic apprehension stole his fears. Would he have to squeeze onto the left bench with MacKenzie, surely under promise to behave himself? Or would he be forced to snuggle with Claude?

"She does not speak," Claude said, interrupting Ward's thoughts on the sleeping arrangements.

"What? Neither do you," MacKenzie said, her eyes comically wide. She pressed her hands on the bench as if she might stand. "You haven't said one word since I got here. Not even 'hi' you freaking statue."

There was no helping it. Ward laughed.

He could feel their eyes on him but it didn't matter. He flopped down on the bench beside MacKenzie and let the guffaws roll. It didn't take long for the contagious nature of laughter to capture MacKenzie. Her scowl broke.

"Don't think you're sleeping beside me, Professor," she said, a grin forming.

"You want me to cuddle with him?" Ward thrust a finger at Claude.

The Frenchman made a face as if they were speaking gibberish.

That was all it took. Ward was lost in another round of laughter. MacKenzie joined him, not with full belly-laughs but enough to lessen the weight of the day.

When the moment began to pass, she said. "Bunk beds, buddy."

Ward's chuckling funneled into an embarrassed smile for having missed the obvious fold-down bench inches above MacKenzie's head.

"Right. I knew that," he said.

The silent void in Claude's corner doused the remaining brevity. The lines on his face were stern as ever but there was something else to his expression which Ward had trouble defining.

MacKenzie must have seen it as well. "I'm sorry about Henri," she said, the sincerity of her words beyond doubt.

Claude's terse response was shocking. "Do not speak his name or pray for his soul."

MacKenzie stiffened as if he'd threatened to strike her. Claude's vitriol was so fierce Ward almost bounded into the center of the room as a barrier in case the big man did attack.

"He was the one who told them where to find us," Ward said to MacKenzie. "Where to find Simon."

"My God, he was the traitor?"

"No, not *Le Traitre*," Claude said. The anger was gone. "Not the thief who took the Vase. My nephew was...he was a foolish boy who betrayed his family and God."

The train lurched into motion, rolling back from the platform. Claude feigned an interest in the window. Ward saw they were in danger of losing him to his grief but they needed answers before they could let the big man indulge his gloom.

"Where do we go after Rome?" Ward asked. "What did Simon have planned?"

Claude seemed to consider his response, or maybe whether or not to respond. At length he explained that they would carry on to Bari in the Southeast. The rest of the plan, he said, would be revealed by Adrien. He then set his jaw, making it clear there would be no negotiating for further details.

When MacKenzie put up her hand as if she might ask another question, Ward quieted her with a wave and shake of his head. He shared what he knew of Bari. It had once been among Europe's great port cities. Peter the Hermit preached for the First Crusade there in the late eleventh century. It was also an oft-contested prize between the Byzantines and the West. Now, however, it was a manufacturing hub, an industrial precinct with only small pockets of historical and residential neighborhoods. The city had been featured in a research paper not so long ago—a publically censored piece, cleared for academia only—but Ward couldn't remember why.

MacKenzie let him talk, seemingly content to let his words drown out whatever was going on in her mind. When he finished she made no motion to for him to continue, nor any attempt to begin a new conversation. It was going to be a long, quiet ride.

After an hour, with the French countryside whipping by the window in sheets of greens and tans and browns, MacKenzie's eyes began the fight to remain open. The lines of grief on Claude's face smoothed. Ward took his leave and folded down his bunk. He hopped up without too much trouble from his injured ankle. As a boy he'd always fallen asleep easily in the car. The train, now that he was lying down, had the same effect. Before he let the drowse pull him in, he peered over the edge of his bunk. Claude remained, like a monument, in sitting in his corner, his head facing the door. A sentry for the night, if he stayed awake. Good enough.

Ward rolled towards the wall and let sleep take him.

"Mommy?"

Eleven year old Raffi peered into the mirror, terrified by what he saw. Nothing. There was no reflection. Neither he nor the room behind him appeared in the empty glass. He wanted to turn away. Spider webs, unseen, held him still, his eyes glued open. Why couldn't Mommy pull him away?

The mirror pulsed. It spun. No—the world spun on the mirror-axis. It was now Rafe facing the absent reflection.

"Mom?"

The bass of his voice throbbed in the mirror, descending into itself, a reflection of a reflection of a reflection...

Mise en abyme. *It's called* mise en abyme, *he thought. Placed into the abyss.*

Warmth fled. Rafe pulled his arms into his core. It was like the null of the mirror had implanted itself in his abdomen. He closed his eyes.

Where's Mommy, Rafe?

The voice was familiar. Yet it wasn't. It was tinny. Sly. Mocking. Somehow—

Mother, mother, mother, mother, mother, mother.

"Stop!" he wanted to scream but he had no voice. He opened his eyes. The mirror glitched.

Little Raffi sat on the edge of his bed. Rafe could see it like he was there, standing where Dad used to stand to whisper goodnight. Yet he could feel it like he was the boy. Himself. So young.

There was no mirror. There was no room. Only a bed. Daniel's bed. And sitting before Raffi, her back to him, her head nearly chin-high to the little boy, was Mommy. Raffi leaned to the side, trying to see even just a bit of her profile, just a glimpse of her face. But there was a shadow cast from somewhere else. Mommy wouldn't turn her head into the light.

She raised her hands, palms up, holding a small bottle, squat and black, chest-high. Raffi didn't like it. It was ugly, not in the way you might describe the opposite of beauty, but in the way deformity was ugly through no fault of its own.

Raffi tried to pull back, but once more was locked in place.

"Your hand," Rafe tried to scream but he had no form. No voice.

Raffi stared at his outstretched hand. Had he heard? His little hand held a big gun. Some black, generic pistol with no features and no weight. He held it against Mommy's right temple.

Raffi cried. The tears, taking turns slipping from each eye, were cold from the right and hot from the left.

Her body motionless, Mommy hoisted her hands higher, the bottle—no, the vase—now rising past her mouth, her nose, her eyebrows. Its mouth yawned above her dark hair.

Raffi blinked, a slow-motion shutter which plunged the world into darkness for far too long.

When the shutter opened, the vase was topped with an ornate, twisted wrought iron cap.

Take me, *it whispered from nowhere. That voice again.* Hold me.

Raffi recoiled as if it were a spider.

Take me! *The voice was earthy and opaque.*

The world hiccupped. It was like a momentary video game freeze or a film's rough changeover.

Raffi winced a hot tear.

Rafe, bodiless save for the cheek he shared with Raffi, flinched as well.

The droplet crawled down their face then plummeted onto their bare left forearm. There was a hiss. The globule, momentarily dispersed by the impact of its descent, reformed like mercury drawn to itself. It trickled down their arm to their wrist. To the back of their palm. To their index finger.

On their first knuckle, the droplet paused. They held their arm out to get the thing as far from themselves as possible.

The heat increased. The droplet bubbled into a blob. It darkened. It grew hotter.

"Mommy," *Raffi wept, though his mouth didn't open.*

The hand that was Rafe blinked out leaving only the child.

The red golf-ball sized blob crept forward to Raffi's fingertip. It weighed his hand down, aching his shoulder. His arm levered forward until it was inches from Mommy's head.

Now crimson and steaming the blob collected itself and leapt from Raffi's hand, perching atop the little vase's black crown.

A siren called from somewhere in the spaceless distance.

The blob let go its form and oozed over the vase, melting the lid with a hiss. The siren grew louder. No, not a siren. A wailing, gravelly and pained.

The vase filled with water. The fluid darkened. It overflowed, slithering down its bulbous body until—

The bed pitched forward as if floating upon a violent wave. Raffi pulled the trigger.

Ward jolted awake. Confusing images of a mirror and a gun disappeared into the darkness of the cabin. His hand lay on his chest, absorbing the riotous heartbeat within. Slowly, incrementally with each breath, his heart returned to a steady cadence.

Had the train stopped and started?

He leaned over the edge of his bed. A line of light from under the door wasn't enough to see if either of his companions was awake. But their even breathing told Ward he was the first up.

He pulled back, not wanting to wake MacKenzie. He rolled onto his back to stare at the unadorned ceiling of their cabin which hovered somewhere above him in the pitch. He tried counting the days since he'd met MacKenzie. Was today Sunday? No—it was Monday. Early Monday morning sometime. He thought about checking the time only to remember he no longer had a Port. He could wake Claude and ask but decided to wait, to lie still, timeless, for a while.

Eventually the sound of MacKenzie rustling on the bottom bunk brought Ward back. Figuring they were no more than a few hours from Rome he listened to his stomach gurgle. He wiped his palm across his forehead and rubbed his eyes. The continued growling from his gut argued that food was paramount but the greasy resin on his hands made a case for showering over eating. He wondered if either was available on the train.

He craned his neck towards the door. Every dozen seconds or so the shadow of a passerby flitted across the light at the bottom of the door. Each fifth or sixth was accompanied by a cough or the sound of a hand or a bag tapping the wall. *Surely there must be a dining car or something,* he thought.

Raising himself up on an elbow he was going to swing over the edge of the bunk. Someone was there, a floating head between him and the door.

"You can't go back, can you?" MacKenzie said.

It took Ward a moment to understand what she meant. He thought, at first, that she was talking about returning to work at the REC. But that wasn't it. And she didn't mean returning to the Republic either. She meant his life. He had signed away all he'd built in the last twenty years. His books. His degrees. His career. Whatever happened next, that Rafael Ward was dead.

"No," was all he said.

"Your house, your job, your students. It all disappeared when you got on that plane with me."

Ward didn't respond. His students. He hadn't thought

about them, not once since MacKenzie knocked on his door in the middle of the night. Italy was six hours ahead of Philly. They'd be going to sleep around now, or maybe still doing some last-minute readings they'd forgotten. In a few hours they'd arrive at their classroom only to find a note on the door saying that class was canceled.

Or had they already been messaged that the course was canceled for the semester? Had an REC Agent spoken with Dean Markinson? Would any of his students message him to see if he was okay or had they been told he was dead, the victim of an unfortunate accident? Or a suicide?

Would his office-mate Ken be forced to explain over and over to inquiring students that Professor Ward would no longer be available on the campus of Carroll University?

Ward had always thought it was the research and the stories—for what was history but the best stories?—that kept him feeling alive at the university. All of a sudden he realized that so much of it was the students. Their questions, the play-acting, even the ridiculous pirate-voices they'd used Friday when playing with their imaginary treasures. He was abandoning them the same as he'd abandoned his mother. The same as he feared he would be forced to abandon Daniel.

MacKenzie shifted. A line of white broke the darkness. A smile, perhaps. Though her eyes seemed not to play along.

Was it a thank you? Forgiveness? Ward hoped the latter. He forced a grin in return but she'd already dropped back to her bunk.

Her voice, barely more than a whisper, floated through the darkness. "I believe you."

Ward held the words for a moment like a salve over the wound of his regret. When he heard MacKenzie return to her bunk he decided to go in search of the dining car. He slid to the corner of the bench to make sure he didn't drop down on MacKenzie, and swung his legs over the edge.

The passing shadows of four or five people fluttered underneath the door. Ward's first thought was that maybe the dining car had indeed just opened. Then he realized the shadows weren't passing the door. They were gathering outside it.

"Claude," he hissed.

The Frenchman lurched awake just as the cabin door ripped open. An assault of light blinded Ward, who reflexively ducked when something metallic—probably the locking bolt from the door—bounced off the wall behind his head.

By the time any of them in the cabin adjusted to the light it was too late. A stocky man in a black business suit, with slick hair and a submachine gun, stood in the doorway. Two similarly dressed men could be seen over his shoulder in the corridor. Though not in tactical gear they were clearly Agents. *It was,* Ward thought, *as if something in the way they stood, the way they tilted their heads, distinguished them as REC. If I'd been recruited sooner, would I be just as recognizable by now?*

The Agent with the slick hair lowered his weapon and turned aside to make room for someone else.

Agent Compano slipped into the room.

"Hi, Rafael," she said, cheerfully. "Fun trip so far. I've got to tell you, I am really looking forward to this promotion."

The slick-haired Agent suddenly raised his sub-machine

gun as if MacKenzie, still on the bunk below, had made a move.

"Ex-fucking-girlfriend, huh Rafe? You stupid dick," MacKenzie said, but didn't do anything else to draw the Agents' ire.

Agent Compano smiled wide. "Ex-girlfriend. That's how you played it off? Smart. I guess I did some good with you after all. Do you miss her, Rafael? Do you miss your 'Em'?"

"Go fuck yourself," Ward said.

Agent Compano, as if she hadn't heard, said, "Follow us, please, folks." The words were pleasant but the tone was as threatening as any of the guns in the room.

Claude clenched his fists. Ward shook his head hoping to cancel whatever move the Frenchman planned. They'd be cut down in seconds in these tight quarters.

"Yeah, Frenchy," Agent Slick-Hair said with a Philadelphia accent. "Don't be stupid."

The Agents drew them out of the cabin, removed Ward's pistol and checked the others for weapons. Finding none the Agents marched them down the narrow hallway. Agent Compano led the way single file, a second behind her with Agent Slick-Hair and another bringing up the rear. Any move they made to escape would leave them trapped in melee range with men holding automatic weapons. Chances were everyone would be slaughtered.

From car to vestibule, and vestibule to car, they marched through the train passed open cabin doors. No passengers remained, though some rooms held half-packed suitcases or spilled and broken coffee mugs. The shadows he'd seen hadn't been passengers in search of the dining car. They'd been passengers being herded to one end of the train so the capture of Ward and his companions could go off without hindrance.

Each step, each empty cabin, increased Ward's anger at his carelessness in getting captured so easily. In the seventh car, Ward again had to shake off a look from Claude which begged for permission to attack.

Finally they entered a spacious car filled with tables and chairs, each set with a white table cloth, water glasses, and silverware. If not the last car in the train it had to be near the end. They proceeded a few feet into the room before stopping so that Agent Compano, with a long-strided strut, could traverse the length of the car and speak with a number of men—surely more Agents—at the far end.

Ward was unable to help himself scanning the dining car for a croissant or maybe even a cocktail-sized liquor bottle. His next thought was to grab a fork or knife as a weapon. This, however, was as blatantly foolish as seeking breakfast or a drink. He pushed both notions aside and tried to assess their situation.

Left with only three Agents guarding them, one in front and two behind, this would be the best time to attempt an escape. If they could overpower these three, they'd have three automatic weapons and about forty feet of rail car between them and the Agents at the other end. It was a good fighting chance.

Then what? There were more than a half dozen Agents at the far end. With no reliable cover other than some dining tables, they would need to find an escape, not try to conquer outnumbering and superiorly trained force. But how do you escape from a moving train? And why was it still running, anyway? Why not stop it and drag them off?

"Bring them," Agent Compano shouted.

Some extrapolation of geometry and calculus from a training exercise more than three years ago told Ward they had ten seconds to act. Adrenaline tightened his muscles.

Two things happened next to discount any attempt at fighting back. First, a detachment of four more Agents, these dressed in standard black fatigues, entered from behind to reinforce the escort. Second, the train banked hard to the right.

Had he been prepared for such a sharp turn, this would have been the time to attack.

He wasn't. None of them were.

Everyone lurched with the train. Agent Slick-Hair in the back lost his footing, reaching out to steady himself on a nearby table and knocking over a water glass. It shattered drawing everyone's attention. That was the moment. Ward, however, missed it as he too had been tossed off balance, barely regaining himself before the Agent had.

Their opportunity was gone.

The four additional Agents were now on them, pushing the procession forward.

Ward did his best to shove his anger aside. He tried to see around the lead Agents as they approached the end of the car, which had been set up for a buffet. A long head table ran the length of the back wall, four large Agents standing sentry behind its chairs, two on either side of a seated figure whom Ward could not clearly see for the guards, and Claude, in front of him. Another table along the right wall held a number of warming dishes. This brought the total number of Agents to thirteen, including the seated one.

They halted just feet in front of the head table. The train banked again. One of the standing Agents behind the table tapped at the screen of his R1 then brought the Port to his mouth like a telephone.

"Tell him to slow this thing down," he said.

The man on the other end of the transmission affirmed the command. The train's speed began to diminish.

The sound of a fork being dragged across a plate drew everyone's attention. It grated on Ward's molars causing him to wince. He craned his neck to see who'd made the sound. An Agent stepped aside, giving a clear view of the head table. Ward's stomach burrowed into his feet.

"There he is," said Ken.

CHAPTER
TWENTY-SEVEN

Ken Hickey held up a glass much as he would at The Barrel on a Friday night. His tone was the same. His grin the same. Even the drink—some yellow fruity thing in a collins glass– was the same.

"Ken?"

It felt like the opposite of when Ward ran into students outside of the classroom. In the different contexts—the grocery store, the gas station, the bar—he often couldn't remember their names. Sometimes he didn't recognize them at all. Now, looking at his office-mate he was suddenly unsure if he really was on a train somewhere in Italy.

"You got it."

The glee in Ken's voice grated on Ward's temples. How could he maintain that obnoxious happiness?

"What are you doing here?" Ward asked.

The bite of a muzzle into the back of his shoulder caused Ward to turn. An Agent with spiky blond hair roughly Ward's height jabbed him again with his submachine gun.

"You're not asking the questions here," the blonde Agent said.

Ward thought of some old gangster film. Black and white. The not-too-smart crony flicks his cigarette at the captive hero. "You're not the one asking the questions here, see?" he says.

Ken's discordant voice pulled Ward out of the Hollywood flashback. "It's okay, Agent…whatever your name is," Ken said. He stood, showing himself to be dressed much the same as he was on any given day at school. A tweed blazer a size too large engulfed an off-white, wrinkled oxford partially tucked in to his also wrinkled corduroy pants.

"What do you say you and I go for a little walk, eh Rafe?" Ken tilted his head to the back door of the dining car, the merriment in his voice betrayed by his darting glances at the four Agents flanking him, their fingers set against their trigger-guards.

Ward could feel Claude and MacKenzie's eyes boring into him. He shrugged, helpless.

"What the fuck?" MacKenzie blurted. She approached as if she might grab him by the throat. Claude seized her arm, yanking her back. The blonde Agent snickered.

MacKenzie's face was a mix of confusion and rage. Ward could imagine her wondering if Ken was the man who had betrayed her father. If he ever actually had a relationship with Agent 'Em' Compano. If their shared laugh and everything else about him was as much a lie as the war the Republic insisted was brewing in France. He opened his mouth to explain but nothing came out. There was nothing he could say that wouldn't make him appear to be exactly what she'd thought earlier—a liar and a traitor.

"Now, now, Miss MacKenzie," Ken said. He finished his drink and slapped the empty glass onto the table. "Why don't you have a seat with your friend there and let Rafe and I work this out?"

MacKenzie's eyes went accusingly wide. With no defense against her thoughts Ward approached the table.

Behind him Agent Compano growled at MacKenzie, "You heard him, bitch. Sit down."

Ward could imagine the threats MacKenzie's eyes were lancing at him and at Agent Compano.

Ken pressed his lips together and raised his eyebrows as if to say, "If she gets out of line she's going to get beat." He motioned to the Agent closest to the buffet table and lifted his glass like a king on his throne. The Agent double-timed it to the buffet, returning with a pitcher of orange juice and a travel-sized bottle of vodka. Ken let the Agent take his glass and mix the concoction.

"Want to join me?" he asked.

Ward wanted to shout at him. To grab the lapels of his blazer and shake him until he explained what was happening. Instead Ward heard himself order a scotch.

"Don't think I saw any of that good stuff over there, buddy," Ken said, taking his refilled glass from the Agent. "How about an amaretto?" Ken sent his errand-Agent back to the buffet to collect Ward's drink. The man returned with an airline-size bottle of amaretto. When the tiny bottle was placed in Ken's hand he stood and held his arm out indicating that they should step around the buffet and enter the vestibule.

Ward did as instructed. They were, as he'd guessed, in the last car. The vestibule was windowed floor to ceiling on three sides, broken only by a waist-high brass handrail, giving a wonderful view of the brightening morning as they rolled through a green, mountainous landscape.

They couldn't be much more than an hour or so from Rome, he figured. A thought crept into his consciousness from someplace that shouldn't have been at the forefront now: *MacKenzie would love this view.* Followed by: *Mom would've loved it, too.*

"Sorry for the guns and all, Rafe," Ken said, entering the tight vestibule. He handed over the amaretto. "You're not pissed, right? I mean, I'm just kind of doing your job."

The smile was gone from his face, though his voice still held that same obnoxious joy. Ward had to fight the urge to punch his friend's throat. Instead he snatched the bottle of amaretto, tore off the cap, and chugged the amber drink. It had a twist of something bitter cloaked in an apricot and caramel sweetness. Too sweet. It went down his throat like children's medicine. No ignition of joy. He threw the empty bottle at his friend's feet.

The smile returned. "You didn't really think you were the only Agent at the university, did you?"

Actually Ward did think so. In fact, he'd been going about it as if he were the only Agent active in the Atlantic District. He saw himself walking about campus with a sense of entitlement. An arrogance in his voice. A tone which he could now hear daring Dean Markinson to write him up the next time he dared utter an architectural comparison between the Republic and some other "forbidden" country.

He wanted to get hit as much as he wanted to slug the smirking Professor H.

The train pitched left. Ward placed his hand against the cool glass of the side window. Ken tried to roll with the motion and stumbled back into the door. As the train straightened he shook his hand as if he'd jammed a finger. He looked out the back window of the vestibule. It was a mannerism Ward had seen before from Ken, a purposeful attempt to avoid eye contact after an embarrassing guffaw.

"Look, you know as well as I you can't say no when they ask you to volunteer." Ken's tone changed as he let the final syllable linger.

"So, what? You've been doing REC work all along?" Ward couldn't believe it. Ken, no matter the situation on the train, was no field Agent. He was a teacher. A bumbling erudite. The man could barely pack a briefcase without destroying half his papers.

And what was I? Ward thought with a snort.

"A month, man. That's all. Right before the semester started, they were just there in my apartment waiting for me. Hey, I'm not one of those guys with guns. They just asked me to do a few small things here and there. You know."

"No," Ward said, hands balling into fists. "I don't know. What things? What the fuck are you doing here? What—"

Then he understood. He didn't need to hear the details.

They recruited his office-mate—a disheveled, muddling professor whose only value could be to do exactly what he did everyday—talk to his recently recruited office-mate. Make sure he didn't blab about his role as an Agent. Make sure he begin struggling with his duty. Make sure that the boy who'd turned in his mother was still front and center in the man who was teaching a generation of Republic Citizens that everything their grandparents believed was just stories. It was part of the interview process. The never-ending background check.

They'd turned the jovial, awkward Professor H into a spy.

And, Ward scolded, I never had a clue. He wanted another shot. Of anything, even the amaretto.

"Come on, man, I never told them a thing. You never gave me reason to. Then they showed up at my house again three days ago and told me I was going to Europe. Like, what the heck, you know. So, tell me what's going on. Why do they need me to come get you?"

"They want you to bring me home?"

Ken shrugged. "That's what they said. Man, those guys are intense. I could do with never having to go down to the Tower again. You've been there, right? It's like walking into a castle, but you don't know if they're going to let you back out again."

"Ken, shut up," Ward interrupted. He ignored the hurt expression on his friend's face. "Did they tell you to bring me home or did they tell you to get something from me?"

"Get something?"

"Just answer the question."

"What would they want me to get from you?"

The train listed a bit. Ken overcompensated and bumped the wall. It was nearly enough to make Ward miss it. He was so angry, marveling at how pathetic an REC operative his office-mate was, that the brief flash in Ken's eyes as he'd asked this last question almost didn't register.

Almost. But it did register.

The train slowed for another curve. Ken, this time, kept his balance. He smiled. It was the same old smile. The same old Ken. Every bit of it, except his eyes.

"You son of a bitch," Ward said. He stepped forward.

Ken pulled a standard issue RT40 and pointed it at Ward's chest.

"Where is it?" The delight in Ken's voice was gone, replaced with a severity Ward had never heard from his friend.

Ward looked past his office-mate at the window in the vestibule door. It was too small to give a full view of the dining car but Ward could see two Agents standing at attention, their focus somewhere other than the door through which Ward was peering.

"Do you even know what 'it' is?" Ward said. He doubted it. He doubted Ken knew any of it. Not the Vase. Not Daniel. Probably not even what he'd done to his mother.

"Just tell me. Then you can go home," Ken pleaded. "Then I can go home."

"Fuck you."

"Yeah," Ken said as if he'd expected that response. "What the heck made you think you could turn your back on the REC and get away? Look, let's make this simple, okay? Tell me or I'll shoot your girlfriend."

"You're an errand boy, Ken. Not a killer."

Ken *was* an errand boy. Ward had been expecting *Le Traitre*. A man who could fool the *conservateurs*. Who could swipe from right under their noses the object they valued, maybe even feared, more than almost anything else.

Ken was certainly not that man.

"Who's pulling your strings, Hickey?"

But the answer was clear. Who pulled all the strings in the District?

Unconsciously the thumb and first two fingers on Ward's left hand came together as if he were rubbing a piece of fine silk. But his mind wasn't feeling silk. It was pottery. A ceramic urn. A vase on a pedestal surrounded by illicit art. Gaustad's office. The vessel that had been ancient Greek and yet not Greek. The air fled his lungs.

He'd touched it. The Vase of Soissons was there in Gaustad's office and he'd touched it. Would MacKenzie embrace him or choke him for having been so close to their goal?

Ward shook away from the vision, finding Ken's grinning face instead.

"Figured it out, did you?" Ken said. "Who's pulling *your* strings?" he mimicked, raising his arms at the elbows like a marionette.

Ken's teasing rotated his palms out, pointing the gun towards the floor. Ward didn't hesitate. He threw his shoulder into Ken's chest, landing two punches against his friend's ribs. The force of the attack propelled the two men into the side window. Ken grunted as his back slammed into the handrail.

The gun clattered to the floor. Ward kicked it to the side and pulled back. Ken collapsed, wheezing. Rotating from the hip, Ward threw his full weight into a blow against Ken's jaw.

"Where's Gaustad?"

Ken's eyes glazed. Blood drooled from the corner of his slack, open mouth. Ward grabbed the pistol and shoved it into his friend's neck.

"Where?"

"Don't kill me, Rafe. Please, don't kill me." The words were garbled but the fear and desperation were clear.

"Last chance."

As he said it Ward wondered if he could kill his friend. He looked again through the window into the dining car. There didn't appear to be any commotion. No one was even glancing at the door. The Agents likely couldn't hear a thing. They probably figured there was no way Ward was stupid enough to do exactly what he was doing now.

Ward craned his neck until he could see MacKenzie. She sat at one of the tables by the door, the blonde Agent casually holding a submachine gun a few inches from her head. He couldn't see Agent Compano. A nagging, almost tearing sensation, like a scotch burn, flared in Ward's chest.

Yes, he could kill his friend if that's what it took to keep MacKenzie safe. He pulled back the hammer.

"Rome," Ken wept. "At the train station in Rome."

They had to get off the train. Ward looked out the window at the greens and browns of the mountains falling into the distance.

Wait for a turn then jump.

Could it work? Logic told him that there was no way. That a jump from a train would kill them. More important, it would mean running away from the Vase. But, he reasoned, it would mean a chance to find the lid first. It was all about the lid.

Wait for a turn then jump.

"Get up."

Ward yanked Ken to his feet and tried to walk him forward, but the man's legs had become jelly. It was all Ward could do to keep him standing. He jammed the gun into Ken's spine.

"You're going to walk into that room like everything is fucking dandy in the world, got it?"

"They said all I had to do was talk to you. Just talk," Ken blubbered.

"Get your shit together, Hickey," Ward said, "or I'll kill you right here."

Ken straightened up and took a wobbly step. Then another. He slid open the door and trembled into the dining car. Ward kept himself hunched behind his office-mate.

"Sir?" one of the Agents said.

"Just talk," Ken whined.

Ward shoved his office-mate to the floor. "Claude," he shouted.

He had no plan. He no reason to believe that either of his companions were prepared to act. Yet before he'd completed the name Claude grabbed the submachine gun from the nearest Agent. Simultaneously MacKenzie spun and punched the blonde Agent in the temple.

Someone fired a weapon. Ward dove behind a table,

pulling it over on its side for the little cover it offered. He rolled as the table settings and glasses crashed about him and came up shooting on the other side, unleashing half a dozen rounds. He didn't care to see who he hit. The sound of automatic fire drove him back behind the table where MacKenzie, holding the blonde Agent's submachine gun, was now crouched.

"We're getting off," Ward said.

He pointed to the vestibule. MacKenzie looked confused. Then her jaw fell open. Another salvo drowned whatever she said next. Frustration crossed her face. She rose to her knees and fired into the center of the car. Ward peered around the edge of the table in time to see MacKenzie's volley hit Agent Slick-Hair in the chest as he moved between tables. At least a dozen rounds tore the man open and flung him against the back wall.

The submachine gun clicked empty. MacKenzie threw it like a boomerang at Agent Slick-Hair's convulsing body. Then she and Ward ducked back behind the table as another burst of fire began.

"No choice," he said into her ear. "We go."

The automatic fire stopped. There was a second of silence before more pistol shots. Ward fired over the top of the table then peered out. Four Agents lay on the floor, two of them burst open by gunfire. Another was contorted by the far wall, clawing towards the back of the car. The Agent's head turned. It was Agent Compano. Half her face was ripped away. Her nose was gone. One eye was jelly oozing down what was left of her cheek.

Ward looked away and found Claude kneeling on the chest of an Agent, his hand held to his neck. Blood poured through his fingers. He aimed a submachine gun at the buffet tables.

In all the chaos Ken was nowhere to be seen.

"Go," the Frenchman yelled.

More gunfire chased Ward back behind the table. They were ten feet from the door. Claude could give them maybe three seconds if they went right now. Ward fired three times over the table. He grabbed MacKenzie's hand, interlacing his fingers with hers, and lunged to the door.

It felt like slow motion.

Each step was like running underwater. It took too long for them to get through the vestibule door. Too long to fire back into the room to give Claude a chance. Too long for the gun to fall from the big man's lifeless hands. Too long for the door to slide shut.

As MacKenzie choked an anguished cry for their lost friend Ward realized they really were in slow motion. The train had decelerated considerably, now banking left for an almost ninety degree turn.

Ward emptied his remaining rounds into the back window. Four tiny holes appeared in the glass, whistling Italian air. For a moment, Ward thought the window would hold, then it crumbled like children's blocks and was sucked out into the landscape.

"Trust me," he said, dropping the gun to the floor by his foot.

MacKenzie looked from the gaping window to him, her

hair twisting wildly in the wind. She let go of his hand, putting hers together under her chin. The train reached the apex of the turn. She held his gaze for less than a second. Then she was gone, leaping into the air without a word.

Ward followed.

PART THREE

THE BELIEVER

That bull was slain; his reeking hide
They stretched the cataract beside,
Whose waters their wild tumult toss
Adown the black and craggy boss

"The Lady of the Lake," by Sir Walter Scott, 1810

Let me be clear: neither the Vatican nor any other person or entity exerted influence over my decision to use our nuclear arsenal to end the war in the Middle East. I alone am the presiding, legal, and righteous president of this great nation.

Celeste Margulies, 44th President of the United States of America, September 1, 2012

You have spoken, America, and I have heard you. We, the New Republic Party, have heard you. No longer will policy be dictated by religious institutions whose doctrines deal only with an afterlife which science denies. No longer will laws be governed by books written thousands of years ago by superstitious authors. No longer will this office strive to achieve any goal but the one which matters most: We will reclaim America!

Samuel Washburn, 45th President of the United States of American, January 21, 2013

CHAPTER
TWENTY-EIGHT

Ward sat up in a haze of dust and confusion. Had they really just jumped off a train? He staggered to his feet, probing his chest and shoulders for damage. He was scraped and bruised but not hurt. His mother would have kissed him on the forehead and called it a miracle. That was her line. How had he not remember that before now? Whether it was him or Daniel. Whether it was falling down the stairs or wrecking their bicycles.

If only she'd left it at that. If only she'd drawn the line somewhere before prayer.

MacKenzie groaned. She sat, half-crumpled in the grass, mouth agape, just beyond the gravel which underlay the tracks.

"Holy shit," she said, the look on her face no less incredulous than Ward's feelings about what they'd just done.

She stood, wincing as she did, but appearing unharmed.

She rolled her shoulders and squinted after the train continuing through its curve in the distance. It was soon lost between the excavated cleft of green hills.

"They're coming back," she said.

It was an obvious truth needing no reply. If he hadn't already the conductor would soon be receiving an order to stop his locomotive faster than he would feel was safe, and throw it into reverse. They needed to move.

Ward's hand went to his jacket's hip pocket, but it was empty. MacKenzie had smashed his R1 in Paris. They were on their own, somewhere north of Rome without anything to guide them. Without Claude, left to die, who was the only one who knew where they were supposed to go in Bari, Ward felt defeated. MacKenzie glared at him. He put up his hand to ask for a moment. He closed his eyes and tried to recall any map of Italy he'd ever seen.

He calculated they might be somewhere around Orte or Otricoli, which meant there were people, roads, and cars nearby. They needed two out of the three. Easy enough…if he'd figured their location correctly.

Realizing MacKenzie had been watching him try to determine their location he offered her his pain pills. When she declined he took three and began the slow hike in the direction, he hoped, of civilization.

After cresting a second sparsely vegetated ridge, at about the time MacKenzie began giving him sideways glares that said she thought they were going to wrong way, the distant hum of a highway beckoned them forward. Over one last hill they found themselves outside the fence of a rest stop along the Autostrada, Italy's motorway.

It was an easy enough task to climb the chest-high fence and trek a few dozen yards to the parking area. Ward's Italian, a byproduct of studying Latin, wasn't as good as his French but it was enough to translate a few signs. They were, in fact, just outside Otricoli, maybe an hour outside of Rome.

"Guess we're borrowing a car," MacKenzie said.

"Guess so."

They walked the rows of the parking lot until MacKenzie stopped them next to an unlocked blue Fiat—*a gas-guzzler!*— at the back edge of the lot.

"They teach you how to hotwire cars in the REC, Agent Ward?" she asked.

He couldn't tell if she was playing at humor but he figured he could give it a shot. Agent Compano had, in fact, taught him how to start a car, but only computer controlled e-drives.

"Just plug your R1 in," Agent Compano had said, "and reset the user ID...Hey, are you paying attention, Ward?"

He hadn't been. His mind had drifted to something else but he'd said yes quick enough to convince her. She'd gone on with her instruction. He'd gone on not listening. Not that it mattered now. This car was older than him. He could try twisting a couple wires together under the dashboard, and hoping. It seemed to work in the movies.

With MacKenzie watching like a store clerk observing a potential shoplifter he climbed in the car and felt around under the dashboard. He found a few wires tucked underneath, but there wasn't enough slack in them for his fingers to grab hold.

"What's the problem, Professor?"

"I'm not sure I have the right—"

"Move over," MacKenzie said, shoving against his shoulder.

Ward slid away from the console and watched as MacKenzie ducked her head between his knees. Halfway under the dash she popped her head back up.

"Not a word," she said.

Ward's cheeks warmed as he tried to prevent a smile.

Back under the dash she went, yanking down a tangle of wires from below the steering wheel. She filtered through the wires like a surgeon working her way through a patient's arteries.

"There we go," she muttered.

The engine spit and sputtered but didn't fire. She kept at it. Ten seconds. Twenty. Finally, the car gurgled to life, belching the grotesque, unsteady discords of an internal combustion engine. Ward backed as far into the springy seat as he could while MacKenzie extricated herself from beneath the dash. He waited until she got settled in her seat, then piloted them out of the parking lot.

"Do you know which way to go?" MacKenzie asked as they settled into the center lane of the motorway.

With the doors now closed the car smelled like wet dog and something else. It was sweet yet pungent. *Probably the gasoline,* Ward thought. He rolled down his window and breathed through his mouth. "Sort of. I mean, I can follow the signs well enough to get us to Bari, I think."

"We can't just go cruising around the countryside. They've got to be looking for us."

"I know," Ward said. He pushed harder on the accelerator, annoyed at the delay between his action and the car's. *Why,* he thought, *would anyone prefer this over the instantaneous response, not to mention the acceleration arc, of an e-cell?*

"Yeah. You know. So what do we do?"

Ward shifted them into the right lane, the slow lane, and checked the fuel gauge. Finally some luck. It was nearly full. He didn't know exactly what that might equate to in terms of miles but they couldn't risk stopping for gasoline. After some quick calculations in his head, figuring as best as he could gas mileage and distance, Ward believed they could make it.

"We can go northeast," he said. "They should be searching to the south, in Rome. Once we hit the sea we can shoot down the coast."

MacKenzie gave her approval by slumping into her seat and turning to the scenery passing outside her window.

Silence accompanied them for most of the next five hours, much of which was spent on the *Autostrada Adriatica* through jagged snow-capped peaks and stretches of flat, unobstructed sightlines to the sea.

In another life, Ward thought as the mountains seemed to move aside for the blue waters, *this is where I would want to live.* Sometime later an exhalation of awe from MacKenzie echoed this sentiment. There was something in the way she *ahh-ed.* Maybe it was something in the way she carried herself in general. He didn't just need her to trust him for the sake of his brother. He wanted her to.

She already has enough reasons to doubt you.

He ignored the warning and said, "They have my brother."

The words came out loud and awkward. He'd hoped saying it would somehow lessen the pain of it. Or at least the confusion of what to do. It did neither.

"What?" MacKenzie said as if she hadn't been listening. Then she added, "Who?"

"The REC. They assigned me to follow you. They didn't even tell me what for. They just said that if I did my job they'd release him."

"They," MacKenzie said. "Your ex-girlfriend?"

"Yes."

"And you want me to believe that you didn't even know about the Vase?"

"Yes."

"Bullshit."

"I didn't even know what you were going to hand me in that basement."

MacKenzie watched him drive the car for a long minute. He kept his eyes on the road but could feel her scrutiny.

"Will you give it to them?"

It was a test. Not the answer he gave. The way he gave it.

"They're never going to let him go."

It hurt to say it but he knew it was the truth. They already had the Vase. The best he could do was offer the lid. The best he could hope for was to get the Vase and Daniel in the same place. Maybe in the chaos of whatever happened next they could get away.

It was a long shot. One likely to end in the death of both Ward boys.

MacKenzie kept watching him drive. She didn't answer.

Neither spoke until they passed a sign which, even to someone who didn't speak Italian, made it clear they were nearing Bari.

MacKenzie watched the sign disappear in her mirror.

"Well," she said. "Now what?"

Ward took the first exit. "What was it your dad and Claude kept saying? Providence, right? Keep an eye out for Providence."

He wasn't sure if he'd meant it as a joke but MacKenzie's sideways glance and slight curl of her lip demonstrated at least partial amusement.

A light on the car's dash pinged on. Low fuel.

MacKenzie leaned across the car to see what the sound had indicated. Upon noting the fuel light she shook her head and turned back to her window.

Ward thought, maybe, she was grinning.

The exit wound them into an industrial quarter. It reminded Ward of North Philly. There were hints of a former populated city neighborhood, but it was mostly smogged brick, broken windows, and an acrid stench that made Ward roll up the window in favor of the still-present wet dog odor.

"Is this the whole city?"

"I don't think so," Ward said. "The old city should be along the coast. That's got to be where we're supposed to go. What was the priest's name?"

"Adrien."

Ward repeated it. He recognized the name as a Latin word, likely with its origins combing roots meaning black water. He wondered, without any cause to, if it was a taken or a regnal name, the way popes adopted new names when there had been popes.

Turn here.

Ward jerked his head to a sign he'd almost missed: *Museo Nicolaino.* The Nicholas Museum? Ward followed the sign's arrow. A few blocks later they entered what appeared to be a university quarter. Just past this was a residential neighborhood, a conglomerate of homes and churches, stuccoed and terraced, covering three or more centuries of architecture. It was as if the landscape had been painted in lemons, gingers, and carrots.

They parked midway along a block of not-quite-ancient row homes. A sign one space ahead of them said they were half a kilometer from the docks. Ward got out and stretched. As MacKenzie exited she too reached her arms to the sky, then rolled her hips and touched her toes.

Ward looked up and down the street, guessing at the best route.

"Which way's Providence?" MacKenzie said. She ran a hand through her hair and swaggered off down the street.

Ward hopped into a jog to catch up. He tapped her shoulder and directed them around a corner, figuring they should be heading towards the docks. He had no good, clear reason for this other than a habit from his childhood. When building a puzzle start with the corners and borders. The docks were Bari's border.

She agreed to the change in direction without a word, continuing for a few minutes before speaking. "So, who was that asshole on the train?"

"Ken Hickey," Ward said. "We share—shared—an office at the university. Apparently they recruited him to spy on me.

He's not a real Agent either. He nearly pissed himself when I pointed a gun at him. But I guess Gaustad needed someone close to make sure I was…I don't know, loyal or something."

"Are you?" MacKenzie said.

It wasn't really a question, more of a snarky jab. Ward didn't answer.

After a moment he said, "Do you really believe we have to destroy the Vase to prevent some kind of…whatever?"

Now it was MacKenzie's turn not to answer for a few seconds. Eventually she asked, "So who's Gaustad?"

They rounded another corner, and the street opened up into Bari's old city. Many of the buildings, short and spartan, were of marble. Even the street itself changed, going from dark macadam to a pearly limestone. The view made Ward think of some old twentieth century film he'd seen bits of, the way it depicted Heaven as built of shimmering white stone.

MacKenzie exhaled. "Whoa."

"I don't know about Providence," Ward said. "But I'm willing to give this place a go."

"Absolutely."

They crossed the street, rotating their heads this way and that. *Total tourists,* Ward thought. After a moment MacKenzie prompted him again about Gaustad. He knew she wasn't going to like what he had to say, and for a moment he considered not answering. But he'd only just begun to earn her trust. If he withheld more information now he might never get her back.

"Commandant William Gaustad of the Atlantic District REC. My boss."

MacKenzie stopped walking. "Oh," she said.

It was a simple syllable but Ward knew what it meant was, "I had no idea it was that serious. This isn't just smuggling artifacts and being chased by some Agents. This is the Republic coming after us."

"There's more," Ward said, needing to get it all out there before she panicked or attacked him. Before he lost his nerve. "I don't know how he got it—maybe Agents confiscated it from your father's traitor—but Gaustad has the Vase."

"What?" she said like someone who'd just been told the monster under the bed was real. "Why didn't you say so?"

Ward inhaled. They were close enough to the sea to taste its salt in the air. "I didn't even realize it," he said. "Not until Hickey said something on the train. Then I remembered." His fingertips came together. "I could feel the power in it."

"Wait. You touched it?"

"It was just a vase. A decoration in his office. He had all kinds of shit he shouldn't have had. I was on my way out, but instead of walking around it I touched it. I…had to."

"Had to?"

"Yes. No. I…maybe. It was weird." The memory was like trying to capture a ray of light as it reflected off the waves in the bay.

Ward got them moving again.

"And he said they'd release your brother if you got them the last piece of the Vase?"

It was close enough to the truth that Ward nodded. They walked shoulder to shoulder to the end of the block without saying anything else, MacKenzie throwing occasional wrinkled-brow glances his way. At the corner she stopped them.

"Let's get some food," she said. "I'm too hungry to process all this."

Ward's stomach growled in agreement. Across the intersection waited a café, a blinking red neon sign in its window advertising *panini*. He was about to suggest they try it when MacKenzie grabbed his forearm.

Her eyes directed his attention to two men half a block ahead on the other side of the street, locals in sport coats talking casually over a Port. Ward raised an eyebrow, confused. MacKenzie kept them walking, slowing their pace just a bit, and motioning again with her eyes.

A woman in black sat on a front stoop. Two men in suits stood together at the corner. An old man walked a curly-haired dog on a leash. He looked familiar. Jeremy? No, that was crazy. Wasn't it?

MacKenzie's squeezed Ward's arm. His eyes, as if directed by her, focused on the two men in suits. The taller of the men looked up from the Port, glanced down the block in their direction, made eye contact with his friend, and looked back to the device. A three second beat passed. The shorter one looked up, to his partner, and back down.

Surveillance.

But who? Agents? Cops?

Ward nearly stopped walking. MacKenzie tugged his arm. He grit his teeth, angry, more so embarrassed, that he'd missed it. They would pass these two men in a couple dozen steps, then likely be passed off to another pair a few blocks down. How many teams were there? How long has they been tailed?

MacKenzie pulled Ward close so she could whisper into his ear. "Meet me back at the car."

Before he could respond she bolted across the street.

CHAPTER
TWENTY-NINE

Ward didn't have to look to know one of the men was in pursuit of MacKenzie.

He spun. The other man—the taller one—was there at the opposite curb. With a military glide the man approached, his hand over his heart for quick access to the weapon in his jacket.

Ward slowed his breathing. *I should be in a library,* he thought. Books. Everything was so much easier in books. But that single lament was all he had time for. Clenching his fists, Ward rushed forward. The man in the black suit halted in mid-step, his balance thrown off by the move. A quick juke got Ward around him. He ran full-out down the block, five deep breaths getting him to the corner. He threw another feint as if crossing the intersection to the right, before angling left. He hoped he'd bought the distance he would need. He slipped around a man walking a cat-sized dog, and a stooped old woman carrying a brown grocery bag. Then the sidewalk was clear for a block.

Nearing an alley, Ward looked over his shoulder. The old man walking the dog suddenly lunged to his left forcing Ward's pursuer to cut hard to avoid a collision. It was just enough to give Ward the lead he needed. But the old man with the little dog – he looked familiar.

The old man winked.

Ward nearly ran into a brick corner, managing to cut hard at the last second into the alley and throw himself against the wall. Had that old man just winked at him? Was he the same old man as at The Barrel? What was his name? But the name was, once more, lost to him.

Forget it, Ward told himself. Focus on the man in the suit. He counted the breaths. Two. Three. He heaved himself off the wall and to the left, leading with his shoulder. He caught the man in the chest as he rounded the corner, both of them tumbling to the pavement.

The man rolled onto his stomach, wheezing. Ward shook off the collision, sprung to his feet and kicked the man in the ribs. The wheezing became a desperate, hollow gasp. Ward pulled the man deeper into the alley.

Too easy, he thought. This was no Agent. One more kick rendered the man unconscious. An uncontested search revealed just over sixty Euro, an Italian model Port, an Austrian pistol, and a badge identifying the man as *Carabinieri*—Italian military police.

"Shit," Ward mumbled. As if killing Agents wasn't enough.

They weren't going to be safe anywhere in Italy now. Maybe not anywhere in Europe.

He took the officer's cash, gun, and Port, a sleek model that was significantly lighter even than an R1. After a look up and down the alley revealed no one taking an interest in the confrontation, he dragged the cop as close to the wall as he could.

A deep breath and a flexing of his ankle were all Ward allowed for recovery. He had to find MacKenzie. He stood and strolled back out onto the street, stopping beside a pizza vendor to access the cop's Port. The first screen showed photos of Ward and MacKenzie, with generic instructions to be on alert for the American *terroristi* who'd escaped from a train near Rome.

"Shit," he whispered again.

A tourist, a slight Asian man in bright yellow, purchased a number of pizza rolls from the vendor on behalf of his plump children waiting in the shade across the street. Ward's stomach complained. He thought about buying two pizza rolls. He could arrive at the car a hero. But a police car crossing through the intersection nullified the idea. Taking a last glance at the pizza, Ward bowed his head into the officer's Port like a tourist and walked on. Taking a circuitous route back to their little Fiat, he searched the Port for a record of a priest, a church, a parish, anything with the name Adrien. He found nothing.

A couple blocks from where they'd parked he dropped the officer's Port into a trash bin. Stay unplugged. He had no doubt that when the time came Commandant Gaustad and his Agents would find them.

He doubled back on his route twice before finally hedging onto the street where they'd parked. MacKenzie was there, across the street and four car-lengths down, perched on an apartment's front stoop. Her hood covered her face, giving her the appearance of a homeless person.

Ward didn't approach. Instead, he whistled, waited until she lifted her head, then crossed the street, passing her without pause as she stood. Deliberately he led her over three blocks and two turns before the streets opened up into the docks. The ocean gleamed as blue as Ward had ever seen.

With MacKenzie keeping enough distance they wouldn't appear to be together, Ward guided them onto Via Venezia, feeling somehow he was going to the right way. The street ran along the sea, its eastern edge an old balustrade which would have once served as a defensive fortification against attack from the sea.

The smell of the Mediterranean, something between a chowder and a warm bath, made Ward's stomach feel hollow. He stopped at the midpoint of the block. MacKenzie joined him a half minute later.

"You get away okay?"

"No problem," she said. "He'll wake up confused and embarrassed in a dumpster."

Ward imagined her catching the cop by surprise in much the same way he'd taken care of his pursuer. But in the fantasy her takedown was graceful and elegant, almost a dance. He withheld a grin and leaned his forearms on the warm stone stockade. After a moment she took up a similar position.

"They were police," Ward said. "Our photos are all over

the country. We're terrorists. But it doesn't look like those two had reported us yet."

"Great," MacKenzie said, stretching the word's vowels. "Should be easy to find this Adrien with the cops after us."

"I tried searching the cop's Port, but I got nothing. You find anything useful on your guy after you dropped him in the dumpster?"

"No," she said through a smile.

Ward felt his own cheeks rise into a smile. "A dumpster?" he breathed a laugh.

MacKenzie straightened up and pulled back her hood. Her eyes had the same flecked proportions of blue as the Adriatic had of green.

"It was there." Another shrug, and within a breath they were both laughing.

The mirth ran its course quickly, but left a lightness in its wake that had been missing since they'd first arrived in Europe.

Ward turned around, leaning his back against the wall. Though he knew they should move, should get out of sight, he didn't want to. Wouldn't it be nice to just relax for an hour and take a walk together through the streets or along the coast?

No time, his conscience prodded.

He snorted.

"Huh?"

"Nothing," he said. He rotated back to the water. He spoke before thinking. "Hannah, I really am sorry about your dad."

She didn't respond for some time, giving the sun an opportunity to grow hot on Ward's face.

When she spoke her voice was hushed, but even. "Is it

weird to miss a man so much when I didn't even know him? I can't remember him from before. He's just a…a ghost. A silhouette in a painting that a voice in my head says was my childhood."

Ward knew that type of painting well. "It's not weird," he said.

At length, she said, "Do you still miss your mother?"

Ward swallowed. He opened his mouth but decided instead to nod an affirmative.

"You said you haven't spoken to her. Where is she?"

Tell her this too and she will never trust you.

Ward took a long breath. "She was arrested. She…" He looked up. The sky was pale and empty. "At the funeral for my father and my brother. I was eleven. Afterwards, she prayed."

"My God."

Do not tell her.

The lines of the waves before him blurred. "It was me."

"What was you?"

Her voice sounded far away. He wondered if she could handle a third confession in less than hour. Daniel. Gaustad. Now Mom. He wondered if he could handle it.

"I called the hotline. I turned her in."

"Rafe," she said, but whatever words came next were lost to a pounding in Ward's head.

His hand made its way to his pocket. He pulled out his mother's necklace. The silver was warm. He wanted to wear it around his neck. He wanted to throw it into the ocean. He wanted to put his hands on either side of MacKenzie's face and kiss her.

Instead, he remembered. He'd still been at the orphanage—before the foster homes—when the breakfast lady, an impossibly thin and impossibly tall woman with a cleft lip, had brought him the only piece of directly addressed mail he would receive until he was an adult.

"Mr. Ward," it began, a bland salutation leading a couple lines of impersonal type he had never forgotten, "Your mother has made amends with the Republic. You may collect her remains within twenty days, after which they will be disposed. Please bring your own 72 ounce vessel."

He couldn't remember if the letter had been signed. Or if Mom had received similar letters for Daniel and Dad.

Ward faced the horizon, letting the memory be drawn out by the sea. He'd never seen such a seamless edge of blues. For a moment, the tiniest sliver of a second, the water appeared as glass, the wind held its breath, and the noise of the world fled. Ward felt as if all the choices of his life had led him to this place. He inhaled. From somewhere the scent of cookies brought him back to the present.

He shoved the necklace into his pocket and turned to examine the city. How were they going to find one old priest, if he was even still alive, in a city on alert for them?

He scanned the shops and restaurants on the other side of the street. The sun glistened off the pointed tower of a church barely reaching over the row of buildings. Maybe they should get some food. They'd think better on a full stomach.

"Rafe," MacKenzie said.

Ward didn't respond. There was something about the church tower. He knew it. He was sure. But from where?

"…some lunch, then figure out what to do."

Ward barely heard this last part. He did know that tower. He darted across the street calling for her to follow. He ran up the block and around the corner until he was standing before a Romanesque, almost fortress-like, church he'd most certainly seen before.

MacKenzie caught up just as Ward pulled from his jacket the photo of the young girl and her father in front of the church. He held it out to her.

She snatched it, her left hand going to her mouth. "Oh my God," she said through her fingers, tears filling her eyes.

"He gave it to me," he said, hoping his smile might keep her from crying.

She turned her back, her shoulders trembling. Ward thought of his mother. He imagined someone handing him a photo of her and little Raffi. His throat swelled.

MacKenzie faced him. "Thank you," she whispered, wiping a hand across her eyes.

Ward found he had no smile this time. Instead he bobbed his head in the direction of the church. She stared, face wrinkled in confusion. Her head tilted to the side. She looked from the church to the photo and back. They were the same. Something between joy and frenzy broke across her face. She kissed Ward on the cheek and, with a bounce he'd not before seen, she dashed into the church.

CHAPTER
THIRTY

The boxy church couldn't compare to the cathedrals of Paris. It featured no rose window. No stained glass. No domes or flying buttresses. It was a castle of impassive whitewashed stone, an aesthetically immobile blockade unconcerned with tourists' opinions. Inside, however, its simple symmetrical layout was lusciously ornamented. It boasted scrolling reliefs, masterful columns, three dominating arches, and a gilded ceiling which held Ward and MacKenzie in mid-step, delaying further access until they'd gaped at the artistry looming above.

When Ward finally dragged his gaze back to ground level he found the church surprisingly deserted, save for a bespectacled teenage girl sitting in an information booth to the left of the entry. He made his way to the booth while MacKenzie shuffled into the nave, her eyes still drawn skyward.

The sign posted above the information booth welcomed them into the Basilica of Saint Nicholas. Ward paged through textbooks and documents and downloads in his mind trying to recall the history of the Basilica. He remembered a news column in one of the university's archives about a plot to steal the treasured relics housed within, the bones of Saint Nicholas the Wonderworker. It was from a European outlet, maybe London's *The Guardian*. Not the kind of article usually accessible in the Republic. However the digital imprint of the column got there, it detailed the failure of the attempt. One of the thieves had been captured, a woman. But she'd committed suicide somehow—Ward couldn't remember the details—before she could be questioned.

Ward wondered if it had really been an REC operation. As Simon indicated, Command had been active in Europe for a number of years. An image of Agent Compano, haughty and confident, defying the Italian police, came to Ward's mind. It was quickly followed by the memory of her crawling across the train car. The look on what was left of her face was a mix of terror and disbelief. She'd stared right at him with her one eye, but what he remembered now was her chin—just bone, streaked and singed, protruding like a shard of marble after a church demolition. He shuddered and refocused his mind on the present.

He scanned the nave and the transepts, finding no parishioners or tourists. No priests. No offices or labeled doors. He couldn't even find MacKenzie, who must have disappeared behind a column or down the transept in her search for the priest, Adrien. Ward cleared his throat. The black-haired girl in the booth, lost in her Port, didn't look up. Ward slapped his hand on the counter.

"*Mi scusi. Como faccio,* um, *trovare Adrien?*"

The girl glared overtop her glasses.

He knew he'd stumbled through the Italian a bit, but he didn't think it was that bad.

A phone rang. The girl, without apology, turned her back.

"*Pronto?*" she said into the receiver as if insulted by the intruding caller.

Ward peered into the nave, still unable to locate MacKenzie. He hoped she was having better a better go of it, but the church was barren even of the sounds of footfalls.

The girl, her back still to Ward, hung up the phone and twirled her finger through her hair.

"*Mi scusi,*" he said, certain his impatience would find its way through the language barrier.

The girl rotated her head a bit. It wasn't enough to make eye contact, just enough to make it known that she would turn all the way around when she was good and ready.

"Fuck this," Ward muttered and went in search of MacKenzie.

He found her at the far end of the nave, before the *cathedra*—the bishop's throne. This particular specimen appeared to be nearly a millennium old. Made of white marble, and with a golden cushion, the seat of the throne was held aloft by sculptures of Classical-styled men in the attitude of Atlas holding the heavens on his shoulders. The step-base of the throne rested on two kneeling lions. It was an impressive piece, one Ward wished he had time to study.

"He's not here," MacKenzie said. "There are a few doors but they're all locked."

Ward didn't like it. Had he made a mistake? Had there been more to the plan that Simon and Claude never got to share? The impetus to quit welled in his intestines.

"Are you sure, I mean really sure this is the right place? I know—the photo and everything but," MacKenzie tilted her head back. "I don't even know where we are."

"The Basilica of Saint Nicholas," Ward said, his mouth dry.

"Saint Nicholas," she whispered.

"Saint Nick," he offered.

"Santa Claus? The fat guy with the beard?"

"You remember who he was? Not many people do."

"Sort of. Wait," she said, looking first to the arches, then to the pews.

"I don't know," Ward said. "Maybe I got it wrong. Maybe this guy's already dead." He wasn't really talking to her. And she wasn't listening. *We should go,* he thought. *If she won't, maybe I should. Maybe if I leave her here, she won't end up dead like everyone else I've cared about.*

"I think I've been here before," MacKenzie said, looking at the throne, not at him.

"Obviously. The photo shows…"

She shook her head. "No, I mean I remember. There was a party. Singing. Dancing. Someone in a big red suit came down from the ceiling on ropes, or something. Dad was here. We…" She darted into the nave, stopping beside a pew halfway back to the entrance. "We sat right here. Dad and someone else."

Ward followed, his resolve returning. "Sounds like a

Christmas celebration."

MacKenzie snapped her fingers. "God, yes. Christmas. Food. Tons of it. And singing. Quiet—no, 'Silent Night.'"

Ward felt a grin tweak his lips. "And presents," he said, though she didn't seem to hear. He wondered how many Citizens could imagine, let alone remember, Christmas. Ward had only ever read about it in books. Real books, not downloads or text threads. He watched MacKenzie replaying the moment. In her mind it was as real as the marble beneath their feet.

Suddenly, without wanting to think it or to feel it, Ward knew he couldn't abandon Hannah MacKenzie. Maybe it was seeing her have to watch her father die. Maybe it seeing her have the opportunity he never did—the chance to say goodbye. Maybe it was simply her. Whatever the impetus, he knew he couldn't sacrifice her to save his brother. Wherever she needed him to go, he'd go. He'd find a way to help Daniel, but not at her expense. And maybe, if he proved himself...

Enough, the voice in Ward's mind declared.

It was right. They weren't out of danger. They seemed to be in the wrong place. Or at least to be here at the wrong time. But with all the riddles and the misdirection, maybe...

"You said you remember your father and a friend," Ward said. "Who?"

"I don't know. He could have been a priest." She combed her fingers through her hair. "It could have been this Adrien, I guess, but he was really old. Like, ancient. He would have to be dead by now. It was more than twenty years ago."

She froze, the last syllable of a word Ward hadn't heard

her begin was stuck in her throat. She peered back towards the *cathedra*. Ward followed her gaze.

"Did you see that?"

Ward saw nothing.

"I swear I just saw—"

The sound of a door slapping shut spun them both to the right. At the far end of the nave waited a double set of brown doors. Locked, MacKenzie had said. But Ward had a feeling they no longer were.

They crossed the church. Ward placed his hand on the cold, wrought-iron handle of the right door and pulled. There was no resistance, only the creaking of wood and the grating of iron hinges. Dank, musty air greeted them, calling them forward to a staircase leading down into darkness.

"Crypts," MacKenzie said.

There was no need to confirm. They descended, passing a sarcophagus on the landing halfway down. In other circumstances it would have borne a thorough investigation. Today, however, Ward wasn't interested in the lying dead. Only the talking living.

At the base of the stairs the crypt lingered. Like the Pantheon, however, this was no ghoulish cemetery. Rather a patterned floor of pink marble titles contrasted with the series of alabaster Byzantine and Norman pillars and vaults which dominated the room. The arches and their supports were alive with masterfully carved flora and beast from every corner of the Medieval world. A perfect place to play hide and seek.

They moved into the room as if drawn by the large iron gate barricading the right side of the apse. Beyond the gate reposed a marble tomb designed more like an altar than a memorial. Saint Nicholas's sepulcher. Somewhere beneath that tomb rested the saint's bones. Behind the altar hung a likeness of Nicholas. It was a beautiful piece done in the Eastern Orthodox style. And it was a fake. Ward knew from his familiarity with the REC archives that the original icon, a fourteenth century masterpiece, had been appropriated during the first of the two failed operations to collect the saint's remains.

The rest of the crypt was empty save for eight pews set in pairs through the center of the room, and two confessional booths in the back corners.

"There," MacKenzie said, pointing to a pillar at the far end of the room.

Ward, again, didn't see it, but sprang after her as she weaved through the columns. He arrived at the far corner of the crypt a breath after her. They were alone.

"I saw it," MacKenzie said. "I fucking saw it. A blur, like someone hiding behind the pillar. It was right here."

Ward placed his palms on the column, his love of pulp fiction giving him a course of action. He pushed. He tapped. He knocked. Nothing. No hidden switches revealed themselves. No secret doors opened.

MacKenzie looked at him like he'd just happily placed his head into a lion's mouth.

"What?" was all he had to offer, not wanting to explain that in plenty of obsolete novels, the solution was just that easy.

She shook her head. "Well, I'm not going to go smacking and licking ever pillar down here."

"Licking? Really?"

"Focus, Rafe," she said, barely containing a laugh.

He held a breath of the crypt's damp air in his lungs. Focus. Sure. On what? He exhaled, spinning in a slow circle as he did, taking in the whole of the room. Columns. Arches. The gate. Pews. Confessionals. There were no exits other than the stairs they'd come down. Had whoever MacKenzie seen drawn them this deep into the crypt only to double back to the stairs? What sense would that make?

It's a trap. The thought came so suddenly Ward felt his body jolt.

"What?"

"Nothing," Ward said.

A sound, a muffled tap like someone knocking on a door a few rooms away, came from behind them. MacKenzie tensed. Ward's hand went to the pistol in his belt.

"You heard that, right?" he said.

The sound repeated. He charged, breaking free of the columns to face the confessional in the opposite corner.

For half a second he considered that perhaps the crypt wasn't a trap; perhaps it was haunted. The thought dissipated as MacKenzie crept up behind him, placing her hand on the small of his back.

There came a single thump, closer this time. Ward and MacKenzie exchanged looks. There was no place the sound could be coming from except through the wall or...

MacKenzie stepped around, planting her feet before the curtained half of the confessional. She produced from beneath her sweater a compact pistol identical to the one in Ward's hand, the one he'd taken from the *Carabinieri* officer in the alley. She waited half a heartbeat then yanked the curtain aside.

It was empty. No seat. No back wall. No anything. The back of the confessional was a void into the foundation wall of the crypt. Ward retrieved his flashlight from his pocket and shined it in. Four feet back, stairs led down into more darkness. With pistol and flashlight locked chin-high he began the descent, MacKenzie a step behind.

Carved from the earth itself, not lain with marble or other finished stone, the stairwell tunnel was narrow with a low hanging ceiling forcing even MacKenzie to crouch. A dozen steps down a landing turned them back in the direction of the crypt. Ward couldn't help thinking about the basement where he'd met MacKenzie just a few days ago. The basement where he'd had to crawl over blood and a severed hand.

MacKenzie tapped him on the shoulder. He hadn't realized he'd stopped walking. He squeezed the knurled grip of the pistol, that familiar feeling slowing his pulse. He nodded and continued down the steps without a word.

By the time they touched down Ward figured they were eight or ten feet within the church's circumference and maybe thirty feet below the crypt's marble floor. The tunneled stairwell opened into a chamber that must have been at least as large as the crypt above, though the ceiling and walls loomed too deep in the darkness to find. Ward's flashlight struggled to reveal more than a few feet of the emptiness that surrounded them. It was disorienting. Ward had to fight the need to reach out for MacKenzie's arm or shoulder for support.

A lantern blazed on chest high at the edge of their vision.

The suddenness of the light cast everything behind it deeper into the void, masking the person holding it but its amber glow offered a chilling vision of their location.

They stood on bare earth, the kind of grayed silt you might find in a dirt floor basement. Ward recognized it as likely being ground level prior to the construction of the basilica above in the eleventh century. Maybe even dating to pre-imperial Rome.

A number of knee-high stones littered the ground, the lantern casting their shadows like fingers reaching for the intruders. The stones didn't appear to have any common source or style, though they were clearly, if roughly, hewn and carefully placed at near-equal intervals. If there were more beyond the lantern Ward couldn't see them, but it was plain that this chamber's purpose was to house these markers.

"Tombstones," MacKenzie said. Her eyes gleamed metallic.

She was correct, Ward knew, despite not being able to see the faces of any of the memorials for the shadows cast by the lantern. This was the true necropolis of the Basilica. Perhaps even the actual resting place of Saint Nicholas' remains. On the heels of that thought came another: *Who else might be buried in this hidden graveyard? Who could be more important than Saint Nick that his or her tomb need be so concealed?*

"Come, children," a voice said from the gloom behind the lantern.

CHAPTER
THIRTY-ONE

Their path through the tombstones set them on a gentle upward slope toward the lantern. Each step brought a little more of this memorial or that one into focus. A hand-carved convex stone. A moss covered one. A chiseled epitaph long illegible. A cracked slab.

Near the crown of the hill the darkness divulged an apparitional hand holding the railroad style oil lamp. The darkness behind the hand shimmered revealing a shadow within the void. No, Ward realized, not a shadow. The black robes…of a priest? Without the white clerical collar the outfit wouldn't be patently illegal in the Republic but it would be daring the REC to notice.

Here in Italy who knew what was acceptable?

"I am pleased you both have come."

The voice was grainy, accented with a mixture of Italian,

French, and something else Ward couldn't recognize. He squinted past the glare and found a withered face, its lines and wrinkles swirling around eyes masquerading as sunken pits.

The old man lowered the lantern, illuminating more of the hill on which they stood. To his right a pillar stretched up into the darkness, certainly a foundation tower for the church above. It might once have been pallid marble or limestone but was now crusted with ancient grime and guano, its fluting long eroded smooth.

To the man's left was a single tombstone, partially obscured by shadow. Still, Ward could see its face was smooth. Its corners sharp. It had the appearance of a well-cared-for memorial.

"Dear Hannah," the priest said. It was barely more than a ragged whisper. "It has been a long time. I offer my sympathies, heartfelt, for the loss of your father."

"Thank you," MacKenzie mumbled.

He shouldn't know about Simon's death, Ward thought. There was nothing in the *Carabinieri's* Port about murder or a dead Frenchman. If the cops didn't know how could an old priest in this dungeon more than a thousand miles away?

As if reading Ward's thoughts, the old man said, "I am aware of everything that has happened with my *conservateurs,* Professor. I am Adrien."

"Prove it."

"The proof is beside me," the priest said, passing the lantern across the tombstone to his left. The face of the tombstone sparkled for the briefest of moments, just enough for Ward to read the name engraved on the marker.

"Adrien Quinque," it read.

Ward rolled the name over and over in his mind. The first name the same as the priest. Okay, fine, coincidences happen. But the full name...He knew it. He knew he knew it. But from where?

"Professor," the old man said, "just as shopkeepers were prepared to lend you their cars, and museum employees risked their lives to shelter you, there is a system in place for communication between Paris and this old priest. I wept for Simon in the same hour as you."

"Sure," Ward said, still confused by the name on the tombstone. How did it prove anything? Was it the priest's ancestor? Father? Who the fuck was Adrien Quinque and why was his tomb atop the hill in a place of honor?

"What do we do next?" MacKenzie said. "Claude and my father, they didn't tell us anything more than we had to come to you. Do you have the lid?"

Adrien said something about peering beneath the surface. Ward didn't catch all of the priest's gravelly words. The engraved name kept pushing its way to the fore of his thoughts.

"When the professor is ready to pay attention..."

"What?" The name fled.

"Jesus, Rafe." MacKenzie said.

"Sorry. I—never mind. Go on."

Adrien placed the lantern on the ground. The new angle cast their faces in shadows, making them specters in this city of the dead.

"The final piece of the Vase waits where it has for almost

four centuries. It waits for you. Others have heeded their callings. The path is set. Answers await you in the depths."

Adrien held the final sibilant syllable, letting it morph into a whistling tune. He turned his back with a flourish, the darkness swallowing his robes. In seconds all that was left of the old man were a few fading, footsteps and a whistled aria that could have been a birdsong. Then he was gone.

MacKenzie's jaw hung open with whatever question she'd wanted to ask the priest. Ward didn't bother trying to stop him or to answer her. He'd already gone back to the name. In the silence it came to him. Adrien Quinque, the deaf, mute mason who discovered Childeric's tomb and treasures in the seventeenth century. The tomb of Clovis' father. It was Adrien Quinque who'd unearthed those exquisite golden bees on display in Commandant Gaustad's office. It was his name Ward couldn't remember in class just a few days ago.

But it didn't track. How was Adrien Quinque's tombstone proof of the priest's identity?

An idea came to Ward that he didn't like. He didn't want it, nor did he believe it, but it was all they had. It led to the only next logical step.

"Fine," Ward said, as if in response to some unspoken command.

"Fine what? What just happened? We're stuck in a damn graveyard, underground, with nothing but another riddle to solve."

Ward picked up the lantern and cast it about. They were alone on the hilltop, a perfect triangle—them, the pillar, and the tombstone.

The light flickered on something metallic behind the tombstone.

"It's not a riddle," he said, accepting what needed to be done, though still refusing to believe why. "If you were Remigius and you had to hide a piece of the Vase from everyone who would come searching for it after Clovis' death, where would you put it?" He didn't wait for an answer. "You couldn't put it anywhere his sons would look, or anywhere their sons, or anyone else, would look for a piece of Clovis' legacy. No, you'd put it somewhere completely illogical. Somewhere no one with a hint of intelligence would consider."

MacKenzie's arms splayed open, her face declaring her impatience.

"In the already completed tomb of Clovis' father, Childeric."

"Great. Another damn dead guy."

"You're missing it. Even if someone had discovered Childeric's tomb, the lid would be nothing. A piece of pottery. No one would connect it to the Vase which Clovis himself didn't lay eyes on until years after his father's death."

"If there's a part of this story that says how we don't have to go running around Europe digging up graves I'd like to hear it."

"Well," Ward said, "we don't have to go running around Europe."

"Jesus, Rafe. Grave robbing? I wasn't serious."

"The good news," Ward said, finding an irrational pleasure in the way MacKenzie's eyes menaced, "is Childeric's tomb was found four hundred years ago."

"So, some other dead guy has the lid now. How is this better?"

Ward held the lantern to the tombstone once more. "I know where he is."

The light gave a full view of the almost waist-high headstone. Its marble was still pink with the glazed sheen of an oft-polished memorial. The Latin block letters of the occupant's name were etched a half inch deep. There was no epitaph, no dates, just a single glyph in the lower left corner, perhaps a crucifix or a dragonfly.

He let her squint at the memorial a moment.

"Another Adrien?" she asked.

Ward shrugged and rotated the light to show what he'd seen behind the tombstone. Two wood-handled shovels.

"Looks like he left us to do the dirty work."

"You're joking."

"Nope. We're digging."

"When we're done," MacKenzie said, picking up a shovel, "the lid is going in a safe deposit box. Somewhere secured. Switzerland or something. Simple. Easy. Just a key."

"What about destroying the whole thing?" Ward knew she wasn't serious, but he couldn't help asking.

While she considered her answer, Ward took up the second shovel. He planted the point into the ground, resting his forearm on the upright handle. In a moment, MacKenzie sliced hers into the raspy earth and lifted a clod of dirt.

"Safe deposit box," she said, splashing soil across his knees.

———◆———

They dug for more than two hours, Ward at the head by

the tombstone and MacKenzie working the foot. The soggy squelches of their cuts and heaves released that pungent taste of mud and earthworms that sits so casually on the tongue and in the nose. Now four feet deep Ward marveled at his partner's stamina. After an hour he'd thought about suggesting a break but she'd been so intent he'd felt embarrassed to do anything but lower his head and fall to. Finally the knock of her shovel on wood announced their goal.

At first neither moved. They gawked at their shovels, then at each other, until the lull became almost absurd. MacKenzie rolled her shoulders then dropped to her knees, swiping at the dirt with her hands. Ward leaned his shovel on the earthen wall and joined her.

It became quickly, and expectantly, clear they were perched on the wood-plank top of a coffin. Though it must have been almost half a millennium old, the wood was in good shape, a grainy burgundy visible despite the loose soil and their shadows cast from the lantern on the lip of the grave above.

MacKenzie stood, stretching her knees and her back. Ward watched her arching body from his crouch while continuing to brush the dirt aside, his fingers seeking the edge of the coffin.

In mid-stretch, MacKenzie said, "Wait."

Ward's eyes dropped to the coffin, expecting to see the wrong name or some other disappointment. There was only the unadorned wood and piles of loose earth.

"There's a dead guy in there. Like, four hundred years dead," MacKenzie said, crouching in front of him.

Ward wasn't sure if she was addressing the potential of discovering a grotesque corpse inside the coffin or simply hesitant to disturb the grave of a man who'd been afforded a place of honor in this ancient, hallowed cemetery. But if what he thought the priest was implying was true there wouldn't be any body in the coffin.

Part of him hoped there was a very decayed corpse inside.

He reached out, intending to place his hand on her shoulder and allay her concern. The wood beneath their feet creaked. It was loud, far louder than should have come from the thin planks of a deteriorated Renaissance-era coffin. They froze, their faces demanding of each other absolute stillness.

A train of snaps, splinters, splits, and cracks echoed through the necropolis. It reminded Ward of Daniel and him climbing a tree at Core Creek Park when they were little, maybe seven and nine years old. The tree was a massive thing begging to be conquered by a brave soul. He'd refused to go higher than the first layer of branches. But Daniel was fearless. He kept going up and up until their mother's voice came screeching from the distance. At that same moment there'd come the sound of splitting wood.

Ward could still remember the silent, open-mouthed look of horror on Daniel's face as he fell.

When the ground beneath the coffin gave way MacKenzie's face held that same look all the way down.

CHAPTER
THIRTY-TWO

There was enough time to hope death wouldn't hurt before Ward crashed shoulder-first into a quagmire of sludge. The hungry mud pulled at his arm, his thigh, his foot. Was this death? Sucked into eternal mud?

With a suctioning pop he rolled onto his back. He imagined his hair soaking up the mud like tiny straws. He didn't care. He just wanted to catch his breath.

They were fortunate to have landed in mud. Another one of his mother's miracles. MacKenzie probably would have said it was a blessing or some other ridiculous Believer's platitude.

Thinking of her knotted his stomach. Where was she? Light filtered in an arc around him but didn't penetrate the darkness more than a couple feet ahead. He tried to stand, managing to get partially upright before losing his balance in the muck. He reached for anything, any support. His hand disappeared into a shimmering waterfall he hadn't realized was there. He went to his knees in a puddle of filth that smelled like wet dog shit.

It took a moment to extricate himself from the growing pond at the base of the waterfall. He tried to wipe the mud from his face but only added more. The tart, brackish water dripped from his eyelashes, his nose, his lips. Sea water. He didn't have time to decide if this was good or bad. He had to find MacKenzie but to the sides he could see only the earthen walls of the pit they'd fallen into. Only darkness ahead. His belly tightened further. Panic was close. A week ago he might have succumbed to it. But not now. Not after these past few days.

He slowed his breathing. He flexed his hands and concentrated on deep breaths. He would find her. First, however, he had to ascertain what had happened.

He started with the light. It shone from the lantern still situated on the edge of the grave maybe twenty feet above. They'd fallen through an oblong shaft, its sides nearly smooth save for occasional dangles of roots and small jutting beams. Nothing low enough or robust enough to offer a handhold for climbing out.

The puddle at the base of the waterfall was slowly becoming a pond. The water was entering the pit from a horizontal crevice a few feet above Ward's highest reach.

The only way out—the only direction to search for MacKenzie—was into the darkness. He slogged forward on all fours.

At the light's perimeter, he paused. *What if she's gone?*

What if she's dead?

"Rafe."

Ward nearly jumped. "MacKenzie! Are you okay?"

"I think so. I can't see. There's wood and splinters everywhere. I—oh God."

"What happened?" Ward scrambled forward, getting only a few feet before he had to stop. The darkness was absolute. He slogged forward, slower. His hand pressed onto a jagged piece of wood. A remnant of the coffin.

"The body. Where's the body?"

"Don't move."

Ward pushed his hands through the mud, oozing them left and right like a blind man. He scraped and cut his fingers on more splinters but found no bone or rotting flesh. Finally, he felt the smooth, cold leather of MacKenzie's shoe.

She bleated at his touch.

"It's me," he said.

"Don't fucking do that."

"I don't think there's a body."

"It couldn't have been empty."

It wasn't, Ward knew. There was a pit in his stomach, growing each time he thought about the priest and the name on the tombstone.

"Rafe, where's your—?"

"Flashlight," he finished, pulling it from his pocket. He had to keep it together. There'd be time to worry about the implications of the old man and the tombstone later, he hoped.

A deep, groan pulsated through the chamber. It sounded like the complaining pipes in an old house.

"What the hell was that?"

"Wait," Ward said. He switched on the flashlight.

MacKenzie lay amidst the wreckage of the coffin. She was muddy but not so much as him. The ground here was drier. Where he could feel the mud caking his hair and face hers was more streaked and splotched. Her hair still shone scarlet.

She tried to stand but winced when she moved her left leg, returning to the ground.

"I think I twisted my knee."

"It's okay. Just give me a minute to find a way out."

Ward rose to his knees and aimed the light over MacKenzie's head. He'd hoped they were in a catacomb or cave system, maybe even a primitive sewer shaft. But there was only another dingy wall at the far end of the chamber.

He refocused his attention on the shaft and the waterfall. The beams sticking out from the shaft looked like support struts, as if the grave had been carefully laid above this pit. Perhaps like a wolf trap to protect the burial from grave robbers.

Which meant there was something worth protecting even if there was no body.

"The Vase," Ward said, shining the light about their feet.

"What?"

There, half sunk in the mire to his right was a smooth surface glinting in the flashlight beam.

"Oh my God," MacKenzie said, crawling—more aptly clawing—forward, her left leg dragging.

Even hobbled she pushed past Ward before he could reach the object. She pulled it free and lifted it into the light.

Covered in dripping mud, the spool-shaped object was a third as tall as its dinner-plate diameter. It wasn't the shape he was expecting but it was consistent with pottery Ward had seen from centuries, even millennia, before Ancient Greece. Remnants of a pre-Hellenic civilization, which had served as the antecedent for much of the Mediterranean world. He remembered the carving on Adrien Quinque's tombstone. It was no dragonfly. And certainly no crucifix. More of the puzzle fell into place. The pit in Ward's gut deepened.

"Tell me this is it," MacKenzie said.

Ward took it from her, running his hands over its impossibly smooth surface. Though unadorned with painted figures or scrolling artwork, its outer edges were reeded like a coin. This was certainly it. The capstone for the Vase he'd encountered in Gaustad's office. The last of the pieces of the Vase of Soissons. An incredible episode of history alive in his hand.

The only word he had was, "Amazing."

MacKenzie snatched it back from him, the corner of her mouth bending upwards. "Now, get us out of here, Professor," she said, the earthenware chiming against the Spear as she slid it into her backpack.

Indeed, Ward thought. *Get us out. But how?*

He returned the light to the shaft, hoping to see a handhold he'd missed earlier. The darkness about the lantern moved. No, it was a shadow. Then another. A third. A fourth. The lantern went out. It was replaced by the sharp glare of a handheld searchlight.

"There he is," a voice sang from above.

For the second time today, Ward couldn't believe the voice he was hearing.

"What are you doing stuck down there, Rafe?"

"Hickey, you son of a bitch. I'm going to—"

"Now, now, buddy. There's no need for name calling. I'm here to help."

Before Ward could respond the walls groaned again, longer this time, followed by the sound of lumber cracking. The ground quivered.

Ward stepped back from the wall. As he did the shaft above the waterfall melted in slow motion, oozing and crumbling into the pit. What had been a stream became a river diving out of the darkness. The water rose over his shoelaces in seconds.

"Uh oh," Ken shouted. "Looks like it's getting dangerous down there. Tell you what, you sit tight and we'll lower a rope. Send us up that little piece of pottery you found and we'll get you out of there before you have to learn how to breathe underwater."

"Go fuck yourself."

Ward would have added more to the retort but hands grabbed the back of jacket and yanked him to his knees. He dropped the flashlight. It rolled away from them, casting eerie shadows about the pit.

"This way," MacKenzie said, crawling through the muck to the far end of the pit.

Leaving the flashlight behind, Ward followed, his knees slapping the rising water.

"Into the tunnel."

"What tunnel?"

She disappeared into the wall before them. Ward squinted. A fissure gaped in the wall, its emptiness nearly indistinguishable from the rest of the pit. Even when he'd shone the flashlight on the wall, he'd missed it.

"Rafe," Ken shouted.

Another section of the shaft collapsed. The water rose to his pockets. There was yelling above, indiscernible over the sound of the deluge.

The water around him erupted as a series of gunshots echoed and re-echoed in the necropolis.

Ward lunged into the darkness, his hands out to brace himself. There was no floor. Face first he tumbled down a steep slope. It was like a muddy water-slide. He covered his head as he sloshed this way and that, waiting for the end.

He splashed down into a pool, twisting against the water pounding above, trying to find a footing. He pushed to the surface. There was no light. There was no sound other than the continuous rush of churning water. There was no way to know how deep underground they were.

The undercurrent dragged him below. It took a moment but finally his feet found the bottom. He stood, the water was to his belt. He was sure it was rising.

"MacKenzie?"

"Yeah." She splashed to his right.

He followed the sound. A hand grabbed his bicep, then worked its way to his wrist below the water. Cold fingers interlaced with his.

The darkness rumbled. The ground pitched. He felt

MacKenzie drop beneath the water. She resurfaced and he pulled her closer. She groaned.

"My leg," she said. The rest didn't have to be spoken. Swimming was going to be their only way out and she might not be able to keep up.

He squeezed her hand. He could feel that she was fighting the current. He searched with his free hand, desperate for anything to grab, any sign of light.

"Rafe," she said, panic creasing her voice.

Ward tried to move with her to wherever the water was pulling her but he stumbled. He went under, losing her hand. The current underneath was strong. He couldn't gain his footing. He clawed at the surface.

Hands pulled at him, catching his jacket, his arm, his mouth. A fingernail caught his neck, raking his flesh. None of them held. His chest ached. Another hand grabbed his hair. He planted his feet and pushed, emerging with a gasp.

MacKenzie wrapped her arms around his waist. The water was now up to his stomach. He imagined it rising to her neck. They had minutes at best.

He wiped the water from his eyes, accomplishing nothing in the darkness.

"Okay, we swim," she said. "Maybe there's a way out underwater."

At the rate the water was rising, Ward figured it was unlikely there was a drainage route. But it was all they had.

"Can you?"

"I will."

"Don't let go of my hand. We go on three. This way," he

said, motioning with the hand that held hers in the direction of the current. If there was an escape route it would likely be there.

He counted them down, took as deep a breath as he could, and dove. They struggled a moment to get in synch, then kicked themselves forward, reaching and groping into the emptiness.

Ward measured their submersion. He reached thirty-six seconds before his lungs ached. He tugged on her hand. They surfaced, with Ward marveling at just how large the chamber must be. They were likely in an ancient catacomb system. Their best hope was that somewhere nearby these tunnels linked into Bari's modern sewer complex.

But even if it did, half a minute of air wouldn't be enough to get them to the surface.

"Give me a second," MacKenzie said.

He could hear her teeth chattering. He reached for her shoulder, then ran his hand down her arm until he touched water. Maybe three inches. They had only one or two more dives until they'd be treading water. Then the question would be how long until they rose to the ceiling, or until MacKenzie couldn't stay afloat.

"Okay, I'm ready."

"Try to go in a straight line. Same direction. We have to find the back wall and work from there. Deep breath."

Another three count and they were under. Twelve seconds in they found the wall. This time it wasn't earth, but stone. Possibly brick. Ward worked his free hand from the surface to the bottom, searching for any imperfection. It was solid.

He tugged on MacKenzie's hand to get her to rise, thinking it was better to start with a full breath.

She, however, yanked back, unwilling to head to the surface. The motion was so unexpected that Ward lost her hand. He groped about trying to find it but couldn't. In a panic, he pushed to the surface prepared to inhale and re-submerge.

Just as his chest inflated he heard her break the surface.

"Where'd you go?"

"I got it."

"Are you okay?"

"Rafe," she said. "I found it."

"What?"

"There's a hole, maybe a foot wide. I could stick my whole arm in and not feel the end. The water's really rushing in. I only knocked a few stones loose, but I think we can break through."

She fumbled about with the sleeve of his jacket before acquiring his hand, pulling him so close the water couldn't get between their bodies.

"Right here," she said, her breath warm on his chin. "On three."

They dove, MacKenzie's hand leading his. They tugged at the wall, making little progress for fifteen seconds. Ward nudged her aside and rotated his position so he could kick at it. He slammed four times, accomplishing little. On the fifth something shifted.

They surfaced and tried again. Three more kicks and a section of the wall dislodged. The entire volume of the room rushed forward into the new void, taking them with it. They were thrust forward then shoved to the left as a second current took over.

It felt like being pushed through a syringe. The tunnel's circumference was wide enough for them and little else. Ward lost his count at nineteen seconds. His ears popped and he battled to keep his eyes closed. MacKenzie's hand was long gone, though their bodies remained mashed together as they accelerated.

Suddenly, they were spinning as if in a whirlpool, only instead of being dragged down they rose. Ward's face broke the surface to a blurred brightness he'd feared he wouldn't see again. He squeezed his eyes closed and re-opened them. Light.

Above them rose a shaft, its walls smooth, terminating in the light source, possibly a sewer grate.

"MacKenzie," he shouted.

The tunnel was filling quickly, the whirlpool diminishing. Once it was gone, the undercurrent would return, sucking them back under.

"Is that a ladder?" She paddled to him.

Ward looked up again. Sure enough, a wrought-iron ladder was embedded in the shaft, its lowest rungs still too high to be reached.

"The water's rising. You'll be able to reach it, right?" MacKenzie asked.

Ward calculated they needed another minute or so of rising water for him to reach the ladder. Each second, however, the water's current grew stronger. He kicked against it, exhausting himself to stay in place. But it was all MacKenzie could do just to keep her head above water. She was being pulled from his grasp.

He wanted to lie and say it would be okay but no words came. Her jaw clenched, telling him she knew the truth.

"Rafe, take this," she said. She let go of his hand and wiggled out of her backpack, holding it out to him. She could barely keep her mouth above water.

Take it, Ward's mind shouted.

"No," he yelled, as much at the voice in his head as at MacKenzie. He needed the lid. Needed its bargaining value. But not at this cost. He'd find another way. "Give me your hand," he said. He stretched as far as he could and still maintain position beneath the ladder.

"I can't fight it. Take this. Go."

Her face dropped below the water to her hairline. She kicked back to the surface.

"Take it."

He reached but not far enough. He didn't want the backpack. He wanted her. He was a strong swimmer. He could grab her, he told himself. He could hold them in position.

You will both drown.

The water was almost high enough.

Daniel will die in prison.

A couple more inches and he'd be able to jump and grab the first rung.

But not while holding her.

No. He would go to her, wrap her in his arms, and let the waters take them. They'd find another way. If there was one ladder there would be a second. He kicked forward.

"Rafe!"

MacKenzie stopped kicking and flung the backpack. It splashed into his arms. For a second her red hair bobbed on the surface. Then she was gone.

CHAPTER THIRTY-THREE

Ward hung from the ladder, his elbow hooked around a thin rung. His boots dangled in the rushing water. The lack of oxygen and the physical exertion of the last few minutes had left his muscles drained. The backpack weighed on his shoulder as if it were filled with lead.

He waited.

He listened.

The water stopped rising. In time it even receded a bit, flowing gently now a few inches below his feet. Still he waited, glaring at the water's impenetrable surface. He searched for anything. Any sign of MacKenzie. A flash of her red hair. An air bubble. A distant scream. Anything to give him cause to let go, to drop into the runnel and save her.

There was nothing. It was time to climb.

He looked up, examining the escape route for the first

time. As he'd surmised a drainage grate waited at the top of the ladder. It was not, however, the exit he'd hoped for. The light extruding through the bars was not sunlight. It was the dull, cool light of fluorescent bulbs. Above was a sewer tunnel or maybe the subway. In either case, it would be dry. For that, at least, he could be thankful.

Allowing for one more glance below Ward climbed the ladder. At the top he levered up the grate with his back and shoulder and pushed himself from the shaft.

It was indeed a sewer tunnel. He shook as much water from himself as he could, then wrung out his jacket and poured a gallon or so from the backpack. Like his flashlight he'd lost his gun somewhere below.

The tunnel was circular, lined with dark brick, and featured a two foot lip halfway up its circumference, no doubt a walkway for the workers who had long ago maintained the tunnel. When water and sewage had flown through here it would have drained at various points through grates like the one from which he'd just emerged, dropping into the older catacombs below and eventually out to sea.

Which meant MacKenzie was being washed out to sea.

He didn't know how far from the Mediterranean he was, or how many miles the tunnels meandered beneath the city before joining the depths offshore, but the thought of her holding onto that last pittance of oxygen in her lungs, praying that she would surface before she had to gasp, hit him like a charging bull. His legs wobbled. He collapsed.

The last few days flashed in his mind like strobe-light visions from a horror film. The Agent at the bottom of the stairs. The tall one in the apartment. The ones on the train. Agent Compano's mangled face. Claude's massive fists covered in a man's brains. Simon's life bleeding into his blue suit. Daniel endlessly heaving his pick.

Ward's hands shook. He wanted a scotch.

He saw MacKenzie's smile.

He retched.

———◆———

Ward hastened through the tunnel, stopping every thirty seconds to listen for any sounds which might offer a way out. He knew it was a pointless exercise. He'd emerged into the tunnel at a dead end. There'd been no side passages offering options. He had no choice but to follow this one tunnel until it took him somewhere.

Eventually the ceiling lowered, though not so much he had to duck, and the walkway-ledge disappeared. The flickering fluorescent lights in the ceiling became spaced further apart, forcing him to traverse moments of near darkness every sixty or seventy steps.

Emerging from one of these blackened chasms Ward faced a T intersection. He peered down the right branch as far as he could. It widened into the size of the original tunnel, sprawling farther than he could see. He looked down the left. It continued with the current, smaller blueprint until it was lost in darkness not far ahead.

Something clacked in the distance. Ward's hand went for the pistol that wasn't there. He couldn't discern if the sound was close or just an echo. If it was from the right tunnel or the left. If it was a person or just a rat. He waited. It didn't repeat. He chose the larger tunnel and hedged forward.

This channel, like the previous, went on and on. It was like being in the endless gullet of a serpent or whale. The thought stopped his feet. Would that be how MacKenzie ended up? Long drowned and digested by some leviathan?

"I'm sorry," he choked, the words louder than he'd expected.

Re-re-re cascaded into the distance, coming back at elongated intervals.

He waited for the echo to cease before trekking forward. He tried keeping track of his steps to count the distance but his mind too often wandered. Why did REC care so much about this relic? Was Hickey really the best option Gaustad had? How could a father choose some broken pottery over his own daughter? What if they never set Daniel free?

Ward was sure he'd walked at least a mile but questions and doubt continued to buzz in his head obscuring his count.

The tunnel ended. Like where he'd entered the system, there was only a brick wall and a grate in the floor revealing still-churning water below. Transfixed, Ward watched the current push on, swelling and rippling without care for whom it swallowed.

Clack, cla-clack, clack.

Ward fell into a crouch, scrambling to push his back against the wall. It was no rat. Agents' boots? The Police digging their way to into the sewers? The great sea beast which had taken MacKenzie and was now seeking her companion?

Stop it, Ward told himself. It was Hickey's Agents, their footsteps echoing in the tunnels. He looped it over and over in his head. Hickey's Agents. Footsteps. His pulse slowed. How many had there been in the necropolis? Three? Four? Enough that fighting wasn't an option. Waiting wasn't an option either, so he stood and settled a breath in his chest before setting off back down the tunnel with quiet, deliberate steps.

Clack, cla-clack, clack.

Agent's footsteps, he reminded himself. Or was it the sound of Daniel's pick perpetually gouging into the world's bedrock? What if it never stopped? What if he had to listen to his brother's toiling labor forever?

Ward's steps accelerated into a trot, then a run. Some vague notion of the ridiculousness of running from a rat thrummed inside his ears. He ran faster. His lungs criticized the choice. A barbed cramp sunk into his ribs.

Clack, cla-clack, clack.

It was wall to wall, omnipresent, coming from everywhere, yet originating from nowhere. *What are you?* Ward wanted to scream. *I'm sorry*, he might have yelled. He couldn't be sure. Still he ran.

His toe caught an uneven brick. He stumbled. It wasn't much. He caught himself on the ledge. But the slap of his palm on the brickwork *ap-ap-ped* through the tunnels.

The clacking ceased.

Ward held his breath.

"Who's there?" he asked of the nothing.

Air-air-air echoed as the only response.

He must be losing his mind.

The clacking resumed. He ran. His thigh muscles flared within a minute. The blood pumping through his veins became a din drowning out even his own footfalls. When he reached the T intersection he pulled to a stop. Ahead was the tunnel without light. Left was back to where he started. Where he'd let MacKenzie drown. There was only one option.

He moved forward, stutter-stepping into an inkiness only an underworld could produce, hands out to touch whatever the dark might divulge. He couldn't tell if he was moving forward or sideways. If he had gone five feet or fifteen. He might well have been dead, imprisoned in some empty purgatory.

His shoulder slammed into a wall, dropping him to a knee. The clacking paused. The world held its breath.

Clack, cla-clack, clack.

Ward pressed his fists to his temples. He was hopelessly lost. There was nothing left to do but wait for whatever was making that sound. It would be on him soon, discovering him hunched like a deer transfixed by headlights.

She gave you a way out.

No, she hadn't. All she'd given him was the backpack with the relics inside. He couldn't see how they could help.

See-ee-ee-ee his conscience seemed to echo.

See? He couldn't see. No one could see in this darkness. That was the problem. It was…

Yes! He fumbled the backpack from his shoulder, tugging at straps and zippers. He found the main pouch, a side pouch, even his own jacket pocket by mistake. Finally his fingers slipped into a small zippered compartment near the shoulder strap adjuster. They were still there, almost weightless, the slender sunglasses MacKenzie had worn in the tunnel in Philadelphia. Night-optics.

Ward put them on. Instantly, the room blazed red. There was a muted whirring in his left ear. The tunnel came alive with greens, yellows, whites, and blues. Far sharper contrasts than the optics he'd trained on, which offered only greens and blacks, and tended to blur with the user's motion, these spectacles made seeing in the dark as natural as daylight.

The wall which had knocked Ward down was actually a corner. The tunnel turned ninety degrees, opening into a wide up-sloping side passage. A sense of decorum and purpose returned, strengthening his legs. He stood, readjusted the backpack on his shoulders, and proceeded ahead.

Soon the tunnel's floor and wall bricks were replaced with smooth subway tiles. The pungent smell he'd gotten used to below faded. He even thought he smelled something like fresh air. Confidence for escape quickened his steps into a full run.

The conviction didn't last. The tunnel dead-ended like the others. A wall and a sewer grate. The dispassionate water continued its course beneath.

Ward kicked a loose stone at the wall and tried to counter his frustration. His breathing slowed, leaving him in silence. No clacking. When had it ceased? He listened for it but heard nothing.

He stared through the grate at the water. Why not? Why not dive in and let it take him to MacKenzie?

It was a senseless thought. A desperate thought. He dragged his eyes from the water and searched for options. There had to be a way out of the sewer. It would be illogical, and likely impossible, to build sewer tunnels that could only be accessed from below. But, like at the other dead ends, there was only…

He squinted through the lenses. They whirred, an encouraging song bringing into focus shallow steps cut into the back wall to form a ladder. He pressed his palms to the wall and looked up. The optics whirred again, adjusting their contrast and presenting a porthole egress.

"Son of a bitch," he muttered.

It could be a manhole cover to street level. It could lead to another tunnel. It didn't matter. He climbed.

The porthole was metal. Its rotating lever-handle, like on a submarine hatch, was warm. He looked at the sewer grate below once more. He'd failed her. It was a simple truth. One that resonated like a verdict in his mind, some ancient karmic decree or sinister knot in fate's thread from an archaic epic. He had the lid. Not her. He held the key to it all. Whatever bullshit everyone believed about this god or that, it was in his hands now. All he had to do was find Hickey. Demand Daniel's release. Hand it over. Walk away.

One-one-one, he'd dialed when he was eleven. "My mom has a bad book," he'd told the hotline operator.

She'd been very polite, with her squeaky voice, but in his memory now it was MacKenzie's voice. It wasn't telling him to stay calm or to trust that the Republic would take care of everything when they arrived. It was deliberate and it was confident.

"You are not done, Rafe," the MacKenzie-voiced operator said. "It is waiting for you."

"What?" Ward screamed at the memory. "What's waiting?" There was no answer, of course. There was no anything save for the gurgling of the water below.

"Fuck Hickey," Ward said. He turned the handle. The porthole clanged. Metal grated on metal. It lifted half an inch. Ward put his shoulder against it and heaved. More metal on metal. The door flung open assaulting him with unbearable light. He nearly lost his footing. Readjusting, he pulled off the optics and squinted.

The hatch opened into a shed not unlike the one Claude had hidden them in back in Paris. Ward climbed into the room and let the hatch slam closed. The shed appeared to be some sort of water authority post with thick pipes running along the walls and plunging into the floor and ceiling. An instrument cluster was built into the back wall opposite the door.

Ward headed for the door. Handle-less it resisted his push. He threw his shoulder into it with a grunt, grinding it open. More light. He put his hands before his eyes and stepped into the fresh air and sun, nearly knocking over an impossibly dark shadow.

"You have lost Hannah. Troubling."

The light dimmed and the shadow dissolved as Ward's eyes adjusted. Adrien, stooped and grimacing, stood only inches away. His breath was humid and sour as it broke across Ward's chin. The priest's withered hand, looking like it might return to dust at the slightest touch, presented a plastic bottle of water.

"How did you find me?" Ward demanded.

The old man opened his mouth as if to answer, then closed it. He squinted at Ward and said, "Would you like a drink?"

CHAPTER THIRTY-FOUR

Ward went for the priest's throat. The old man backpedaled as Ward's hands battled the thick robes for a grasp of anything human. They slammed into a wall. The plastic bottle hit the ground. Adrien wheezed.

"I should tear your fucking eyes out," Ward growled. "She's dead."

Adrien's face, floating within his hood, cracked into a horrible grin. His skin, the color of vellum, sagged and stretched unnaturally. His eyes, set wide above a crooked nose, were the gray of no color at all.

"She chose death, did she not?"

Ward knew the old man was right but he didn't want to care about right. He wanted to choke the life from the old man, mostly because there was no one else to blame for MacKenzie's death. No one but himself.

His grip on the priest's robes loosened

"We do not have long, Rafael," the priest said. "There are other deaths to prevent, yes? And they are coming for you."

Ward's hands dropped to his thighs. He backed off. Other deaths? Could the priest mean Daniel? *No*, Ward thought. Even Simon and his museum ushers couldn't have known about that. They couldn't have told Adrien about that. He must be referring to Ward's own death. Maybe to the deaths of everyone on Earth if he believed the same narrative as Simon.

"You have the dome—the lid for the Holy vessel?" Adrien asked, stepping from the sun-bleached stucco wall into which Ward had hurled him.

"You know I do," Ward said. "Why didn't you get it yourself?"

"Each of us has a role to play, Professor. Today, yours was to dig."

"More of this 'chosen' bullshit? Chosen by who?"

"Where will you stand as today becomes the past, Rafael?" The priest held out his hand, palm up, fingers curled as if holding a ball. "You may give it to me."

Ward hooked his thumb into the shoulder strap of the backpack. *Why not just hand it over*, he thought, *and walk away?* This misguided Believer's quest was no longer his business. Hannah was gone. Simon. Claude. All dead. There was no way he could play the REC alone, force them to turn over his brother, even if he had the lid. They'd probably just shoot him and take it. The thought caused his legs to weaken. They were nearly trembling. The only option he saw was handing it over to Adrien and walking away. He could disappear into the

Italian countryside. He could rebuild his life in a free country.

MacKenzie's voice, superimposed over the hotline operator's voice in his memory, came back to him: "You are not done, Rafe."

Yes I am. He had nothing left to give. Even the anger now had fled. His chest was empty.

Adrien, likely responding to Ward's immobility, lowered his hand. "Very well. There is, perhaps, time for the answers you seek. Come."

The priest led Ward through the deserted, cobblestoned alley. Through the peach-colored buildings rising two and three stories on either side. Past the uncaring eyes of windows and fenced balconies absent of gawkers and nosy neighbors. They moved at an old man's pace, exiting the lane to a view like a tableau. A baroque-style hotel sprawled to their left. The rest of the landscape was open. Open to the sky. To the sea. To the air. Ward inhaled, surprised at how much his body craved the brisk, salty air.

The priest walked them across a congested two lane road running parallel with the shore, paying no mind to the cars and scooters whipping by, horns bleating. Ward cringed as the vehicles weaved angrily about them. Somehow they arrived safely on the other side where Adrien knifed through row upon row of pedestrians bustling about in bright colors, paying no mind of the black-robed priest and the wet American. In brief interludes, like pulsing flashes from a strobe light, Ward was impressed with the old man. He strutted and strolled as if his steps were the only ones which knew their place.

Finally free of the crowds Adrien paused to look at the

sun, hanging lazily past its zenith, before continuing. Ward assumed they would head to the pier which jutted to their left. Or maybe hail a taxi. Instead the priest guided them to a precisely manicured park of vibrant green hedgerows and plumed palm trees.

"Where are we going?"

Adrien remained mute, meandering through the hedges which had been laid out to give a labyrinthine impression. At the center of the park, shaded by the palms, posed four wooden benches, two each on opposite sides of a concrete slab. A harried-looking woman, hair frizzing from beneath a purple hat, sat on one of the far benches, her back to the sea. She held an infant to her chest beneath a pink and yellow blanket.

Adrien again glanced up at the sun. Satisfied with whatever he saw, he chose the left on the near side, the one facing the woman. He sat stiffly, his back straight, hands resting atop his knees. He looked like an effigy of a king on his throne.

"Sit, Rafael."

Ward obeyed, placing the backpack on the ground between his feet. He stared beyond the woman, taking in the view of the Adriatic. Traffic and pedestrians bustled behind them. Ships lazed in the distance. But here, by the pier, there was little activity.

"The artifact, please." The priest's voice was dry, his words dispassionate.

It was the placidity of the old man that reinstated Ward's rage. He grabbed the priest's robe by the shoulder, twisting so that his face nearly entered the hood.

"Hannah's dead and all you care about is this fucking

piece of pottery."

The woman on the bench glared at Ward, muttering something in Italian. She gathered her things, keeping her child tight to her chest, and fled the park.

"Professor, you know well enough that no single death can be allowed to derail this quest. Simon made this clear, did he not?"

"Then there's nothing to stop me from killing you."

Adrien laid his hands on Ward's, the touch of the old flesh loosening his grip on the robes.

"Every one of us is willing to give our lives in this service. The *conservateurs*, young Hannah, even those who now possess the Vase—they too will accept death for the moment that fast approaches. Are you willing? Was your family willing?"

"What the fuck do you know about my family?"

"I know your mother wasn't the only one with faith. I know your brother still holds his."

Ward stood. But once to his feet he couldn't move. He was paralyzed between rage and grief. The priest knew. What did it mean? Was there hope for Daniel? For himself?

Ward heard his own voice, pleading and weak. "Just tell me what it is. What the Vase of Soissons really is."

"It is far older than Soissons, my friend. But you know this. You have seen it. You have seen enough else these past days to know where we go next. Sit. Please."

Ward was about to protest when the memory of the Vase returned. Greek but not Greek. First millennium BCE, yet clearly older. These flashes were followed by an image of the headstone carving in the necropolis. He'd almost forgotten.

He did know.

"Crete." He sat.

"Ah," Adrien said. "You do understand. Excellent."

Normally Ward would have enjoyed this moment of validation. With only seconds of contact in Gaustad's office he'd recognized that the Vase was too old to be Greek. Too old even to be Mycenaean. Now he saw it. The Minoans were the cultural source of both societies, dating back nearly five thousand years. And though the style of figures painted on the Vase didn't fit this timeline—they actually appeared more modern, more like artifacts discovered from the golden age of Athens—the "dragonfly" on Adrien's tomb supported the hypothesis. In the sewer tunnels he'd recognized the icon for what it was. Not an insect, or a crucifix, but a rendering of the sacred double-headed axe of the Minoans.

How many others could have deduced all this?

How much of it didn't matter now that MacKenzie was gone?

How much of it did with Daniel's life still at stake?

Am I actually allowing myself to believe in all this?

"However," Adrien said, "we go not to the Minoan temples on Crete. We go to Thera."

Ward repeated the name. It was familiar but he couldn't place it. Like Adrien Quinque's name when he first saw the tombstone, it danced just out of reach.

"The source."

"Of what?" Ward asked. "The Minoans were gone long before the bible. If the Vase is theirs, your biblical God is irrelevant."

Adrien didn't respond. He seemed to be watching an odd yellow bird with a blue tail flutter across the cement slab at their feet. When it reached the sand it chirped. Adrien whistled. The pair repeated the duet.

Once more indignation biled up in Ward's throat.

As if sensing this Adrien turned his head. The bird flew off. "The bible is but a book, Rafael. Man's attempt to relay events and words beyond his understanding. We go in search of Truth and of Him."

"So, God."

"Who is God?"

"There is no God," Ward said. "You, all of you, are fucked up believing in something that doesn't exist. And it got Hannah killed." But even as he spewed the words he could hear the conviction lessening in his voice.

"Are you angry at her belief or mine?"

Ward didn't know the answer.

"Rafael," Adrien said, "who is God?"

Like with Commandant Gaustad days earlier, Ward recognized the rhetorical bait. Unable to resist he thought his way around the question and offered a response.

"Jehovah," Ward said, the first name for the priest's god that popped into his head.

"You understand." The old man clapped his hands once. "Now go older."

"Older? You mean like Adonai. Yahweh. Elohim."

"Ah, Elohim. You know it?"

"I just said it."

"Then you know it is plural as well as singular."

Ward considered this, then said, "So what?"

"'Let Us make man in Our image,' the book says."

"You said the book doesn't matter."

"Then who is God? Older, Rafael. Older."

What was older? They were all names for the same being. God of Abraham. Father of Jesus. It didn't matter what moniker he offered, they were just pseudonyms for a make-believe creator. He might as well say Chaos, Uranus, or Brahma. The nameless Bull God of the Minoans. His counterpart, the Great Mother. It was all the same. And none of them could bring her back.

"Rafael," Adrien prompted, stretching the syllables.

"For fuck's sake, I don't know." But he did. The answer had been with him his whole life. His name, in Hebrew, was *Repha'El*. He'd discovered this fact in graduate school while researching the supposed trumpet Sur, belonging to the archangel Raphael. Legend said it was this trumpet the angel would sound on Judgment Day. His name, Ward had learned, translated as: God has Healed.

"You mean El," Ward said. "The Semitic God. Canaanite. Pre-Abraham."

"Pre-everything but Him. You are ready."

"For what?"

"To understand," Adrien said. "You know the creation myths. They are all alike, yes? From Chaos comes light and dark. Day and night. Land and sea. And soon appears characters. Gods. Goddesses. Or, from Genesis, materializes Eden. The tree of good and evil. The tree of life. Adam." He paused.

Ward thought he saw the pattern the old man was suggesting. "Eve," he said. "Man and woman. That's what you're going for? Father. Mother. The double-bladed *labrys* on Quinque's tomb. Duality. Sure. Very pagan but not biblical. It's one God. One Vase. Don't give me your 'Our image' shit. It's the royal 'Our.' It's translation. It's crap."

"You are rash."

"You aren't telling me anything."

From somewhere inside his robes Adrien produced a small golden pendant. He held it out in his palm. Expertly sculpted it depicted two bees, their faces and stingers coming together to make a circle. Though of different design it was reminiscent of the bees in Gaustad's office.

"Rafael, from whence did El come?"

Ward stared. "What difference does it make? There are Agents out there looking for me. For this. Why are we sitting her in the open? If they take it, Daniel dies."

"We all die eventually."

"That's great coming from a walking fossil."

Adrien responded as if he'd expected the adversity. "Very well. Here it is: all religions—the Mediterranean, the Levant, and beyond—come from the same source. A culture touched in ancient times by the only God. An entity which, in truth, is two. Can you actually believe a universe built on symmetry is the realm of a singular identity? All is binary. Balance. Matter and anti-matter. El and Ba'el."

Ba'el. The word struck Ward like a slap against his cheek. What was it Simon said? The beast—Ba'el, the bisected diarchy. It started to make sense. It was right there, like a flavor on the wind. Then it was gone. The indignation was back.

"No," Ward said. "I'll buy that El is the Biblical God. Sure. Most scholars agree. I'll even take El as the Bull God of the Minoans if you want to push it that far. There's plenty of evidence suggesting Minoan influence on Mesopotamia and the Middle East. But Ba'el is nothing. A minor pagan deity. A generic word for 'lord' or 'lady.' You can't tell me that 'Thou shalt have no other Gods before me' means 'before us.' It doesn't work. It doesn't make sense. None of the texts say God is a dual act."

The ridiculousness of the conversation made Ward shake his head. He was arguing with a Believer about the natures and names of gods that even Believers didn't talk about. They might as well be debating the nature of comic book superheroes.

Adrien twisted his position to look once more at the sun. He stared a moment before refocusing his attention on Ward. "Hear this, Rafael. El and Ba'el are one. And they are two. Like a coin, or day and night, they are simultaneous." He held up the bee pendant once more, tapping it against the air. "They are the Bull God. *And* they are the Mother."

"Fine. Which is male and which is female?"

"Both." The bees disappeared back into the priest's robes. "Neither. It does not matter. What matters is you understand that it was to those living on Crete—those we call Minoans— that the Dual-God made itself first known."

"Great. So what happened to Ba'el? Why does he, or she, or whatever, get the shaft in the bible?"

"Even gods quarrel. Even gods, Rafael. And when mankind was ready one chose to bless the Minoans while the other chose to bless the Semites. They clashed as only gods can. It was then that El betrayed his companion, constructing a prison and casting Ba'el within. This vessel he dropped from the heavens and destroyed the people Ba'el loved. The victor was thus free to offer His covenant to Abraham."

"You're telling me that Ba'el is inside the Vase?"

"This was Truth until the prison was shattered at Clovis' feet. For over two millennium the Vase was like a battery of culture to the Mediterranean, inspiring art and science and philosophy. The Mycenaeans. The Greeks. The Romans. There are no coincidences. Only the will of a God denied form who wished to give His people, and their descendants, these gifts. Ba'el has given art and culture to the world. El has given only law and fear."

Ward's skepticism told him to walk away but his academic brain craved more. "But when the Vase was destroyed wasn't Ba'el released?"

"He, too, was shattered. When did the Dark Ages begin, hmm? You know the answer. The moment the Vase fragmented was the moment Western culture, Ba-el's culture, arrested. Ba'el became but a whisper, splintered, agonizing through the centuries. This is our quest. Rebuild the vessel. Rebuild the God."

"Yeah, and destroy it like Simon said. To what end? Another Dark Age?"

Adrien snorted. "We are still in the Dark Age."

"Whatever," Ward said. "What happens if we leave it in pieces?"

"Scripture demands the eternal destruction of Ba'el as the

first step towards El's Kingdom of Heaven."

There it was. Ward knew that interactions with Believers always came back to one principal: the victory of their righteous god over heathens, heretics, and wicked atheists. Good and evil. God and his great adversary, Satan.

"Good and Evil are nothing," the priest snapped as if reading Ward's mind. "There is El and Ba'el. Once coupled, now asunder. All other morality is a fiction."

"So let's just destroy the lid right here. Smash it or toss it to the bottom of the ocean. No Lid. No Vase. No God. Over. Done."

"Do you believe none have tried? No one knows what forces allowed the Vase to be shattered. Perhaps the soldier's axe was a gift from El. Whatever the case, Remigius made many attempts to complete the destruction, all in vain. Finally he prayed and received the answer. He was told to scatter the pieces until the time came. We stand upon the precipice of that hour."

It was ridiculous. Ward was a scholar. He knew no god was going to appear and turn the world to ash. Yet he also knew that MacKenzie didn't throw her life away for nothing. It was an innate knowledge, like hunger.

But what did that say about his mother? About Daniel?

Adrien placed his hand on Ward's shoulder. "You will understand, Rafael," the priest said. "I promise."

A shadow crossed Ward from behind, followed by a cheery voice.

"Hey, buddy."

Ward's stomach sank. His legs tried to push him up from

his seat but the old man's hand on his shoulder, far stronger than it should have been, kept him pinned to the bench. The best he could do was tilt his head toward the voice.

Ken Hickey, hands on his hips and a ridiculous grin painted across his face, stood flanked by four black-suited Agents.

"This would've been easier if you'd just worked with me on the train."

Adrien brandished a dagger, its steel glinting yellow in the sun. "Now you understand what is at stake," the priest said. "And how powerful Ba'el, the virtuous creator, is."

The dagger pressed into Ward's ribs. He was surprised to find he had no anger left. Two of the Agents rounded the bench. It was too late to run. Too futile to fight. He knew what was coming next. The black bag.

He couldn't help but wonder if all darkness was the same. If MacKenzie's was somehow blacker as she'd died.

He closed his eyes and waited.

CHAPTER
THIRTY-FIVE

He was on a ship. The roll of the sea made this evident even with the acrid black bag over his head. They'd dumped him into a feverous closet. Hands bound behind his back he could kneel and sweat. It was all the confines allowed. No standing. No laying. He'd long ago lost track of the hours. Long ago felt the wailing in his legs and spine give way to numbness.

At first fear had turned the darkness into an assault of nightmare visions. MacKenzie drowning. Daniel's flesh splayed open by rod and whip. His own execution in one of the horizontal slots of a Crematorium. A blazing Bull God consuming the Earth.

His tongue tasted of charcoal and tears.

Eventually, with his body's numbness, came serenity. The heat dissipated. He thought of his mother. Was this how she'd felt when they came for her? Had loneliness and the dark been her only companions as they took her to the fire?

The sound of a door opening brought the smallest hint of clean air but no light. He tried to turn.

A thousand needles lancing his limbs.

A horrible goring in his spine.

He cried out, and received a mouthful of the fibrous, sweaty bag.

"I bet you're thirsty."

He was. He'd give anything, even tear off a chunk of himself, for some water.

"Listen, Rafe, just agree when he comes. The rest of it doesn't matter anymore. Just say yes."

He knew the voice, shrill and falsely confident. Hickey.

"Just go along, man. Say you will and he'll let you out of here. Water. Air conditioning. Whatever. He'll even let us go back to the university."

It sounded nice. Easy. Ward inhaled, nearly—irrationally—giggling as fibers from the bag over his head tickled into his throat. He imagined sunlight. A glass of water. He thought about books. Files and text threads. Codices—the real, tangible, dusty, heavy bound books that lurked in the university's storage cellars. The ones in his apartment. Just say yes and he could read all the books he wanted.

The image of a particular book came to him. The one his mother had read from that day. The one that had been taken away with her. She'd never protested the fate her son, little Raffi, prescribed for her. She'd only looked at him like any mother might look at her child after he'd made one of those terrible, necessary, mistakes that come with innocence and idealism. Mournful. Hopeful. Loving. Maybe even—he clenched his already closed eyes—proud?

"No." He choked on the word. Choked on the bag. Choked on his own desiccated lips and tongue.

He imagined choking the life out of the deplorable Ken Hickey and grinned inside the bag. It stuck to his lips, picking off pieces of flesh.

"Just do it, okay?"

The door closed.

Minutes spiraled by. Hours. His head grew heavy as if it was filled with gelatin, bowing and swirling within his skull.

He inhaled the bag, gnashing his teeth on the burlap. Sucking his own sweat out of the fabric. It burned his palate. His throat flexed for it, clamored for it, begged, but it was gone, absorbed, before ever getting past his tongue.

Had it been a day?

How many days since the woman with the red hair—he'd forgotten her name—had come to his home?

When the door again opened, he didn't turn.

"I'll make you a deal, Mr. Ward."

He knew this voice, too, though he couldn't find its name afloat in his mind. A title instead. Commandant.

"We approach the endgame but if you tell me everything you know about Simon's congregation, his *conservateurs*, I'll get your brother on a chopper right now. His will be the first face you see when we dock. Hell, I'll make you dean of your university. We'll have you home in a day."

Ward wanted to be angry but his chest was bereft of

hatred. All he felt was duty. Familiar and comfortable yet somehow alien. It wasn't the duty to his superior or to his government that he'd known his entire life. It was bigger. Greater. A duty to death.

How many deaths since he'd entered that basement?

How many deaths had he been complicit in over the years as a Citizen, as a professor, preaching the Republic's dogma?

How many deaths had his mother died in his heart? His father?

He felt a duty to reconciliation. To balance. To vengeance.

For his mother. For the redheaded woman.

So much death that it now demanded of him something else.

Silence.

"Very well."

The door closed.

Thirst abandoned him as hunger previously had. As pain before that. The lapping of waves—why hadn't he heard them earlier?—metallic and hollow against the side of the ship, became his world. An anthem for his wrongs. He wished to drown. What better way to find oblivion than in water? What better way to avoid the fire?

A third time the door opened. He didn't hear it. Didn't taste the crispness of that new air but he knew it had opened. The cells within his blood all whispered at once. There was a visitor.

"Men are not expected to survive by conviction alone. Drink, Rafael."

The bag was rolled partially up his face, exposing Ward's

mouth. The sweat on his bristled chin evaporated, tickling his flesh.

A bottle, plastic and sterile, was pushed between his lips. He drank. He choked. He drank. His veins iced from within. Had there been more he might have breathed it into his lungs. Drowned by a bottle of water? Why not?

The empty bottle was ripped away.

"The gift of a soul. Deceiver and Believer. She told you of this, yes?"

It was the priest speaking.

A finger, cold like winter cement, pressed into the dimple between Ward's lip and nose. At its touch, Ward found himself seeing the world in that video game split-screen mode again. The half on the ship was still cast in darkness. The other half peered down into a pit of dirt of mud.

A monk stood in the pit, brown hood lowered around brown shoulders. Dark hair matted with sweat. He hefted a pick, a cumbersome iron tool, and swung it at the earth with all his might. Again and again until he fell to his knees. There was no sound with the vision but Ward knew the monk was listening to a voice in his head. He knew he was looking at Adrien Quinque just before his discovery of King Childeric's tomb. That four-hundred-year-ago moment Ward had enacted in his classroom a few days ago. That moment the monk would discover the real treasure in the pit—the lid to the Vase of Soissons.

It was truth Ward understood—at least as much truth as the priest Adrien believed. The crazy old priest really thought *he* was Adrien Quinque, a man his contemporaries thought to be touched by God. But not God, Adrien believed. Not El, but Ba'el. Not touched but chosen for this centuries-long mandate to protect the lid until the other pieces could be found.

Ward watched the monk swing his pick again and again, like Daniel in the quarry, each slice releasing an aroma. Flowers? The look on the monk's face was sublime. It was deranged. Yes, touched by God is what they would have said four hundred years ago. It was the only euphemism they had for crazy.

But with all he'd seen, with all he'd heard, was it really so crazy that this priest could be Adrien Quinque?

An idea came to him, a memory—an anonymous manuscript dismissed as hyperbole by scholars. A scanned image of an incomplete scrap, the original long lost. An Italian monk writing about a gift from God. How did it go? The Latin words began to coalesce before him like a title superimposed over a movie scene. Could they be the words of Adrien Quinque? Of Adrien the old priest?

The split screen blinked out leaving only darkness. Ward's chin drooped to his chest.

"Good," Adrien said. "All that remains is the giving. And then you will be free. You will stand with me in glory by Ba'el's side."

Ward wanted to refute it. He begged death to take him before the desire for more water took over. Before he conceded.

Death wasn't listening.

He bobbed his head once.

He was given more water. He clamped his teeth down upon the bottle's neck and didn't let go until he'd gotten all there was. His belly burned.

"Thank you, Rafael."

Ward's face was consumed by the bag once more. In the darkness Ward saw Adrien Quinque's face from the vision. The face of the man whose grave had lain empty beneath the Basilica of Saint Nicholas for centuries. He saw that face grown withered and ashen with the passage of unnatural centuries.

He saw the gnarled face of the priest, Adrien.

Those strange words his mother had spoken in Daniel's bedroom came to him. Foreign syllables. Harsh. Elusive. Beautiful. He never knew which prayer it was. He'd never tried to find out.

He wept.

PART FOUR

THE VASE

And the king commanded... bring forth out of the temple of the Lord all the vessels that were made for Baal... and he burned them without Jerusalem in the fields of Kidron.

Book of Kings, 23:4

And I stood upon the sand of the sea, and saw a beast rise up out of the sea, having seven heads and ten horns, and upon his horns ten crowns, and upon his heads the name of blasphemy.

Book of Revelation, 13:1

...currently enjoying the longest sustained domestic and international peace in the history of both the United Republic, and its predecessor the United States of America. And with continued approval ratings for New Republic Party presidents, senators, and congressmen consistently in the high 90% range, there appears to be no end coming to our Pax Americana.

The American Vision: A Textbook History of the Republic, Volume II, 2029

CHAPTER
THIRTY-SIX

Rafael Ward marched along a steep, grainy path. His hands were still bound. He still wore the black bag. His legs trembled and his head pounded. He stumbled often, dragged back to his feet by silent hands. Prodded forward again and again by muzzles and stocks of assault rifles.

He had, at least, been given water and a few standard ration bars when they'd disembarked from the ship. Now, maybe an hour along the route to wherever, he felt some strength returning to his limbs, some clarity returning to his thoughts. He did his best to count footsteps and voices, coming up with at least five people in the procession, two or three of them lugging something heavy up the incline.

Hickey was definitely among them but he didn't hear Gaustad's or Adrien's voices. He wondered if maybe he'd imagined them on the ship.

Gulls mocked the prisoner from somewhere to his left, the direction of the sun warming his face even through the black bag. A balmy wind whipped his jacket's collar against the back of neck.

"How much farther, Agent, um, Givers?"

It was Hickey's voice.

"Gibbons," the Agent corrected. "We're close." His tone discontinued further discussion.

A few minutes later they halted. Someone shoved Ward to the ground. His hands were cut loose. The bag was jerked from his head, abrading his face.

The light hurt. He clenched and lowered his eyes before slowly reopening them. Six pairs of feet, five booted and one in loafers, made an arc before him. Ward lifted his head, keeping a hand across his brow for the glare of the afternoon sun.

They were situated by the edge of a promontory overlooking an endless blue body of water. They could have been fifty feet above sea level. They could have been fifty miles into the sky.

Four Agents stood before him, two on either side. The other feet belonged to Hickey and Commandant Gaustad. Behind these two a tan blanket draped over what had to be the Vase. Ward thought about Agent Compano. She'd surely died of her grotesque wounds on the train, but had she survived, would she be among this chosen lot?

"Agent... I'm sorry, Mr. Ward. How nice to see you again," the Commandant said. He stood like a statue. Not motionless but with a sober gravity that only bronze or marble could offer. He held in his left fist an iron rod. No, not a rod. MacKenzie's

Spear of Destiny.

"Sir," Ward said, the word choking off in his throat. He kept his head down but his eyes on the Spear. He imagined plunging it into the Commandant's neck. *About as fair a trade as he would get for MacKenzie*, he thought. *That will be good, yes?*

Gaustad laughed. "Still holding to rank, eh, Ward?"

"I got it for you, sir," Ward said, not hiding his rancor. "Let my brother go."

Commandant Gaustad laughed. Ward expected as much. But for reasons he couldn't quite explain he needed to offer that one haughty demand.

"I'll tell you what," Gaustad said. "One last chance. Perform the duty I ask and I'll release your brother. I'll even give you this." He held up the spear like a scepter.

Ward knew the offer of the Spear was supposed to show some magnanimity on the Commandant's part, offering to give away what would otherwise be a central piece of the collection in his office. He rolled his shoulders and cracked his neck.

"What duty?" he asked, finding it difficult to draw his eyes from the gleaming tip of the Spear. It was no longer razor sharp as when it was first came off the forge but it would do.

Hickey approached and dropped MacKenzie's unzipped backpack onto the dusty earth before him.

"The Vase requires a gift," Gaustad said. "Didn't Simon tell you?"

"He said you thought it was a weapon," Ward said.

"A weapon? Simon and I never spoke of such things. It's a power source, Ward. A means to do away with weapons. Surely Simon explained his 'battery' theory—the Vase emits energy, providing me with unlimited potential. The Republic will do more than flourish. With the power of the Vase we will dominate the world like no empire before."

Ward was still groggy but he was sure Gaustad was delusional. Simon had never mentioned being in the Republic. He'd never mentioned meeting the Commandant. When would the two of them have discussed the Vase?

"He begins to comprehend, William."

It was Adrien's voice. The priest moved into Ward's vision, a blackened wraith within his rippling robes.

Despite the priest's assertion Ward was not comprehending. He was confused. Only the *conservateurs* had known of the Vase. Only Simon, Claude, and…

"Yes," Adrien said. "He does see."

"William," Ward said, almost laughing at himself. "Guillaume. *Le Traitre*."

The Commandant feigned affront. "Traitor? Come now, Ward. I discovered contraband while on an operation. No different than you. I did my job and confiscated the artifact. That is no betrayal."

"Your job?" Ward said.

But he already knew the explanation. His mind read it as if from a script while William Gaustad spoke the words. He'd never been a Parisian university student any more than Ward was a smuggler. He'd been on assignment, undercover as Guillaume, and tasked with obtaining relics in Europe before they could be smuggled into the Republic. What luck to make friends with a man like Simon. And when the time came Guillaume's staged arrest returned him to the Republic, to a fast-track career within the REC where he kept tabs of Simon's progress. Eventually, the theft of the Vase pieces, thus eliminating a powerful threat to the Republic, secured his ascension to Commandant.

"What made the real difference," Gaustad added to the narrative, "was that I saw things in France no one in the Republic could understand. There are powers on this Earth far beyond what any government can hope to attain. Forget religion. All of them have been false. The Vase…" He pointed at Ward. "The Vase is real. No more religion. Just power from the heavens. Power only great men can harness. Alexander. Charlemagne. Tamerlane. But Simon saw only fear. He wanted to destroy the Vase. Not me, Ward. I see the future. Now get up and do what I say. It's the only redemption you have available."

Ward remained on his knees, clenching his jaw in defiance. It was most certainly not the only redemption available. If he couldn't save Daniel—if he couldn't save himself—he could at least make sure he killed Gaustad before it was over.

Gaustad sighed. "Agent Hickey."

Hickey advanced. Ward tensed for a blow. Instead, his former office-mate moved around him. He grunted with the weight of something, eventually dragging an unconscious form into Ward's peripheral view. He continued dragging the body all the way to the Vase where he let it flop to the ground. It rolled onto its back, red hair spilling across its face.

"Hannah!" Ward scrambled to her.

"She wasn't easy to find," Hickey said. "We had more than a dozen divers down there but I picked the right spot. They brought her out right to me. Mouth to mouth, Rafe. I saved her life."

Ward barely heard him. He rolled MacKenzie onto her back and laid his ear on her chest. She was breathing, soft and shallow but alive. He placed his hands on her cheeks and whispered her name. She didn't respond. It didn't matter. She was alive. He kissed her forehead.

An Agent chuckled. The one on the far left, a young man about Ward's height, with cropped black hair and red cheeks. Ward's chest solidified like molten iron. He sprang to his feet, surprised at the strength his body still held. He knocked Hickey aside and smashed his fist into the Agent's throat. The man dropped as if he'd been shot.

The other three Agents were on him before he could defend himself. They pummeled him to the ground, each blow rocketing pain through his body. It was all Ward could do to cover up and wait until Gaustad ordered them to cease.

Hands dragged him from MacKenzie, raking his body across the earth. He didn't fight it, didn't open his eyes until they pulled him to a kneeling position. He was once more groveled before the backpack. His head throbbed. His left eye didn't want to remain open. Each breath sent bolts of pain through his chest. He spit out a mouthful of blood causing his abdomen to constrict. He'd never had a broken rib but Agent Compano had taught him the symptoms. It felt like he had at least two.

"Mr. Ward," the Commandant said, "if you want to survive the day don't do that again. Now pay attention."

Adrien approached, pulling back his hood enough to show his crooked nose and murky eyes. "Do you know where we are?"

"Thera," Ward said. Somehow his addled brain made the next leap he hadn't been able to in the park. "Santorini," he added.

"Ah," The priest said, exchanging satisfied looks with Gaustad. "And do you know why we are here?"

Ward didn't answer.

With a nod from Gaustad Hickey stepped forward again, his face radiating an intense satisfaction. This time he drew back his arm and slugged Ward's jaw. It was a soft blow compared to the beating the Agents had given him. Ward offered only another painful spit of blood in response. The pleasure slipped from Hickey's face.

Adrien yanked Ward's head back. The sun burned his eyes. The priest ran his thumb through the blood drooling from Ward's mouth. He then dragged his thumb across Ward's forehead. It felt like a blade. The motion was repeated, crossing over the first tract. The blood burned.

The priest jabbed his thumb again to Ward's lip, splitting it open. He traced over the crossbeam a second time, widening it.

Ward knew the image as if he was looking down at his own prostrated form. The Minoan double-bladed axe.

Adrien let go. Ward's head drooped. He saw six of something. Three of the object. Two. He blinked his vision into focus. Just one—the backpack, the earthen lid peering out like a forgotten piece of candy.

"We are on an island within the Santorini caldera, Rafael." There was a disturbing sense of pride in Adrien's voice. "We overlook the place where El cast Ba'el's prison to Earth more than three thousand years ago. History records the moment as a great volcanic eruption, the event which ended Minoan reign over the Mediterranean. But we know the truth, do we not?"

I know the truth Ward wanted to say. *I know you're completely insane* but he kept his mouth shut. With MacKenzie alive he had to rethink his plan. He couldn't just throw his life away for the satisfaction of killing Gaustad. She would die too. His head throbbed. His conscience was silent. It took a second for him to realize that fear—the fear of doing something that would hurt MacKenzie—was just as immobilizing as his injuries.

Commandant Gaustad swaggered beside the priest, the Spear still gleaming in his hand. "What's going to happen is very simple. You are going to sacrifice Miss MacKenzie, spilling her blood into the Vase. Are you hearing me, Mr. Ward? You do this willingly and you and Daniel will live."

"Fuck you."

"Let's try this again. Do it willingly and you live. Do it not," Gaustad tilted his head to one of the flanking agents who obediently knelt beside Ward, an R1 in his palm, "and you watch him die."

Ward looked at the screen. The man he'd seen before, the man on the mustached Agent's Port, was standing against a wall. Shackled. Daniel. There was no doubt.

To Daniel's left stood a man in something like police riot gear. Another stood on Daniel's right holding a pistol to his temple.

"All I have to do is tap the screen and you get to watch his brains exit his skull."

Ward's resistance fled. He was trapped. He couldn't save both Daniel and MacKenzie. He knew he couldn't survive the loss of either of them again. There was nothing left but the seconds before he'd be forced to choose. The moments between that choice and the act. So little time yet it was all he had left. He was desperate to hold onto them, those few seconds. But what good were they when all he wanted was an end?

"Tell me you understand."

"I understand," Ward said, the words as bitter as the blood in his mouth.

The three Agents still standing closed the perimeter.

Adrien, his voice eager like a starving man's, said, "You offer this gift for Ba'el to consecrate the vessel, to return form to the formless?"

Ward tried to hesitate. To say something else but the voice in his mind consumed his thoughts.

Yes, it said.

It was the only answer to give.

"Yes."

Adrien spun, his robes flourishing outward like a cape, obscuring Ward's vision. There was a glint of metal followed by a grunt. Somewhere gulls cackled.

The priest's pirouette spiraled him to the side, leaving Gaustad standing before Ward. The Commandant dropped the Spear. His hands clutched his own throat. Blood spewed through his fingers. His eyes raged wildly side to side. His mouth gaped like a fish, gurgling blood and half-formed words. He collapsed, his boots twitching on the gritty earth.

There was no pause. Adrien plunged the bloody dagger into the nearest Agent's stomach. The others gawked, their weapons half raised.

Ward stared. Was he imagining it all?

Attack, his conscience shouted.

Ward launched. There was no thought to it. No plan. His right hand grabbed the Spear from the dirt beside Gaustad's twitching body. His shoulder slammed into Hickey's chest, knocking the wide-eyed professor to the ground. A sidestep brought him the closest Agent. He drove the Spear into the man's ribcage, losing his grip on the weapon as the Agent fell.

The remaining Agent aimed his pistol at Adrien as the priest turned, the dagger held forth as if it could stop bullets.

Ward tackled the Agent's legs. A single shot bellowed into the sky. The two men rolled over each other until Ward freed his hand and landed consecutive blows to the Agent's temple. The skull felt like it gave way beneath the assault. The Agent went limp.

Ward rolled onto his back, sucking in as much air as he could.

"Providence," Adrien said, raising the dagger in salute. In his other hand, he held the Port, the one which could order Daniel's death. There was no noise but the wind.

"Why?" Ward asked.

Adrien didn't answer. The Port disappeared into his robes as he approached the prone Agent who'd laughed at Ward's kiss. Without a word, he raked his dagger across the man's throat. All that remained was Ward's former office-mate.

"Don't let him kill me," Hickey said, cowering as he had

on the train.

Adrien advanced, holding the dagger like a gun. "Remove the covering from the Vase," he said.

Shaking, Hickey shuffled to the Vase, just feet from the cliff, and did as Adrien ordered. He dropped the blanket on the ground beside the urn. A breeze, the first significant wind since they'd arrived at the summit, carried the covering over the edge.

"Rafe," Hickey said, his eyes frantic, "don't let him kill me."

Adrien turned to Ward. "Would you like to?"

Ward considered his erstwhile friend. Tears dripped from Hickey's cheeks and chin. His hands and legs trembled. He shook his head like a child trying to ward off the monster in the closet.

No, Ward didn't want to kill him. He was surprised by this fact but accepting of it. Enough death. He likely wouldn't be able to stop Mackenzie's or Daniel's. Or his own. But maybe someone other than Adrien could walk away from this rock. Even if it was only Ken Hickey.

"Very well," the priest said.

"Rafe," his office mate pleaded.

Ward grabbed the old man's arm. The priest turned, his dark eyes showing something akin to amusement, but he didn't pull away.

As the two faced off they missed Hickey creeping forward. They didn't see him pull the Spear from the Agent's chest. They didn't hear him take his first menacing steps towards them.

It was Adrien who finally saw it. His head tilted. Ward spun. Hickey charged, the Spear before him like a bayonet.

Ward pounced. It wasn't an action of desire. It wasn't even a choice. He'd been taught thirteen years ago during basic training to defend himself. He'd been coached more recently by Agent Compano to use deadly force. In the past few days the rote mechanics of those lessons had become part of his nature. His muscles recognized the coming threat. They acted.

He closed the distance before Hickey could aim, evading the Holy Lance and grabbing his office mate's forearm. They whipped to the ground. Ward captured Hickey's wrist. Without thought—or was it?—Ward, in one motion, gripped the Spear, yanked it free, and plunged it into his friend's lung.

Ken Hickey, lying beside Commandant Gaustad's body, choked up three blood-soaked breaths. His eyes enlarged. His chest shuddered, then deflated.

Ward sat up, fixated on his own hands. Dirt clumped in the blood that covered his fingers. Another murder. He wiped his hands on his jeans. The blood remained, like spilled crimson glue. His stomach clenched. He ground his fists against his jacket, accomplishing nothing, until a shadow crossed him.

Adrien stood over him, the lid in his hand, the dagger inches from Ward's ear.

"Get up, Rafael. We are not done with blood just yet."

CHAPTER
THIRTY-SEVEN

The ocean, so far below and extending so far ahead, barely rolled. It could have been a sheet of cerulean glass stretching for the horizon. Ward thought of throwing himself over the edge. Let the world be damned by Ba'el or whoever else. It seemed a peaceful way. A painless way. A far better way than by blade, bullet, or bonfire.

In the periphery of his vision, Ward became aware of a voyeur. A tourist standing idle atop the plateau watching the chaos play out. An old man. Once more, the forgotten name came to Ward. Gabe. With it came recognition. Gabriel. The messenger of God, according to the Old Testament. The Man in Linen. Interpreter of Dreams.

Am I dreaming? Ward thought.

He turned his head to see the old man but there was no one there. Just a view of the Earth's curve. And a feeling of certainty in Ward's gut. He wasn't going to toss himself over the side in a futile attempt to escape the coming end of this game.

The priest knelt before Ward, beside Gaustad's body, drawing his attention from the old man that wasn't there. What was his name again?

The dagger leveled at Ward's eyes erased the last residue of the mysterious old man's face from Ward's thoughts. He saw only Adrien now. Only Hannah and the Vase now.

With his free hand, Adrien touched a finger to Gaustad's forehead. He traced the finger down the Commandant's nose, and lingered it upon his lips. Ward watched, enthralled. When the priest bent over to kiss Gaustad's lips, Ward saw in detail for the first time what he had presumed to be a scar on the Commandant's neck. It was, in fact, the trailing line of a tattoo, a script that would forever be illegible as it had been torn in half by Adrien's blade. The mark of a Believer. Not in the bible or the scriptures of El's church, but in Ba'el, the Lord who had used and betrayed him. The priest stood with surprising nimbleness and retrieved the lid of the Vase of Soissons. This he dropped into the dirt beside Ward. "Pick it up," he said.

Ward clutched the lid to his belly and rose, keeping his motion slow to steal a glance at MacKenzie. The breathing motion of her chest was now visible. Her leg twitched. His earlier thought reoccurred: *All I have left is time.*

"Bring it to the Vase," Adrien said, the dagger bobbing in his hand to a tune only the priest could hear.

The use of the dagger—both men knew it—was unnecessary. The threat was not to Ward's life. It was

MacKenzie's suffering should he disobey. It was Daniel's life should he disobey. He didn't. He took lingering steps, matching the old man's pace behind him, maybe even slowing it, working deliberately around the bodies cluttering the ridge.

When he stood before MacKenzie's prone form he asked, "Why?"

Adrien leaned into Ward's shoulder. His breath was putrid. "So that you can slice her throat and fill the Vase with her blood, Deceiver."

Ward's insides constricted as if trying to squeeze themselves into nothingness. He was trapped in a nightmare. The one of the funeral. The one of the little jar in his hand. His whole life. A nightmare.

"But that is not your question, is it? Your question is why kill poor William." Adrien's wrinkled face snaked closer. Spittle gleamed in the rumpled corner of his mouth. "Because he was a fool. He wanted to own the Vase. To create an empire. This is not Ba'el's wish. We are not here to draw lines on a map. We are here to unleash a God. We are here to witness Ba'el reconquer and consume El. We are here to engender the ascension of a singular Lord. He will restore order to the Earth. Or incinerate us all and begin anew. It matters not which. His will shall be done."

"You're a lunatic," Ward said. Time was all he had. He could buy a little more.

Adrien shoved the dagger into Ward's side. It sliced through his jacket with ease, sinking into the fatty part of his waist. Ward struggled to keep the lid in his arms while clenching his jaw against the pain.

Time, he repeated silently.

"You didn't answer my question," Ward said. "Why me? Us? Why not just dig up the damned lid yourself?"

Adrien made a face as if he'd just been asked why water was wet. "It was not His will," he said.

"And I am?"

"Believe." Adrien stretched the word. "Deceive."

"Deceive what? I told her everything. I—"

"These are El's rules, Rafael. He made the prison. Blame Him."

"Bullshit. The lid sat there for what, four hundred years? That's what you want me to believe, right?" Ward knew his next words would either buy him the few seconds he needed or get him killed outright. "Adrien the priest. Adrien Quinque. Whatever your fucking name is. Guardian of the lid but not special enough to dig ten feet for it. Ba'el's special pet, right?"

The priest did not react. No sneer. No rage in his voice. He words were measured, nearly emotionless.

"Long Ba'el has spoken to me, bade me wait until the nations of the book weakened. Then He came to me. For the first time not just a voice. A vision. The lightning-helmed Lord of the Minoans. The charging Bull God. The golden spider reeling His threads leaf to leaf. All and none as only a God can be. 'Find the daughter of El's chosen,' He told me. 'Find her and the Deceiver will be revealed.' And here you are, Rafael. Here you are."

Mackenzie groaned.

"Now," Adrien continued, "it is time we open the prison. It is time we do our part in returning Ba'el to the heavens."

Ward shot a glance, eyes only, to MacKenzie. She rubbed her palm over her eyes. She bent her left leg, pointing her knee to the sky.

"Slice open her throat." A small knife was placed in Ward's right hand. "Catch her blood upon the lid. Give her soul and close the Vase. Do it now and she dies quick. Painless, and you get to enjoy life in the shade of Ba'el's favor. Your brother gets to live. Do it not and I will make good on William's promise. Just as all he needed to do was push a button so can I. You will watch Daniel die. Hannah will suffer unimaginable horrors, begging each day for death and cursing you each night for inflicting those tortures upon her." He withdrew the dagger from Ward's abdomen, and pressed it against the base of his neck.

Ward sucked a breath through gritted teeth. The blade was warm with his own blood, the drops running down his back. He swallowed hard to fight off the accompanying nausea. It occurred to him that the air brimmed with the aroma of something familiar. Sweet. It smelled like…

Return the Vase, Rafael.

The voice boomed. Ward flinched, almost dropping the knife.

"You see," Adrien said, his voice thick with glee. "He tells you Himself."

"He?"

"Long He has spoken to me. Long has He spoken to you."

The voice that had been with him since his earliest memories? His conscience and companion? This was Ba'el?

It couldn't be. Could it?

Return the Vase.

No. This voice was different. New. Feminine. Beautiful. Familiar?

But then, what voice had been with him before? What voice had been directing him all those years? He tried to remember it but all he could hear was this new voice.

MacKenzie coughed. Ward forgot the voices.

"Cut her throat and catch her blood upon the lid," the priest said with a snarl.

"Promise you'll let me live," Ward said. There was time. There was a chance.

"Give the soul, Deceiver, and you will have your life. Give it freely. Say it."

MacKenzie's body shivered. Her eyelids fluttered.

"I do this freely." Ward extended his arm, holding the knife over the prone MacKenzie.

The press of the dagger on his neck disappeared. The priest chanted something indecipherable. Guttural. Throaty.

Ward watched MacKenzie's lips move but she made no sound.

There was little time but there *was* time.

The priest repeated his recitation.

"Rafe?" MacKenzie's voice was shaky but her eyes were open.

Adrien began a third invocation.

Return!

"Run," Ward shouted.

He spun his body counterclockwise, rising and bringing the lid around like a shield.

The dagger entered his chest up high. It didn't matter. The lid continued in its arc catching Adrien in the temple. Both men howled. Ward's right hand plunged the little knife into the priest's gut.

Adrien lunged, his seemingly brittle bones delivering a crushing blow to Ward's abdomen. They grappled, somehow still standing, clawing furiously at each other's flesh. It was all Ward could do to hold off the frenetic priest, to give MacKenzie time to escape.

Ward tried parrying with the lid. It was futile. Fists and claws found their marks. He was forced backwards, nearly to the Vase. He should have been standing on top of MacKenzie. He broke line of sight with his attacker, glimpsing a shock of red hair far from the edge. It was enough. Clutching the lid to his chest with one hand, he grabbed Adrien's robes by the throat with his other. With all the strength in his legs he spun and threw himself at the Vase. In a violent tangle they all went over the cliff.

——————◆——————

Fear—that cold systematic clenching of all bodily systems— was absent. As the Mediterranean approached Ward exalted in the deafness the buffeting wind granted. He reveled in the tears being pushed back into his eyes. He felt like an angel swooping past startled gulls.

Content, he embraced the Vase and waited.

He hit the water.

He should have died.

This was his first thought. His second was to wonder if MacKenzie had escaped.

Then all thoughts were slammed aside as pain gushed into his chest. The water went dark. Something pulled at his flesh.

The priest.

Ward's thigh ignited in pain. The water around him warmed. The salt and the blood stung his eyes. It was like trying to see through smoke. He kicked and twisted until the priest's gnarled teeth snapped at his face.

Ward released the Vase. It was pure reaction. He surged forward to reclaim it before it sank. But it did not sink. Somehow it floated between the two men as if waiting.

The blade came. Ward managed to thrust himself aside. The attack missed. His lungs raged. His vision dimmed.

He couldn't find the priest. Had the old man swam for the surface? Had he sunk into the abyss?

Let go.

It was the new voice. Peaceful like a song. An aria. His eyes closed. Was this death? Was he about to drown as he'd thought MacKenzie had?

Let go.

He knew this voice. He'd been waiting to hear it nearly his whole life. And he understood.

The Vase waited for a gift.

Ward reached out blindly, finding only water, water, water. Just as his lungs were about to open and accept whatever might surge in, his fingertips brushed something solid. He stretched. He grasped the rim of the Vase.

His eyes flashed open. The water was clear.

In his other hand, though unaware of retrieving it, he held his mother's silver necklace. As if drawn by a magnet, the pendant sought out the hollow of the Vase. Ward let go. His sight faded to light and shadows.

Was that the lid placing itself upon the Vase?

Forgive, Raffi.

He was sinking. A thousand agonized voices screamed in his head. His eardrums burst. His body jolted, caught in the wake of some shockwave from the depths.

Was he rising?

The shadows fled, leaving only an approaching light.

How wonderful it would be, he thought, *to touch that light for just an instant before the darkness comes.*

CHAPTER
THIRTY-EIGHT

He was dreaming.

Perhaps he was dead.

He had no body. He existed only as hearing. An auditory wraith. The sound he heard was beautiful.

"I've got you, Rafe."

The voice, close yet echoing with great distance, was familiar. He longed to see the lips that made those words.

He willed his eyes into existence. Pushed them open. It was too much.

His form dispersed.

———◆———

Rafael Ward awoke. The sun barbed at his eyes. They shut without permission.

"Rafe?"

A hand brushed at his hair, shielding him from the light.

He tried again. At first all he saw was her. A redheaded, befreckled seraph, hair blowing about recklessly. For a moment he thought it was another woman, an image from a past too far away to touch. But the thought faded. Only the redhead remained.

She was bruised. Her cheek darkened. Her eye swollen. But she smiled, the lines at the corners of her mouth and beside her eyes somehow deeper than he remembered.

"Hannah." It hurt to speak.

"Shh."

He looked past her to the sky. The cloudless sky. Blazing red. Not the red of sunset or of impending storm. It was like the Earth itself was on fire and the atmosphere could only reflect the color helplessly.

He tried to sit up, managing to lift his head only inches. A pounding reached across his temples, blurring his vision.

"No, no, no. Relax."

A hand cradled the back of his head, lowering it to the ground.

"I have to see." He struggled forward, propping himself on his elbows. "My God," he said, unable to help the words.

He was laid out on a beach a few feet from the water. The cliff from which he'd thrown himself loomed overhead. The water was perfectly still. No waves. No ripples. And it was the same scarlet as the sky.

"What happened?"

"You'd drifted almost to the beach by the time I got down here," she said.

"No. The water…"

As he watched, a void opened in the sea. A gaping hole, perfectly black, just off shore where he'd hit the water. Where the Vase had hit the water.

"There," he said, pointing.

"Lie back. I've got you."

"Don't you see it?"

His vision dimmed. The sky and the sea blended together, the colors fading to ash. His insides turned.

Was he about to see Ba'el rise?

There was a buzzing in his ears.

Had they done this? Had he?

His vision darkened. His head began to roll. His limbs disappeared. He was falling again.

This time it was okay. Hannah was here.

She would catch him.

PART FIVE

THE TOWER

In shards the sylvan vases lie,
Their links of dance undone;
And brambles wither by the brim,
Choked Fountain of the Sun!
The spider in the laurel spins,
The weed exiles the flower,
And, flung to kiln, Apollo's bust
Makes lime for Mammon's tower.

"The Ravaged Villa," by Herman Melville, 1891

EPILOGUE

The air in the capital city of the Atlantic District tasted different than he remembered. Not smog or pollution or even the river. It was something else. Something viscose and musty.

Rafael Ward looked up and down the block as he'd done on every street he'd crossed for the last six months. Pristine macadam. Gleaming sidewalks. Polite, blank-faced pedestrians. Reasonably-paced traffic.

The Republic wound on.

Still, the taste bothered Ward. Identification was coming, he could feel it meandering its way to that point in the brain which turns image into word but it was taking too long. He missed that voice in his mind, his companion, always quick with an answer or a warning.

He was still getting used to the silence. Peaceful, but sometimes so empty. So lonely.

He crossed to the opposite sidewalk. He again peered up and down the block. She wasn't there. He rounded the corner.

The REC field office, the Tower, sat like a boulder in a wheat field. Its tenth floor window glared down at Ward as if it knew why he'd come. Ward didn't hide from its stare. He stepped to the middle of the sidewalk and turned his back on Republic Hall. He straightened his shoulders, lifted his head, and dared the window to stop him.

Recognition arrived. The taste. Only it wasn't just taste. It was smell, too. And texture and sound. It was a knowing that undercut everything, the way you can discern a storm coming. He'd felt it looking out of that window, which now menaced above him. He'd felt it on the afternoon he'd been conscripted into the REC. He'd felt it that summer over a decade ago when he'd received his first Citizen's ID.

But it went back farther than all of that. He could remember it as a teenager, as a child, as an infant. It had always been there, every day of his life. An invisible fact, oppressive like August humidity.

He saw it now on the faces of those who walked by. The men and women in business suits and spring jackets. The pedestrians who crossed the street rather than pass in front of the Tower's doors. It wasn't politeness. It wasn't a zombie-like blankness.

It was fear.

And, Ward understood, it was so palpable because it no longer controlled him. He wondered what the air had tasted like before the Reclamation.

A black RM sedan, like the one Ward and MacKenzie had

met for their tickets to Paris all those months ago, exited the parking garage to the right of the field office. Ward hooked his thumbs into the straps of his backpack, turned and made a play of examining the Center Square flags. Row upon row of flags rippling in the light breeze. *So temporary,* he thought, *like leaves.*

The car passed without a hiccup in the purr of its e-drive motor. Ward watched it turn the corner then found an unoccupied bench on which to sit and prepare. He unslung his backpack and placed it on the sidewalk between his legs. He checked each of the five small pockets situated on the shell of the bulging pack. Unzip. Zip. Unzip. Zip. There could be no catches. No zipper pulls too small or awkward to grab while under duress.

It wasn't necessary. He'd done his diligence, confirming and reconfirming everything was operational. Each piece of equipment was in place and accessible. But it wasn't the confirmation that mattered. It was, rather, the moment. The opportunity to pause and recommit. To exhale the fear.

He lifted the backpack onto his lap and opened its main compartment. Crammed with a submachine gun, two pistols, ammunition, and four orange brick-sized blocks of Semtex, it looked like a child's puzzle box. Remove one item and the rest collapses into a chaotic pile. Ward touched each article, confident in their placement and his ability to extract them when needed. The last item he placed his hand on was unlike the others. Lean and long and wrapped in a towel, it was nearly tall enough to point out the top of the backpack.

MacKenzie's Spear of Destiny.

When Ward had woken on the beach a third time, she'd still been there cradling his head in her lap.

"I've got you," she said.

He'd tried to ask her about the burning sky. He'd tried to ask her about the abyss in the sea but she'd only whispered to him like he was a child afraid of what lurks beneath the bed.

"It's okay, Rafe. It's okay."

He'd looked to the sky then, and to the water. Blue and blue. Carefree clouds and drowsy waves. It was as if he'd imagined it all. Yet he knew he hadn't.

He'd reached for her hand but found the Spear instead.

"You kept it?"

"I don't care what your scans said." Her tone changed, only for an instant, from nurturing to reprimanding. "I know what I felt when I first held it. I know what it is."

"But it's—"

"Just call it a good luck piece, okay? Now close your eyes. I've got you."

When he'd next opened his eyes she was gone. She'd dressed his knife wounds and pulled him farther from the waves.

And she'd left the Spear beside him in the sand, his right hand over its shank. It was a promise. He didn't need a note or a text message to tell him. It was a promise that she'd be back. That he'd see her again.

He closed the backpack and looked up and down the block. Men and women in business suits went about their day like any other, grouped together, heads buried in their Ports, not speaking to each other. Isolated. Isolating.

Except for one old man across the street. He looked familiar to Ward, standing there, hands in his pockets, shaking his head like a father telling his son not to touch a hot stove. He looked familiar. Like someone Ward should know. Should listen to.

Inexplicably Ward thought of The Barrel. He thought of the last time he'd had a drink there with his friend Ken Hickey. Someone had been there. Someone talking about war.

A car passed, drawing Ward's eye. When he looked again to where the old man had been, the sidewalk was empty. Had there really been someone there?

Ward looked up and down the street. No one appeared to be taking any interest in him. Why would they? The days of fearful vigilance were gone. The news feeds made it clear that the only unrest was across the ocean. Thank goodness for the stability of the new America.

The Republic wound on.

Ward stood and hefted the bag onto his shoulders. It was heavy and took a moment of shifting before its weight was properly distributed. The Tower's window still spied from above. Now it seemed the window, the REC's eye, was daring him to enter.

Ward reached into his jacket's pocket and tapped his ID card. It would work, he told himself. Reprogrammed half a dozen times by half a dozen hackers between the Mediterranean and here the ID would get him past the field office's first two security checks. That was all he needed. Labor Camp data should be accessible through any terminal in the building, including the research posts on the lower levels.

While the building was virtually impregnable from the outside its internal structural foundations were quite vulnerable in both the southeast and northeast corners. A bathroom and a medical supply closet.

For this much the ID would work.

Ward thought of Gaustad's office, now belonging to the new Commandant Massen. Gaustad's contraband had surely been removed from display by now but some pieces could still be in the building. Perhaps in the basement. The thought of destroying them was hard to stomach but not impossible. *Not if he could rescue one of them,* he thought. *Maybe one of Childeric's Bees.*

He crossed the street and positioned himself to the right of the Tower's entrance. From here there was no angle to see the window ten stories above. There was no angle for it to see him. He adjusted the backpack and looked up and down the street.

He inhaled, holding the breath high in his chest. He took out his ID card and exhaled, pushing out more air than he'd taken in. It was time. He approached the outer doors. He thought of that door in the cellar hallway half a year ago. The door that had led him to MacKenzie. To the truth about Daniel. He'd been certain that door would be the last he'd ever walk through.

Today, he was certain these metal and glass doors wouldn't be.

Rafael Ward took a step forward. The doors slid open with a sound like a parent shushing a child.

He turned up his jacket's collar, smirked at the pop-noir move, and looked over his shoulder once more. She wasn't there.

It was okay.

He would see her again.

ABOUT THE AUTHOR

Michael Pogach began writing stories in grade school. He doesn't remember these early masterpieces, but his parents tell him everyone in them died. He's gained some humanity since then, even occasionally allowing characters to escape his stories alive. Michael lives in suburban Philadelphia with his wife and daughter. *The Spider in the Laurel* is his first novel. www.michaelpogach.com